Praise for
THE BODY FARM SERIES
BY
NEW YORK TIMES
BESTSELLING AUTHOR
JEFFERSON BASS

"The real deal."
Kathy Reichs

"Bass is a fresh voice in the crime novel arena."
Seattle Post-Intelligencer

"[Bass] takes the Bill Brockton series into
Steve Berry territory with this story of an ancient
mystery and a modern-day lunatic's quest to reshape
the world. . . . Brockton is as appealing as always,
and the story . . . is clever and compelling."
Booklist

"*The Inquisitor's Key* combines medieval history,
religious conspiracy, and murder
with . . . authentic forensic investigation."
Huntsville Times

"[The Body Farm] is a place for terrific
thrills, chills and other accoutrements of
mysteries. And that's a good thing."
Asbury Park Press

"[Bass] is a solid storyteller who inspires credibility
with scientific expertise. . . . [*The Inquisitor's
Key*] provides plenty of food for thought."
Kirkus Reviews

Books by Jefferson Bass

Fiction
THE INQUISITOR'S KEY
THE BONE YARD
THE BONE THIEF
BONES OF BETRAYAL
THE DEVIL'S BONES
FLESH AND BONE
CARVED IN BONE

Nonfiction
BEYOND THE BODY FARM
DEATH'S ACRE

JEFFERSON BASS

FLESH AND BONE

A BODY FARM NOVEL

HARPER

An Imprint of HarperCollinsPublishers

HARPER

An Imprint of HarperCollins*Publishers*
10 East 53rd Street
New York, New York 10022-5299

Copyright © 2007 by Jefferson Bass, LLC
Excerpt from *Cut to the Bone* copyright © 2013 by Jefferson Bass, LLC
ISBN 978-0-06-227737-4

First Harper premium printing: June 2013
First Harper mass market printing: January 2008
First William Morrow hardcover printing: February 2007

HarperCollins® and Harper® are registered trademarks of Harper-Collins Publishers.

Printed in the United States of America

Visit Harper paperbacks on the World Wide Web at
www.harpercollins.com

10 9 8 7 6 5 4 3 2 1

In memory of Officer Ben Bohanan
1975–2004

FLESH
AND
BONE

PART 1
BEFORE

CHAPTER 1

THE CHAIN-LINK GATE YOWLED like an angry tomcat in the watery light of dawn. Once my jaw unclenched, I made a mental note to bring grease for the hinges next time I came out to the Body Farm. Don't forget, I chided myself, just as I had each of the past half dozen times I'd mentally made and mislaid that same damn note.

It wasn't that my memory was failing, or so I liked to believe. It was just that every time I headed for the Anthropology Research Facility, as the University of Tennessee preferred to call the Body Farm, I had more interesting things on my mind than WD-40. Things like the experiment I was about to rig with the body in the pickup truck Miranda was backing toward the facility's gate.

It never ceased to amaze me, and to frustrate me, that the Body Farm remained the world's only research facility devoted to the systematic study of postmortem decomposition. As an imperfect human being, with failings and vanities, I did take a measure of pride in the uniqueness of my creation. As a forensic anthropologist, though—a "bone detective" who had branched out into seeking clues in decaying flesh as well—I looked forward to the day when our data on decomp rates in the moist, temperate climate of Tennessee could be compared with rates from similar research facilities in the low desert of Palm Springs, the high desert of Albuquerque, the rain forest of the Olympic Peninsula, or the alpine slopes of the Montana Rockies. But every time I thought a colleague in one of those ecosystems was on the verge of creating a counterpart to the Body Farm, the university in question would chicken out, and we would remain unique, isolated, and scientifically alone.

Over the past twenty-five years, my graduate students and I had staged hundreds of human bodies in various settings and scenarios to study their postmortem decay. Shallow graves, deep graves, watery graves, concrete-capped graves. Air-conditioned buildings, heated buildings, screened-in porches. Automobile trunks, backseats, travel trailers. Naked bodies, cotton-clad bodies, polyester-suited bodies, plastic-wrapped bodies. But I'd never thought to stage anything like the gruesome death scene Miranda and I were about to re-create for Jess Carter.

Jess—Dr. Jessamine Carter—was the medical examiner in Chattanooga. For the past six months she'd been the acting ME for Knoxville's Regional Forensic Center as well. She'd been promoted, if that's the right word, to this dual status by virtue of a spectacular screwup by our own ME,

Dr. Garland Hamilton. During what no one but Hamilton himself would have described as an autopsy, he had so badly misdiagnosed a man's cause of death—describing a superficial accidental cut as a "fatal stab wound"—that an innocent bystander ended up charged with murder. When his mistake came to light, Hamilton was promptly relieved of his duties; now, he was about to be relieved of his medical license, if the licensing review board did its job right. Meanwhile, until a qualified replacement could be appointed, Jess was filling in, making the hundred-mile trek up I-75 from Chattanooga to Knoxville anytime an unexplained or violent death occurred in our neck of the Tennessee woods.

The commute wasn't as time-consuming for Jess as it would have been for me. Her Porsche Carrera—fire-engine red, fittingly enough—generally covered the hundred miles in fifty minutes or so. The first state trooper to pull her over had gotten a quick glimpse of her badge and a brisk talking-to about the urgency of her mission before she left him standing on the interstate's shoulder. The second unfortunate officer, a week later, got a verbal vivisection, followed by scorching cellphone calls to the highway patrol's district commander and state commissioner. She had not been stopped a third time.

Jess had phoned at six to say she'd be in Knoxville this morning, so unless she'd been called to a Chattanooga murder scene in the past half hour, the Carrera was streaking our way now, closing like a cruise missile. I hoped I could get the body in place by the time she hit Knoxville.

As Miranda eased the UT pickup toward the fence, the backup lights helped me fit the key into the padlock on the inner gate. The inner gate was part of an eight-foot wooden privacy fence, erected to deter marauding coyotes and squeamish humans—or voyeuristic ones. Originally we'd had only the chain-link fence, but after a couple of years, a few complaints, and a handful of thrill seekers, we topped the chain-link with barbed wire and lined the entire half-mile perimeter with the wooden barrier. It was still possible for nimble critters and determined people to climb in or see over, but it took some doing.

The padlock securing the wooden gate sprang open with a satisfying click. I unhooked one end of the chain from the shackle and began walking the gate inward. As the opening widened, the chain began snaking into the hole bored near the gate's edge, like some metallic noodle being slurped up with clattering gusto. *Sucked into the maw of death,* I thought. *Is that a mixed metaphor, or just a nasty image best kept to myself?*

As I held the wooden gate open, Miranda threaded the narrow opening with ease, as if she made deliveries to death's service entrance on a daily basis. She practically did. For the past three years, thanks to a spate of television documentaries and the popularity of *CSI*—a show I'd watched only one incredulous time—we were swamped with donated bodies, and the waiting list (as I called the ranks of the living who had promised us their bodies eventually) now numbered nearly a thousand. We'd soon be running out of room; already, in fact, it was hard to take a step without stumbling over a body or stepping on a patch of greasy ground where a corpse had recently decomposed.

About half the bodies were simply brought out here to skeletonize. It was a little slower but a lot easier to let time, bacteria, and bugs—especially bugs—do the messy work of separating flesh and bone. Thanks to nature's efficiency at reclaiming her dead, all that remained for us to do after a body's residence at the Farm was to scrub off and deodorize the bones, take detailed measurements, plug those into our forensic database, and tuck the skeleton into our growing collection. The University of Tennessee now possessed the world's largest assemblage of modern skeletons of known age, sex, and race. That was important not because it gave us bragging rights, but because it gave us a huge and continually evolving source of comparative measurements for forensic scientists to consult when confronted with the skeleton of an unknown murder victim.

The body in the back of the truck, though, was destined to contribute more than just his skeleton. He would shed crucial light on an unanswered forensic question. About fifty bodies a year were used in faculty or student research projects, usually exploring some variable affecting the rate of decomposition. One recent experiment, for instance, demonstrated that people who died shortly after undergoing chemotherapy decomposed far more slowly than what I'd since begun to think of as "organic" or "all natural" bodies. Chemotherapy, in other words, bore more than a passing resemblance to antemortem embalming, which was not a particularly comforting notion.

Once Miranda had cleared the opening, I closed the gate behind her and fed the chain back through its hole, leaving the padlock open so Jess could get in when she arrived. Miranda was already out of the truck, unlatching the camper shell and tailgate. She turned the latches slowly and opened the back of the truck almost gently, a gesture that seemed right and thoughtful in the peaceful morning. It was early yet; the hospital's day shift hadn't begun arriving in the adjoining parking lot, so the only traffic noise was the distant drone of cars on Alcoa Highway, a mile away on the west side of the medical complex. Tennessee was waking up softly, with just enough chill in the early March air to cloud our breath. I also noticed mist rising from several of the fresher bodies—not from breath or residual heat, but from the teeming masses of maggots feasting on them. It pleased me, for some reason, to possess the arcane knowledge that feeding was exothermic—heat-producing—for the supposedly cold-blooded maggot. Few things in science were as black and white as terms like "cold-blooded" implied, and I wondered, in passing, if the chemical reactions in the bugs' digestive tracts produced the heat, or if metabolizing calories to fuel their wriggling muscles was what warmed them up. Maybe someday I'd explore that.

Above the innumerable maggots, the oaks and maples dotting the hillside were beginning to leaf out. In their branches, a chorus of cardinals and mockingbirds chirped and trilled. A pair of squirrels played chase up and down the trunk of a ninety-foot loblolly. There was life abundant out here at the Body Farm. Long as you could see beyond the hundred-odd corpses lying about in various stages of disrepair.

Miranda and I stood in silence awhile, soaking up the birdsong and the golden early light. One of the frolicking squirrels began to fuss at the other for breaking some rule of their game, and Miranda smiled. She turned toward me and her smile widened. It caught me by surprise, blindsided me, like a two-by-four upside the head.

Miranda Lovelady had been my graduate assistant for four years now. We worked well as a team—in the decomp lab, as we sorted through the skeletal wreckage of some highway fatality or murder victim, our movements often seemed choreographed, our unspoken communication akin to telepathy. But lately I worried that I'd crossed some invisible line with her; that I'd let her grow too attached to me, or maybe that I'd grown too attached to her. Although she was technically still a student, Miranda wasn't a child by any means; she was a smart, confident woman of twenty-six now—or was it twenty-seven?—and I knew the ivory tower was chock-full of professors who had taken up with protégées. But I was thirty years older than Miranda, and even if that difference might seem tolerable to her at the moment, I couldn't imagine it would remain so forever. No, I reminded myself, I was a mentor, and maybe a bit of a friend, but nothing more. And that was best for both of us.

I reached into the back of the truck and busied

myself with a pair of purple nitrile gloves, forcing my thoughts back to the experiment we were here to set up. "Jess—Dr. Carter—should be here soon," I said. "Let's find a good tree and start tying this fellow up."

"Ah, Dr. Carter." Miranda grinned at me. "I *thought* you seemed a little nervous. Are you intimidated, or infatuated?"

I laughed. "Probably a little of both," I said. "She's smart and she's tough. Funny, too, and easy on the eyes."

"All true," said Miranda. "She'd sure keep you on your toes. About time you found somebody to do that, you know."

I knew all too well. My wife of nearly 30 years, Kathleen, had died of cancer more than two years ago, and I was only now recovering from the blow. The prior autumn, I had felt the first stirrings of interest and desire. Those stirrings had been kindled, I was embarrassed to recall, when a student impulsively kissed me; fortunately and mortifyingly, the kiss had been cut short by Miranda's appearance in the doorway of my office. Shortly after that inappropriate but memorable kiss, I'd invited a woman closer to my own age—none other than Dr. Jess Carter—to have dinner with me. Jess had accepted the invitation, though she had to cancel at the last moment, when she got summoned to a murder scene in Chattanooga. I hadn't worked up my nerve to ask her out again, but the notion occurred to me every time our overlapping cases—her fresh homicides, my not-so-fresh ones—brought us into contact.

Miranda's question brought me back to the task at hand. "Does it matter what kind of tree we strap this guy to?"

"Probably not, but she said the victim was tied to a pine, and we've got several of those, so we might as well make it realistic. Doesn't cost any extra." I pointed at the tree where the squirrels had been scampering. "How about that one?"

Miranda shook her head. "No, not that one," she frowned. "That one seems too . . . exposed. Might be hard on the campus cops or on visiting researchers if this experiment was the first thing they saw when they walked in the gate." She had a point there. "Besides, didn't you say the victim was found way back in the woods?" She had a point there, too.

"That's my understanding. Prentice Cooper State Forest. Covers some pretty rugged terrain along the Tennessee River Gorge, just downstream from Chattanooga." I pointed farther up the hillside, to another tall pine near the upper boundary. "There you go. That look secluded enough?"

Miranda nodded. "Yeah, that seems better. Bit of a haul to get him up there. But good exercise, I guess."

"If it doesn't kill us, it makes us stronger?"

"Right," she said. Then she stuck out her tongue at me.

In unison, we leaned into the back of the truck and each grabbed one of the straps sewn onto the sides of the black body bag. We slid it out over the tailgate until it hung about a foot off the end. "Ready?" I asked.

"Ready," she said, and with that, we each grabbed

another strap, about two-thirds of the way down. Sliding the bag farther off the tailgate, we gradually bore more and more of the corpse's weight. It was heavy—180 pounds, which was roughly the weight of the victim whose death scene we were about to re-create. The more faithfully the re-creation mirrored the crime—not just the victim's weight, but his injuries, clothing, and positioning—the more accurate our eventual time-since-death estimate would be, allowing the police to focus their investigation more precisely.

We hadn't gotten more than fifty feet up the hillside before I broke a sweat in the chilly morning. I could tell Miranda was straining, too, but I knew she'd collapse before she complained. That was okay by me; I was willing to whine for both of us. "You wanna rethink that first tree? Sure would be convenient."

"Hun-uh," she grunted through gritted teeth, shaking her head for emphasis.

"Okay," I gasped, "you're the boss. If I stroke out before we get up the hill, use me for some especially spectacular research."

"Gladly," she huffed.

We stopped twice to catch our breath and mop our brows, but even with the rest breaks, we were half dragging the bag by the time we reached the pine near the upper fence. Still, as I opened the long, C-shaped zipper running around three sides of the bag, I had to agree that a secluded location was much more appropriate for this particular experiment.

We had prepared the body in the morgue, so I

knew what to expect, but even so, I took a sharp breath when I folded back the flap to expose our subject. The blond wig had shifted a bit, sliding down over the face and concealing much of the trauma I'd inflicted, but what remained visible was strong stuff. According to Jess, most of the bones of the victim's face had been shattered by blunt-force trauma—she was guessing something fairly big, maybe a baseball bat or a metal pipe, rather than something smaller, like a tire iron, which would have left sharper, more distinctive marks in the bone. I couldn't bring myself to wale away on a donated body with such violence, so I'd settled for cutting through the zygomatic arches—the cheekbones— and the lower jaw in several places with an autopsy saw, then smearing a liberal amount of blood on the skin in those areas to simulate the bleeding that perimortem trauma would have induced. Miranda, being more skilled in the art of makeup, had applied base and rouge to the cheeks, plus violet eye shadow and a pair of long false eyelashes. I doubted that the makeup would affect the decomp rate, but I didn't want to throw any unnecessary variables into the equation.

Procuring the leather corset that we'd cinched around our subject's torso had proved far easier than I expected. Less than twenty-four hours before, Miranda had spent five minutes Googling and web surfing, then demanded my UT credit card. A few more keystrokes and she announced, "Done. One extra large bustier arriving at six A.M., First Overnight, thanks to the efficient teamwork of FedEx and Naughty&Nice.com." I foresaw some red-faced explaining to the UT auditors once the American Express bill arrived, but such was the occasional price of original research.

"Have you got the rope," I asked, "or do I need to go back to the truck and get it?" Miranda was wearing a black jumpsuit that bristled with pockets.

"No, I've got it," she said. She reached down and unzipped a big pocket just above her left knee and fished out a package of nylon cord and a big, military-looking pocketknife. With one twist of her thumb, she flipped open a wicked serrated blade.

"Whoa, that's some serious cutting power," I said. "What is that, a six-inch blade?"

She snorted. "Do men really believe that's what six inches looks like? Try three and a half." With the tip of the blade she deftly flicked off the package's plastic wrapper, then unspooled about six feet of cord—or was it three and a half?—and cut it with a swift stroke. "You wanna tie his hands while I do his feet?" I took the piece of rope and began to bind the corpse's wrists in front of him. Miranda sliced off another length of cord and lashed the ankles together. The rope snagged on the fishnet stockings as she cinched it taut above the stiletto heels. "I've never understood the appeal of cross-dressing," she said, "either for the guys who do it or for the people who go to drag shows. But I also can't understand how anybody could get so enraged about it that they'd beat a guy to death for putting on a wig and some slutty clothes."

"Me neither," I said. "The one thing I understand, after all these years and all these murders, is that there's a lot I don't understand about human nature."

Once our stand-in was trussed up like the Chattanooga victim, the next task was to tie him to the tree. "Jess said his hands were up over his head," I remarked, half to Miranda and half to myself. "Hard to get 'em up there without a ladder, though." I spied a low branch. "Maybe if I throw a rope over that limb, we can use that like a pulley to hoist him up." Miranda whacked off another length, which I tossed across the branch where it joined the trunk. Then I tied one end to the wrist bindings, and together we hauled on the line. The nylon cord was thin, so it bit into our hands as we pulled, but once we had him upright, the friction of the rope on the branch helped support his weight.

"You think you can hold him," I asked, "while I fasten his legs to the tree?"

"Yup," said Miranda, taking a turn of rope around one hand.

Kneeling at the base of the tree, I pulled the feet close to the trunk and began tying them there. A yellowjacket circled my still-sweaty face, and with one hand I waved it away. Suddenly I heard a sharp exclamation—"*Dammit!*"—followed by a slapping sound. Then: "Oh, *shit*, look out!"

With a thud, the corpse toppled forward, draping himself over my head and shoulders and knocking me flat. Wriggling like some giant bug, I lay trapped at the base of the tree, pinned by the garishly dressed corpse. "I am *so sorry*," Miranda said, and then she began to snicker. But the snicker died suddenly, and I soon saw why.

A pair of rattlesnake boots, topped by black leather jeans, entered my peripheral vision and planted themselves a foot from my face. I knew, even before she spoke, that the snakeskin boots were coiled around the feet of Dr. Jess Carter. After a moment, her right toe began to tap, slowly and, as best I could tell, sarcastically.

"Don't let him get you down, Brockton," she finally said. "I think you can take him. Best two out of three?"

"Very funny," I said. "Y'all mind getting this guy off of me?"

Jess reached down and grabbed the rope around the dead man's wrists; Miranda seized a leg. Together they gave a heave that rolled the corpse onto his back beside me. I regained my feet and as much of my dignity as I could. Jess winked at me with the eye Miranda couldn't see. I would have blushed, but my face was already red.

"This wasn't one of the questions you asked me to research," I told her, "but I'm thinking maybe more than one person was involved in the murder. Pretty tough to tie his arms that high on the tree without some help."

"I see what you mean," she said, "but the forensic techs couldn't tell. Ground's pretty rocky around there, and we had a dry spell for a couple weeks, so nothing useful in the way of footprints."

"I'm sorry I wasn't in town when he was found," I said. "My secretary said you called right about the time my plane was taking off for Los Angeles."

"Damned inconsiderate of you to help the LAPD with a case," she said. "We may need to fit you with one of those electronic ankle monitors to make sure you don't leave Tennessee."

"Can't do it," I said, pointing to my faded jeans and work boots. "It would spoil my fashion statement."

"Nonsense," she said. "Word is, Martha Stewart's coming out with a designer line of corrections apparel and accessories. I'm sure the Martha anklet will look fabulous on you." Jess handed me the rope. "Shall we try this again?" This time, once we'd hoisted the subject upright, I took the precaution of knotting the rope to the branch immediately. I tied off the legs, Jess pronounced herself satisfied with the positioning, and Miranda trimmed the loose ends of the rope.

"The strange thing is, the head and neck were in better shape than I'd expected," she said. "Lots of trauma, but not much decomp, considering how much blood there was to draw the flies. That would lead me to think he wasn't out there all that long, except there was almost no soft tissue left on the lower legs."

"You think maybe carnivores did that? Coyotes or foxes or raccoons?"

"Maybe," she said, "but I didn't see a lot of tooth marks. I'd like you to take a look at him, though, see if maybe I missed something."

"Sure," I said, "I could probably come down to Chattanooga later in the week. One thing I was wondering about, though: Why are you even working the case? I checked the map, and Prentice Cooper State Forest is across the line in Marion County, isn't it?"

She smiled. "I bet you were a whiz at map-and-compass back during your Boy Scout days, weren't you?" I grinned; she was right, even if she was just joking. "Cops got a report of an abduction from the parking lot of Alan Gold's one night a couple weeks ago. Alan Gold's is a gay bar in Chattanooga. Has the best drag show in East Tennessee. A female—or female impersonator—fitting the victim's description was seen being forced into a car and speeding away. We're working on the theory that the crime began in Chattanooga." She paused briefly, as if considering whether to say something else. "Besides," she said, "Marion County is rural and has a small sheriff's office. They just don't have the forensic resources to work this."

"Makes sense," I said. "Okay, I think we're ready to let nature take its course here. We'll check this guy every day, track the temperatures. The forecast for the next fifteen days—if AccuWeather can be believed—calls for temps about like what you've had in Chattanooga over the past couple weeks. So the decomp rate here should track the victim's pretty closely. Once this guy's condition matches your guy's, we should know how long he was out there before that poor hiker found him."

Jess took another look at the corpse tied to the tree. "There's one more detail we need to make the re-creation authentic." I looked puzzled. "I didn't tell you about this," she said. "You were already skittish about the trauma to the head and face, so I figured this would send you clear over the edge." Reaching down to her belt, she unsheathed a long, fixed-blade knife from her waist. She stepped up to the body, yanked down the black satin panties and stockings we'd tugged onto him, and severed his penis at the base.

"Good God," Miranda gasped.

"Not hardly," said Jess. "I'd say this was more the devil's handiwork." She took a deep breath and blew it out. "Bill, you sure this guy is clean?"

I struggled to speak. "Well, I can tell you he didn't have HIV and he didn't have hepatitis. That's all we screen for, though. I can't promise he didn't have syphilis or a case of the clap."

She eyed the penis. "I don't see any obvious symptoms," she said. With that, she peeled off her left glove, dabbed her bare thumb on the severed end of the organ, then carefully rolled a print onto the shaft. As Miranda and I stared in disbelief and horror, she pried open the corpse's jaw and stuffed the penis into the mouth.

"There," she said. "*Now* it's authentic."

CHAPTER 2

"KNOXVILLE POLICE."

I pulled the telephone receiver away from my ear and stared at it dumbly, as if KPD were the last place on earth I'd have expected to reach when dialing criminalist Art Bohanan. Art and I had collaborated on dozens of cases over the past twenty years. Besides being remarkably eagle-eyed at murder scenes, Art had shown himself to be a whiz in the crime lab as well, teasing out clues from minuscule bits of carpet fibers, upholstery, bullet trajectories, and random (to me, though not to him) spatters of blood. He had also become one of the nation's leading fingerprint experts, devising equipment and techniques that even the FBI's crime lab had adopted to reveal latent prints—including seemingly invisible ones on the skin of a body.

"Knoxville Police Department. Can I help you?" The guy on the other end of the line—I pictured an aging, overweight sergeant easing toward his pension—sounded annoyed, despite his offer of help.

"Oh, sorry," I stammered. "I was trying to reach Art Bohanan. I expected either him or his voice mail."

"Sir, he's not available. Can I take a message?"

"Do you know when he'll be in?"

"No, sir, I do not. All I know is that he's unavailable. Do you wish to leave a message or not?"

"Uh, yes. Please. Tell him—ask him—to call Dr. Brockton when he gets a chance, if you would."

"Dr. Brockton? Hey there, Doc." Suddenly the guy was all warmth and cheer. "This is Sergeant Gunderson. I was the one found that guy under the Magnolia Avenue viaduct about ten years ago. You 'member that case?"

"I sure do," I said, smiling at both the memory and my deductive powers. Gunderson was indeed a fat sergeant coasting toward retirement. One reason the case had been memorable was that it featured Gunderson in the unlikely act of running. "You were chasing a burglar that night, if I remember right?"

He chuckled. "Was, till I tripped over that damn body and went ass-over-teakettle. Scared the hell out of me. I 'bout messed my britches. Fellow I was chasing let out a yell just before I went sprawling, so he musta seed it, too."

"Pretty scary thing to stumble across in the moonlight," I agreed. The body turned out to be one of the local winos. Judging by the advanced state of decomp—his skull was nearly bare, though a fair amount of soft tissue remained on his torso and limbs—he'd been ripening beneath the viaduct for about a week of midsummer nights and days. His outline was traced with greasy precision on the concrete by the dark fatty acids that had leached from his corpse, marking the splay of his arms and legs, even the spread of his fingers. There was heated speculation among the officers on the scene about who might have wanted him dead, and what sort of bludgeon had shattered his skull with such devastating force. Then I pointed to an uncapped empty bottle of Mad Dog 20/20 perched on the rail of the viaduct above us—a bottle Art later found to be covered with prints from the dead man's hands and lips. I often used my slides from that case in police trainings, to underscore the importance of looking all around, and up and down, at death scenes.

"Art's on special assignment right now, Doc," Gunderson said, "but I'll page him and have him call you."

"Thanks," I said. "Good to talk to you, Sergeant. Watch your step. You never know where the bodies are."

He chuckled again. "I've got a pretty good fix on where most of 'em are buried here at KPD, though. See you, Doc. Don't be a stranger."

Two minutes later my phone rang. "Bill? It's Art."

"Art Bohanan, Man of Mystery?"

"Maybe, maybe not. Who wants to know?"

"Nobody, now that I think about it," I said. "You available for a quick fingerprint consult?"

"I've gotten sorta sidetracked, but I could spare a few minutes. You got something really gross, as usual?"

"I wouldn't dream of bringing you anything less."

"Got a pen?" I surveyed my cluttered desktop, finally found a nub of a pencil. "Close enough. Why?"

"2035 Broadway. Come inside."

"Why? Where *are* you, anyhow? What are you doing?"

"Can't talk right now. Oh, you got a boom box there in your office?"

I wouldn't have called it a boom box—I kept it tuned to the UT public radio station, which played classical music, and the volume was cranked down so low it was almost subliminal—but I said yes.

"Bring it."

"What for?"

Art didn't explain; he'd already hung up.

For the second time in two phone calls, I found myself staring stupidly at the receiver in my hand. Then I hung up, too. My boom box was sitting atop a file cabinet just inside the door of my office. The cord, shrouded in cobwebs and dust, disappeared behind the cabinet, which was snugged tight against the wall, or tight against the plug, at any rate. Curling both hands behind the back of the filing cabinet, I gave a tug. It did not budge; many years and many pounds' worth of papers had accumulated in it since I had plugged in the radio and shoved the cabinet back in place.

I shifted my grip, crossing my wrists, which somehow seemed to equalize the force I could apply with each arm. Then I hoisted my left foot up onto the doorframe, nearly waist-high, where my hands clutched the cabinet, and strained to straighten my leg. With a rasping sound that set my teeth on edge, the cabinet scraped forward by six inches. Triumphantly I reached into the gap I had created, wiggled the plug free, and extricated the cord and my arm, both covered with cobwebs and grime. "This had better be good, Art," I muttered.

CHAPTER 3

A CENTURY AGO, BROADWAY had been one of Knoxville's grand avenues, lined with elegant Victorian mansions on big, shady lots. The street had long since gone to seed, though, especially in the vicinity of the address Art had given me. Heading north from downtown, I passed two of the city's homeless missions. The missions didn't open their doors for the night until five o'clock, so for most of the day their clientele roamed Broadway; some hung out, or passed out, in nearby cemeteries. A few neighboring streets, buffered from Broadway's blight by a block or so of rental houses, had made a comeback over the past couple of decades. Those pockets of gentrification, sporting pastel houses with gleaming gingerbread, were poignant reminders of how lovely Old North Knoxville had once been, before I-40 had cut a swath through its heart and Broadway itself had become a commuter artery lined with liquor stores and pawnshops.

I was having trouble pinning down the location

Art had summoned me to. "Dammit," I groused to myself, "why don't people put numbers on their buildings anymore?" I passed the turnoff to St. Mary's Hospital—where my son Jeff had been born during a blizzard, back in the decades before the planet's thermostat had ratcheted upward—and finally spotted a number on one of Broadway's few remaining mansions. It was now a funeral home, one that had sent a fair number of the Dearly Departed to the Body Farm.

Judging by the funeral home's address, which I should have remembered from all the thank-you notes I'd sent them, I'd overshot Art's location by several blocks. I whipped into the parking lot, circled the gleaming black hearse, and doubled back toward downtown on Broadway. Traffic backed up behind me as I crept along, scanning for numbers. Finally, running out of options, I turned into a small, run-down shopping center whose anchor tenant was known throughout Knoxville as "the Fellini Kroger" because of the surreal cast of characters who shopped there. A fair number of graduate students lived in Old North Knoxville, since it was fairly close to campus and offered housing that tended toward interesting but cheap. One of my forensic students who'd never lost his interest in cultural anthropology liked to time his shopping at the Fellini Kroger to coincide with the delivery of Social Security disability checks. On those days, he swore, the line at the check-cashing counter could rival any circus sideshow on earth.

Just down from the Kroger, I idled past a Dollar General Store numbered 2043—at last, a

number!—and parked the truck. Feeling conspicuous and more than a little silly, I hauled the boom
box off the passenger seat, as well as the small
cooler Jess had brought from Chattanooga, and
headed along the row of shops. At the far end of the
shopping center, beside a kudzu-choked drainage
ditch, I found myself facing a door marked 2035.
The door and windows were coated with reflective
film; a hand-painted sign on the window glass announced the store as BROADWAY JEWELRY & LOAN.
Puzzled, I tried to enter, but the door was locked.
I set the boom box and cooler down, pressed my
face to the door, and cupped my hands around my
eyes to screen out the sunlight; inside, I discerned
a hulking man behind a counter. I rapped on the
glass and he looked up, then pointed emphatically
to my right. A doorbell-type button was mounted
to the doorframe. "Good grief," I muttered, but I
pushed it. Inside, I heard a metallic buzz—I was
mildly surprised that it worked—then a loud click
in the doorframe. I picked up my belongings and
pushed through the door. Within the narrow store-
front, one wall was lined with shelves laden with
stereos, televisions, and power tools; set out from
the opposite wall was a long glass counter on which
the guy who'd buzzed me in was leaning. His beefy
forearms rested on a sign that read DO NOT LEEN ON
COUNTER.

"I'm sorry to bother you," I said, "I think I must
have been given the wrong address."

He looked me over, then his eyes settled on the
boom box. "Depends," he said. "Who gave it to
you?"

"My friend Art. Art Bohanan. He's with the police department."

The big man vaulted the counter like a dog going after a UPS guy. Before I knew what had happened, my nose was flattened on the glass, my right arm torqued up between my shoulder blades. "I want to know who the fuck you are, mister, and what you mean coming in here talking about the damn police."

"Bill? Bill, is that you?" Art's voice floated out from the back of the store. "It's okay, Tiny. He's on our side."

Tiny released my arm, milliseconds before the bone was about to snap. "Dammit, Tiffany, why didn't you tell me you had somebody coming? And why'd you bring him here, anyway? You know better than that."

Tiffany? I was more confused than ever. Art emerged through a curtain at the back of the shop. "I'm sorry; I meant to tell you, I just forgot. Tiny, this is Dr. Bill Brockton. Bill, this is Tiny."

"Tiny and I have met," I said, rubbing my arm.

Tiny looked me over again, seeing something different this time. "You're the Body Farm guy?" I nodded. "Hey, it's an honor to meet you, Doc," he said, seizing my hand and pumping my mangled arm. "I'm sorry I got a little excited there. You're a better class of customer than what we're used to dealing with here at Broadway Jewelry & Loan. You had me worried our cover was blown."

Suddenly I grasped where I was, and why Art had told me to bring the boom box. "So you're running an undercover sting operation here? Dealing in stolen property?"

"Tiny is," said Art. "I'm camped out in the back, putting some of the inventory to good use. Come on in. Welcome to my world. And Tiffany's."

As I stepped through the curtain into the back of the store, my eyes irised open to compensate for the dimness. The only light, besides what leaked around the doorway curtain, came from two large computer monitors. When I realized what was on them, I felt my stomach clench. "Oh *Jesus*, Art." One screen showed a paunchy middle-aged man. He was stark naked, and he was not alone. He was with a girl who couldn't have been more than eight or ten. The other showed the same man with a boy who appeared even younger, possibly even six or seven.

"Sickening, isn't it?" said Art. "I spend hours every day looking at filth like this. It's getting to me, I have to tell you."

"I can't even begin to imagine. How on earth did you get into this? And for heaven's sake, *why*?"

He sighed. "You remember that little girl who was abducted, raped, and murdered a few months back? The perp represented by your buddy Grease?" I nodded, grimacing; Art had been deeply distressed by the case, especially the fact that the abductor's lawyer, Burt DeVriess—"Grease," most of the cops called him—had delayed the search of the car in which the child had been kidnapped. "Well, when we finally searched the guy's house and his computer, we found tons of child pornography. Not surprising—a lot of child predators trade kiddie porn over the Internet, and some of them troll for victims in online chat rooms." I nodded. "After that case, the chief decided that it was time for us to go after guys like that before they struck, rather than after. Guess who won the coin toss?"

He sounded bitter about the assignment, but I knew Art better than that. What he was bitter about was the existence of child predators. Spending his days and nights in their virtual company would be bound to take a toll on him, but I knew he would pursue them with relentless zeal.

"So what's with the 'Tiffany' business?"

"That's one of my chat room IDs. I'm a thirteen-year-old girl who hates her parents, loves to chat, and can't wait to find out what love is really like. I've got a dozen dirty old men across the state just dying to initiate me into the pleasures of the flesh."

"Clearly they have a different picture of you than I do," I said, eyeing Art's stocky body and graying hair.

"Oh, absolutely," he said. "I'm actually tall and slim, but all the boys say I have nice boobs and a great ass."

I shuddered. "Yuck. I can't believe you have to think like that."

"Tell me about it. One of these creeps is about to talk me into sneaking away to meet him. Some jerk down in Sweetwater who thinks I'll be there this weekend visiting my aunt, who just so happens to live near the Motel Six. I can't wait to see the look on his face when I kick in the door of the motel room, flash him my badge, and say, 'Hi, asshole, I'm Tiffany, and you're under arrest.'"

I had to laugh, in spite of the seamy subject. "But

Sweetwater's fifty miles south of here. Isn't that a little outside your jurisdiction?"

"Not anymore," Art said. He picked up a badge from the desk and handed it to me. It was a five-pointed gold star encircled by the words UNITED STATES MARSHAL.

I whistled. "U.S. Marshal? How'd a lowly KPD cop swing that?"

"We're working with the feds," he said. "FBI and postal inspectors. I've got arrest powers anywhere in the state. Believe it or not, this"—he swept his arm in an arc that encompassed the dingy space—"is the headquarters of the Tennessee Task Force on Internet Crimes Against Children. Mainly me and a couple of stolen computers so far, but we're about to get some serious money and manpower."

"Good for you," I said. "Reminds me of my own job—the work stinks, but somebody's got to do it. Can't think of anybody who'd do this with more commitment and integrity."

"Not sure how long I can take it, though," he said. "I'm only two months in, and already my blood pressure's through the roof, I'm having trouble sleeping, and once I do get to sleep, I have awful nightmares."

Knowing what a decent guy Art was, that didn't surprise me. "You're on a rough diet right now," I said. "Nothing but rotten fruit from the tree of knowledge."

"Isn't there supposed to be some good fruit on that tree, too? Last time I read the Bible, it was called the tree of knowledge of *good* and evil."

"Yeah, but the good stuff's on branches neither

one of us gets to pick," I said. "Speaking of bad fruit, let me show you what I need you to print. You might want to glove up for this." I reached into my pocket and pulled out a pair of latex gloves for him, plus a pair for me. Then I opened the small cooler Jess had given me. Inside, propped on a bed of ice and sealed in a plastic bag, was the Chattanooga victim's penis. A bloody thumbprint—bigger than the one Jess had planted on our research subject— showed clearly through the bag.

If I'd known Jess was bringing this grisly piece of evidence with her, I'd have asked Art to meet us at the Body Farm. I didn't mind playing courier, though, as I hadn't seen Art in weeks and I welcomed the chance to catch up with him, even briefly.

When he recognized the object in the baggie, Art's eyes widened and he gave a low whistle. "Ouch, man. Well, you've certainly come to the right place," he said, nodding toward the computer monitors. "Feels like we're in the theme park from hell here. What's the story? There is a story, right? I mean, it's not every day somebody brings me a severed pecker on ice."

"Sure, there's a story. We just don't know what it is yet. The guy this belonged to was found tied to a tree in a state forest outside Chattanooga. He was wearing a woman's wig, makeup, and leather corset. Head and face were bashed in pretty bad. And this was stuffed in his mouth."

"I can think of a few more guys that deserve the same treatment," he said. Then: "Sorry—I don't mean that this guy did. I shouldn't let what I'm working on here poison my thinking about other cases."

"It's okay," I said. "Be tough not to."

"You thinking homophobic hate crime?"

"Well, that's sure what it looks like. First glance, anyhow."

Art switched on a small desk lamp beside one of the monitors; mercifully, he also switched off both monitors. Holding the severed organ gingerly in the palm of one gloved hand, he leaned close and studied the bloody print. "Not a bad print, considering," he said. "If your killer is considerate enough to have prints on file, we might just get a match. I'll need to take it back to the lab, though. You wanna come along?"

"Don't you need to stay here . . . *Tiffany*?"

He glared at me, then cupped a hand behind one ear. "I think I hear my mean old mom calling me," he said. "She says I have to log off and do my stupid algebra homework. Like, what a total bitch?"

He switched the monitors back on, prompting me to flee to the front of the pawnshop, where I inspected Tiny's merchandise. The glass display case contained several iPods, a handful of heavy gold neck chains, and at least a dozen handguns, ranging in price from one hundred dollars to three hundred. I couldn't tell any difference between the least expensive and the most expensive, so I asked Tiny to explain. "This here's a Hi-Point," he said, pulling out the hundred-dollar gun. "Lots of 'em out there, 'cause they's so damn cheap. Some folks say they're bad to jam, but that's mostly because of cheap ammo, is what I think. 'Course, if you can't afford but a hunnerd-dollar gun, you probably got to buy cheap ammo, too. So either way, you could be screwed." He pulled out the expensive gun. "This is a SIG Sauer," he said. "Everything about this weapon is top-notch. If I'm needin' to shoot some sumbitch, I want to be able to trust my piece. Don't you?"

"Um, sure," I said. "Damn right I do."

"Okay, Deadeye, let's go," said Art. "I have to do homework for a whole hour, and then I've got a chat room date I have to get back for."

CHAPTER 4

THE KNOXVILLE POLICE DEPARTMENT was housed in a gray and tan concrete and brick fortress of indeterminate vintage—late 1960s or early '70s, maybe, the heyday of "urban renewal," when whole blocks of old buildings were razed to make way for parking lots and stark, boxy structures. Situated a stone's throw from two of Knoxville's low-income housing projects, it probably saved the city thousands a year in fuel costs just by virtue of its location.

As Art and I passed the front desk I looked for Gunderson, the sergeant I'd joked with earlier in the day, but evidently his shift was over, for the desk was staffed by a young Latina woman. She waved at Art, studied me and my cooler briefly, then pressed some button that opened the elevator for us.

For years the fingerprint lab was down in the basement, but these days, it inhabited quarters on the second floor. Art nodded at a countertop, which I took as a sign to set the cooler down. It was a good guess; he opened the top and lifted out the bag containing the penis.

"Are you going to fume it?" I asked. I didn't know a lot about fingerprinting, but I knew Art had patented a gizmo for creating fumes of superglue which would stick to latent prints on whatever object was placed in the chamber that filled with the fumes, tracing the loops and whorls in crisp white.

"No," he said, "for this I'll use leuco-crystal violet. Shows up better than superglue. It reacts chemically in the presence of blood—the hemoglobin actually catalyzes a reaction between the LCV and hydrogen peroxide—to produce a bright purple. Even if the blood were a lot dimmer than what's on this guy's pecker, it would be very dramatic."

From a cabinet of bottles and boxes and bags of supplies, he took down a brown plastic bottle of ordinary hydrogen peroxide and a bottle of a clear solution; in a small beaker he mixed 50 cc's of the leuco-crystal violet—a couple of ounces, maybe—with another 200 cc's of the peroxide. Finally, he slid an oblong pellet the size of the end of his pinkie down the side of the beaker into the mixture.

"What's that? The magic ingredient?"

"Close," he said. "The magnetic stirrer." He set the beaker on top of a small instrument with a round, flat platform on top and rotated a switch on the instrument's face. The pellet began to spin, slowly at first, then faster and faster as he cranked the dial. "Good for mixing drinks, too, as long as you're not hoping to chop ice." He poured the liquid from the beaker into a plastic spray bottle, aimed the bottle into a sink, and pumped the trigger a few times to prime it. "Okay, let's take a closer look at our boy here."

From a box of latex gloves on the counter, he took and donned a pair. Then he took a pair of forceps from a tray, opened the bag, and reached in with the forceps to extract the penis. "You mind switching on that light for me?" He gestured, using the penis as a pointer, toward a lamp that consisted of a large magnifying glass encircled by a fluorescent tube. I held the red button on the base, and the tube flickered on. "I don't suppose we know what size this thing was when the print was deposited, do we? I mean, it makes a difference whether a balloon is inflated or deflated when the artwork gets applied." It hadn't occurred to me until he brought it up, but size really did seem to matter in this particular instance.

"I don't think we have any idea," I said. "At least, no one's mentioned a photo or a note about dimensions at the moment of amputation."

He studied the print closely. "Well, this looks to be about the same size as my thumbprint," he said. "Not, mind you, that there's any other resemblance. I would guess, unless the person who lopped it off was incredibly sneaky, the poor bastard was probably not in a state of arousal."

"I would guess," I said, "that if I saw somebody coming at my private parts with a butcher knife, I'd be shriveling fast and trying to make like a turtle."

Art laughed. "Yeah, I can recall a couple of occasions when I wouldn't have minded being able to do the emergency retraction. Once when I was a kid, I was peeing out a double-hung window, and the sash fell shut. A very narrow escape, not to mention a big mess to clean up. Another time, when I was nineteen, I'd gone to visit my girlfriend at the women's college in Mississippi where she'd just started. We hadn't seen each other in two months, and she had finally caved in. Just at the wrong moment, a bright flashlight shone through the car window right at my proud manhood. My first and most humiliating law enforcement experience."

He rotated the penis, bringing the head into sharper focus. "Too bad this guy was circumcised," he said. "If the foreskin were intact, there might be enough fluid underneath to let us get a swab and check for saliva or other fluids from recent sexual contact. We've gotten DNA matches that way in a couple other murders, though the penis was still attached to both of those stiffs. So to speak."

With that, he took the penis and the spray bottle over to an exhaust hood, where he tapped a floor switch to turn on a light and the exhaust fan. Then he gently misted the severed penis with the mixture from his spray bottle. Almost immediately, the severed base of the organ turned a bright purple. A second later, so did the faint reddish brown of the print an inch away from the stump. Rotating the organ, Art sprayed a fine mist around its entire girth, and as he did so, other prints—previously little more than faint smudges—leapt into view. "Look at that," said Art. "We've got a complete set. He had a pretty good grip when he lopped it off. There's the thumb on top, closest to the base, and a row of fingertips running up the side. See the pinkie, there near the head? And look at that line in the thumbprint—this guy had cut his thumb recently."

"I'll be," I said. "If this guy's prints are on file, you think you can match one of those?"

"Bill, if this guy's prints are on file, *you* could match one of those. These are nearly as good as we get when we print a new hire upstairs in Human Resources."

"So all cops' fingerprints are on file?"

He nodded. "We put those in AFIS—the Automated Fingerprint Identification System—so if they show up at a crime scene, we know it's because they were working the scene, not committing the crime. In theory, at least."

"Any other noncriminals in the system?"

"Sure. Soldiers and firefighters—sometimes helps identify bodies if faces are damaged beyond recognition. People think all that's done with DNA these days, but prints are still a lot faster and cheaper."

"Anybody else?"

"Gun buyers," he said. "Teachers and child care workers—background check to make sure they're not sex offenders."

He pulled the penis out from under the hood and laid it on an absorbent paper pad on the counter. Then he gently patted it dry with another pad. "I think the best way to capture these prints would be to press this flat under glass and photograph them," he said.

"You don't lift them with tape?" I asked.

"LCV doesn't lift like powder," he said. "The

photos should work fine, though. Besides, we'll still have the prints themselves. I can pop Little Johnny Doe in the freezer and he'll stay fresh for years. I can't wait to show this to a jury in court."

"Well, I'm happy to leave it in your capable hands," I said. "Just write me an evidence receipt so Jess Carter doesn't ream me out for losing her penis."

"Jess? Is she still filling in as ME up here?" I nodded. "Well, if you do lose her penis, I suspect Jess could lay her hands on another one just about anytime she wanted to."

"I suspect if she heard you say that, she might lay her hands and her scalpel on yours."

"I don't doubt it," he said. "She's a feisty one, that's for sure. Take a mighty gutsy cowboy to climb into that saddle. Big cojones or a death wish, one." For emphasis, he pointed at me as he said it. With the purple-spotted penis he still held in the forceps.

"Hmm," I said.

What I didn't say was that Jess was coming to my house for a drink and a steak in a couple of hours. As I rode the elevator down from the second floor and walked out of KPD, Art's comment kept looping through my mind, and I couldn't help wondering: Who was having whom for dinner tonight? I found Jess intriguing, admirable, and exciting— she was smart, competent, confident, and funny, and she was good-looking, too: wavy auburn hair, green eyes, and a petite but athletic-looking build. But there was an edge to Jess that I found intimidating. I hadn't dated in decades, and the prospect of dating made me nervous even in the abstract. In the concrete—in the flesh, rather, of Jess Carter, who projected a take-no-prisoners toughness—the idea seemed downright perilous. Not so perilous, though, that I'd declined when she suggested I cook dinner for her. Just perilous enough, perhaps, to keep me on my toes. And according to Miranda, who was pretty smart herself, maybe it was time for a woman to keep me on my toes.

CHAPTER 5

THE WESTBOUND LANES OF Kingston Pike were as clogged as a fat man's arteries as the late afternoon traffic crept into the bedroom community of Farragut. I reminded myself of the oath I'd taken years before—never never *never* go to Farragut between 3 P.M. and 7 P.M.—but deep down, I knew I had no choice today unless I wanted to find myself a new accountant.

I was on permanent probation with my accountant, and with plenty of cause. I was undoubtedly his worst client. For one thing, I tended to take a grocery bag full of receipts and deposit slips to his office every year around the first of April—early enough for me to feel virtuous, but far too late for him to have any hope of filing my tax return on time. For another, anytime he chastised me for sloppy record-keeping or dumb investments, I tended to say, "Don't act smart with me; I used to change your diapers."

My accountant was my son Jeff. His firm, Brockton & Associates, included two other CPAs and several seasonal tax accountants. They specialized in medical practices and rich physicians, so besides being his worst client, I was probably his poorest, too—a minor but meaningful distinction.

I'd arranged to drop off my grocery bag—two whole weeks earlier than usual—at Jeff's house so I could piggyback a visit with his kids. My grandsons. Tyler was seven; Walker was five; both were rambunctious and confident little boys, unscathed enough to fling themselves at life unreservedly, certain that life stood ready to catch them with unfailing arms.

Tyler flung open the door for me. "Grandpa Bill! Grandpa Bill! Mom, Grandpa Bill's here!" I set my paper bag down and scooped him up, and he hugged me hard. He felt warm and moist and smelled slightly nutty and pungent—that mix of clean sweat and fresh dirt little kids exude when they've been playing hard. Walker came tearing around the corner from the den and grabbed my legs, pinning me in place. He, too, felt and smelt like a busy boy. Both boys were wearing soccer uniforms, which explained the sweat and the dirt.

"Grandpa Bill, Grandpa Bill, I was playing Sonic and I got *three more lives*," Walker said.

"Three more? Three is three-mendous," I said. I had no idea what he meant, but if he was pleased, I was pleased.

He giggled. "*Tree*-mendous, silly."

"Three is nothin'," said Tyler. "I got *seven*."

"Oh yeah? I got . . . I got seventy-*seventy*-seven," said Walker.

"Did not. Besides, there ain't no such number, poopy-breath."

"Tyler *Brockton*," came a warning voice from the kitchen. "*Isn't any* such number. And no name-calling, or no computer." Jeff's wife Jenny appeared in the doorway holding a pizza box in one hand and a Diet Coke in the other. "Hey there," she said. "We got in from a soccer match in Oak Ridge about two minutes ago. Will you eat some Big Ed's with us?"

"Sure," I said, "if there's enough."

"More than enough," she said. "Jeff just called; he's bogged down in some surgeon's huge tax return—big surprise, huh?—so he probably won't be home for a couple more hours. You can have his share. Walker, let go of Grandpa Bill's legs so he can move. Tyler, you come help me set the table."

I set Tyler down, and he staggered into the kitchen as if it required his last ounce of strength. Actually, considering the way boys tend to run hard until the moment they give out completely, that might have been the case.

Jenny moved around the kitchen with an easy, athletic grace. She had played soccer in both high school and college; she, not Jeff, was the parent who helped coach the kids' teams. By training and trade, she was a graphic designer; she worked part-time, freelance, from an office over the garage. I'd seen some of her pieces—mostly corporate brochures, but some magazine ads and even a few album covers—and liked them. From a distance, they looked like thousands of other pieces of commercial art: children and dogs, perfect couples, rolling farmland in buttery light. But when you actually looked at them, something small and quirky always caught the eye and prompted a smile: a doggie treat in a kid's mouth, a piece of corn wedged in a husband's smile, a cow squirting out a fresh pie in one corner of the pasture. The deadpan humor was Jenny's approach to life and marriage and motherhood, as best I could tell, and I knew it had been good for Jeff. Jenny loosened up the tidy, stuffy streak that allowed Jeff to spend two thousand hours a year happily adding and subtracting digits that represented other people's money.

The pizza—extra cheese, extra pepperoni—had a thin but yeasty crust, dusted underneath with cornmeal. Big Ed's Pizza had been an institution in the nearby town of Oak Ridge for as long as I'd been in Knoxville. It was housed in a cavernous, high-ceilinged building that dated back to the town's Manhattan Project days, and it looked like the floors hadn't been refinished, and possibly hadn't been swept, since the atomic bomb was dropped on Japan. Big Ed himself had died a few years back, but his blocky caricature and his signature line—"I make my own dough"—remained on the job, as did the recipe for his memorable crust. The pizza was heavy, greasy, and extremely good. We ate fast and appreciatively.

"I haven't seen your name in the paper lately," Jenny said, taking a third slice. "Things pretty quiet in the seamy underbelly these days?"

"Things are never quiet in the seamy underbelly. Just quiet in the press, thank goodness."

"What's an underbelly?" asked Tyler.

"This is an underbelly," I said, and reached down and tickled him.

"Where's *my* underbelly?" Walker asked, so I tickled him, too.

I asked Jenny about her recent projects, which were safer dinnertime fodder than my work. The winter had been slow, but she had just landed a contract to design a collection of brochures and ads for UT, which was launching a billion-dollar fund-raising drive. "Be sure you use some good photos of my research subjects," I said.

"I like it," she mused. "Tell folks if they don't pony up, this is the fate that awaits them. I think the money would roll right in." Then she shared war stories from a photo shoot with the UT herd of dairy cattle. Apparently, getting that photo I'd seen of the rolling pastures and the pooping cow took multiple shoots. "Who'd have thought, with all those cows, it would take us a whole week and the magic of PhotoShop to get that pooping cow in the picture?"

"Poopy cow, poopy cow," crowed Walker.

"You're the poopy cow," said Tyler.

"Huh-uh, *you're* the poopy cow."

"I hope," I said, "we're not having chocolate ice cream for dessert."

"Ooooh," said everyone.

Jenny finally hauled us back to civility. "Tyler, do you want to tell Grandpa Bill about the project you're doing for school?"

"Sure," he said. "It's a PowerPoint about sea turtles."

A PowerPoint? The kid was in second grade. I

had tried making a PowerPoint presentation once, and I ended up needing a new hard drive in my computer. "Sea turtles? I like sea turtles. Can I see it?"

"Course," he said. "C'mon." I followed him into the den, where Walker had already settled into a video game involving some whirling, twirling, spiky-furred creature. Sonic, I presumed, living his three more lives at warp speed.

Tyler clicked the mouse on the Apple computer sitting on a table in the den, and the big flat-panel display—which until recently had been Jenny's graphic-design monitor—came alive. The screen's background image consisted of a collage of photos of Tyler and Walker from babyhood on. In one close-up, Walker stared, transfixed, at a monarch butterfly perched on his index finger; in another, Tyler peered out from behind an enormous sphere of purple bubble gum, half the size of his head. Every photo showed a child alive with wonder, and I suddenly felt a stab of fear and sadness. All that joy and innocence reminded me of the two other children whose faces I'd seen on computer monitors just a few hours before: the young boy and girl being sexually abused by a paunchy, middle-aged man.

It took everything I had to focus on Tyler's slide-show about sea turtles—their long lives, the remarkable homing instincts and nesting habits of the females, the way many of the species were being driven to extinction by hunting and beachfront development. Finally he finished, and I praised his work extravagantly and excused myself. I found

Jenny in the kitchen, packing the next day's school lunches. "Can I ask you something?"

She looked at me closely. "Sure; what's wrong? You look upset."

"I've gotten a little too close to the seamy underbelly lately," I said. "My friend Art is working on Internet crimes against children—he's chasing down pedophiles who troll for kids online." She looked upset now, too. "We didn't have to worry about this when Jeff was growing up, thank God. How do you deal with that kind of threat, and that kind of fear?"

"Eternal vigilance," she said. "I love the Internet; I couldn't do what I do, the way I do it and where I do it, without e-mail and Google and all those other things. But cybertechnology is the best of tools and the worst of tools. Besides allowing people to do things faster and better than ever, it allows people to do things faster and worse than ever. Including letting kids get in way over their heads way before they realize it."

"I know you can't put the genie back in the bottle, but how do you protect the kids? I mean, I don't do that much on the Internet, but even so, I'm always getting e-mails promising to enlarge my penis or show me girls gone wild. Are there ways to filter that stuff out, keep kids from seeing it?"

She made a face. "In theory. We've tried both CyberPatrol and Net Nanny, which promise to block that kind of stuff. But the reality is, even if they're ninety-nine percent effective, which they're not, even one percent of what's out there is an enormous amount of smut. Hell, you know me, Bill;

I'm a free-speech advocate, I give to Planned Parenthood and the ACLU, and I opposed the death penalty until I started to hear about the kinds of people whose handiwork you end up dealing with. But I swear, bleeding-heart liberal though I am, the parent in me thinks we need to get a whole lot more restrictive about what's on the Internet."

"I agree," I said. "But meanwhile, what do you do to protect Tyler and Walker?"

"We don't let them go into chat rooms. We don't let them download files—if they come across some reference to something they need, Jeff or I will download it for them. We only let them e-mail with a very limited group of friends—we've created a list of approved contacts, and the computer blocks anything to or from anybody who's not on that list. Mostly, though, we try to keep a pretty close eye on what they're doing—that's why neither one of them will ever have a computer in their bedroom. Not till they're in college, anyhow."

"Sounds like you're being super careful."

"We are," she said, "but we can't be with them all the time. They have computer access at school, at the library, at friends' houses. We do our best to make sure those places are pretty strict, too, but sooner or later they're bound to get curious and get into stuff I wish they wouldn't. All we can do is hope and pray that by that time, they're pretty well grounded."

CHAPTER 6

I HEARD A SHARP rap at my front door, but before I could get there, the door rattled open and Jess Carter's voice rang out, "Bill? I'm here and I'm hungry. Where are you? Or where's the food?"

"Back here in the kitchen," I called. "Straight back." Her boots clomped on the slate floor of the entryway. I realize it's just a function of the materials used to make the heels, but I've always found it fascinating that women's shoes tend to announce themselves so much more loudly than men's. The designers' strategy, if that's what it is, works well, at least on me.

She appeared in the kitchen doorway holding a cloth shopping bag in each hand. She set them down on the granite counter. "You still a teetotaler?" I nodded. "As I suspected. I came prepared." She reached into one of the bags, pulling out a fifth of vodka and a bottle of cranberry juice cocktail.

"What's in the other bag? After-dinner cigars?"

She made a face. "Yuck, no. Something much tastier. You mentioned steak and asparagus and potatoes, but you didn't promise dessert." She fished a low, wide box out of the other bag. The picture showed a golden brown fruit pie, which the label proclaimed as "Razzleberry."

"What kind of berry's a razzleberry?" I asked. "Never heard of it."

"Them," she said. "Two kinds, raspberry and blackberry. Good on their own, fabulous together. The perfect couple, you might say. Much like us." She faced me dead-on and raised her left eyebrow by what seemed to be an inch, while the right remained perfectly stationary.

I laughed. "How'd you do that?"

"What, this?" She did it again, this time with her right eyebrow.

"Yeah. That's amazing. How'd you learn to do that?"

"Diligent practice. While the other med students were dissecting cadavers, I was perfecting facial gymnastics in the mirror. Honing indispensable skills like this." One side of her mouth suddenly turned upward in a big smile; the other side drooped in an exaggerated, clownlike frown; it was as if invisible hands were tugging in opposite directions on either side of her face. I shook my head in astonishment. "It's just muscle isolation," she said. "Like belly-dancing, only higher-brow." She did the eyebrow again to underscore the pun.

I tried to duplicate the maneuver. I felt my whole face contort with the effort. She grimaced in mock horror. I took another run at it; this time, I felt my scalp shifting and my ears twitching. "Ow. I think I just pulled a muscle I didn't know I had."

She shook her head and patted my arm. "There, there. We all have our special talents. I'm sure you'll discover yours one of these days."

"Hmph," I said. "Now you're patronizing me."

"Everybody needs a patron," she said.

I opened the cabinet and pulled out a tall glass, then filled it with ice cubes from the freezer and handed it to her. She set it on the counter and half filled it with vodka, which she topped off with cranberry juice.

"You don't need to measure?"

"It's not chemistry lab," she said. "Plenty of margin for error." She took a long pull and smiled happily. "Ah, just what the doctor ordered. You sure I can't corrupt you?"

"Pretty sure," I said. "I can barely keep up with you sober. I wouldn't have a prayer if I were impaired."

"You would if I were more impaired," she said, taking another swig.

I took this as a sign that it was time to put the steaks on. I opened the fridge, took out the steaks, and unwrapped the white butcher paper. They were big, thick filets, nearly as tall as they were wide, wrapped in bacon. I'd picked them up at the Fresh Market, the grocery store on the edge of Sequoyah Hills. Sequoyah is Knoxville's ritziest neighborhood, unless you count some of the suburbs to the west, in Farragut. Normally I shopped at Kroger— not the Fellini Kroger, but a far closer and far tamer one—but the Fresh Market's meat was the best in town. It was actually worth paying Sequoyah Hills prices for.

My house was *in* Sequoyah Hills, but it was not *of* Sequoyah Hills, to borrow a prepositional distinction Jesus once made to his followers about their relationship to the world. I had an archetypally common ranch house—an extraordinary house, I sometimes called it—which shared a shady circle with a half dozen other ranchers. The only remarkable thing about them was the way they were surrounded by hundreds of mansions. Whenever things got dangerously ostentatious in the neighborhood—a fancy symphony party or political fund-raiser at the Versailles-like palace around the corner, attended by glittering people in formal wear—it comforted me to imagine our modest homes as pioneer wagons, circled for self-protection. If our protective circle were ever breached, it probably wouldn't take long before every ranch house on the street got torn down and replaced with some stucco-slathered behemoth three or four times as big, crowding its property lines and its equally steroidal neighbors. Not that I was bitter or anything.

Plopping the steaks on a plate, I sprinkled both sides with salt and pepper, rubbing the seasonings in, then dashed some Worcestershire sauce on top to add a little zing.

Jess nodded approvingly. "You gonna put some sizzle in that steak?"

"Gonna try."

"How you cooking them?"

"I'm a guy; on the grill, of course."

"Gas or charcoal?"

"Be a waste of a good steak to cook it over gas," I said.

"Indeed," she said. "Gas is great for a crematorium, but a steak just cries out for the extra flavor of those charcoal carcinogens."

"You do have an eye for the tarnished lining. Anybody ever tell you that?"

She looked down at her drink. "Ouch. Actually, I've been told that's one of my special talents," she said. She looked up again, and I could see hurt in her eyes.

"I was just joking," I said. "Who said it that wasn't joking? And why does it make you look so sad all of a sudden?"

"My ex-husband. My most recent ex-husband, to be clinically precise."

"You introduced me to a lawyer husband a couple years ago; that the one?" She nodded. "How many other exes you got scattered around?"

"Just one other. If you're only counting husbands."

"And if I'm counting other significant others?"

She rolled her eyes. "It'd take me some thinking to tally them up. Four or five semiserious guys, and one experimental woman."

The world had changed in the several decades since I'd last dated, I decided. "A few months back, you told me you were happily lesbian. Was that the experiment?"

She laughed. "Naw, that was just to fend you off in case you were harboring any designs on me. You seemed so bogged down in your grief over Kathleen still, I knew you weren't ready for anybody yet. Or maybe I just didn't want to get tangled up in all that sadness."

"And now?"

"Now you seem over it, or at least through the worst of it. Not exactly giddy with joie de vivre yet, but then again, that'd be a stretch for a guy in your line of work. You seem . . . solid now."

"Did I seem solid a few months ago, when we had that near miss with a dinner date?"

"Solid enough," she said, "at the center. A little gooey around the edges, maybe, but who isn't sometimes?" As she said it, she cocked her head and shrugged slightly, and smiled not so slightly. I could have sworn I felt myself getting a little gooey around the edges but stirringly solid at my center. I took a step toward her and reached up a hand to touch her cheek. When I did, she nodded her head up and down, rubbing against my hand. I closed my eyes to concentrate on the feel of her skin. "So you didn't mind that I invited myself to dinner to-night?" My eyes still closed, I shook my head. "So why didn't you ask me out again after I had to skip out all those months ago?"

The truth was, I'd gotten scared, but I wanted to appear more suave than that. "I was playing hard to get," I said. As I said it, I heard my voice crack like that of a boy just hitting puberty. So much for suave. I laughed. "I've heard nothing interests a woman more than acting indifferent."

I felt a palm smack my face, but it was a playful smack. I opened my eyes and saw Jess shaking her head, but she was grinning as she did it. "You are such a lying piece of shit," she said. "You are a seri-ously bad liar. But a seriously good man."

She moved closer to me and turned her face to mine. Maybe some things in the world hadn't changed all that much, because I had no trouble interpreting an invitation to kiss her. With her boots on, her mouth was nearly at the level of mine. Just enough lower that it felt good to reach a hand around to the back of her neck, threading my fingers through her thick auburn hair.

I felt a pleasant tingling in my loins for a moment, then it stopped. Then it returned, and I realized the tingling was not actually within my loins, but against them.

"Oh, *damn*," murmured Jess. "It's my pager." I felt the buzz one last time, then she pulled away and jammed a hand into a pocket of her jeans. As she fished out the pager, it gave another buzz, like an angry insect—a cicada spinning helplessly on its back, I decided. "Shit, it's Homicide," she said. "I have to call them." From her other pocket she fished a cellphone and flipped it open. "Dispatch," she snapped, and I heard the cellphone play a tune of dial tones as it obliged. "This is Dr. Carter," she said. "You got one for me?" As she listened, she winced and shook her head. "Shit. What time was the call? . . . Okay, I'll be there in an hour. Tell 'em to cordon off the park, keep the TV cameras out, and don't touch anything." She flipped the phone closed and began scooping up her bags. "A murder in Riverfront Park."

"That's the park that stretches along the Tennessee from downtown all the way up to Chickamauga Dam?"

"Yeah. Seven or eight miles. This was right near the downtown end, a stone's throw from the aquarium and the art museum."

"What happened? A tourist mugging that turned violent?"

"No. A local. A runner with a dog. Dog's dead, too." She got an odd look on her face. "I think maybe I've been in this job too long, Bill. I'm upset about this."

I touched her arm. "That just shows you're not jaded."

She shook her head. "No. What I'm upset about is the dog."

She turned to go, then veered back and gave me a quick peck on the lips. "I'm sorry to cut and run," she said. "I was looking forward to dinner. And dessert."

She clomped back through the entryway and out the front door. As it latched shut behind her, the timer on my microwave beeped to tell me the charcoal was ready. I picked up the plate of steaks and headed for the back porch.

CHAPTER 7

THE RINGING PHONE SOUNDED far away, and I felt myself swimming up from a deep and viscous sleep to answer it.

"Bill? It's Jess."

Her voice and her name jolted me awake. "Jess? What time is it? Where are you? Are you okay?"

"It's about four. I just got home from the scene. Bill, could you . . . could you just talk to me for a few minutes? Talk me down a ways?" Her voice shook and her nose sounded stopped up, as if she'd already done some crying.

"Sure, Jess. Of course. Tell me what's wrong."

"I might have to work up to it," she said. Her breathing started to run away with her; I could hear her struggling to rein it back in. "It was a bad scene. Brutal. Like some biblical retribution. Blood everywhere. Stab wounds all over the victim. Multiple dog bites. Two slaughtered dogs."

"Two?"

"Two. One was the victim's; other belonged to one of the killers."

"Was it a dogfight that spread to the people?"

"No. Other way around. We got the story from a couple of witnesses. A homeless guy who spends a lot of time sleeping under this bridge where it happened, and a bike rider who was just up the hill. Apparently there was some history between the victim and this handful of punks who liked to hang out in the park under the bridge. The victim was a runner; they'd been hassling him for a while. If he'd had any sense, he'd've found some other place to run his dog."

"People don't always do what's in their own best interest," I said. It sounded stupid as I said it, but I didn't know what else to offer. Didn't know what she needed to hear.

"The detectives talked to his girlfriend. Guy was a science teacher, turns out. Early thirties. Idealistic. Just started teaching last fall at one of the inner-city magnet schools. Gonna save the world—or at least inner-city kids—through education. He'd moved in from Meigs County to take the job. Used to have a place out in the country, with a big yard for the dog, the girlfriend says. Australian shepherd. He felt bad about keeping it cooped up in an apartment. Figured he owed it a run somewhere every day with grass and trees to make amends."

"And that got him killed? That is sad," I said.

"It gets sadder," she said. "The girlfriend says when these punks first started hassling him—a week or so ago, she thinks—he tried to reason with them. I mean, these are the big brothers of the kids he's teaching every day. But they wouldn't leave him alone, and he wouldn't back down. Like dogs, stalking around all stiff-legged with their hackles up. She begged him to steer clear of the park, but he said once you start running away, you never stop. So he bought a knife to carry on his runs. A lot like that serrated number Miranda was packing yesterday."

"That wouldn't do much good against a gang, would it?"

"Well, we haven't done the lab work yet, but actually, I think it did. There were three blood trails leading from the scene. He put up a hell of a fight."

"You think maybe his dog did some of the damage? Gave his life protecting his master?"

"No," she said, "I don't. He . . ." She began to draw raw, gasping breaths. "The guy . . . the victim . . . he cut his own dog's throat," she said, "just before they got him."

"*What?*"

"One of the witnesses saw him do it," she wept. "They chased the guy down, surrounded him. One of them had a pit bull on a chain. Big, mean junkyard dog. As they closed in, he knelt down and slashed his dog's throat. He knew, Bill, he *knew* . . . neither one of them would get out alive . . . and he wanted . . ." I could barely hear her, but I didn't dare interrupt. "He wanted to make sure . . . it didn't *suffer* . . . Oh God, Bill . . . what a horrible, hopeless, loving thing to do."

She was hyperventilating into the phone now; I knew she must be getting dizzy and she'd soon black out. "Jess, stay with me here," I said. "Jess?

Slow down. You've got to slow down, Jess. Have you got a towel or a blanket or a shirt handy? Even your shirtsleeve or your hand, Jess. Put something over your mouth and breathe through it. Anything to slow you down, make it harder to breathe." She didn't answer, but her breathing suddenly got muffled, and gradually it slowed. I heard a long, hard sniffle through a runny nose, then a sustained burbling, bugling blast from her nose. "Good girl, Jess. Slow and steady. Slow and steady."

She took in a deep breath, heaved it out. "God-*damn*it, I hate to cry," she said. "Where can all this come from? Gallons of snot and tears. Every time I think there can't be any more in me, the damn spigot opens again. Funny; I see a hundred dead people a year, and it's the dog that breaks my heart. No, not just the dog. The guy's love for his dog. A guy that would do such a thing for an animal he loved, even as he saw death bearing down on him." She set the phone down, blew her nose again, then drew and exhaled out a long shuddering breath. "It was like something straight out of Nero's Coliseum," she said. "They turned the pit bull loose on the guy. Nearly tore his left arm off. He managed to cut that dog's throat, too. Even with his arm being ripped to shreds, he remembered his anatomy and found the jugular. Then the two-legged beasts closed in. Four or five, we're not sure; the witnesses were backing off fast. Looks like he took stab wounds from several directions while he was still on his feet. More after he fell. Lotta overkill. Maybe the pit bull's owner was pissed; maybe one of the creeps he cut—somebody was mad enough to do extra damage." She sighed again. "Autopsy's gonna be a bitch. Could be my first with triple-digit stab wounds." She laughed mirthlessly. "Shit. Soulless cowardly no-count fuckers."

I took the anger as a good sign.

"Dammit, Bill, this isn't the first killing like this we've had this year, and it won't be the last. I'm afraid we've got a growing problem here— hell, I think we've got a growing problem across America—but nobody wants to talk about it."

"What do you mean? Murder rates rising?"

"Not yet. Our rate's actually way down, for now, but I'm afraid it can't last. I'm afraid the anger's building among these young black males. Half of them are high school dropouts. You know what the nationwide unemployment rate among black high school dropouts is?" I didn't. "Seventy percent, and rising. White dropouts, thirty percent unemployment. Hispanics, just nineteen percent. A lot of these young urban black guys have no prospects. No hope. Nothing to live for and nothing to lose. So it's nothing to them to take a few of the fortunate down with them as they go."

"You think the police will get these guys?"

"Maybe. Be pretty easy to find out who owned the pit bull. And I think we can match some of the blood at the scene to two or three of the attackers, if we can find them. But if the witnesses disappear and clam up, we might have trouble making a case. Hell, these guys could even get together and argue self-defense: big, bad white man came at 'em with a knife and they feared for their lives. Not the truth, but if four or five guys say it on the stand with believable emotion, be hard to find a jury that would call them all liars."

Jess was a medical examiner; her role was to determine causes of death, not to win convictions. But she was a human being, too, with a strong sense of justice and injustice, and I understood her frustration. "Maybe it'll turn out better than that." I said it with more optimism than I felt.

"Yeah, right. You know what else makes me furious about this?"

"What?"

"This plays *exactly* to all those goddamned racist stereotypes I've spent forty years in the South resisting," she said. "If it had to happen—if this guy had to get murdered by a pack of feral punks, why couldn't they be *white* punks, Bill?"

"I don't know, Jess. I don't know. I think you're right, if something doesn't change, we may be headed for a huge problem. And we don't seem to have the wisdom or the will, even after all these years, to fix it."

We both fell silent for a while.

"God, I'm so tired, Bill. Tired and cold. When I get this tired, I get cold all over. All I want to do at this moment is crawl under the covers and sleep for a week." Her breathing had grown deep and even by now; I felt my own breath slowing to mark time with hers, my mind slipping back toward drowsiness with surprising ease.

"You think maybe you'd be able to sleep now?"

"Maybe," she said. Her voice sounded drained of its horror and rage, though the sorrow remained. "I think so. I hope so. I need to."

"If you can't," I said, "call me back and I'll give you one of my osteology lectures. 'Morphological Characteristics of Shovel-Shaped Incisors in Native Americans.' Guaranteed to put you under in five minutes or less. Okay?"

The only answer was a gentle, ladylike snore at the other end of the line.

I listened to Jess sleep for a long time. Eventually I began nodding off myself, drifting in and out, as if I were floating down a slow-moving stream, easing from sunlight to shade and back again. In one of the waking moments, I realized that it was the first time I'd slept with a woman, even long-distance, in the two years since Kathleen had died. The intimacy of it—the vulnerability and trust and simple physical communion—nearly burst my heart.

"Sleep well, Jess," I whispered, easing the phone back into its cradle.

CHAPTER 8

MY STUDENTS WEREN'T GOING to be happy.

A week ago, I had announced that today's class would focus on the forensic case that had proven to be my most popular with students over the years: my slides from Knoxville's most infamous serial-killing spree. Four women's bodies had been found on a wooded hillside a stone's throw from I-40, about seven miles east of downtown. The newspapers dubbed the man charged with the murders "Zoo Man" because that was his nickname among Knoxville's prostitutes. The name referred both to his sometime place of employment and also to the location of a barn where he often took hookers for sex. "Watch out for the Zoo Man," hookers warned one another, because he often beat the women he hired for sex. He also liked to kill them, according to police and prosecutors. The murder trial—the longest and costliest in Tennessee history—ended in a mistrial, but Zoo Man had been sentenced to sixty-six years in prison for a series of vicious rapes, so the streets of Knoxville were safe once more. Safer, anyhow.

Hunters had stumbled upon the first of the four bodies in the woods; a grid search by police and my anthropology students yielded the remaining three. The photos from the case showed the victims in various stages of decomposition, ranging from fresh (one body was only a few days old) to almost fully skeletonized, and the contrasts—plus the notoriety of the case—always sparked keen interest among students. But over breakfast, I'd decided to scrap today's lesson plan.

I had slept badly and awakened tired and frustrated. Jess's Chattanooga cross-dresser case was nagging at me—the police didn't seem to be making any headway, from what Jess had told me, and I wasn't sure that our reconstruction of the death scene was likely to give them much more to work with. If they'd been trying to confirm or refute a potential suspect's alibi, it might help for me to nail down the time since death. But with no suspects anywhere in sight, I couldn't see that it would jump-start the case for me to say something like "He'd been dead five to six days by the time he was found."

So I was already cranky when I sat down with my bowl of instant oatmeal. Then, when I opened the *Knoxville News Sentinel*, one of the stories in the national news section tipped me into full-blown rage. An Associated Press wire story related how the state Board of Education in Kansas—a state where I had once taught, early in my career—had voted to require science teachers to criticize evolutionary theory. In undermining evolution, the board members were indirectly championing "intelligent design," a sneaky, pseudoscientific term for creationism: the theory that life is too complex to have evolved without the guiding hand of a whip-smart Creator. In adopting the new policy, the Board of Education ignored the advice of their own science committee, as well as the pleas of the National Academy of Sciences and the National Science Teachers Association. They also ignored the accumulated evidence of a century and a half of painstaking scientific research.

I fumed as I drove to campus and gathered my materials for class. I fumed as I made my way down the stairs and out of the stadium; I fumed as I ascended the sidewalk to McClung Museum, which housed the lecture hall where the class met; I was still fuming as I strode into the auditorium, which was filled to capacity.

"Good morning," I said. "I have bad news. I'm postponing the lecture about the Zoo Man case." Groans and good-natured boos erupted around the auditorium. "I'll show those slides a week from now. Today, we're going to talk instead about unintelligent design."

A hand shot up in the third row. The young man spoke without waiting to be acknowledged. "Excuse me, Dr. Brockton," he said with an air of proud helpfulness, "don't you mean *intelligent* design?"

"No," I said, "I mean *un*intelligent design. Dumb design." Someone giggled briefly. "People who don't believe in evolution are always talking about the brilliant design of the human body," I continued, "about what a cosmic genius the designer had to have been. Well, today we're going to talk about a few design features you and I have that would suggest some inefficiency, some inattention to detail, or some downright shoddy work in our design." I scanned the room; clearly I had their full attention.

"Let's start with teeth. Show me your teeth." I opened my mouth as wide as it would go, retracted my lips, wiggled my mandible back and forth, and tilted my head in all directions to flash my not-so-pearly whites. Some of the students rolled their eyes, appalled at the silliness, but most of them mimicked what I was doing, if a bit less comically. "Good," I said. "Most of you still have some teeth. Clearly UT's admission standards have gone up lately." I heard a few chuckles, saw a few more teeth. "Okay, now I want you all to stick a finger in your mouth and run it all around your upper and lower jaw to count how many teeth you have. This is an experiment; we'll gather some data on evolution, or 'secular change,' as we usually call it in physical anthropology." I demonstrated, reaching my index finger back to my upper right molars and tracing a line around my mandible, counting aloud as I went: "Un, oo, ree, or, ive, ix," ending at "unny-eight." I went to the chalkboard and wrote "28" in foot-high numerals. I turned back to face them. "By the way," I added, "if you've had your wisdom teeth extracted, or any other teeth, add those to your total. Ready? Count."

A few students tried counting with their tongues; most used an index finger, as I had done, but a sizable subset of the girls used the long nail of a pinkie so as to be more delicate about the procedure. As the students fished around in their mouths, it looked as if they were trying to dislodge popcorn hulls from their teeth. Then, almost as if choreographed, a hundred fingertips rubbed across pants legs and skirts to wipe off traces of saliva.

"Okay," I said, "now let's analyze our data. How many of you had thirty-two teeth, which is what's considered normal for an adult human?" A sprinkling of hands shot up, representing about a quarter of the class. "How many had twenty-four?" I saw roughly the same number of hands. "And how many had twenty-eight?" Half the students raised their hands.

"See, this is interesting," I said. "Only a quarter of you have thirty-two, which is considered a full set of teeth—for *modern* humans. But for our ancestors thirty or forty million years ago, the norm was forty-four—which, by the way, is still the standard for most mammalian teeth. If you'd lived forty million years ago, you'd have had twelve more teeth. Where would you put them? Anybody in here feel like they've got room enough for a dozen more molars?" I shook my head dramatically. "And why is that? Because our jaws have gotten smaller. And why is *that*?" Faces went blank; shoulders shrugged.

I had started slowly, but now I was gathering momentum, like a rhino on the run. "A couple hundred million years ago, our ancestors, the first mammals, began evolving from swamp lizards," I said. "They were small mammals about the size of squirrels or shrews, called 'preprimate insectivores'; they lived on the ground and ate bugs. They had long snouts, sort of like anteaters, and their eyes were on the sides of their heads." I tapped both temples for emphasis. "Well, at the same time, another group of animals was emerging: the dinosaurs. Now, what happens when a tyrannosaurus or a brontosaurus steps on a preprimate insectivore?" I smacked one palm down on top of the other. "*Splat*," I said. "So some of the brainier insectivores decided they'd be safer up in the trees, where they wouldn't get stepped on. Good idea; more of those survived. But not all. If you're skittering around in the trees, jumping from branch to branch, it's hard to see which branch to grab if your eyes are on the sides of your head and you've got a big snout in the middle of your face. So some of these critters fall out of the trees and get eaten. Or stomped on." I made the *splat* again. "So over time—remember, we're talking millions of years—the survival rate, and the reproductive rate, is higher in the ones with smaller snouts and eyes closer to the front of their heads. But to lose that snout, they have to lose some teeth—if you've got forty-four teeth, you're going to have a mighty big snout. So natural selection favors those with smaller snouts. Fewer teeth. The fossil record documents all these changes in great detail."

The young man in row three raised his hand again. "But you're assuming the fossils were formed over millions of years. What if they weren't? Painters and sculptors can easily create works of art that look very old, even though they're not. If they can do that on a small scale, why couldn't God do it on a much bigger scale?"

I was dumbfounded, and didn't even know where to begin to respond. We had just leapt from science to faith, and although those two spheres weren't always in conflict, I could tell that in this instance, they would be.

"Okay, forget the fossil record," I said. "Let's talk about modern humans, people who have lived within the past two hundred years. People whose birth dates and death dates we know. The Terry Collection at the Smithsonian contains nearly two thousand human skulls, belonging to individuals born as far back as the early 1800s. Here in Neyland Stadium, in the UT collection, we have about six hundred skulls so far, belonging to individuals born as recently as twenty or thirty years ago. Comparative measurements of those twenty-five hundred skulls show that in just the past two hundred years, the average jaw is getting smaller, and the average cranium is getting bigger. We think of evolution as something occurring over thousands or millions of years, but this is an example of evolutionary change that's almost fast enough to see in our own lifetime."

Just as he was winding up to reply, I saw another hand go up at the back of the room. Grateful to shift interrogators, I pointed. "Yes, there in the back?"

"You mentioned 'dumb design.' What's dumb about having fewer teeth?"

"Good question. There's nothing dumb about having twenty-eight teeth instead of thirty-two, or forty-four. The way we eat nowadays, we could probably get along just fine with twenty, or even twelve. What's dumb, or inefficient, or problematic, is that our jaws are shrinking more rapidly than our tooth count is. The two evolutionary changes are not in sync. So we wind up with too many teeth in too little space. That's why so many of us have to have our third molars—our wisdom teeth—yanked when we're fifteen or twenty or thirty years old. Which is a bad thing for most of us, but a good thing for those of you who are heading for dental school." I noticed a few smiles, which I guessed might belong to pre-dent students.

"Enough about teeth," I said. "Let's talk about a couple of other design flaws. I won't embarrass anybody by asking who's had either of these problems, but I would bet some of you have, and I guarantee that more of you will: hernias and hemorrhoids. A hernia is a failure—a blowout, you might say—in the abdominal wall. Back when we moved around on all fours, our internal organs had it easier. I'll show you why." I clambered onto the table at the front of the auditorium on my hands and knees. "You see how my belly is hanging down here?" I heard a few good-natured "oohs" and "yucks" from the students. "The point is, when you're in this position, the abdomen makes a nice, roomy sling, like a hammock, for the organs." To underscore the point, I swayed back and forth a few times. Then I stood up on the table and put my hands on my belly. "But when we went vertical, what happened? Anybody?"

"Everything sank down to the bottom," ventured a girl in the front row.

"Exactly," I said. "And that increases the pressure on the lower abdominal wall. So it's more prone to tear. Same thing with hemorrhoids. The lower end of the large intestine gets more pressure now than it did in our four-footed ancestors, so it's more susceptible to blowouts, too, which is basically what hemorrhoids are." I heard more exclamations of disgust. "Varicose veins—how many of you have seen varicose veins?" A lot of hands went up. "Now that we're upright, the heart has a lot more work to do. It has to pump blood with enough force to push it from the bottom of your feet all the way up to the top of your head, a distance of five or six feet, or even more. That's a lot tougher than pumping it three feet uphill, which is about how tall we are when we're on all fours. It's interesting," I said. "To try to compensate for the circulatory problem we created when we stood up, we've evolved this complex system of tiny flaplike valves in our veins, whose job is to keep the blood from flowing back downhill in the pause between heartbeats. But as we get older, those little valves tend to leak a bit, so blood pools in the legs, and the extra pressure makes the veins swell up and sometimes burst."

An especially tall young woman—she was one of the star players on the Lady Vols basketball team—raised her hand. I pointed to her. "Yes?"

"So do other mammals—dogs and lions and whales—not have those little valves in their veins?"

No one had ever asked that before. I had never asked it myself. "To be honest," I said, "I don't know. I'll find out before our next class. Good question." She beamed; it was considered a coup to stump me.

"Okay, now let's talk briefly about the pelvis and the spine," I said. "Some of you women will doubtless have babies at some point. The good news is, obstetric medicine is getting better all the time."

"What's the bad news?" a female voice called out.

"The bad news is, babies' heads are getting bigger and bigger," I said.

"Ouch, man," the same voice said. "C-section, here I come."

"Lots of women are having cesareans these days," I agreed. "Purely as elective surgery, not because there's any medical complication that calls for it. And frankly, skittish as I am about the idea of having my belly sliced open, if I were a woman, I might consider it, too."

"If you were a woman, Dr. Brockton," called out a guy who had emerged as the class clown, "I don't think pregnancy would need to be high on your list of concerns." Much laughter ensued, including my own.

"Okay, last dumb-design feature," I said, opening the box I had brought with me. "There are others, but we'll stop with this." I reached into the box and fished out an articulated pelvic girdle, the bones held together with red dental wax. The pubic bones arced together in the front; in back, the sacrum—the fused assemblage of the last five vertebrae—angled between the hip bones. "Notice the shape of the sacrum," I said. "As you get down to the end of the spine, the vertebrae get smaller and smaller. So it's shaped like a triangle, a wedge. Now, what do you use to split firewood?"

"Um, an ax?" offered someone.

"Well, yes, but I was thinking of a wedge. When you apply pressure to a wedge, it tends to force things apart, doesn't it? You see where the hip bone, or the ilium, joins the sacrum here on each side? That joint is called the sacroiliac joint. When you put pressure on this wedge, the sacrum—with the weight of your entire upper body—it pushes down, and it tends to force these hip bones apart, and strain that sacroiliac joint. That's a common cause of lower-back pain in people my age and older."

I looked directly at the intelligent-design proponent in the third row. "So you see," I said, "there are all sorts of structural features in the human body that suggest slow, imperfect evolution, rather than instantaneous, intelligent design."

He raised his hand, his face showing a mixture of regret and defiance. "But think about the eyeball, and the brain, and the heart. Those are complicated and amazing structures. The eyeball is a marvel of optical engineering. The brain is more sophisticated and powerful than any computer on earth. The heart makes any man-made pump look flimsy and crude." I nodded, trying to acknowledge that we shared an admiration for those organs. "Besides," he challenged, "what's wrong with teaching both theories? Isn't that what education is all about? Let both sides of the controversy make their case, and let people make up their own minds?"

"There *is* no controversy," I thundered. "Evolution is no more controversial than the Copernican theory of the solar system, or the 'theory' that the Earth is round. Just because a few people make an opposing claim, loudly and often, that doesn't make the issue a legitimate scientific controversy. There is nothing scientifically testable or provable about creation theory. Hard-core creationists claim the fossil record—fossilized evidence showing that animals and plants evolved over many millions of years—was created right alongside Adam and Eve. That's hocus-pocus, a fictional geologic backstory, conjured up out of nothingness: 'Fossilized remains just *look* millions of years old'—you said as much yourself not thirty minutes ago—'because God *made* them look millions of years old.' Logically, you can't argue with that. It's perfectly circular reasoning, the ultimate 'because God said so.' Only it's not really God who's saying so. It's people claiming to speak for God. Well, maybe God spoke to me this morning as I was reading the paper, and told me to tell everyone that Charles Darwin was right, and that anybody who says otherwise just isn't paying good attention.

"Don't get me wrong," I said. "I'm not dismissing the possibility of some higher principle or higher power operating in the universe, something that's far beyond my meager powers of comprehension. I can't explain the 'why' of evolution, but the fact that I don't fully understand how it works doesn't keep it from working. I don't begin to understand how pictures appear on my television screen, but that doesn't keep them from showing up. And it doesn't mean God put them there. The laws of physics—and people who are smarter about those laws than I am—put them there.

"And if we need any further proof of unintelligent design," I said, really getting wound up, "all we need to do is look at the Kansas Board of Education. Those people are the very incarnation of dumb design." I waved the morning newspaper.

My opponent was not ready to give up. "We are made in the image of God," he insisted.

"Then God must be evolving, too," I snapped. "And I hope he's got some divine dentist up there in heaven to extract his wisdom teeth, because once they get impacted, God's gonna have one hell of a toothache." I wadded the newspaper into a ball.

I heard a gasp, and then a snicker, and the class jester called out, "Amen, brother!" And then someone at the back of the room began to clap. Slowly, steadily. Soon more of the students began to clap, and before long, almost all of them were clapping.

The young man in row three stood up. I opened my mouth to tell him to sit down, but then I noticed his face. It was a bright mottled red, and he looked on the verge of tears. He stared at me for a long moment, with eyes full of hurt and betrayal. Then he walked up the aisle and out of the lecture hall, accompanied by catcalls and whistles.

I gathered up my notes, the pelvis, and the crumpled newspaper, and exited by the lower door. As I traipsed down the sidewalk from McClung Museum to the underbelly of Neyland Stadium and the stairwell to my office and my collection of still-evolving skeletons, I accused myself of going too far, speaking too harshly, because I'd gone into class already mad about the newspaper article. It was important for scientists to defend good science and expose pseudoscience. But it was also important to do it gently, at least when students were involved. "Damn, Bill," I said to myself, and *at* myself. "Damn."

CHAPTER 9

TESTIFYING AT A HEARING to revoke a physician's medical license wasn't exactly the same as testifying in court, but it was damn close. This hearing looked like a trial and it quacked like a trial, complete with lawyers and oaths to tell the truth.

The Tennessee Department of Health and Environment had a lawyer whose job was to ask me easy questions, and Dr. Garland Hamilton—the medical examiner whose license was on the chopping block, so to speak—had a lawyer whose job was to chip away at my answers.

The case that had prompted the state to try to revoke its own regional medical examiner's license was a fascinating one. A man named Eddie Meacham called the 911 dispatcher in Knoxville one Saturday night to say that his friend had just collapsed. By the time the ambulance arrived, Billy Ray Ledbetter was dead, with a bloody wound in his lower back. Dr. Hamilton performed an autopsy, found copious amounts of blood in Ledbetter's right lung, and pronounced the cause of death to be a stab wound in the lower back, with the blade penetrating the lower lobe of the right lung.

Trouble was, it turned out that the "stab wound" was inflicted by a big shard from a glass-topped coffee table, which Billy Ray had shattered when he collapsed onto it. I had the dubious pleasure of getting involved when I did an experiment at the Body Farm that showed it would have been impossible for a knife blade—even if there had *been* a knife wound, which there wasn't—to puncture the back on the left side, cross the spine, and then veer ninety degrees into the right lung. The real cause of the lung hemorrhage, it turned out, was a bar fight a couple of weeks before Billy Ray's death, when he got severely boot-stomped, breaking multiple ribs and puncturing the lung with a sharp piece of bone. My testimony had served the dual purpose of clearing Billy Ray's friend of an unjustified murder charge—which pleased me—and of spotlighting Dr. Hamilton's incompetence—which displeased me on two counts: first, that he was incompetent, and second, that I was now part of the effort to strip a longtime colleague of his license to practice medicine.

Hamilton had confronted me furiously after the trial, so I was prepared for the worst when I entered the hearing room. He stood up and stepped toward me; I braced for an assault, verbal or even physical. Instead, he stretched out his right hand. Startled, I took it and shook. "No hard feelings, Bill," he said with a smile and a squeeze of my hand.

Surprised at his change of tone, all I could come up with was, "I hope not, Garland."

Up at the front of the room, which was just a large conference room in one of the state office buildings in downtown Knoxville, a panel of three physicians—members of the Board of Medical Examiners—sat behind a long table. To one side, a stenographer perched at a much smaller table, her fingers poised over the odd little machine she used to transcribe words. I was fascinated by the technology. Her machine, a stenograph, looked more like an old-fashioned adding machine than a computer or typewriter; as she typed, though, she would often press two or three keys at once, like playing a chord on a piano. I had once asked a court reporter to explain and demonstrate the technique to me. "I'm transcribing sounds, not words," she'd said, and she had me speak a few words at a time. She showed me what combinations of keys she used to transcribe the various sounds I had uttered—sometimes a "chord" represented a syllable; sometimes an entire word; in one case, even an entire phrase. It beat the hell out of anything I'd ever seen: as if she'd had to master a new language and a musical instrument all at the same time. Ever since, I'd had great admiration for court reporters' abilities.

"Dr. Brockton, are you ready?" The state's lawyer brought my mind back to the business at hand. He had already briefed me on the charge against Hamilton: "significant professional incompetence, with actual or risk of immediate harm," the most serious charge possible. In this case, the harm was not to the patient, since Billy Ray was long since dead by the time Hamilton got to him; the harm was to the friend who faced life in prison for an unjust charge of murder. Pretty harmful, all right. If the examiners upheld the complaint, Hamilton's license could just be suspended temporarily, but it was more likely to be revoked for good. And it would be good, judging by some other shoddy autopsy reports I'd seen.

I'd brought diagrams of the spine, rib cage, and lungs, showing the impossible "wound path" Hamilton had described the knife taking; I had also requested that a teaching skeleton be on hand so I could further illustrate the impossibility in three dimensions. The state's lawyer led me swiftly through a recap of the experiment I'd done, in which I had been unable even to approximate the path Hamilton had described. He ended by having me describe finding the shard of bone, from Billy Ray's own splintered ribs, that had pierced the right lung. The examiners on the panel asked a few questions: Might a thinner blade have been able to make the requisite turns? Was there any sign of a knife mark on the detached bone shard? Was there any possibility the shard had punctured the lung during postmortem handling of the body?—but they seemed satisfied with my answers.

Then Hamilton's lawyer got his turn. I had been cross-examined by the Knox County district attorney about this same case, so I felt reasonably confident, well prepared, but his first question threw me off-balance. "Dr. Brockton, did you examine the decedent, Mr. Ledbetter, for evidence of scoliosis? Curvature of the spine?"

"Well, no," I said, "but I think I would have noticed—"

"I'm not asking what you *think you would have*

noticed, Doctor; I'm asking whether you took measurements or X-rays or conducted any other sort of investigation that would have yielded an objective indication of scoliosis?"

"Then I'd have to say no," I said.

"And did you examine your research subject, the one you stabbed in the back, for evidence of scoliosis?"

I felt my cheeks flush. "No," I said. "He appeared to be a normal individual. He was a marathon runner. I don't imagine someone with scoliosis would have an easy time running marathons."

"You ever see photos or news stories about amputees, wearing artificial limbs, running marathons?"

"Yes," I said.

"Do you imagine they have an easy time doing it?"

"No, I don't. I'm not sure I understand what you're getting at, though."

"What I'm getting at, Dr. Brockton, is this: You don't actually know for a fact that Billy Ray Ledbetter's spine was normal, and you don't know for a fact that your research subject's spine was identical in shape to Mr. Ledbetter's. What I'm getting at is the fact that a knife *could* have followed a different path in Mr. Ledbetter's body than in the body of your experimental cadaver if their spines were curved differently. Couldn't it, Dr. Brockton?"

I was not willing to back down completely. "Slightly," I said. "If one of them had severe curvature and the other did not. But neither of them had severe curvature."

"You've just said you didn't measure or X-ray either spine for scoliosis," he shot back.

"I haven't measured or X-rayed *your* spine, either," I said, "but that doesn't keep me from noticing that you probably have some anterior deterioration and compression in your cervical disks. That's why your head juts slightly forward of your shoulders. Do you have neck pain? You might be a good candidate for cervical fusion."

"We are *not* here to talk about my spine, sir," he all but shouted at me.

"No, sir, we're not," I said levelly. "What we're here to talk about is truth and competence, and what *I'm* getting at is that after studying thousands of skeletons, I don't have to take X-rays and measure angles to notice a deformed spine. Neither of these two individuals had a deformed spine."

He sputtered a bit, and tried to regain his advantage, but he had clearly played his one trump card, and it wasn't quite the ace he'd hoped it would be. After a little more sparring, the physician who was leading the hearing called a halt, thanked me, and pronounced me free to go.

As I left the hearing room, I noticed Hamilton's attorney rubbing his neck; the sight made me smile. Then I caught the stenographer looking from me to the attorney and back again. She gave me a wink and a smile; she crossed her legs at the same time. I wasn't sure if that was just a happy coincidence, or if it was some sort of reward for providing a bit of entertainment. Either way, I smiled bigger and returned the wink.

Then I saw Garland Hamilton looking at me. I met his gaze, and he gave me a brief nod. It wasn't as friendly as his greeting had been, but it was fairly cordial, considering that his professional life was on the line here and I was part of the effort to terminate it.

The state's lawyer led me out of the hearing room. In the marbled hallway, seated on a bench outside the double doors, was Jess Carter. If I'd given the matter any thought, I'd have realized Jess would be testifying as well, since she had reautopsied the body of Billy Ray Ledbetter before I examined the bones. But I'd been too preoccupied with the Chattanooga case, and with my heavy-handed treatment of my creationist student, to think about it.

"Hey, stranger," she said. "Fancy seeing you here. You free by any chance tonight?"

This was the second question today that had caught me off-balance.

"Well, I could be," I said, my thoughts lagging half a beat behind my words. "I mean, I am. I think. Are you?"

She laughed at my clumsiness. "Ah. Sorry, no. Some guy in the hospital for routine foot surgery died the night he checked in, and the family's screaming lawsuit. I gotta get back and do his autopsy this afternoon."

"Oh. Right. Me too, now that I think about it. I mean, not an autopsy. I have some test papers to grade, so I can give them back tomorrow morning."

"I thought UT was out on spring break this week?" She raised a quizzical eyebrow at me. Underneath both brows, her eyes were dancing.

Damn. Why did her processor always seem to work so much faster than mine? I was glad it hadn't been Jess cross-examining me in there just now.

"Don't let me keep you from your testimony," I said, nodding at the state's attorney, who was looking anxious.

"Oh, what I have to say won't take long," she said. "I'll just tell them how I took one look at those rotting remains and handed them straight over to the eminent Dr. Brockton."

She winked, turned, and disappeared through the doorway. In her wake she left a swirl of hair, perfume, and female pheromones. Also an unmistakable aura of wit, intelligence, and professional competence.

CHAPTER 10

I WAS HALFWAY THROUGH a stack of a hundred test papers, and already my stomach was paging me. I checked my watch; it said ten-thirty, which was too early for lunch even by my standards, though not by much. Besides, the nearest cafeteria, in the athletic building across the street, didn't start serving lunch until eleven. If I stayed focused, I could grade the remaining fifty papers—it was a multiple-choice and fill-in-the-blank test—and still be the first person through the lunch line.

There was a knock at my door. I always kept the door ajar when I was in, and most students just barged right in. Not this time. "Come in," I said. Miranda leaned her head around the door and scanned the room. "Since when do you knock?" I asked.

"Since I walked in on you *kissing* someone," she said, rolling her eyes.

"Ah," I said, regretting the question. "That was a once-in-a-lifetime lapse. I was overcome with grief at the time. She was just trying to comfort me." Unfortunately—mortifyingly—"she" was an undergraduate student who had asked a question that had released a flood of sadness over my wife's death. In trying to console me, the young woman had given me a kiss that began as compassion but swiftly turned to passion. It was probably fortunate that Miranda had appeared in my doorway when she had; otherwise, I might have crossed even farther over the line.

"Comfort, huh," Miranda snorted. "Hmm. Sort of like that jailer I read about in the *News Sentinel* last week? The guy caught comforting one of the female prisoners? She was grief-stricken over being arrested for prostitution, if I remember the story right."

"No," I said, "not like that. There was no nakedness involved in this comforting."

"Might've been if I'd walked in five minutes later," she said. "Speaking of the capable and comforting Miss Carmichael, how is she? Still at the top of her class?"

"I don't know," I said. "She's taking two cultural anthropology classes this semester. I hope she hasn't gone over to the Dark Side."

"Hmm. I suspect she'll circle back to physical anthropology. She just seems the physical type, you know?" Miranda smiled sweetly as she said this, to let me know she was joking. Sort of.

"I'm glad to hear you say that," I said with an answering smile. "I was getting worried about her. You've given me such . . . comfort."

She glared, then laughed. "Okay, okay, I'm sorry.

Truce. I'm not still jealous of her." She paused for half a beat. "Smart, cute little bitch." She laughed again. So did I. Miranda had a way of tipping me off-balance, then catching me just before I went sprawling. "Actually, I didn't come by just to stomp on your feet of clay," she said.

"Oh, I'm sorry to hear that. I was so enjoying it. What other delights await me?"

"Our research subject, oh-five thirty-one?" I was instantly alert; 05–31 was the case number we'd assigned to the corpse tied to the tree at the Farm, because he was the thirty-first forensic case of 2005.

"What about him?"

"He's getting pretty interesting. You might want to come out and take a look."

"I was planning to head that way after I finished grading these papers and eating lunch," I said, "but somehow those seem less compelling now. Let's go."

The department's pickup truck was parked a flight of stairs away, near the tunnel that penetrated the stadium at field level, at the north end zone— the tunnel the UT football team ran through to the cheers of a hundred thousand people on game days. The truck was angled nose-first between two of the columns holding up the stadium's upper deck. I backed around, tucking its rear bumper between two other columns, and threaded the one-lane service road that ringed the base of the stadium, weaving a path around several students and an on-coming maintenance truck.

Turning right onto Neyland Drive, we paralleled the river, driving downstream. The morning was sunny and unseasonably warm for mid-March—at least, what used to pass for unseasonably warm—and there were already a fair number of cyclists and runners on the greenway that bordered Neyland. The School of Agriculture's trial gardens—a couple of carefully landscaped acres radiating from a large circular arbor—were already ablaze with daffodils, forsythia, and tulips. I slowed to admire the view, which was just as well, because a hundred yards ahead, a truck hauling a long horse trailer was making a leisurely right turn into the entrance of the veterinary school.

"Hey, speaking of horses, whatever happened to Mike Henderson?" asked Miranda. "He was doing research on the effects of fire on bone a while back. Worked at the vet school part-time, and used to burn horse and cow bones to study the fracture patterns, didn't he? Laying the groundwork for a big project with human bone."

"Well, that was his plan," I said. "His M.A. thesis had some problems. He burned a lot of bones, and he got some nice pictures showing the difference between how dry bone and green bone fracture in a fire. But I'm not sure he added much in the way of interpretation or analysis."

"I saw some of those pictures at a poster session at the forensic conference a year or two ago," she said. "Really interesting. The dry bones he burned fractured in a sort of rectilinear pattern, like logs in a campfire. But the green bones fractured in a sort of spiraling pattern, right?" I nodded. "How come?"

"Not sure," I said. "Nobody is. You wanna know my personal theory?"

"Oh yes, please, Doctor," Miranda whispered huskily. "I love it when you share your personal theories with me." I'd laid myself wide open to that brickbat of sarcasm.

"Okay, smart-ass, I think it has to do with the collagen," I said. "There's still a lot of collagen in fresh bone. I don't think anybody's done research that supports this yet, but my theory is, the collagen matrix has a little twist to it. That would make the bone stronger. Sort of like those twisted pine trees you see growing on windy cliff-tops, you know? The spiral grain makes them a lot tougher than the tall, straight trees that grow where the wind doesn't blow so hard."

"Nature's a pretty good structural engineer," she agreed.

I turned onto the entrance ramp that would carry us up to Alcoa Highway, which spanned the river and led to the medical complex and the Body Farm. "It's not too late to change your dissertation topic," I said. "I bet if you took comparative X-rays and MRIs of bones when they were fresh and then after they'd dried, you could shed some light on the structure of the collagen."

"Sure," she said. "Just flush all my data on osteoporosis down the toilet and start over." I nodded. "So when I hit the seven-year mark as a graduate student, can you get me tenure?"

"If it means I get to keep you as a colleague," I said.

"Ha," she said. "You'd feel threatened by me if I were a colleague."

"Ha," I said. "I feel threatened by you already."

I laughed. "I guess that means I'm either brave or foolish."

"Guess so," she said. She didn't indicate which one her money was on.

As we crossed the bridge over the river, I noticed the water level had risen during the night. Every winter, the Tennessee Valley Authority lowers the levels in its chain of reservoirs so that there's room to accommodate plenty of runoff during the rainy season. By mid-March, though, the rains tend to taper off, so TVA begins refilling the pools to their normal summertime highs. Some of the lakes up in the mountains—Norris and Fontana, especially— dropped ten or twenty feet in the winter, expos- ing high layers of red clay banks ringing the green waters. Fort Loudoun, though—as a mainline res- ervoir that had to be kept open to barge traffic— only dropped about three feet. It was enough to expose shoreline for arrowhead-hunters, but not enough to strand boats on the mud like beached whales.

The redbuds and dogwoods along Alcoa High- way were starting to bloom. Normally the redbuds came first, then—just as they were winding down— the dogwoods burst out. Some years, though, when the botanical planets aligned in some magical way, the two species bloomed in unison, and this was shaping up as one of those glorious years. Maybe it was just because I was finally getting clear of my two-year grieving spell over Kathleen's death, or maybe because I felt the stirrings of desire for Jess—encouraged by what I took to be flirting on her part—but this spring seemed to reek of wanton, shameless fertility. The air was almost indecent with the scent of blossoms and pollen. It was the sort of spring that had inspired pagan festivals in other cultures, other centuries.

UT's College of Agriculture had a dairy farm beside the hospital, bounded by a big bend in the river; on a morning like this, with the trees in full flower and the black-and-white Holsteins arranged on the emerald grass, the view was like something out of a painting: *Tennessee Pastoral*, it might be titled. Tuck the Body Farm into one corner, and it would be like one of those seventeenth-century memento mori paintings featuring a skull or bludgeoned animal nestled among the dewy fruits and vegetables to remind us of our mortality. Sort of like the role I played at UT faculty meetings, I supposed.

I parked beside the entrance and unlocked the padlocks on the chain-link fence and the inner wooden gate. We didn't have any redbuds or dogwoods inside the Body Farm, but we did have dandelions galore in the clearing, bright splashes of yellow amid the new grass and old bones.

As Miranda and I trudged up the path toward the upper end of the facility, I noticed a new body bag a few feet off the trail, with one hand and one foot exposed. "Is that the highway fatality?"

"Yes," she said. "We brought him out from the morgue yesterday morning."

I knelt down beside the body and folded the bag back. As I did, a small squadron of blowflies swarmed up from around and beneath the black plastic. "And he was walking on I-40?"

"Yeah, wandering along that elevated stretch downtown where there's no shoulder. Stumbled into the traffic lane, and some high school student smacked right into him. I feel sorry for the kid—apparently he's pretty torn up about it."

"Be hard not to be," I said. "I ran over a dog once, and it made me throw up. I can't imagine accidentally killing a person."

"He's lucky he was driving a big SUV. Otherwise, he might've been killed, too. The front end was pretty smashed up. Smaller car, this guy might've come right over the hood and blown through the windshield at sixty or seventy miles an hour."

I studied the dead man, who looked to have lived four or five tough decades before dying in the fast lane. One side of the face and head had been crushed; shards of glass and paint were tangled in the hair, and a number of teeth had snapped off at the gum line. The left arm, shoulder, and ribs appeared shattered as well. I noticed clumps of white fly eggs, which looked like grainy paste or Cream of Wheat, scattered across his many wounds. Twenty-four hours from now, his entire body would be swarming with newly hatched maggots.

"Looks like a coin toss whether he died of brain damage or internal injuries," I said. "I guess Jess could pin it down, if it mattered."

"The family said they didn't want an autopsy, and they didn't want the body, either," Miranda said. "He'd been living on the street for a while; problems with drinking and probably mental illness. Apparently no love lost between him and his relatives. The death certificate simply lists 'multiple injuries from automobile impact' as the cause of death."

"Well, it's too bad," I said, "but he'll be an interesting addition to the skeletal collection. Good example of massive blunt-force trauma, and how you can tell the direction of impact from the way the bones are fractured."

"Also a good example of why it's not a good idea to drink and walk."

"That too," I said.

I folded the body bag back over the man, nudged his hand and foot beneath its shade. The shade would keep the skin from turning leathery-tough, as it would in the sunshine; it would also keep the maggots—which shun daylight, and the predatory birds that accompany it—munching busily around the clock. With that, we turned and headed up the path again toward our Chattanooga victim's stand-in.

As we got close, I saw why Miranda had been eager to bring me out for a look. The body still hung from the tree, its head sagging forward nearly to its chest. Despite the facial injuries I had replicated—bloody injuries that would normally prompt a feeding frenzy by teeming maggots—most of the soft tissue remained. Even the exaggerated eye makeup remained intact. But the body's feet, ankles, and lower legs had been reduced almost to bare bone.

"Wow," I said, "he's looking a lot like the murder victim, except that his abdomen is still bloated. Another couple days, maybe, and I'd say he'll correspond almost exactly." I knelt down and checked the feet and legs for signs of carnivore chewing, but

I didn't see any—again, just like the Chattanooga victim. All I saw were maggots, fighting over what little tissue remained on the lower extremities.

We had set an infrared camera on a tripod, aimed at the body; it was rigged to a motion sensor so if a nocturnal animal managed to breach the fence and chew on the body, we'd capture a photo of it. "Have you checked the camera?" Miranda nodded. "Has anything triggered it?"

"Nope. Not a creature was stirring, not even a mouse."

I stood up to study the face more closely. I had to crouch slightly, and look up from below the dangling head, to get a good view. As I did, I felt a tiny maggot drop onto my cheek. And then another. And another. I jumped back, shaking my head like a wet dog, then brushing my cheeks for good measure. "Woof," I said. "I think I understand now why there's such differential decay between the upper body and the feet."

"Yes?"

"Yes. Once the blowfly eggs hatch, the maggots fall off. There's no good horizontal surface, the way there is when a body's lying on the ground." I pointed down at the feet. "They fall down there, and the feet are easy for them to reach. Some of them manage to crawl up the ankles, and a few even make it partway up the lower leg. But the higher you look, the fewer you see."

Miranda leaned in, but not so far as to place herself beneath the rain of maggots drizzling down from the head. "You're right," she said. "You could graph the distribution as an asymptotic curve. As

X—the distance above the ground—increases, Y—the number of maggots—drops from near infinity to near zero."

I stared at her. "Asymptotic curve? What language are you speaking?" She stared back, puzzled at my puzzlement, then we burst into simultaneous laughter.

"Okay, I admit it: I've become the world's biggest, weirdest nerd," she said. "But it *is* a nice curve, and a classic asymptote." She raised one index finger high overhead, traced a near-vertical line downward, then gradually, gracefully swooped it toward horizontal.

"Very nice indeed," I agreed. "Actually, you probably could get a paper about this published in the *Journal of Forensic Sciences*. Especially if you include a video of yourself tracing the asymptotic curve in the air like that."

She made a face at me. "Eat maggots and die," she said.

I didn't die, but I did suddenly feel my scalp itching in half a dozen places.

CHAPTER 11

THERE WAS A LIGHT tap on my doorframe, and a millisecond later—even before I had time to look up—a female voice said, "Knock knock."

"Come in," I said, not yet looking up. I was writing a note on a student's test paper, and I wanted to finish the sentence before I forgot the second half of it. As I tapped the period into place, I realized that the voice was familiar, but that it was also not one I was accustomed to hearing in the dingy quarters of Stadium Hall.

My first glance explained the disconnect. The voice belonged to Amanda Whiting, and I had never heard it except in the walnut-paneled confines of the President's Dining Room and the similarly veneered interior of the UT president's home.

"Uh-oh," I said. "I must be in some mighty deep trouble if you've come all the way down here looking for me." Amanda was a UT vice president; she was also the university's chief counsel, its highest-flying legal eagle. "What did I do this time? I've tried to cut back on the dirty jokes in class. Really, I have."

"I wish it were as simple as a coed offended by your Neanderthal sense of humor," she said. "This is about Jason Lane."

"Jason Lane? He's one of my students; I do recognize the name. But beyond that, I'm drawing a blank."

She heaved a sigh. "Jason Lane is a devout young man. A devoutly fundamentalist Christian young man." I suddenly saw where this was heading, and I didn't like what I saw. "He believes the Bible to be the literal, unerring word of God. He believes the Book of Genesis to be the definitive account of the creation of the earth and of all the life-forms therein."

"And in class the other day, I begged to differ," I said.

"Begged to differ? Hell, Bill, you stomped all over this kid's belief system in front of a hundred other people." She folded her arms across her chest and gave me a stern look over the top of her reading glasses.

"You're right," I said. "I was hard on him, and I feel bad about it. But dang it, Amanda, I'm a scientist. Am I really supposed to check my brain and my education at the classroom door, pretend that everything we know from paleontology and zoology and molecular biology is idle speculation? And if some kid says everything was conjured up in six days, am I supposed say, 'Gosh, Jason, maybe you're right and the Nobel laureates are wrong'? When did that become UT's policy on academic freedom?" I glared at her; she glared back, and then she softened.

"I know," she said. "Intellectually and scientifically, you're right. And you do have the freedom to teach what you think is right. Nevertheless, we do have a problem."

"So what do I need to do, apologize? In private, or in front of the class so my humiliation corresponds to his?"

"That's not it," she said. "He's not after a pound of flesh."

"Then how many pounds is he after?"

"How many pounds you got?" she said. "It's not just you, and it's not just him now. That's why it's a problem. This student is just the convenient opportunity, and you're just the door about to get knocked on, or knocked down."

"What do you mean?"

"You ever heard of Jennings Bryan?"

"William Jennings Bryan? Sure. Lawyer, senator, and presidential candidate in the late 1800s. He argued the case against evolution at the Scopes trial, just down the road in Dayton, didn't he?"

"That one did; this one was born at least a hundred years later, and he's very much alive and kicking. No relation to the monkey-trial attorney, by the way, but many parallels. He's a lawyer, too. And an antievolutionist as well. A philosophical chip off the old Bryan block. Even has political aspirations—he and that former Alabama Supreme Court justice, the Ten Commandments judge, are getting some buzz as the dream ticket of the far right in the 2008 presidential election."

"Then even I might start praying without ceasing," I said. "So how does young Jennings Bryan, Esquire, fit into this?"

"As best I can tell, your student Jason called home upset about what you said in class. His parents, who are of the same persuasion as Jason when it comes to matters of faith and evolution, called their minister. And their minister's flock just happens to include Mr. Bryan, who has been making a name for himself in fundamentalist circles by spearheading several successful efforts to teach creationism—or at least undermine evolution—in public schools."

"Was he part of the campaign out in Kansas that got the state Board of Education to muzzle science teachers?"

"Behind the scenes," she said. "He's also filed friend-of-the-court briefs in half a dozen cases involving public education, evolution, and intelligent design. The scary thing about him is, he actually knows the scientific issues pretty well, so he can target what he sees as the Achilles' heel of evolution."

"Like what?"

"Well, like the gaps in the fossil record. As I understand it, you'd logically expect fossils to show steady changes over millions of years, but instead, they show long periods with small changes and few transition species, then *boom*, this explosion of new species or variations appears."

"Evolution proceeds in fits and starts," I said. "Just because we don't yet understand why, that doesn't mean we should chuck it."

"Believe me, Bill, I agree with you completely.

I'm just saying, Bryan is shrewd. He knows how to frame the issues in ways that resonate with middle-of-the-road people. Including judges and juries."

"So how does Mr. Bryan propose to complicate our lives, exactly?"

"In three ways, from what I'm hearing through various grapevines," she said. "First, by filing a class-action suit against you, the university, and the state for discriminating against students who believe in the literal truth of the six-day creation story. Second, by petitioning the board of trustees to adopt a policy that would require any evolution-oriented instruction to be balanced by alternative theories."

"Swell," I said. "I've always liked the Native American alternative, which holds that North America is carried along on the back of a giant sea turtle."

"It's easy to see the absurd side of this," she said, "but I tell you, I can't promise which way the vote would go if the trustees started getting a lot of pressure."

That was two ways. "What's the third circle of hell he wants to consign us to?"

"Legislation, modeled after a 1980 Louisiana law that requires teachers who discuss evolution to also present scientific evidence for creation."

"But there's no such evidence," I protested. "Besides, the U.S. Supreme Court overturned that law years ago."

"Exactly," she said. "Twenty years and six justices ago. The Court's changed since then, become a lot more conservative. Today's Court might uphold a law similar to the one overturned by the 1987 court. This proposed Tennessee law—and I'm told he's already got sponsors in both the House and the Senate—is crafted with enough differences from the Louisiana law that the Supreme Court might be willing to hear the case."

"Damn," I said, "wouldn't that be ironic if Bill Brockton—a guy whose scientific career is founded on evolutionary change in the human skeleton—handed the creationists a landmark victory in the Supreme Court?" She gave me an enigmatic Mona Lisa smile. "Even more ironic," I said, "if eight decades after the Scopes trial, where science won the battle for public opinion, Tennessee's educators and legislators turned their backs on science."

She stood up to go. "You know the most important thing you can do now to keep that from happening?" I waited. "Keep quiet."

CHAPTER 12

I HAD JUST PARKED my truck outside the loading bay behind UT Medical Center when Miranda stuck her head out the door. "Peggy called," she said. Peggy was the Anthropology Department's overworked secretary. "She says Dr. Carter wants you to call her at her office in Chattanooga. ASAP."

I hurried in, trying to imagine what could prompt the added note of urgency. I came up empty. "Jess, it's Bill," I said. "Is something wrong?"

"I just got a call from Nashville," she said. "From the Board of Medical Examiners." It was the group weighing the fate—and the medical license—of Dr. Garland Hamilton, the disgraced Knoxville medical examiner whose vacancy she had been filling for weeks now. "Bill, they chickened out. They voted to suspend him for ninety days. From the date of the complaint. The complaint was filed eighty-three days ago. That means in another week, he's back on the job."

I groaned. How could they have let him off with such a token punishment? Hamilton's incompetent autopsy had put a man on trial for a "murder" that hadn't been committed. It was the sloppiest post-mortem examination I had ever seen, and while it was the worst of his lapses, it was by no means the only one. I had testified for the wrongly accused defendant in the "murder" case, and Hamilton had confronted me angrily, even threateningly, outside the courthouse afterward. But by the time of last week's licensing hearing, he seemed to have gotten over his animosity; he had shaken my hand, and assured me he bore no hard feelings. Even so, I didn't relish the idea of having him restored to the position of medical examiner for Knox County and eighteen surrounding counties.

"Well, damn," I said. "We were just getting used to having a competent ME up this way. I know all the driving between Chattanooga and Knoxville has been hard on you, but we'll sure miss you." I hesitated, then added, "*I'll* sure miss you."

The line fell silent, and I felt panic rising, then she said, "Doesn't mean we can't still see each other. Just means we have to find time outside of work." I felt a rush of relief and hope.

"We're both smart people," I said. "We ought to be able to manage that sometimes."

"Don't overestimate us," she joked. We chatted a few more moments, then Jess got paged so we hung up.

Almost the instant I put the handset back in its cradle, the phone rang again. "Hello, this is Dr. Brockton," I said.

"Bill? Garland Hamilton. Listen, I wanted you to hear this from me. The Board of Medical Examiners voted to put me in the stocks for ninety days, but they gave me credit for time served. So I'll be back in the office a week from today."

"Well, I know that must come as good news to you," I said carefully.

"Oh, I'm dying to get back to work," he said. "Listen, Bill, I meant what I said the other day. I know we didn't see eye to eye in that Ledbetter case"—I almost laughed at the understatement; it was like saying George Bush and Al Gore didn't see eye to eye—"but I hope we can put that behind us and start with a clean page."

I hesitated. Again I sought refuge in ambiguity. "A clean page would be nice."

"Great," he said. "What'd I miss? Any interesting cases come through while I was out?"

I wasn't sure I wanted to brief him on Jess's work. "Well, I've been working on a homicide, but it's from Chattanooga, so it's in Jess's jurisdiction anyhow," I said. "Other than that, it's been pretty quiet lately."

"Glad to hear it. Listen, I won't keep you. Just wanted to touch base, and let you know I'll be seeing you next week."

"Right. Next week. Thanks."

As I hung up the phone, I felt my heart sink. I wasn't sure how much of the heaviness was because Garland Hamilton would be coming back soon, and how much was because Jess Carter wouldn't be.

Oh, buck up, I scolded myself. *You haven't seen*

the last of her yet. You're going out with her tomorrow night. Another inner voice butted in. *Yeah, but it's work. And you better wear your bulletproof underwear.* The first voice squawked, *I* really *didn't need to know that.*

CHAPTER 13

THE DRIVE FROM KNOXVILLE to Chattanooga passed in a hundred-mile blur of white and fuchsia blossoms. Dogwoods and redbuds both loved sunlight and limestone, so wherever I-75 cut through layers of rock, the highway was lined with enough flowering trees to make Home & Garden Television—which was based in Knoxville—and HGTV's entire army of landscapers and gardeners hang their heads in shame.

As I crested East Ridge and started the swooping S-curve that led down into the valley floor cradling Chattanooga, I replayed the morning's conversation with Jess, who had called to finalize the arrangements for our research outing.

"I booked you a room at the Marriott downtown," she had said.

"A hotel room? I need a hotel room?"

"Trust me," she said, "you won't want to *think* about driving back to Knoxville by the time things wind down at this nightclub."

But driving back to Knoxville had not been what I'd been thinking about. What I'd been thinking about, and hoping for, was an invitation to spend the night at Jess's. I tried not to show my disappointment. After all, so far we had exchanged only one kiss. It was a memorable kiss, and I hoped it wouldn't be the last. Still, it was only one—a pretty meager foundation for a sleepover invitation.

"Ten o'clock seems like a pretty late starting time," I said.

"Trust me, the party doesn't really get going until midnight at this place."

And so it was that I now found myself checking into the Marriott, a sleek tower of black glass, hours before Jess and I were scheduled to visit the nightclub where she hoped we might pick up the trail of her drag-queen murder victim.

I parked in the garage beneath the hotel, checked into my room, and decided to wander down toward the Tennessee Aquarium, one of Chattanooga's main tourist attractions. I'd brought Jeff's boys to the aquarium during their last Christmas break, and the facility's design had struck me as ingenious. I welcomed the chance for a return visit.

The main building's exhibits began five or six stories above the entrance level. There, beneath a huge glass pyramid, was a convincing re-creation of a Tennessee mountain rain forest. Technically, the Great Smoky Mountains were classed as a temperate rain forest, which explained the lush vegetation and rushing streams; in the aquarium's topmost exhibit, mist swirled and water dripped convincingly from trees into streams and pools. Within those streams and pools, brook trout and salamanders and otters darted behind glass walls.

Descending through the aquarium's series of exhibits, level by level, was like journeying down a river to the sea, through a succession of realistic habitats. Within them dwelled hundreds of species, not just aquatic life but birds and reptiles as well, including one monstrous eastern diamondback rattlesnake, whose body was as thick as my forearm and whose tail sported fifteen rattles, which I counted twice in disbelief. In one tank, two scuba divers were feeding fish by hand; one of the fish—clearly well fed—was a five-foot-long catfish that probably weighed as much as I did. When the fish opened its mouth to feed, its maw looked nearly big enough to engulf the diver's entire head.

After completing my journey downriver, through the delta, and out into the ocean, I swam outdoors into a steamy southern afternoon—a spring day that felt like high summer. Running along one side of the aquarium's exterior, from the entrance plaza down the hillside to the Tennessee River, was a cascade of water designed as a tribute to the Cherokee Indians, the first human inhabitants of eastern Tennessee. The cascade originated as trickles of water representing the Trail of Tears, the brutal march that evicted the Cherokees from Tennessee and forced them onto a reservation in Oklahoma. As the water coursed down the hill, it grew in volume, fed by hidden spigots, into a respectable-sized stream, dropping over ledges into shallow pools. Children in shorts and bathing suits and rolled-up jeans waded in these; alongside, parents and older siblings and babysitters lounged on the concrete terraces, a few brave souls sunbathing in bikinis amid scores of little sneakers and flipflops.

When I reached the bottom of the cascade, I crossed the street to Ross's Landing on the river itself and found myself wandering upriver along a wooden boardwalk, the beginning of the long ribbon of park that stretched for miles up to Chickamauga Dam. A paddle-wheeled riverboat moored at the landing gave a blast on its whistle, and a handful of tourists responded by scurrying toward it. A runner passed, sheathed in sweat, and I remembered Jess saying that somewhere along here, a man and his dog had died a gruesome death. I began walking faster, with more purpose now, until suddenly I stopped. Perhaps a quarter mile upstream from the aquarium and Ross's Landing, the riverwalk passed beneath a pair of bridges, then zigzagged up a steep hillside toward a striking contemporary building—the new wing of the art museum—cantilevered daringly off the edge of the river bluff. Here beneath the bridges, an odd little amphitheater had been terraced into the hillside, and on one of the lower terraces, yellow and black fragments of crime scene tape clung to bridge supports, and the tan pea gravel still bore traces of blood. I studied the low space beneath the bridges as I would any other death scene, trying to decipher patterns in the bloodstains, but the gravel had been rinsed and raked and scuffed too much to tell me anything. I pictured this place at dusk, rather than in the bright light of midafternoon, imagining what it must have felt like to be set upon by malevolent young men for no other reason than that I was a handy target for years of anger and despair.

My gloomy reverie was interrupted by the hum of rubber tires on the riverwalk. A brightly clad cyclist pedaled past on a mountain bike. When he reached the sharp switchbacks angling up the bluff, I expected him to dismount; instead, in a display of balance and precision I would not have thought possible on two wheels, he made one hairpin turn after another—at least twenty in all—before topping out near the museum and speeding off. I laughed in amazement and delight and ascended the hill myself, huffing and sweating by the time I zigged and zagged clear to the top. Once there, I wandered the neighborhood—an assortment of galleries, cafés, and inns clustered near the art museum—and ate dinner in the courtyard of a restaurant. By the time I ambled back to the Marriott, my legs were tired, my feet were sore, and I had just enough time to shower and change before meeting Jess in the lobby for our research excursion.

As we pulled away from the hotel, Jess steered me right on Carter Street, then right again on Martin Luther King Boulevard. After maybe a mile, she directed me left onto Central, then right onto McCallie Avenue. I was vaguely familiar with McCallie, as I'd been invited several times to guest-lecture at McCallie School, a prestigious private academy whose graduates included media mogul Ted Turner, Senator Howard Baker, and televangelist Pat Robertson. The prep school, though, was farther to the east, nestled at the base of Missionary Ridge; our destination, a nightclub called Alan Gold's, was in a flatter, more blue-collar section of town. As we crossed a viaduct over a railroad track and a city park began spooling darkly past on our left, she said, "Okay, slow down, slow down; there it is on the right. Turn onto that side street and park anywhere you can."

The building was a drab old brick structure, two stories high; at first glance it looked more like an electrical supply company than a trendy night-spot. The only distinguishing feature of the façade fronting McCallie was a line of spherical white lights about fifteen or twenty feet off the ground. As we turned onto the side street, though, things picked up dramatically. A hundred or more cars and trucks were jammed into a patchwork of tiny lots. Dozens of people—singly and in couples of every possible combination of age, gender, ethnicity, and edginess—milled about. Music throbbed intermit-tently from the side entrance, a door that opened and closed every few seconds to admit or disgorge more patrons. We got lucky—a PT Cruiser backed out of a parking spot just as we approached at an idle. "Somebody must have paired up early," Jess said. I raised my eyebrows, for what I suspected would not be the only time tonight.

Jess paid the ten-dollar cover charge for us, and we entered through a long, narrow hallway, congested not only by the ceaseless ebb and flow of custom-ers, but by the tunnel's terminus, a small alcove just outside the club's restrooms, where people hovered and chatted, blocking traffic. From here, a branch-ing pair of hallways let into the club's main areas, a small back bar and the main bar, fronting the dance floor, which a crowded mezzanine overlooked.

Jess and I had decided to split up and work the room separately; we each had several copies of pictures of the Chattanooga murder victim, as envisioned by a police sketch artist. One version showed him as a normal male, in regular street clothes. The other version showed him in the kinky outfit in which his body had been found.

Jess made for a cluster of young men in biker gear—black leather trimmed with an abundance of zippers, rivets, chains, and skulls. Some of the skulls sported wings, which I found particularly intriguing.

I felt a need to acclimate before interrogating anyone in this crowd, so I eased toward the bar and found an opening. The bartender looked up from the drink he was shaking. "What'll you have?"

"Coke, please," I said.

He smiled slightly. "A Coca-Cola, or some coke?"

It took a moment for the distinction to sink in. "Ah," I said. "Just the legal soft drink, if you would."

"Certainly, sir." He smiled again, indulgently, when he handed it to me, waving aside the five-dollar bill I had fished out of my wallet. "Soft drinks are free," he said. "All you pay for here is the hard stuff." He winked as he said it. Perhaps, I thought, I should have stuck close to Jess.

I turned around and leaned back against the bar. As I scanned the room and its occupants uneasily, I heard a soft female voice to my left side. "You look like you're looking for somebody," she said. "And like you haven't found him yet."

I turned and found myself facing a beautiful young black woman. Her skin was the color of strong coffee cut with lots of cream. Her shoulder-length hair had been straightened; it had a bit of wave to it, and where it swept across her forehead, the blue-black was streaked with golden highlights. Her brown eyes were warm and liquid, and her gold evening gown showed an impressive amount of cleavage. It took some willpower not to stare. "Well, I'm not sure who I'm looking for," I said.

She gave a dramatic sigh. "Oh, honey, ain't that *always* the way. I been looking half my life, and I ain't found my loverboy yet. But we *gots* to keep lookin'. Don't you give up, now. You gon' find him real soon. Maybe even tonight, right here."

I felt my face redden. "I'm not looking for a man . . . like that," I said. "I'm looking for somebody who might be able to tell us whether a specific young man was hanging out here a while back. Do you come here a lot?"

"Why yes, I do come here every now and then," she said, "but most times, I come when I'm in my big brass bed with some big, strong man." She reached out and gave my left shoulder a squeeze. "Oh my, *yay*-es," she said, batting her long lashes at me.

This conversation had clearly spun out of my control. I knew she was making fun of me, but I had to laugh. Actually, she seemed to be making fun of both of us, which is why I was able to laugh. Was she flirting? Probably so. Was I flirting back? Not yet, I decided, but I was strongly considering it. "What specific young man you looking for, sweetheart? Lossa young mens hang out here."

"This one," I said, fishing the two portraits from my pocket. "He might have been dressed in men's clothing, or he might have been wearing women's clothing and a wig. In drag."

She looked at me archly. "Darlin', I *know* what drag means."

"Right," I said. "Anyhow, we're wondering if anybody here might have seen him."

She glanced at the pictures, then looked at me and across the room at Jess. "Y'all the po-lice?"

"No," I said. "She's a medical examiner; I'm a forensic anthropologist. I teach up at UT-Knoxville."

"A pro-fessor? Oh my, I do love a man with a great big . . . brain," she said. She laughed, a musical sound that started high and cascaded down, like a series of handbells pealing in quick succession. As she did, she laid a hand on my chest momentarily; her nails were long and cobalt blue, with flecks of gold that matched her dress and the highlights in her hair. I caught a whiff of perfume, something floral and citrusy. Not too heavy or sweet; fresh, but also exotic. It suited her, I decided. "Mr. Professor, I am Miss Georgia Youngblood, and I am delighted to make your acquaintance."

"Thank you," I said. "I'm Dr. Bill Brockton. Sorry; that sounds stuffy. I'm Bill." I wanted to be sure I'd understood her enunciation correctly. "Did you say *Miss* Youngblood? Not *Ms.*? I've spent years learning to put that *z* on the end for my female students and colleagues."

"Oh no no *no*," she said, "I am most definitely an old-fashioned 'miss.' In fact, most of my friends call me Miss Georgia, which I like, because I grew up just over the line, in the Peach State." She cocked her head, studying my face. "I think I'll call you Dr. Bill. I don't usually enjoy receiving doctor bills, but I feel myself inclined to make an exception in your case."

She talked like a character out of some Tennessee Williams play, but the dramatic flourishes seemed to fit somehow. I wasn't sure what all she meant by "receiving," and I didn't have the nerve to ask, so I waved the pictures to remind her that I'd asked about them. "So how about it, Miss Georgia," I said, "do you recognize either version of this fellow?"

She frowned. "No, I can't say as I do," she said. "Mind you, he's not the sort of boy who would catch my eye. I prefer my men to have a little more maturity and *experience* under their belts." She looked at me suggestively; in response, I tried raising one eyebrow at her—I'd been practicing Jess's trick, with occasional success. The half-guilty knowledge that Jess was barely twenty feet away, also armed with the sketch artist's renderings, made it harder to achieve the needed muscle isolation.

"What about this version, where he's in drag?"

"Honey, I *know* I ain't seen *that* li'l bitch," she said, "if you'll 'scuse my French. Look at that cheap-ass Dolly Parton wig. And that S&M bustier? Tha's some kinda white-trash *ho* getup. Miss Georgia wouldn't be caught dead in that."

"Well, he was," I said. "Somebody murdered him a couple weeks ago, and we'd like to find out who he was and who killed him."

"I'd like to find out why he wearin' that trashy getup," she said. "He probably killed by the fashion po-*lice*. A crime of fashion in the first degree." She laughed again, the peals ringing out above the din of the bar. Just then the lights in the place flickered, briefly, and she glanced at her watch, then laid a hand on my forearm. "Baby, you gots to 'scuse me for just a little bit. Don't you go 'way, though. I want to come back and hear all about your Ph.D. and your arthropology."

"*An*thropology," I corrected, but she was already headed through a doorway at the end of the bar.

Suddenly the lights flashed again, then dimmed, and the noise level in the room dropped by a good ten decibels. "Ladies and gentlemen," an amplified voice boomed from speakers in the ceiling, "Alan Gold's is proud to present Chattanooga's favorite entertainer, the one and only Miss Georgia *Young*-blood!" Many of the people in the bar whistled and whooped and clapped as my new friend, microphone in hand, strutted onto a small stage occupying one end of the room. She curtsied deeply, bending over far enough to expose plenty of cleavage—and to incite a fresh round of cheers. As she straightened up, she half hid her face behind one bare shoulder, feigning shyness. The crowd responded again. She clearly knew what they liked, and she clearly liked giving it to them. Then she shushed them, and I heard a recording of violins fade up on the sound system. A spotlight flicked on, causing Miss Georgia's mocha skin and glossy hair to glow, and then she began to sing. Her voice started out delicate and tentative, then quickly grew powerful and poignant. "Don't . . . know . . . *why*/There's no sun up in the sky/Stormy weather/Since my man and I ain't together," she sang. Her voice rang with sadness and longing—a tragic version of the bell-pealing laugh she'd let loose only minutes before.

Out of the corner of my eye I glimpsed Jess, who had edged through the crowd to me. "Isn't he great? Most of them just lip-sync, but this one's really belting it out, isn't he?"

"He?" I looked at Jess and I saw disbelief, amusement, and pity flash across her face in quick succession. Then the amusement won out over the other expressions.

She leaned close so she could speak softly in my ear. "Oh, *Bill*. You really didn't know you were talking to a she-male?"

"A she-male?"

"She-male. Transvestite. Female impersonator. Miss Georgia there has been a local celebrity ever since she burst onto the scene a year or so ago. People drive all the way up from Atlanta to see her." Jess hoisted an eyebrow at me. "She seemed to be taking quite the shine to you, by the way," she said. "You must have set your charm-phaser to 'stun.' I was about to come over and scratch her eyes out."

"Oh, stop," I said. "I was just trying to find out if she's seen your murder victim."

"And?"

"Apparently not. She said version A wasn't the sort of guy she'd notice, and that she had definitely never seen version B's 'cheap-ass wig and trashy ho getup,' if I'm quoting her correctly, on anybody around here. Said he was probably executed by the fashion police. No, sorry: the fashion *po*-lice," I corrected myself.

"Miss Georgia does seem to have a good knowledge of the laws of fashion," Jess said. "She's a *knockout* in that gown." Jess looked down at her own outfit, which consisted of her usual black jeans, topped by an elegant blouse of what I guessed to be blue silk. "Her tits are better than mine, aren't they? Come on, tell me the truth—I'm a big girl; I can take it."

I stared at her. Had I had been living in suburbia and the ivory tower far too long? This evening had gotten way too surreal for me.

Up on the stage, Miss Georgia's torch song was flickering out, her voice getting small again and breaking a bit. "Can't . . . go . . . on/Everything I had . . . is gone . . ." she quavered, sounding as if she meant it from the bottom of a broken heart. "Keeps raining all the time/Keeps raining all of the time."

The violins faded, and Miss Georgia hung her head and let the microphone drop to her lap. The crowd applauded and cheered wildly. I hesitated, still embarrassed and confused by my stupid mistake. I looked at Jess; as she clapped, she grinned at me and rolled her eyes and shook her head. I found myself grinning back, then laughing out loud at my silliness. Then I found myself clapping so hard my hands hurt.

Miss Georgia performed several more numbers, ranging from a booty-shaking, foot-stomping rendition of "R-E-S-P-E-C-T" to a haunting blues lament. "She cries alone at night too often," she sang. "He smokes and drinks and don't come home at all/Only women bleed/Only women bleed/Only women bleed." Somehow those words seemed to take on an added layer of poignancy, coming from a young black man who envisioned himself, for whatever reason, as a woman. On the inside, at least, he was surely bleeding, too.

I still couldn't claim to understand why a man would want to dress in drag. But I could now intuit at least some of the pain involved in taking that drastic step. My bewilderment was tempered by compassion. And I could even, at least in Miss Georgia's case, appreciate the stunning results that a willowy frame, a flair for fashion, and an outsized personality could yield.

At the end of the set, the spotlight switched off and the lights in the bar came back up, though not all the way. The gray noise of a hundred conversations ramped up as well, but also to a more subdued level than before. Something about the songs, and the singer, seemed to soften the tone of the entire bar.

"I'm gonna go work the other side of the room," said Jess. "If you can get your mind off Miss Georgia for a minute, how about talking to these folks around the bar?" Without waiting for an answer, she threaded the crowd and began at a table in the far corner.

I made my way from patron to patron. I got a lot of odd looks, a few lewd propositions, and one pinch on my butt, which was swiftly followed by one of the lewd propositions. Taking a moment to collect myself after that, I scanned the opposite side of the room. I saw Jess engaged in an animated conversation with none other than Miss Georgia.

Jess pointed at Miss Georgia's chest and then at her own, laughing and shaking her head. Then, as I watched in astonishment, Jess reached up and cupped Miss Georgia's breasts in her hands, giving them an appraising squeeze and admiring nod. A moment later, Miss Georgia returned the gesture, squeezing Jess's breasts, then fanning herself dramatically.

I didn't know whether to be amused or jealous. The truth was, I was both.

I checked my watch. It was 2 A.M.—a good three hours past my usual bedtime. It suddenly felt much later. It suddenly felt too late for me.

CHAPTER 14

THE CHATTANOOGA MEDICAL EXAMINER'S office occupied a small building on Amnicola Highway, several miles northeast of downtown. Unlike the Regional Forensic Center in Knoxville, which was part of UT Medical Center, Jess Carter's facility was a freestanding structure, a nondescript, discreetly labeled rectangle of concrete block and glass that could have housed anything from a paint store to a software company. Its location always struck me as odd, too: its closest neighbor was the city's police and fire department training facility, an adjacency that possessed a certain logic. Other nearby businesses seemed far more random, though, including a grain elevator, a chemical plant, a lumber company, television station, and trucking firm. On the other hand, I reflected as I turned into the small parking lot, death was no respecter of persons, nor of occupations; seen in that light, this blue-collar setting for the morgue made as much sense as any other.

In both square footage and staff, Jess's facility was only half the size of Knoxville's, but—also unlike the Knoxville center—it wasn't handling cases from surrounding counties. The young murder victim dressed in drag whose body was found in the state forest in neighboring Marion County was an exception. Jess, and the Chattanooga police, had gotten involved because there was evidence to suggest that the victim had been abducted in Chattanooga.

Until a month ago, Jess's staff of five had included a forensic anthropologist, Rick Fields, who was one of my former students. But Rick had just taken a similar position at the Regional Forensic Center in Memphis, which represented a big step up, in salary and in caseload: Memphis had about 150 murders a year, compared with Chattanooga's 25 or 30. While Jess sought a replacement for Rick, I was filling in down here, just as she had been filling in as ME in Knoxville since Garland Hamilton's suspension for incompetence.

I said hello to Amy, the receptionist separated from the lobby by a window of bulletproof glass. Amy pointed to my right, toward the end of the building that contained the autopsy suite, and buzzed me in through the metal door on that side of the lobby. Jess was just stitching up the abdominal cavity of an elderly white female. "Don't tell me you've got another homicide," I said.

Without looking up from her sutures, she answered, "No, just an unattended death. Colon cancer. She had just gone home from the hospital to die. The irony is, she was supposed to be in hospice care, but somehow the paperwork got lost, so they were scrambling around to get her signed up. If it had worked like it was supposed to—if there'd been a seamless handoff from the hospital to hospice—I wouldn't have needed to spend two hours confirming what we already knew about her cause of death."

Jess was wearing faded jeans—blue, not black— and a maroon scrub shirt. She looked more tired than I'd ever seen her look. Also less guarded and more human, somehow. It made me want to take care of her, ease the load she was carrying. "No offense, but you look about halfway toward needing hospice care yourself," I said.

"You silver-tongued flatterer, you," she said, but the smart-ass words lacked her usual smart-ass crackle.

"Seriously," I said, "you okay?"

"Tired. Really tired. In the past week I've done six autopsies here, four in Knoxville, and made a trip to Nashville. I've only had two days off, both of them Sundays, in the past month. I desperately need to hire a morgue technician, but our budget's so tight the only thing keeping us out of the red is those two vacancies, the tech and the anthropologist." I had never stopped to consider what a load Jess carried; her willingness to do double duty up in Knoxville was remarkably generous, and it was wearing her down fast.

She had her hair pulled back in a short ponytail, but a wisp had gotten loose and fallen across her face. She couldn't reach up and brush it away because her gloves were a mess, so I did it for her. Then I laid my hand on her cheek. She leaned into it, and it felt good, so I put my other hand on her other cheek, cradling her face in my hands. She closed her eyes and took a long, deep breath, then puffed it out. As she did, she dropped her head deeper into my hands, her shoulders sagging with fatigue. Her gloved hands hung at her sides. I moved my hands from her face to her shoulders, then wrapped my arms around her and pulled her close. She did not resist, and in a moment she laid her head on my chest. "I'm sorry you're so tired, Jess," I murmured. In response, she gave a small shiver, or maybe it was a sob. But then she stiffened and began to pull away. I held tight, and tried to soothe her. "Shhhh," I said. "Just relax for a minute."

For some reason I didn't understand, it was the wrong thing to say. She began to struggle against me, and put her hands—messy gloves and all—on my chest and pushed me away. "Stop," she said sharply. "Not here. I cannot be this way with you here."

The words stung, or maybe it was the physical rejection that stung. Whichever the case, my face burned with disappointment and humiliation. "Dammit, Jess, then where? Not at my house— that wasn't the place, either. Alan Gold's? Those were somebody else's hands on you there. Your house? You haven't invited me there. Where does that leave? I'm confused and frustrated. I didn't start this; *you* did. Unless I completely misread that dinner invitation you extended to yourself last week."

Now it was her turn to flush. "Right now I'm *working*," she said. "Would you do this in the middle of teaching a class?" She looked away and chewed on her lower lip. "No," she said at last. "You didn't misread. I'm confused, too. When I saw you last week, I thought you were finally over Kathleen's death and ready for another relationship. What I failed to think about was whether or not *I* was ready."

"Your divorce? How long has it been?"

"About six months. No; eight. But we'd been on the skids for a couple of years. Hell, I was on the verge of jumping ship myself. So how come it hurt so much when he beat me to the punch?" I saw tears welling up, something I'd never expected to see in the eyes of Jess Carter. I reached up to wipe them away, but she took a step back and held up a warning finger. Then she raised her arms, one after the other, and wiped her eyes with the sleeves of her scrubs. "I'm sorry, Bill," she said. "This is harder than I thought, and I'm too tired and strung out to be smart about it." She looked at the bloody smears her gloves had left on my chest. "I'm sorry about the shirt, too," she said. "Go change into some scrubs, and while we're looking at this forensic case, I'll get Amy to run it through the wash."

By the time I had changed, handed my wadded-up shirt to Amy, and returned to the autopsy room, Jess had rolled the cancer victim back to the cooler and rolled out the gurney on which our male murder victim lay. When the body came in eight days ago, she had taken X-rays and autopsied him; at this point, I wasn't sure I'd be able to see much that she hadn't already spotted, but I was willing to give it a shot.

The crime scene photos hadn't done justice to the violence inflicted on this battered body. The cranium—largely covered in the photos by the blond wig—had been hit with great force, more than once. Bone fragments had been driven deep into the brain; brain matter had oozed out like the insides of a smashed pumpkin. The zygomatic arches—the cheekbones—were both shattered; so were the nasal bone and the outside rim of the left eye orbit. From the X-rays Jess had clipped onto a light box on the wall, I could see that several ribs were broken, too.

I glanced from the body on the gurney to the cranial X-rays, then turned to Jess. "So was it the head trauma that killed him?"

"Superb deduction, Sherlock," she said. "Massive brain trauma and acute subdural hematoma. I'm hoping you can give us an idea what the murder weapon was."

"I'll do my best," I said, "though with blunt-force trauma, it's sometimes tough. The impression left by a baseball bat looks a lot like the impression left by a length of galvanized pipe. If we're lucky, it might be something like a hammer, which leaves a nice round mark, or even an octagonal one, if the hammerhead is shaped that way—a wound with a distinctive signature. But from what I can see right now," I said, bending down and peering at the face and cranium, "I don't think we're going to be that lucky." It was a relief, after the awkwardness and tension of a few moments before, to burrow into the puzzle of a challenging case.

I did an overall visual exam first. The corpse's

most noticeable feature—aside from the battered skull with the top sliced off and the brain removed—was the differential decay: the stark contrast between the bare bones of the lower legs and the extensive soft tissue remaining on most of the body. The insects had managed to do a moderate amount of damage to the eyes, the nasal cavity, and the shoulders and base of the neck—an area that offered the only sizable horizontal surface on the upright body; otherwise, they'd been largely frustrated in their attempts to feast on the body that had been served up to them.

I rolled the body over. I saw numerous scratches on the back, and bits of pine bark embedded in the flesh, but those all looked like superficial abrasions, exactly what you'd expect to see on the back of a body lashed tightly to a tree.

"I don't see anything, here or in the X-rays, that would suggest the manner of death involved anything other than the blunt-force trauma," I said.

"Think you can tell what did it?"

"Hard to know till I get the soft tissue off," I said. "Are you finished with him?" She nodded. "What I'd like to do, if you're willing, is remove the head, take it back to Knoxville, and deflesh it so I can get a good look at the bone."

"I was hoping you'd say that," she said. She rolled over a tray of instruments. I chose a scalpel to begin cutting through the windpipe, esophagus, and muscles of the neck. When I had exposed the cervical vertebrae, I switched to an autopsy knife; scalpel blades were thin and relatively fragile, and all it took to break one was a little sideways pressure when the blade was wedged deep between two vertebrae.

As I began to cut between the second and third vertebrae, Jess moved to the corpse's head and grasped it with both hands. She tilted it back, and also pulled slightly so that as the knife cut deeper, the gap between the bones widened. "Thanks," I said. "That helps. Reduces the risk I'll nick the bone, too."

A few more strokes of the knife and the spine was severed. That left only the muscles and skin at the back of the neck, and those were easy to cut, especially as Jess continued to apply tension. When the head came completely free, she rotated it to study it, as if for the first time. As she gazed at it, I was reminded of a religious painting I'd seen once, of Salome holding the head of John the Baptist. But in the painting I'd seen, Salome looked exotic, youthful, and richly dressed; in the harsh fluorescent lights of the morgue, Jess—in her jeans and soiled scrub shirt—looked shabby, exhausted, and middle-aged. For the first time in the days since I'd found myself peering at the toes of her snakeskin boots, I began to despair of our chances at any sort of romance.

"I'll bag this and put it in a cooler for you," she said.

"Thanks. Do you still want me to go out to the death scene?"

"If you're still willing," she said.

"Sure," I said. "How far away is it?"

"Only about ten miles as the crow flies," she said, "but probably twice that by road. And some of it's gravel. So it'll take forty-five minutes or an hour to get there."

I checked my watch; it was already midafternoon. "Guess I better make tracks, then."

"Yeah. Why don't you wash up and change— we've got some denim shirts with our logo on them; I'll tell Amy to give you one—and I'll pull together what you need to find your way out there." She started toward the door, then stopped and turned back. "Bill? I'm sorry I'm a mess right now. Any false advertising was unintentional. Please don't give up on me." She took a step toward me, stood up on tiptoe, and kissed me quickly on the cheek. Before I could react, she was out the door of the autopsy room.

I looked down at the eyeless severed head on the gurney as if it had somehow witnessed the scene. "Well, unlike you," I said, "I'm not *quite* dead yet."

After I washed up and changed into the shirt Amy had given me, I found Jess in her office, at the other end of the building. She opened her desk drawer and fished out a set of keys and a handheld electronic gadget. She switched on the gizmo, and after a few seconds an image flashed onto an LCD screen the size of an index card. The image diagrammed a dozen points; lines from each of the twelve converged on a point at the screen's center.

"Looks like a constellation," I said, "except the dots aren't connected in the shape of what's supposed to look like an animal, but never does."

"That's us at the center," she said. "We're receiving GPS signals from twelve satellites. More satellites is good for the accuracy; you shouldn't have any trouble pinpointing the spot."

Her fingers flicked rapidly over the buttons, and the image changed to a small color topographical map, this one bearing two dots: one at the center, and one in the lower left corner. "That dot in the lower left? That's a waypoint marking the death scene. The center one is us. That's the thing I like best about GPS: it always acknowledges that I'm the center of the universe." She laughed at herself. "God, how can I have such a gigantic ego and such stunted self-esteem at the same time?"

"Well, as Thoreau said, consistency is the mark of small minds," I said.

"Actually, that was Emerson," she said. "And he said 'little minds,' actually: 'A foolish consistency is the hobgoblin of little minds, adored by little statesmen and philosophers and divines. With consistency a great soul has simply nothing to do.' If memory serves."

"Very impressive," I said. "How come I thought that came from Thoreau?"

"Same vein, sort of," she said. "Thoreau's trademark line is 'different drummer,' which is even more famous. 'Why should we be in such desperate haste to succeed, and in such desperate enterprises?'—almost nobody quotes that lead-in, which is a shame. 'Why should we be in such desperate haste to succeed, and in such desperate enterprises? If a man does not keep pace with his companions, perhaps it is because he hears a different drummer. Let him step to the music which he hears, however measured or far away.' Too bad he didn't copyright that; with the royalties, he could've bought up Walden Pond and everything for miles around. Built himself a fancy mansion instead of that tatty shack he cobbled together out of scrap boards and recycled nails."

Jess's mixture of scholarly erudition and quirky irreverence always caught me by surprise, like topspin on a serve in tennis or Ping-Pong. But I liked it, the way I liked iced tea on a hot day. "They teach you all this in med school over at Vanderbilt?"

"Naw," she said, "this is what I have to show for my four years at Smith. Scraps of poetry and philosophy. Oh, and that one unfulfilling foray into dating within my own gender."

"Ah. I had almost managed to forget," I said, feeling awkward and sounding prudish.

"Come on, Bill, that's an experiment I did once, twenty years ago. Don't turn it into something that defines me. Hell, I tried all sorts of things when I was young, didn't you?" She was glaring at me now; I had pressed one of her hot buttons without intending to. "I mean, isn't that part of how we grow and learn who we are, by trying things on and seeing what fits? I tried on another girl, and she didn't fit. Big deal. I got drunk a few times in college, too, but that doesn't make me an alcoholic. I cheated on a biology test in high school, but that doesn't make me a cheat. I stole a candy bar when I was six, but I'm not a thief."

I felt ashamed of my small-mindedness. "I'm sorry, Jess. I don't judge you for it. Or maybe I do, but I don't like the part of me that does. I came along, what, ten years ahead of you? I grew up in a small town, where even straight sex was practically immoral. I went to a conservative college, and I settled into a traditional life—marriage and family—right after graduating. My horizons got drawn a little nearer, a little narrower, than yours. Doesn't mean I want my mind or my heart to be narrow." She still looked mad. "Please," I said, "this is important to me. You are important to me. I'm not sure exactly how yet, but I'd like the chance to figure it out. I think maybe you would, too. At least, I hope you still do."

Her eyes bored into mine, fiercely still. And then, almost imperceptibly, something softened, yielded just a fraction. I smiled. She smiled. I laughed. So did she. "God," she said, "you make me so mad sometimes. But you also make me feel so human."

"That's a good thing, right?"

"I haven't decided yet," she said, but her eyes were smiling as she said it. "Do we never really grow up? Sometimes I feel as clueless and confused inside as I did when I was fourteen, and first started feeling these inexplicable, thrilling, terrifying stirrings."

"Oh my," I said. "It thrills and terrifies me just to imagine you at fourteen." I leaned toward her, angling for a kiss. She placed a hand on my chest and held me off. "Not here. Not now," she said. "But soon, I hope. You need to get going if you want to have any daylight when you get out to Prentice Cooper." She ended the conversation by reaching down and hefting something from beneath her desk. It was a small cooler, and as she handed it to me, I felt something round and heavy shift inside. It was the dead cross-dresser's head.

I set the cooler down on the desk long enough to stuff the keys and GPS receiver in the roomy pockets of my cargo pants. Then I hefted the cooler in hand, found the four-wheel drive Bronco Jess had offered me for the trip, and set out for Prentice Cooper State Forest, hoping I wouldn't have a cooler-smashing accident or get pulled over by a curious cop.

Prentice Cooper lay barely ten miles west of Chattanooga, but it was a world away, both topographically and culturally. Most of its 26,000 acres lined the slopes and rim of the Tennessee River Gorge, a thousand-foot-deep gash the river had carved through the southern foothills of the Appalachian Mountains. In addition to the GPS, which would guide me to the exact spot where the body was found, I had a printed topo map of the area, too. To reach the forest, I would head west for about five miles on state highway 27, which was nestled between the base of Signal Mountain and the river's north shore. Then the highway would veer north, up a smaller side gorge carved by Suck Creek, which—according to the topo map—would split into North Suck Creek and South Suck Creek. The highway angled and corkscrewed up the side of South Suck Creek, finally topping out—for two or three miles—near Suck Creek School. If I missed the turnoff to the state forest, I would quickly find myself descending the west flank of the mountain through Ketner Gap, which looked every bit as steep as Suck Creek, and appeared to offer few opportunities for a U-turn.

I needn't have worried. The left turn to Prentice Cooper was well marked, as was another left through a meandering collection of small rural houses. Civilization dropped away fast, though, as soon as I crossed the boundary into the forest. Asphalt gave way to gravel; yards gave way to woods.

I rolled down the windows on the Bronco. The weather was sunny but cool, and the air up here was as crisp and sweet as a good apple.

Suddenly I heard a gunshot. Then another, and another. I hit the brakes, and the Bronco rasped to a stop, enveloping me in a cloud of my own dust. The dust kept me from seeing my assailant coming, but it also hid me from sight, and from aim, so I figured I was no worse off than I'd been.

Just as I was about to back around and hightail it back to civilization, the dust settled and I saw it: RIFLE RANGE, said a brown and white sign pointing down a side road to the right. The direction of the gunshots. Amused and appalled by my paranoia, I wiped a fresh layer of dusty sweat—or was it sweaty dust?—from my forehead and headed south again. Suck Creek Mountain was more plateau than peak, so the road ran surprisingly straight over gently rolling terrain. Two or three miles in, I bisected a cluster of forest service structures, including a fire lookout tower on a rise to the right. "Well, I might be paranoid," I said out loud, "but at least I'm still on Tower Road." Then I said, "I might be turning into a guy who talks to himself, though." After a pause, I added, "Yep. I've been meaning to speak to you about that."

Jess had told me that the body was found just off a Jeep trail near Pot Point. The name had concerned me—in the course of my last case involving a body in a mountainous rural area, I'd learned firsthand that where there were pot patches, there were often booby traps, too, ranging from shotguns with trip wires to poisonous snakes staked out with fishhooks through their tails—so I had asked Jess if "Pot Point" referred to illegal agriculture. "No, I'm pretty sure the name is some historical reference," she had answered, "but I don't know the particulars."

On the little GPS screen, it hadn't looked far from the forest entrance to Pot Point, but on the ground, it seemed to be taking forever. The road was good, but it was gravel, so my speed rarely topped twenty miles an hour. I perked up when I passed Sheep Rock Road, as that meant I was more than halfway there.

Two miles later, I reached a fork in the road. Tower Road, the main artery through the forest, bore right; Davis Pond Road—my turn—angled left. The terrain became hillier, which meant I was nearing the edge of the plateau. The road began to pitch and curve, and the woods closed in. After an undulating mile, I passed a small pond on the left, and the gravel road suddenly became a dirt road. Then it forked into two smaller dirt roads and I stopped, unsure which way to go. The GPS display showed only one road here, bearing east near the rim of the gorge; my printed topo map showed two roads, roughly parallel, which I assumed were branching from the spot where I'd just stopped: Upper Pot Point Road and Lower Pot Point Road. Unfortunately, the waypoint marking the crime scene was on the GPS, so I couldn't tell which of the two roads to take.

I pulled out my cellphone to call Jess for clarification, but I wasn't getting any signal bars. Civilization, or at least cellphone service, had dropped away as I had threaded my way up Suck Creek, and my journey into the forest hadn't done much to restore either one. I got out of the Bronco and flattened the USGS map across the hood, hoping a side-by-side comparison of the two maps might help. And indeed it did, though not quite as I'd expected. A white Ford 4×4 pickup came slewing off of Upper Pot Point Road; when the driver saw me, he stopped alongside me and rolled down his window. There was a Tennessee Department of Forestry logo on the door of the truck—the tree in the center tipped me off—and the shoulder of the man's tan shirt bore a patch with the same logo. I caught a brief snatch of country music—"I know you're married, but I love you still," wailed a woman—before he switched off the radio and leaned out the window. He was tall and lanky, with curly red hair going to gray, and a short beard that had already gone to white. His face was weathered and ruddy except in the deep crinkles that years of smiling or squinting had etched in it. He glanced at the official logo on the side of the ME's vehicle, then at me and my map. "You returning to the scene of the crime?" he asked.

"Not returning. Headed there for my first look," I said. "But I can't tell from the map whether I want Upper Pot Point Road or Lower."

"Well, you want Lower Pot Point, but you

don't want it much. Gets kinda rough in spots, but you should be all right in that Bronco. Take your right-hand fork here for about a mile; there's a turnout just past a little water crossing. Then you got to bushwhack about a hundred yards to the rim trail . . ." He trailed off, studying me and my navigational aids doubtfully. "Tell you what," he said, "let me show you the way. If you haven't been there before, I'm not sure you'll find it on your own."

I thanked him, and started folding up the big topo map. "Oh, one other question, if you don't mind," I said.

"Fire away."

"Why is it called Pot Point? Does the name refer to marijuana, or Native American artifacts?"

"Neither," he said. "Back before TVA built Nickajack Dam, there were three big rapids in the river just below that overlook. The one farthest downstream was called the Frying Pan, the middle one was called the Skillet, and the uppermost was called the Boiling Pot. Pretty ferocious, supposedly—there's a house on the shore there that was built partly from the wreckage of old riverboats. I guess the Boiling Pot must've been the biggest, since the overlook is called Pot Point. Me, if I'd been naming the rapids, I'd have called the *middle* rapid the Frying Pan and the next one downstream the Fire. Get it? Out of the Frying Pan, into the Fire?"

"Oh, I got it," I said. "Yep, that's a good one, all right."

"Hey, can I ask you a question?"

"Fire away," I said.

"The body's been gone for a week. What are you hoping to find?"

"Couple things," I said. "Be better to show you than try to explain. You want to hang around and see?"

He checked his watch—it was close to three o'clock, and I could practically see him calculating how long before his workday ended, and subtracting the half hour it would take to drive back to the highway. "It won't take more than an hour, will it?"

"I don't think so," I said. "And if it does, you can leave me on my own. I was expecting to be out there by myself anyway."

He put his truck in reverse, cut his wheels sharply, and eased back until his rear bumper nudged a sapling at the edge of the woods. Then he spun the steering wheel to the left and edged forward, narrowly clearing the Bronco's fender as he turned. Motioning for me to follow him, he idled down the narrowing dirt track.

The road was a fresh reddish brown cut through the woods, a wound whose edges had not yet healed; its newness explained why it hadn't shown on the GPS map. Rutted clay alternated with stretches of tan sand and exposed sandstone. After several minutes, we bumped across a rocky little stream, then the pickup nosed into a cut in the treeline where the bulldozer that carved the road had shoved a pile of dirt and roots twenty feet into the woods. The F-150 pulled far enough forward to allow me room behind him, and we got out.

A crisscrossing of knobby tire tracks testified to a spate of recent traffic here, but otherwise, there was no hint that a crime scene lay nearby. "I'm mighty glad I ran into you," I said. "I'm not sure I'd have found this on my own. Probably not."

"Glad to do it," he said. "Gives me an excuse to get out of the truck and walk in the woods on a nice day. Name's Gassoway, by the by. Clifton. Call me Cliff."

"Cliff, I'm Bill Brockton. I'm a forensic anthropologist from UT-Knoxville." We shook hands.

"Are you the one with all the bodies?"

"That's me," I said. "Some folks collect antiques; I collect corpses." I glanced back at the Bronco, considering whether to show him the contents of the cooler in the rear floorboard, but decided that might be too much, too soon. "Lead on."

We followed the small stream for a short distance; there was no clearly defined path, but the leaves and underbrush looked recently trampled. After a hundred yards or so, we intersected a well-worn trail marked by blazes of white paint on tree trunks every so often. He turned right, and I followed. "Looks like we're not as far off the beaten path as I'd thought," I said.

"We're near the southern end of the Cumberland Trail," he said. "It's still a work in progress, but eventually it'll stretch three hundred miles along the Cumberland Plateau, clear up to Kentucky. We don't get as many hikers as sections a little farther north—Fiery Gizzard and Devil's Staircase and the Big South Fork have some spectacular scenery— but I like seeing the river gorge here."

As he said it, I began noticing gaps in the vegetation to our left, gaps that soon widened to reveal a spectacular view. A mile to the south, a steep mountainside rose in a dark, concave curve; at its base, the Tennessee River made a wide U-turn, flowing south from Chattanooga, deflected back to the north by this immovable geologic object, then finding passage to the west in an S-curve two miles long.

The overlook where we stood consisted of a half dozen sandstone ledges carpeted with moss and straw from a grove of widely spaced pines. Some of the trees looked healthy; others had fallen victim to pine beetles and violent winds, which had snapped their trunks ten feet above the ground.

The ledges adjoined one another, each one slightly higher or lower than its neighbors. The geometry reminded me of Fallingwater, the famous Frank Lloyd Wright house whose many balconies jutted daringly above a rocky stream and waterfall in Pennsylvania. Near the edge of the westernmost terrace, only a few feet from the bluff, stood a large pine swathed in yellow and black crime scene tape. I looked from the tree to the river gorge.

"Murder with a view," I said. "You think that was intentional?"

"Maybe," he said. "Otherwise, I can't quite figure why this particular spot. Be a pain in the ass to get a body out here."

"Sure would," I said.

"Also," he added, "it's not much of a hiding place. Not nearly as isolated as some areas over in the western side of the forest. Hell, over toward Long

Point and Inman Point, I don't know that I've ever seen another vehicle or a person. If I wanted to dump a body, I'd take it over thataways."

"So maybe the killer wanted the body to be found," I said. "Just not right away."

"I think you're right," he said.

I studied the mountain across the river. The top looked unnaturally flat, with a stone or concrete dike-looking wall along the edge. I pointed to it. "What's that?"

"That's Raccoon Mountain," he said. "TVA has a big pumped-storage reservoir up there, a lake nearly a mile wide. They pump water from the river up there at night, or whenever there's not much demand for power. Then, whenever the demand for power ramps way up—hot summer afternoons, cold winter mornings—they draw it down, letting the water spin generating turbines down there by the river." He pointed down into the gorge, to the shore directly opposite us; several buildings and a parking lot had been set at the base of the steep mountainside, and I saw water churning out a spill-way and into the river channel.

"You're a good tour guide," I said.

"Not many people have this kind of view from their workplace," he said. "I eat lunch out here probably once a week if the weather's decent."

"I'm surprised you didn't find the body, then," I said. Looking to my right, I eyed the crime scene tape staked out around the big pine.

"I was out here on a Monday about three weeks ago," he said. "Then I was off for a week—not that week, but the next one. Hiker found him on a

Sunday, day before I got back. So it could've happened anytime during those thirteen days. Pretty big window of time."

I did the arithmetic; at the outside, the murder had occurred twenty days ago; at the inside, a mere eight—but that seemed too recent, given the decomposition of the lower legs. "Well, if we're lucky, we can narrow it down a little more than that," I said. I walked slowly toward the tree, bent over to study the ground closely. After stepping over the tape, I knelt and continued the last six or eight feet on all fours.

Jess had shown me the report from the evidence techs who'd worked the crime scene. They'd done a reasonably good job, it sounded like, including collecting some key insect evidence. Since the creation of the Body Farm—and partly because of research conducted there—forensic entomology had advanced remarkably. In our first pioneering study of insect activity in human corpses, one of my graduate students had spent months studying the sequence of bugs that came to feed on bodies, making detailed notes about what bugs appeared, and precisely when. While observing and collecting bugs, he also fended off food-crazed blowflies, the first and most numerous visitors, as they landed on his face and tried to crawl into his own nostrils and ears and mouth. Within seconds after a body bag was unzipped, he had documented, the blowflies began homing in on the fresh scent of death; within minutes, some of the females would begin seeking out the body's moist orifices or bloody wounds as ideal spots to lay masses of eggs, which looked rather like dabs of grainy white toothpaste. And sometimes within only a few hours after a fly laid her eggs—especially in warm weather—they would hatch into hundreds of tiny maggots, the larval form of the blowfly.

Now, years later, most crime scene techs knew to collect the largest maggots they could find on a body, as those would probably have hatched from the earliest flies to find the body. By collecting and preserving those maggots and sending them to a forensic entomologist, the crime scene techs could get a pretty good idea how long ago the murder had occurred. The best-trained techs would also keep a few of the largest maggots alive, and make careful note of when they encased themselves in a pupa case, or puparium—the inelegant maggot's version of a caterpillar's cocoon—and record when the metamorphosis into the adult insect occurred. The only difference was that instead of a beautiful butterfly emerging from its cocoon, what would emerge from the puparium would be a young blowfly, which would promptly home in on the body, too, if the body were still there. So far, Jess said, none of the live maggots collected from the body had pupated yet. That meant, if the collected specimens did indeed represent the earliest fly hatch, the murder had occurred less than fourteen days ago.

Even from several feet away, I could see the dark stain at the base of the tree, marking where volatile fatty acids had leached from the body as it began to decay. Drawing closer, I thought I saw the first piece of additional evidence I was hoping to see: a faint line of stain leading from the base of the tree into the edge of the woods. The crime scene report had given me reason to hope I would see this.

"Sharp eye, wrong interpretation," I muttered.

"How's that?" I had forgotten the forester was with me.

"Oh, sorry," I said, "I was talking to myself. You see this faint trail of dark fluids?"

"Yeah," he said. "A drag mark. One of the crime scene guys pointed it out to me. Said it showed the killing occurred over there at the edge of the woods—said that was the primary death scene, and the tree here was really the secondary death scene."

"I don't think so," I said. "You see how the stain is darkest here at the tree, then fades as it leads over there?"

He studied the faint trail. "Maybe, now that you mention it. So what?"

"What I think we're looking at here is a maggot trail."

"A maggot trail?"

"Sometimes, when the maggots get ready to cocoon and turn into flies, they crawl away from the body to find a more protected place. Probably so they won't get gobbled up by birds. And for reasons we don't understand, when they do that, they all tend to head in the same damn direction, like a herd of sheep or cows, or a bunch of lemmings."

"Huh," was all he said.

"The reason the trail gets fainter as it leads away from the body is that they're coated with goo from the body at first."

"Goo?"

"Goo. That's a technical term we Ph.D.'s like to throw around to impress folks," I said. "More or less interchangeable with 'gack.' Also with 'volatile fatty acids.' Anyhow, they're all greasy with goo when they first crawl off to cocoon, but as they wiggle along the ground, the goo gets wiped off, leaving that trail we see. But by the time they get where they're going, sometimes they're scrubbed off enough that they've stopped leaving a trail. I bet if we head in that direction, though, we can find where they ended up."

The trail of dark stain led to the west, in a remarkably straight line about a foot wide, so I followed it into the edge of the woods. Within a few feet it began to fade dramatically, so I dropped to all fours again and crawled along through the brush. Cliff followed me upright. Just when I reached a thicket of mountain laurel that seemed impenetrable, I began to see them, mostly tucked under a protective layer of last fall's leaves. I beckoned Cliff closer and pointed. "You see those little torpedo-shaped things, about a quarter inch long?"

He frowned, squatted down, and then said, "Oh yeah, dark brown? With little rings around 'em? What are they?"

I picked up one with my right thumb and forefinger, taking care not to crush it, and cradled it in the palm of my left hand. One end had a small round opening, revealing the cylinder's hollow interior. "It's a puparium—a pupa case. This one's empty, which means the fly has already chewed his way out. So that means the body was out here at least two weeks ago."

"So you're saying these things tell you that the murder occurred maybe just a few days after I was out here?"

"Looks that way to me," I said. Taking a small vial from my shirt pocket, I flipped off the cap with my thumb and tipped in the puparium from my cupped palm. Then I plucked several more from the ground, snapped the lid closed, and buttoned the vial into my shirt. "We've re-created the death scene at my research facility up at UT-Knoxville, using a donated cadaver. It's been tied to a tree for nearly a week now, and it's starting to reach the same stage of decay as the body here was in when it was found. So that argues for the same timetable."

Out of the corner of my eye, I caught a tiny movement among the leaves. I looked down in time to see a tiny fly, newly hatched, crawl onto a reddish brown leaf from a chestnut oak. It joined several others already on the leaf's broad surface, which was catching the afternoon sun. I pointed to them, and Cliff leaned down for a look. I waved a finger above them; they scuttled to and fro, trying to get away, but remained on the leaf rather than flying away. "When they first hatch," I explained, "their wings are still damp and soft. They have to dry awhile before they're stiff enough for flight. If you look around on some of the tree trunks here, you might see a bunch more. Once I worked a death scene where the south-facing wall of a building was covered with thousands of little flies, all drying their wings."

He scouted around, then called my attention to a couple of tree trunks. "Not thousands, but probably hundreds on these two trees." I nodded. He looked thoughtful. "So next time I bring my lunch out here," he said, "these guys are gonna be all over me, huh?"

"Some of them," I said. "Unless they've caught wind of something, or somebody, that smells more interesting someplace else."

"And these came from the maggots that were feeding on the body, right?"

"I think so," I answered. "What do you think?"

"I think it's time to find myself another lunch spot."

I retraced my steps to the tree where the body had been lashed. Stooping down, hands on knees, I scanned the ground. I didn't see what I was seeking, so again I dropped to my hands and knees and began crawling outward from the base of the tree in a series of ever-widening arcs.

"What are you looking for now?"

Just as I was about to say it wasn't there, I spotted what appeared to be a shriveled, curled leaf sitting by itself atop the carpet of moss and pine needles. "This, I think," I answered. I picked it up and rolled it between two fingers, gently but with enough pressure to crumble a dead leaf. It did not crumble. I uncurled it ever so slightly and held it up to the light. The sun shone through it, giving it an amber glow, and in that glow I could discern a pattern of creases and swirls I would recognize anywhere.

I walked over to Cliff, bearing it like some holy relic. In a way, it was: the identity, potentially, of the young man who had been beaten to death here in this spot. I held it up to the light so he could look through it. He studied it, frowning, and then a look of understanding and wonder dawned on his face. "Looks like fingerprints," he said. I nodded. The frown returned. "But how . . . ?"

"About a week after death, the outer layer of skin—the epidermis—sloughs off of the hands," I explained. "It comes loose from the underlying layer, the dermis, and peels off almost like a surgical glove. I can take this back to the lab, soak it in water and fabric softener overnight, and tomorrow morning somebody in the crime lab can put his fingers inside these fingers—put this glove on *his* hands—and get a set of prints."

He whistled. "I don't think the deputies from Marion County know that trick."

"Well, it's not something you run across very often," I said. "And this guy might not have prints on file anyway. But if he does, we should be able to ID him." I took another, larger vial from my hip pocket, slid the husk of skin inside, and sealed the lid.

I took one last look around. I noticed blood and bone shards and bits of brain matter lodged in the bark of the pine tree. Did that add anything to what I already knew? Maybe not, but it confirmed something: the trauma, or at least the cranial trauma, had occurred out here, not someplace else. It occurred to me that the rural deputies might not have thought to collect samples for evidentiary purposes, and that a slick defense attorney—someone, say, like my sometime nemesis Burt DeVriess—might use that omission to plant seeds of doubt in the minds of jurors. Taking out my pocketknife and one of the several ziplock plastic bags I'd brought, I unfolded the larger of the two blades and pried loose a few scales of the flaky pine bark, catching them in the bag as they fell. The bark was dark brown, almost black on top; underneath, it was the rich, rusty red of cinnamon. I made sure to get enough so that Jess could preserve some unaltered and send some off for DNA analysis, to confirm that this material came from the same shattered skull sitting in a cooler in my truck, a few hundred yards away.

As I sealed the bag and zipped it into the side pocket of my cargo pants, I noticed the sun was dropping down toward the S-curve in the river. I checked my watch and calculated that I had been out here for well over an hour; closer to two. "I thought you wanted to head for the barn before this," I said to Cliff.

"I wasn't sure you'd find your way back out," he said. "Didn't want to get called out at midnight to find you." He saw the look of chagrin on my face and added, "Besides, this is interesting stuff. I learned a lot more from you than I did from the deputies who worked it last week." He seemed to mean it, so I thanked him and decided to quit worrying that I had imposed on him.

By the time I coasted and corkscrewed back down Suck Creek Mountain to Chattanooga, Jess was already gone for the day, so I left her a note saying I was taking the skin of the hand back to Knoxville. It was extremely delicate, and I didn't trust anyone but Art Bohanan to handle it. I got Amy to buzz me into the autopsy suite, where I filled the plastic evidence jar with warm water and added a few drops of Downy. Finally, before hitting the road, I signed over the bone shards to Amy, who gave me a receipt for them and locked them in the evidence room. Then I bid her good-bye, asked her to relay my regards to her boss, and—cooler and head in hand—headed for my truck, and the drive back to Knoxville.

CHAPTER 15

THE SUN WAS GONE and the evening star—Venus—was hanging like a pearl in an indigo sky as I clicked the keyless remote to unlock my truck. The drive to Knoxville would take two hours, and even though it was all interstate, I wasn't looking forward to doing it in the dark. Although I still had a bit of an adrenaline buzz from finding the empty puparia and the degloved skin, that buzz was fading fast, and underneath it, I was deeply tired.

As I cupped my fingers under the handle of the driver's door, they encountered a soft but unexpected obstacle. A piece of paper had been folded up and tucked into the hollow beneath the door handle. I unfolded it and saw that it was a page off MapQuest.com, an Internet site that offered maps and driving directions to anyplace in the nation. The word START was superimposed on what I recognized as the location of the ME's office, where I was now parked. The word END occupied a street address in a neighborhood a few miles away, which the map labeled as Highland Park. A wide, purple-shaded line—the computer's version of a highlighter mark—led from one to the other. I puzzled over the map's meaning, but then my eye caught sight of two lines of text in a small box just above the map. "B—I hope it's not too late to invite you over for dinner. J."

As the meaning between the lines of the brief message sank in—or at least, the meaning I hoped lay between the lines—my fatigue dropped away. My breath quickened as I climbed into the truck, and I noticed as I fiddled with the key that my hand was shaking slightly. "Easy, fella," I said to myself. "Drive safely so you'll get there in one piece, and don't expect too much once you're there."

Highland Park proved to be a charming neighborhood, one that I guessed dated back to the late 1800s. The houses ranged from gingerbread-clad Victorians to simple shotgun cottages. Jess's house was a simple but elegant old two-story, a design I seemed to remember being called a foursquare— four rooms up, four down, with a chimney flanking each side and a deep porch stretching the width of the front. The exterior of the ground floor was clad in lapped wooden siding, painted the green of baby leaves; the second floor was sheathed in cedar shakes, barn red. A second-floor balcony nestled beneath the roof, tucked into an alcove between the two front bedrooms. I could picture Jess sipping her morning coffee there, reading the newspaper before heading into the morgue. The image of her engaged in such an act of cozy domesticity surprised and pleased me.

A stone staircase led up to the front porch. The porch was surrounded by a waist-high balustrade whose wide rail was completely covered with ferns and spider plants and red geraniums. The simple lines of the house contrasted with the elaborate front door, which featured leaded glass in the door itself, in a pair of sidelights that flanked it, and in a wide transom above. The dozens of panes, beveled at the edges, diffracted the golden light from inside the house, giving each partial image a rainbow-like aura.

I rang the bell, and in a moment glimpsed a fragmented, beveled figure approaching. The door swung wide and there was Jess, unfragmented now, smiling at me. She was wearing a navy Harvard sweatshirt, three sizes too big, whose sleeves were streaked and spattered with putty-colored paint that matched the living room walls. Underneath the shirt she wore gray sweatpants, nearly as baggy as the shirt; their fleece had an odd, nubby nap, like a much-loved teddy bear, or a bowl of oatmeal that had been drying on the kitchen counter for a few hours. Instead of the sharp-toed footwear I was accustomed to seeing on her feet, she wore soft clogs of wool or felt. Her hair was pinned up and damp, as if she'd just gotten out of the shower, and her face had been scrubbed free of makeup. She looked utterly beautiful.

I touched one of the smears of paint on her sleeve. "I like the way you've accessorized," I said. "Picks up the color in your walls."

She plucked at the sleeve and smiled. "Thanks for noticing. I pulled out all the stops for you. How'd things go at the crime scene—any luck?"

With a flourish, I produced both containers from my pockets. "Eureka," I said. "Empty puparia, which argue for an earlier death than the maggots you're incubating at the office. And the grand prize, the skin from one of the hands."

She clapped. "You are amazing," she said. "I knew there was a reason I liked you."

"You mind if I take this skin back to Knoxville and let Art print it? The lab folks here might do fine with it, but Art's probably got more experience printing degloved hands than all the criminalists in Chattanooga put together."

"Anything that might help us ID the guy," she said. "Oh, have you eaten?"

"No. Have you?"

"I picked up pad thai on the way home. I already scarfed some down, but there's leftovers. You want?"

"Sure, thanks." Normally I wasn't an adventurous eater, but I knew pad thai was pretty safe—an Asian version of spaghetti—and I had worked up an appetite traipsing around the woods at the death scene. I followed Jess through an arched doorway and into the kitchen, which was a composition in blond wood, black granite, and stainless steel, lit by small lights with cobalt blue shades. "Jeez, I feel like I've just stepped into the pages of *Architectural Digest*," I said. "I didn't realize you had such an eye for style. Guess I should've figured, though, from the car and the shoes and all."

She gestured at her sweatpants and clogs. "Fashionista, that's me, all right." She popped a covered bowl into the microwave and hit the one-minute button. "Actually, I wanted to be an architect, but I couldn't draw worth a damn. I used to dream these great buildings when I was in college—spaces Frank Lloyd Wright would have given his left nut to've designed—but when I'd wake up and try to sketch them, they'd look like some kindergartner's drawing. If I'd had some way to hook a VCR to my brain while I was dreaming, I'd be rich and famous today."

"Judging by this, I'd say you work pretty well in three dimensions. It's elegant, but not at all frilly. It suits you."

"Thanks," she said. "I never have been much for frills. You know one of my favorite things about this house?" I shook my head. "Guess who created it?"

"Let's see," I said. "Surely I can dredge up the name from my encyclopedic knowledge of Chattanooga architects of the early 1900s . . ."

"Wasn't a Chattanooga architect," she grinned. "Sears."

"Sears? *Who* Sears? From where—New York?"

"Not 'Who Sears'; 'Sears Who.' Sears Roebuck, the department store," she said, pointing to a wall. There, she'd hung a framed page from a century-old Sears catalog, showing an ad for the house I was standing in. It bore the catchy name "Modern Home No. 158," and a price tag of $1,548. "Houses by mail order," said Jess. "This house came into town on a freight car, in pieces. Probably ran four grand, all told, for the kit plus the caboodle."

"I'm guessing it's appreciated some since then."

"Well, *I* appreciate it some," she said.

The microwave beeped, and she pulled out the bowl and handed it to me, then reached into a drawer and fished out a pair of chopsticks. I made a face; I had never mastered the art of using them. "What, you got no forks?" She shook her head and handed me the chopsticks. The noodles, a reddish brown, smelled of garlic and peanuts and scallions and shrimp and hot oil, all swirled together so richly and tantalizingly I'd have eaten with my bare hands if I had to. Clutching the chopsticks awkwardly, I hoisted a wad of pad thai toward my mouth. Halfway there, the sticks went askew and the tangle of noodles plopped back into the bowl.

"Here," she laughed, "let me show you a better way to hold those." She took my hand in one of hers, and with the other, she pried the chopsticks from my fist. "Very simple," she said. "One of them is fixed, the other moves. Sort of like a fencepost and a gate. The fixed one nestles down in the V between your thumb and forefinger, like so, and between the tips of your pinkie and your ring finger." She demonstrated. "Hold the other one almost like you would a pencil, but not quite so near the point." She gripped the second chopstick with the tips of her thumb and first two fingers, then made a great show of waving it to and fro, then clicking the tips together like a lobster claw. "Okay, try it." She laid my hand, palm up, in her own palm, then arranged the two chopsticks for me. I studied them awhile. She looked at me, puzzled. "Still confused?"

"No," I said. "I think I've got the concept. I just don't want to move my hand right now."

She laughed, then looked shy, but she stretched up and gave me a quick, warm kiss on the mouth. "Eat," she said. "You might need your strength." I looked up at her, hoping she meant what I thought she meant. In response to my quizzical look, she hoisted a suggestive eyebrow at me. Newly inspired, I snagged an enormous clump of noodles with the chopsticks and managed to get most of them into my mouth, with only a few stragglers draping my chin. "Easy, Popeye," she said. "Take your time. I'm not going anywhere. Be bad for an ME's career if you choked to death in her kitchen."

I slowed down slightly but still managed to empty the bowl in about two minutes flat. She rinsed it, put it in the dishwasher, and came back to stand in front of me, close enough that I could feel the breath from her upturned face. I put a hand to her cheek, because she seemed to like that when I did it earlier, at the morgue. She seemed to like it again, so I put my other hand on her other cheek. She didn't seem to mind that, either—she turned her face slightly and kissed my palm—so then I pulled her face to mine and kissed her. She kissed back, and she kissed me like she meant something by it.

After a long spell of meaningful kissing, I slid my hands down her neck, over her shoulders, and down her sides to the bottom of the sweatshirt. Then I burrowed them under the loose-fitting hem and began easing them back up: up the nubby sweatpants, over the top of her hips, till I felt the bare skin of her waist. It seemed magical, miraculous somehow, that within this huge, shapeless tent of a sweatshirt could be something so slender, so smooth—so female—as the sculpted curves and hollows of this waist. I touched the tips of my thumbs together, and my fingers stretched halfway around her back. I grazed my thumbs around the rim of her navel, imagining its vertical cleft; I pressed the taut flatness of her belly, slid the waist-band of the pants down to grip the solid flare of her hip bones. It had been more than two years since my hands had held a woman's hips like this, but I remembered what female hips felt like, and I could tell these were splendid hips, to match the splendid belly. It augured well for what the rest of her would be like, too. Just to be sure, I slipped my hands higher, and I knew I'd guessed right. Her breath caught as I began to trace the curves of her breasts, which were bare beneath the baggy shirt. It seemed almost as if I were living two lives at the moment: one life, my visible life, was a baggy, frumpy sweat-shirt sort of life; the other, lived by my mouth and hands, was an exotic, dizzying swirl of tongues and fingertips, rounded breasts and hardening nipples. I pulled away from the kiss so I could see Jess's face, and I was glad I did, because it radiated a combi-nation of tenderness and desire and wonder I had never glimpsed before.

"That is the single most gorgeous thing I have ever seen on this earth," I whispered, and she buried her face in my neck and began to kiss softly. "You know what?" I murmured eventually.

"No, what?"

"You did such a good job showing me how to work those chopsticks, I'm thinking maybe you could teach me a few other skills."

"What did you have in mind?"

"What's the best way to take off a pair of sweatpants—standing up, or lying down?"

"Come upstairs and I'll show you," she said.

And so I did, and she did, and we did. And we liked what we did so much that we did it again. Finally, happily tired from all we'd done, we laced our arms and legs together and lay still. Within minutes Jess was asleep, a sweet, childlike snore accompanying the rhythmic rise of her chest.

I watched her sleep, savoring the peaceful expression on a face that was often as focused and intense as a laser. Eventually I must have dozed off, because I noticed a murky awareness of awakening. The clock read 4:47. Unknotting myself from her embrace, I recovered my far-flung clothes and got dressed, leaving off my shoes so I wouldn't make noise. I found some paper and a pen, and wrote a note. "Dear Jess—Sorry to go. I have an early meeting, and I couldn't bear to wake you. Call me when you wake, if you want." I thought a moment, then added, "You took my breath away, and then you gave it back again." I didn't figure I needed to sign it.

I folded her sweats and laid them on the foot of the bed, setting the note on top. Then I bent and kissed her cheek. She made a soft sound, somewhere between a coo and a laugh, and I hoped maybe she was dreaming of the love we had made.

I tiptoed out of her bedroom, down the stairs, and out the front door. Sitting on the top step of Modern Home No. 158, I put on my shoes and walked to my truck. I had parked on the street, and the truck was headed down a gentle incline, so I coasted a ways before cranking the engine. I pulled onto I-75 North toward Knoxville just as the sky's velvety darkness began to yield to a voluptuous red in the east.

CHAPTER 16

I'D ARRANGED TO MEET Art at KPD headquarters at 7:30 A.M.: just before his undercover shift at Broadway Jewelry & Loan began; just before he waded into the sewers of cyberspace, trolling for the creeps who troll for kids, pursuing the monsters who peddle kids. Art was waiting just inside the glassed-in lobby of the building; he took the plastic jar—now containing both the skin and the solution that had rehydrated it—and inspected it, nodding in approval or optimism. We took the elevator up to his lab and he set the jar on a tabletop, then donned a pair of snug latex gloves.

Unscrewing the lid, he extracted the skin with a pair of tweezers, then unfurled it slowly on a tray lined with paper toweling, studying each fingertip in turn, gently blotting it dry. Finally he spoke. "All of the fingers are torn in places, so we won't get any prints that are completely intact. The center of the fingertips are intact, though, so I'm pretty sure we can get enough details for a match, if this guy's prints are in aphids."

"Aphids," I asked, "like the rosebush-eating garden insect?"

"No, Dilbert," he said. "AY-fiss, A-F-I-S, like Automated Fingerprint Identification System." He frowned, then corrected himself. "I mean I-AFIS. They tacked an *I* on the front end a while back—stands for 'Integrated'—but I still call it AFIS. Force of habit."

"Easier to say 'AY-fiss' than 'EYE-ay-fiss,' too," I said. "Especially for an old dog like you."

I remembered that AFIS was a database created by the FBI six or eight years earlier. Before its creation, I could recall Art squawking about the weeks or even months it took the Bureau's fingerprint lab to analyze prints. The delays often meant that by the time a match was found, a suspect who had been arrested or detained for questioning was no longer in custody—and nowhere to be found. These days, he told me, it was possible to get a match—a name—within two hours in criminal cases, and within twenty-four hours for civilian requests such as employment background checks.

"How big is their database by now?" I asked.

"Pretty darn big. Last time I looked, they had prints from nearly fifty million people on file."

"That is big. I didn't realize so many of our friends and neighbors were criminals."

"They're not. Remember, a big chunk of those are people required to submit fingerprints as part of their employment—teachers, military personnel, firefighters, gun buyers, all sorts of folks. Mine

are in there; yours probably are, too, aren't they?"
He was right, I realized. When the director of the
Tennessee Bureau of Investigation had asked me to
serve as a TBI consultant, I had filled out a long
questionnaire and had been fingerprinted, presumably to make sure the agency wasn't hiring a fox to
help guard the henhouse.

As I watched in fascination, Art carefully fitted
the dead man's skin to his own right hand, then
walked to a laptop computer sitting at the end of
the table. Beside it was a thin rectangular gadget,
slightly smaller than the laptop's keyboard, with a
blue pad on top. Using his left thumb and forefinger
to stretch the skin taut over his right thumb, he laid
one edge of his thumb on the blue pad and rolled
it in a half revolution, from one edge of the nail
to the other. After a few seconds, a six-inch-high
swirl of tightly nested lines appeared on the laptop's screen.

"Hey, where's the roller, the ink, the glass plate?"
I asked.

"Bill, Bill," he said. "Ink-on-slab is so last-century.
This is optical scanning. No fuss, no muss. Digitizes the prints directly, and lets us upload them
directly to AFIS. We can print out hard copies on
standard fingerprint cards so Jess and the Chattanooga PD can add them to their files, but this is
a lot quicker and easier than the old way. Shoot,
the new criminalists we hire these days, kids fresh
out of school? Some of them have never rolled a
set of prints in ink. Or if they have, it was just as a
history lesson, a demonstration of how things were
done back in the day. Like letting kids milk a cow

or churn butter by hand to show them the pioneer way."

"You sound disgruntled," I said, "but I notice you've switched over."

"Hard to argue with results," he said. "Hey, do me a favor, since I'm using both hands? Come hit ENTER on the keyboard there, to accept the print and let me get the next one."

I did, for the thumbprint and each of the four fingerprints. Once he had finished scanning the prints, Art returned the skin to the jar, screwed the lid on snugly, and handed it back to me. Then he peeled off his gloves and tossed them in a container labeled BIOHAZARD. He went back to the laptop and clattered the keys for a few minutes, then hit the ENTER button with a flourish. "Okay, they're sent," he said. "We should have an answer within a couple hours."

"How can it be so quick? You said there are nearly fifty million sets of prints in the database, right? That's nearly five hundred million fingertips to compare."

"I guess the software's pretty powerful, and their mainframe has a lot more horsepower than our little personal computers," he said. "I mean, it's easy to narrow it down." He hit a few more keystrokes, and the thumbprint reappeared on the screen. "Prints have one of three basic patterns," he explained, "whorl, loop, and arch. Whorls are concentric circles—like a target with a bull's-eye at the center, or the cross section of an onion. A loop pattern is more complicated; the ridges come in from one side, make a U-turn, and go back out the same side. In an arch pattern, the ridges come in from one side, go up in the middle, and then go out the other side."

I studied the pattern on the screen. "So our guy has a whorl pattern," I said. "At least on his thumb."

"Bingo," said Art. "So when the AFIS software is looking for a match for this particular print, it searches only right-hand thumbprints, and only those with whorls. That means it only needs to compare this print with, I dunno, maybe twenty million others. Still a lot, but there are other criteria and features that can progressively narrow that down tighter and tighter." He pointed to two areas on the print where the circular pattern of ridges gave way to a triangular intersection, as if the whorl had been shoehorned into an arch pattern. "See those? Those are called deltas. Pretty easy to tell if the deltas on one print are spaced differently from the deltas on another. I'm not a software guy, but I imagine it would be fairly straightforward to program a computer to recognize features like deltas and compare their locations on an X-Y coordinate system."

Art promised to let me know later in the day if AFIS returned any hits on the prints. "I can't access AFIS from the computers at the pawnshop," he said, "but I'll dash over here at lunchtime and see if we got lucky."

He rode down the elevator with me and we walked out into the crisp morning sunshine. I was headed to UT to teach Tennessee's brightest and best. He was headed to Broadway Jewelry & Loan to stalk Tennessee's darkest and worst. "Thanks, Art," I said. He nodded and headed for his car. "Hey," I called after him. "Go get 'em, Tiffany." Without looking back, he raised one hand in a parting wave. His middle finger was extended. The gesture was aimed not at me, I knew, but at the men who were his quarry. The predators out there lurking in cyberspace, waiting to pounce.

CHAPTER 17

AT 10:50 A.M., I strolled around the curve of Circle Drive toward McClung Museum, where my eleven o'clock forensic anthropology class met. An event of some sort seemed to be taking place outside the museum. The small plaza at the museum's entrance was filled with people and banners. As I got closer, I realized that the event was a protest, and what I had thought were banners were actually neon-hued picket signs.

I took mental inventory of the museum's current exhibits, wondering which of them could have sparked controversy. The exhibition of nineteenth-century Samurai swords, prints, and other artifacts? Surely not. "UT Goes to Mars," photos, videos, and models documenting the role several UT faculty played in NASA's Mars Rover landings? Doubtful; I'd not read of fans of, say, Venus lobbying NASA for equal time. "The Origins of Humanity," a show that included fossil remains from human ancestors, as well as two life-size reconstructions of early hominids? Hmm. That could fit, I realized, judging from my own recent brush with the hornet's nest of creationism.

As I drew near enough to read the picket signs, I spotted a disturbingly familiar word on many of the signs. It was my own name, and I realized with a jolt that the picketers weren't protesting an exhibit; they were protesting me, Bill Brockton, Darwin's loudest local mouthpiece. DR. BROCKTON HAS NOT EVOLVED, read several of the signs. BROCKTON MONKEY'S WITH GODS CREATION, read a few others, combining dubious theology with appalling apostrophe usage. Some simply bore a stylized drawing of a fish, an ancient symbol of Christianity. And one, carried by someone wearing a gorilla costume, even featured a life-size photo of my head pasted atop the cartoonish body of a chimpanzee. A television news crew was on the scene, getting close-ups of the picketers as they marched in an oval, blocking the doors to the museum.

A half dozen UT police officers were arrayed a tactful distance from the protesters. I sidled up to the closest one to learn what I could about the group. "When did this all start," I asked him, "and who are these folks? They don't look like UT students." Except for the gorilla suit, their clothing was more conservative than anything I'd ever seen on UT students in decades. The boys and men wore dark pants, white shirts, and ties; the girls and women wore long dresses and clunky shoes, and there was not a pierced navel or tattoo anywhere in sight.

"They showed up about twenty minutes ago," the officer said. "They must have known your class schedule. A church bus pulled into Circle Drive and unloaded, then drove off to park, I'm not sure where."

"Did you notice what church it was from?"

"Nothing I ever heard of. 'True Gospel Fellowship,' or maybe 'True Fellowship Gospel'? I never heard of the place, either. Some town in Kansas."

"Kansas," I said. "Why am I not surprised?"

"That guy in the monkey suit seems to be the cheerleader," the officer said, "but I'd say the fellow off to the side there is calling the plays."

I followed his gaze. Standing apart from the knot of protesters, his hands clasped in front of a double-breasted gray suit, stood a well-groomed man of middle years. His hair was dark, going to silver; it was swept back from an imposing forehead, and either it was naturally wavy, or it had been carefully styled to look that way. I noticed French cuffs and gold cuff links peeking out the ends of his jacket sleeves, and his trouser cuffs draped over sleek black shoes that spoke of money in an Italian accent.

I took a wide detour so as to come up behind him. "Nice signs," I said as I eased alongside. "My favorite is the one with the picture." He gave a brief, practiced chuckle, then turned toward me to make conversation. When he saw my face, he looked startled but quickly recovered his composure. "I'm Bill Brockton, anthropologist and evolutionist," I said. "I'm guessing you're Jennings Bryan, attorney and creationism activist?"

"Not creationism," he said pleasantly. "Intelligent design. Please." He smiled slightly, as if acknowledging a worthy adversary. "The famous Dr. Brockton," he said. "Please forgive me for not shaking hands. It would complicate things for me, for the cause, if the newspapers or TV captured a handshake on film."

"Well, I'd hate to complicate things," I said. "I struggle even when they're simple."

"I hear otherwise," he said.

"Well. For whatever it's worth, I am sorry I embarrassed that boy in class."

"I'm not," he said. "You did us a huge favor."

"So I see," I said. "I'm sorry about that, too." He gave me the little smile again.

A crowd numbering a hundred or more had gathered at the edge of the protest, and the TV crew was dutifully capturing their images as well. Some were mere onlookers, but I recognized most of them as my forensic anthropology students. I checked my watch; it read 10:59, and I had always drilled punctuality into my students. "You'll have to excuse me, Mr. Bryan," I said. "I have a class to teach." I stepped forward, toward the museum, toward the protesters. I hadn't gone more than ten feet when I heard Bryan call from behind me, "Here he is!"

Every head, every camera, swiveled in my direction. I kept walking, closing the distance. When I was perhaps twenty feet away, the protester in the gorilla suit began screeching like a chimp. It must have been a prearranged signal, because when he did, his comrades reached into pockets and bags and fished out overripe bananas, which they began lobbing at me. Most of them missed, but a few caught me on the shoulders and chest, and one splatted open on my head. Banana mash dripped down my face and into my collar. My feet had stopped moving when the banana barrage began; I felt rooted to the spot. Someone in the crowd of picketers produced a cream pie from somewhere and handed it to Gorilla Man; he scampered forward, monkey-style, and ground it into my face. It, too, was banana, and I was surprised to find that it wasn't half bad.

As I took out a handkerchief and wiped pie from my eyes, I saw the UT police officers racing toward me. They formed a circle with their backs to me, their arms and hands outstretched. The TV cameraman scrambled to the edge of the circle, zooming in on my dripping face. I looked at the protesters, their expressions a mixture of joy and hatred, and then I looked at the crowd of spectators and students, who now far outnumbered the picketers. Suddenly a young woman pushed through the crowd and jogged toward me, holding a crudely made sign high over her head. It was Miranda Lovelady, and the sign bore a hand-drawn image I recognized from a bumper sticker on her car: a stylized fish, its body filled with the word DARWIN; below the body, the fish had sprouted legs.

A cheer erupted from the students, and they fell in behind Miranda. The officers fanned out into a wedge, and we walked forward—the police, the students, and I—through the picket line and into the building.

I made a quick stop in the restroom to clean the pie off my face and neck. Then, for the next ninety minutes, I taught, and I'd never felt prouder or more privileged to be a teacher.

CHAPTER 18

MY PHONE RANG JUST as I was getting into bed. It was my son Jeff. "Turn on Channel 4," he said.

"Why? What's on?"

"Local news. The tease, just before they went to a commercial, mentioned you, creationism, and a mouthwatering controversy, whatever that means. Did you go looking for trouble today?"

"Oh, hell," I said, "no, trouble came looking for me. Sort of. I guess you might say I did some pot-stirring last week. But not enough to justify what happened today."

"Yikes," he said. "Sounds serious. Call me back after the story airs." With that, he clicked off.

I pulled a bathrobe over my boxers and made my way into the darkness of the living room, where I switched on the floor lamp beside the recliner. The remote was, as always, on the arm of the chair. I settled heavily into the leather, leaned halfway back, and switched on the television. I caught a loud local spot for a group of car dealerships out by the airport calling themselves the "Airport Motor Mile," followed by an equally noisy ad for a wholesale furniture warehouse, then the newscast resumed.

Characteristically, though, they didn't start out with the story about the protest. It was one of the things that annoyed me most about television news: the way they'd repeatedly tease a story they figured lots of people would stick around to watch—something involving cute animals or slapstick comedy or a racy scandal—and not show it until the very end of the newscast. I chafed through weather, sports, and, oddly, a reprise of the weather (which I tuned out the second time as well) before the announcer—who tended to look cheery even when relating the death of a child—assumed a concerned expression and asked, "Is Tennessee headed for another monkey trial?" The picture then switched to a full-screen close-up of the guy in the gorilla suit, followed by a series of shots of other protesters, singly and in twos and threes and sixes. The way they strung the images together, without zooming out to show the group as a whole, made it appear as if scores, maybe even hundreds of people were wielding picket signs, rather than the dozen or so that had actually picketed. The reporter played up the "controversy," splicing in angry accusations by protesters; he mentioned "an angry counterprotest" as the camera showed Miranda arriving with her DARWIN sign.

Then came something I didn't expect. During a series of short interviews with bystanders, Jess Carter's face flashed onto the screen, with her name and title superimposed as well. I hadn't even known she was there today. "These people are a small minority of small-minded, self-righteous busybodies," Jess said directly to the camera lens. "If they want to check their brains at the door, fine, but they shouldn't be trying to force other people to do that, too. Dr. Brockton does more good in the world than this whole group of anti-intellectual protesters put together. They need to get back on the bus they rode in on and head back to whatever Kansas backwater they crawled out of." I smiled at her feisty eloquence and her defense of me, but at the same time I winced, and hoped she didn't get tangled up in this mess along with me. In the background, over her left shoulder, I could see Jennings Bryan, the lawyer who was orchestrating the event. For the most part, his face was an expressionless mask, but I saw his eyes lash with anger as she spoke. Bryan's sound bite, which followed hers, decried the co-opting of public education by soulless intellectuals and secular humanists whose chief aim was persecuting people of faith. *Damn*, I thought again, *me and my big mouth.* But then I thought, *No, I've got nothing against faith—just against willful, bullying ignorance.*

The story's final shot, played in excruciating slow motion, showed a screen-filling cream pie arcing toward my face and then smashing into it. Filling slowly radiated from the edges of the pan; streams of yellow and white dripped lazily from my nose and chin. The picture froze at the moment I wiped my eyes and blinked out through the mess. The announcer came back on-screen, his earlier look of concern now replaced by merriment. "If the protesters have their way," he said, "Professor Brockton, whose classroom comments set off the controversy, might soon be eating his words, too." His eyes twinkled. "That's it for this edition of *Nightwatch*. Good night—and good eating!"

I clicked off the television in disgust and called Jeff. "Not exactly a shining moment for higher education, was it?" I said.

He laughed. "Well, no, but at least you're not getting burned at the stake, like Copernicus."

"Not yet, anyhow," I said. "But that wasn't Copernicus. Copernicus died quietly in his sleep, I think. It was Bruno who got toasted for spelling out the implications of the Copernican theory—for speculating that there might be other worlds, orbiting other stars, inhabited by other, more intelligent beings." I sighed. "Sometimes we don't look like particularly stiff competition."

"But hey," said Jeff, "that Dr. Carter—she seems pretty bright. Leapt to your defense mighty strongly, too. Isn't she the one you were planning to bring with you to my house for dinner a few months ago?"

"The same," I said. "She has a way of getting paged anytime I have a dinner date with her. Happened again last week—I was actually cooking dinner for her at my house. Just as the coals were getting hot— in more ways than one—she got beeped."

"Maybe you should let me fix you up with Sheri," he said.

"Who's Sheri?"

"One of the accountants at my firm. Completely unavailable three months out of the year, but starting April 16, she's got a lot more time on her hands. And I have never, ever paged her. Not a whole lot of emergencies come up on tax returns. Except for yours." This was an unexpected and unwelcome turn in the conversation. "Dad, I've been through this box of what passes for your financial records, and I can't find bank statements for August, October, or December."

"Look again," I said. "They must be in there somewhere."

"Dad, I've looked twice." I could tell he was upset; he tended to preface his sentences with "Dad" whenever he was put out with me. I heard "Dad" a lot every year at tax time. "I've sorted and organized everything. Dad, they are *not there*."

"Dang," I said. "Then I have no idea where they are."

"Clearly."

"Maybe they got lost in the mail," I offered. "Can't you just call the bank and ask them to send you copies?"

"No," he said, "they can't do that; it's not my account. Why don't you just go online and download copies, then e-mail them to me?"

"Online? That stuff's online?"

"Only for about the past ten years," he said. "You should have a user name and password filed away somewhere."

"Well, I don't know where. Check that stuff I brought you. Maybe somewhere in there."

"Dad, you're hopeless," he groaned. "I'd fire you, except that I'm the only thing standing between you and the complete loss of my inheritance."

"And what makes you think you're in my will, smarty-pants?"

"Oh, I don't know. Lucky guess, maybe. Or maybe it was that copy of the will that was stuffed into this pile of papers."

"Ah," I said, "I was wondering where I'd put that. Hang on to that for me, would you? I need to see how best to cut you out of it."

"Right. Okay, I'm hanging up now. Good night. See if you can program yourself to dream where those bank statements might be. Oh, and Dad?"

"Yes, son?"

"Good luck with Dr. Carter."

"Thanks," I said. "Good luck with my tax return."

The next morning I called Jess at her office. "Hey," I said when she picked up, "thanks for leaping to my defense on the news."

"Do I get Brownie points for that?"

"Thousands," I said. "What were you doing there? I didn't even know you were in Knoxville."

"Quick trip," she said. "I came into the morgue early that morning. Couple unattended deaths up your way, and things were quiet down here, so I dashed up on the spur of the moment. I was just getting back into my car to head back to Chattanooga when Miranda came rushing out and asked for a ride to campus. She made the Darwin poster on the drive over."

"Well, I appreciate the show of support," I said. "I just hope they don't cram a pie in your face, too."

"Oh, I wouldn't mind that part. I like banana cream pie. It's the other stuff I'd like to avoid."

"What other stuff?"

"I got half a dozen phone calls last night," she said. "Same guy every time."

"What guy? Did he say his name? Did you recognize his voice? Did you get a number on your caller ID?"

"No name, blocked number, muffled voice."

"Tell me about the calls."

"Well, after the nasty names he called me during our first chat, I decided to let the rest of the calls go to voice mail. Some of the messages just consigned me to a very unpleasant afterlife. Others promised me some pretty hellish experiences this side of the grave. Leading to the grave, too."

"Death threats? My God, Jess, did you call the police?"

"Naw, it's just some pissed-off coward blowing off steam," she said. "Not worth wasting any more time or energy on it."

"Don't take any chances," I said. "Call the cops."

"If I called the cops every time somebody hassled me, I'd be the girl who cried wolf. If it keeps up, I'll call the phone company and get a block or a trace. If anything else happens, I'll tell the police. Okay?"

"Okay," I said, but it didn't feel okay.

"Uh-oh," she said. "I gotta go—Amy's making her 'Somebody important is calling' face at me. Talk to you soon."

"Okay. Be careful, Jess," I said. "Bye."

"I will. Bye."

CHAPTER 19

AS I REACHED INTO my briefcase, I thought, This *could be my best work ever.* Thirty seconds later, I was certain I'd been right.

I'd just taken a huge bite of my masterpiece—possibly the finest sandwich ever made—when the phone on my desk rang. I briefly considered spitting the mouthful into the trash, but the individual ingredients were splendid on their own—smoked turkey, smoked Gouda cheese, spicy brown mustard, crisp kosher pickle, and tomato on nutty oat bread—and the whole was even tastier than the sum of its parts. In short, I couldn't bear to waste it. Instead, I gave three quick chews as I reached for the receiver, then two more as I slowly raised it, jamming wads of food into my cheek pouches.

"'Lo, ih Dah Rockuh," I mumbled.

"Bill? Is that you?" I was relieved to hear that it was just Art.

"Eh, ih ee," I grunted.

"Are you sick? Are you hurt? Hang on. I'm calling 911."

"Nuh," I said. "'Ait ussa min't. Ea'in unh." I gave a few more hurried chews, then swallowed the first of three installments. "'orry. 'ang on." Chew chew swallow; chew chew swallow. "Okay, sorry. Had a mouthful there."

"Bill, Bill, have you forgotten everything you learned from Gomer Pyle?"

"What? Gomer Pyle? You called me up to talk corny old sitcoms?"

"No. I'm just thinking you did not chew thirty-four times before swallowing, like Grandma Pyle taught Gomer to do. Shame, shame, shame, shame, *shame*."

"Well, Shazam," I said, "call Barney Fife and have me arrested."

"Wrong jurisdiction. Barney's over in Mayberry. Anyhow, the reason I called is, we got lucky on the prints."

"Tell me," I said, my sandwich suddenly forgotten. "Who was he?"

"Well, for starters, he was a teacher."

"So his prints were on file from his background check? Damn. I hate to think a teacher got killed just because he liked to dress funny."

"He had another set of prints on file, too. The guy was also a pedophile, Bill. He had an arrest record for aggravated sexual battery."

I sat bolt upright in my chair. "Jesus Christ," I said. "I thought that wasn't supposed to be possible. I thought the whole point of the background investigations and fingerprint checks was to keep people like that from working with kids."

"It is," he said, "and it did. Sort of. The system worked, within its limits. The guy was a teacher first, and a pedophile second. At least, that's the order in which he was printed. Reality is, he probably became a teacher so he'd have easy access to kids. But he'd never been caught at the time he was hired."

"How much information did you get?"

"Enough to know the basics and start tracking down the details. Guy's name was Craig Willis; thirty-one years old. He applied for a teaching job three years ago—in Knoxville, by the way, not Chattanooga. Got hired just down Middlebrook Pike from you, at Bearden Middle School." I felt my insides go cold. That was the school my son had attended. Jeff was there three decades ago—he was a student at Bearden Middle around the time this Craig Willis was born—but the coincidence brought the danger closer to home somehow. "He taught English and social studies for two years," Art went on. "Then, last summer, he was arrested for molesting a ten-year-old boy at a day camp where he was a counselor."

"That's terrible," I said. "How come I don't remember reading about that in the newspaper?"

"Wasn't in the newspaper," said Art. "His lawyer—guess who?—managed to keep it all very quiet."

"Grease?"

"None other. He got a gag order on the arrest information, claiming his client would suffer irreparable damage if the arrest were made public, and then he got the case dismissed on a technicality—apparently the arresting officer was so upset he manhandled Craig and forgot to read him his rights. But the judge refused to expunge the arrest record, and the school system dropped him like a hot potato. He moved to Chattanooga last fall."

I was almost afraid to ask, but I did. "And what was he doing in Chattanooga?"

I heard Art draw a long, deep breath, which he exhaled in a slow, angry hiss. "He had just opened a karate school. Like teaching, only better, for his purposes—doesn't require a background check. And it's mostly boys in the classes."

I thought at once of my grandsons, who were five and seven—and who were both taking karate lessons in West Knoxville. "God help us," I said.

"Maybe he did," Art replied. "They say he moves in mysterious ways. Maybe it was a mother's prayer that steered some queer-hater with a violent streak to cross paths with our boy Craig when he was all dolled up like a tart."

"See, I don't buy that," I said. "I think the buck stops here on earth; good and evil arise from the choices we make, the things we do. I don't pretend to understand why some people are motivated to do wonderful things, while others are driven to commit unspeakable acts. But I think we're the ones who do the deeds, and we're the ones who deserve whatever credit or blame comes due."

"Mostly I agree," said Art. "Couldn't be a cop if I didn't believe in holding people accountable. Anyhow, it sure adds an interesting twist to this case."

"Did you call Chattanooga yet—the detective, or Jess?"

"Nope. You found the skin that gave me the prints, so you earned the first call. I'll phone Jess right now."

"Wait. One more question before you go."

"Shoot."

"I'm assuming you still haven't gotten any hits on that thumbprint you got from Craig's severed penis?"

"Right."

"So the killer's prints aren't in the AFIS database either in Tennessee or at the FBI?"

"Maybe not," he said, "but then again, even if the print's right, the size could be wrong."

"Huh?"

"We can't be certain that the size of the pecker when I printed it was the same as the size when the killer grabbed it," he said. "So I need to shoot some enlargements and reductions of the thumbprint, send those in, too. What I send in has to be within ten percent of the size of the prints on file, or AFIS won't see it as a match."

"You know," I said, "it would be quite a coup to ID both the victim and the killer from the prints on a husk of skin and an amputated penis."

"Yeah," he said, "don't think I haven't thought of that. But that would take a real stroke of luck. Maybe more luck than I've ever had before, all put together."

"We make our own luck," I said. "I believe that, too. 'Chance favors the prepared mind.' Louis Pasteur."

"The pasteurized-milk dude?"

"The same."

"He say that to explain how he came up with the idea?"

"No," I said, "he said it years before he came up with the idea. The idea proved his point, you might say."

"Looks that way," Art agreed. "Speaking of ideas, I've got an idea the Chattanooga PD or the ME's office will release Willis's name either today or tomorrow."

"Probably," I said. "They're bound to be feeling some pressure to show they're making progress on the case."

"I figure the Knoxville media will pick up the story, too," he said, "since Willis lived in Knoxville till a few months ago."

"But of course," I sighed. "Local angle on a kinky case."

"I keep thinking about the parents of that kid," said Art. "This is going to dredge up some intense feelings for them. Rip the scab right off the wound—if they've even managed to get as far as scabbing over. Maybe the newspaper isn't the best way for them to hear about it."

I tried to put myself in the position of the parents. I imagined my son Jeff and his wife Jenny; I pictured what it would be like for them if Tyler or Walker had been sexually abused by a trusted adult, and how they might feel if they read about the abuser's death in the paper. "That would be intense," I said, "but not necessarily negative. Might be the best news in the world to them. Might be just what they need to set it behind them and get on with their lives."

"You don't ever set this sort of thing behind you," Art said. "It's a lot like the death of a child; it haunts you forever. The pain dulls after a while, but it doesn't take much—a birthday, a scene in a TV show, a crayon drawing you find in the bottom of a drawer—to put a sharp edge on it all over again."

I suddenly realized what he wanted to do. "You're planning to go tell the kid's parents yourself?"

"Not exactly," he said. "Not me. We."

"We? You and me? Why?"

"We ID'd the body," he said. "That makes us the logical messengers. We're witnesses to the death, in a way; we're the two people who can say, with firsthand knowledge and absolute certainty, 'The man who molested your son is dead, and here's how he died.' Besides," he added, "telling them is the decent thing to do, and we're the only decent guys I can think of at the moment."

I could think of several, but I knew Art well enough to know that his mind was made up. And his reasoning, if not strictly logical, was emotionally compelling. "Okay," I yielded. "When?"

"Tiffany doesn't get home from school and cheerleader practice for another couple hours," he said. "How about I pick you up at your office in half an hour? That gives me time to call the folks in Chattanooga."

"You want me to be waiting down by the end-zone tunnel?"

"I'll call you when I'm turning onto Stadium Drive," he said. "That should give you time to wash bone cooties off your hands and come downstairs."

Half an hour later, he called back. "Okay, I just

turned off Neyland onto Lake Loudoun Drive, and I'm turning onto Stadium now. Hey, what's going on in Thompson-Boling Arena? I see a ton of media trucks."

"A creationist rally," I said miserably. "I mean, 'intelligent design.' Oh, and thanks for rubbing salt in the wound."

"Sorry," he said. "I'll use lemon juice next time. Or maybe lemon meringue pie." He snorted with laughter.

"Bye," I said, and hung up. I made a pit stop in the bathroom that adjoined my office—a useful vestige of Stadium Hall's former life as a dormitory—then locked up and headed down the stairwell.

Just as I walked out of the building, Art rounded the end of the stadium and stopped at the chain-link gate to the end-zone tunnel. He was driving an un-marked gray Impala I hadn't seen before. Unlike the battered white sedan he usually drove, this car had glossy paint and clean upholstery, and the inte-rior did not reek of spilled coffee and stale cigarette smoke, the way police cars often do. "Nice wheels," I said. "How'd you rate a fine steed like this?"

"Blackmailed the chief," he said. "Not on pur-pose, though. He asked me last week how the un-dercover work was going, and I said, 'Pretty good, Chief; by the way, I see you're doing a little under-cover research on adult web sites yourself.' Hell, I was just messing with him, but he turned red and broke into a sweat. Next thing you know, I get a call from the motor vehicle pool telling me to come swap my old beater for this thing. I guess you were right," he added.

"About what?"

"Chance does favor the prepared mind."

"I don't think Internet porn and accidental black-mail were what Louis Pasteur had in mind when he said that."

"No, but it makes me feel better about driving the car if I can quote something highbrow to justify my accidental good fortune."

"You think the chief's into any of the really bad stuff?"

"Naw," he said, "he's a good guy. But he's a guy. The percentage of adult males with Internet access who have never visited a porn site is about the same as the percentage of adult males who've never jerked off."

"Hmm," I said. "Once again, I find myself outside the mainstream."

"Which one you talking about? No, don't tell me—I don't wanna know."

Art drove north on Broadway, in the direction of Broadway Jewelry & Loan. A few blocks shy of the shopping center, though, he turned left onto Glenwood, then left again onto Scott. A sign on one corner announced that we were entering Old North Knoxville. Scott Avenue, like most of the neighborhood, was a street in transition. At one time, it had been an elegant neighborhood of two- and three-story Victorian homes occupying large, shady lots. Over the decades, though, many of the homes had gone to seed; some had been carved into apartments and smothered in aluminum siding; others had burned and been replaced with bleak brick boxes. The past few years had brought something of a rebirth, in a scattered, piecemeal sort of way. We drove past several houses in varying stages of decay, their lawns overgrown, tree branches clutching at sagging roofs. Then we passed a pocket of beautifully restored homes. Some of these were painted in neutral colors or subtle pastels; others, decked out in vibrant, contrasting colors—one combined turquoise siding with gold windows and orange gingerbread—were what my colleagues in the Art and Architecture Department called "painted ladies." They reminded me of the drag queens Jess and I had seen at the nightclub in Chattanooga, and the analogy made me smile. I would never paint a house so boldly, but I could appreciate the way they livened up a neighborhood.

"So tell me about these lucky folks we're about to drop in on," I said. "And how do you know if anybody's even home?"

"I called the house just before I phoned you," he said. "Woman answered; I said, 'Sorry, wrong number,' and hung up. I didn't want to get into it by phone." I nodded. "Parents are named Bobby and Susan Scott; kid's name is Joseph. Joey. Dad's a contractor of some sort; mom works part-time as a dental hygienist."

"Any other kids?"

"Don't know." He slowed to check a house number. "Must be the next one on the right."

The next one on the right was a three-story Victorian with an immense porch that stretched the width of the house and then wrapped around one side. Two of the bedrooms on the second floor had covered, columned balconies as well, and the third floor—which might have been servants' quarters a century ago—was a marriage of slate roof and dormer windows. The house was a microcosm of the neighborhood itself: a work in progress; a study in transition. One side of the façade was freshly painted, its cedar shakes an elegant blue-gray with white trim; the other side was sheathed in a tower of scaffolding through which I glimpsed a patch-work of peeling paint and new, unpainted shakes.

A minivan was parked beside the house, beneath a porte cochere whose roof was supported by fluted white columns. "Now that's what I call a carport," said Art. "They just don't make 'em like that any-more."

"They don't," I agreed, "but I bet your heating bill in the winter is about one-tenth what theirs is. Look at all those windows with all those little bitty panes of glass. Some of 'em missing, too, looks like. Probably no insulation in the walls, either—I bet when the winter wind blows, you can feel it inside the house."

"Cuts down on the germs," he said. "Toughens up the immune system, too." He parked at the curb and cut the engine. "Okay, you ready?"

"No."

"Me neither. I never am, for this kind of thing. You just have to take it slow; don't dump too much on them at once." He took a deep breath, and I did the same, and then we walked slowly up the side-walk and climbed the porch stairs.

The front door was a massive slab of fine-grained oak and bubbly, rippled old glass. The wood—hand-carved in a motif of leaves and vines—had been meticulously stripped and refinished to a lustrous golden hue. The glass was screened on the inside with a curtain of white lace dense enough to give privacy but sheer enough to let in plenty of light. The doorbell, like the door, was clearly original: a keylike knob set into the center of the door, just below the panel of glass. Art gave it a brisk twist, and it responded with a fusillade of clattering dings. I jumped, and Art smiled. "Sorry, I guess I got a little carried away," he said. "They don't make 'em like that anymore, either."

Inside, we heard the distant clatter of hard-soled shoes on hardwood floors. They drew nearer, then stopped, and a manicured hand pulled back the lace curtain. A woman who appeared to be in her mid-thirties peered out at us. Her expression was somewhere between neutral and slightly guarded—about what you'd expect to see on the face of a woman who looks out her front door to find two strange men on her porch. Then I saw something register in her eyes, and her face collapsed into panic and despair. She wrenched open the door and put a trembling hand up to her mouth. "Oh God," she whispered, "what's happened now?" My heart went out to her, and I suddenly grasped the full import of what Art had said on the phone: some wounds never heal; some ghosts haunt you forever.

"Everything's fine, Mrs. Scott," Art said quickly. "Nothing's wrong, I promise. We just have some information we thought you might appreciate hearing from us." She looked from Art to me and back again. "May we come in?"

She gave her head a quick shake, as if shrugging off a bad dream. "Yes. Of course. Forgive me."

We stepped into a soaring entry hall. On the right side, a wide oak staircase ascended to a broad landing halfway to the second floor, then made a left turn and topped out at what looked to be a sitting area. On the foyer's left side, a wide columned archway opened into a parlor that could have been transported from the 1890s. Unlike the house's half-renovated exterior, the interior—at least, what little I had seen so far—looked completely restored. She motioned Art and me to a velvet-covered sofa, its back formed of three ovals framed in walnut. She took a wingbacked armchair, but rather than settling into its embrace, she perched tautly on the front edge.

Art introduced himself, then me. She nodded as he described my work as a forensic anthropologist, and said, "I've read about you. Your work sounds interesting and very important." There was a hint of a question in her eyes and her voice as she said it.

I glanced at Art; he gave me an almost imperceptible nod: permission to speak. "A man was murdered a couple of weeks ago in Chattanooga," I said. "There was no identification on the body. The authorities down there asked if I could help figure out who he was and when he was killed." Mrs. Scott's eyes flitted back and forth as she scanned the universe of possibilities, trying to see where this might be leading.

"Ma'am, Dr. Brockton and I have just identified the body of that man," said Art. "It was Craig Willis." She inhaled sharply, and both hands flew to her mouth this time. Her eyes were wide, and I could almost swear I felt electricity crackling from them. Her hands began to shake, and the shaking traveled up her arms and into her shoulders and face and chest, and she dropped her face into her hands and began to sob—soundlessly at first, then with a sort of ragged, gasping noise which gave way to a high, sustained whimper that was more animal than human. I remembered a line from a movie—"the sound of ultimate suffering"—and I knew that was the sound I was hearing. I looked helplessly at Art, then pantomimed a question— *Should one of us go to her?*—but he shook his head slightly, motioning for me to sit tight.

She finally wound down, in a series of shuddering aftershocks, and lifted her head, staring out bleakly between her fingers. When she looked at Art, he reached into his jacket pocket and pulled out a clean handkerchief, which he held out to her. She wiped her eyes, her cheeks, and her dripping nose, then blew into it twice. By now the handkerchief was sodden, so I handed her mine, too. She repeated the maneuvers, looked at the mess she'd made of both hankies, and gave a sort of embarrassed half laugh. Then she drew a series of deep breaths, as if she had just sprinted half a mile. "I have imagined . . . this scene . . . a thousand times," she managed to say. "A thousand different ways. Dreamed it, day and night. Lived for it, when I couldn't hang on to anything else to live for. Prayed for it."

"Yes, ma'am," said Art. "I expect you have."

"So as much as I've rehearsed it, why does it still feel like my insides have just been torn out?"

"Because they have," he said. "This time it's not make-believe."

"God, we've worked so hard to put that behind us," she said. "Months and months of therapy. For Joey. For Bobby. For me. For me and Bobby together. For all three of us together. The abuse damn near killed us; now, the recovery's about to bankrupt us."

"I understand," said Art. "I'm sorry. I know it might not be much consolation, but this case—Joey's case—inspired us to work harder and smarter to catch guys like Craig Willis. We've created a new task force to catch people who use the Internet to target children or trade child pornography. If we can catch them in cyberspace, we can charge them with federal crimes. It's a small program right now, but it will only get bigger. And we're closing in on several of these people right now."

She looked both distressed and grateful to hear that.

Art checked his watch. "It's about three o'clock right now," he said. "What time will your husband be home from work?"

"Probably not till seven or eight. He's working a lot of overtime—that's how we're paying those therapy bills."

"Would you like us to come back this evening and tell him about this?"

She shook her head. "No," she said. "He'll be upset—he'll need to be upset, just like I did—and it would be hard for him to do that with you. If I tell him, I can hold him while I tell him, and maybe that will make it easier for him. More bearable, somehow." She smiled slightly. "He's a pretty manly man," she added. "He might actually hit you if you told him. With me, I think maybe he'll be able to cry instead."

Art smiled back. "Sounds like he's married to a wise woman with a big heart."

She teared up slightly at that. "If this is wisdom, I'll take foolishness any day." Suddenly she frowned. "Joey gets home from school at three-fifteen," she said.

Art stood up. "We were just leaving."

She looked relieved and grateful. "He can spot a cop a mile away," she said. "I'm afraid he'd get really scared if he saw you here. I'll call his therapist and ask how much we should tell him, and when."

"Just remember," said Art, "it's likely to be in the newspapers as early as tomorrow. So if you don't tell him pretty soon, he might hear it some other way."

"Damn," she said. "I think I see an emergency therapy session in our future this evening."

"I know it's not easy," said Art, "but it looks like you're doing all the right things." He looked around the room. "Sort of like fixing a big old house that's had a hard life. You just keep plugging away, one room at a time, one problem at a time."

"Yeah," she said. "Plugging away. That's us."

She walked us to the door. I held out my hand, and she took it in both of hers and squeezed it warmly. Art held out his arms, and she let him enfold her for a moment before propelling us out onto the porch and down the steps.

As the Impala reached the corner of the block, a school bus turned the corner, braked to a stop, and flashed its caution lights. Three children—two girls and a boy—stepped from the bus. By the time the bus lights stopped blinking and the STOP sign had folded back against the side of the bus, Susan Scott was at the corner, a smile on her face and an arm around the boy's shoulder.

"I think that was a good thing we did just now," I said.

"I think maybe you're right," said Art.

CHAPTER 20

I WINCED WHEN I unfolded the newspaper. MURDERED DRAG QUEEN WAS FROM KNOX, screamed the headline above the lead story in Friday's *News Sentinel*. POLICE PROBE POSSIBLE HATE CRIME IN CHATTANOOGA, read the subhead.

The article was by a crime reporter I didn't know, one whose byline had first begun appearing in the Sentinel only a few weeks earlier. I pored over the article.

Chattanooga police made a crucial breakthrough yesterday in a murder that has shocked the city's gay community to its core, but now a wave of fear could ripple through Knoxville. The battered body of a young man dressed in women's clothing and a wig was found two weeks ago outside Chattanooga, tied to a tree in Prentice Cooper State Forest. Chattanooga's medical examiner, Dr. Jess Carter, yesterday identified the victim as Craig Willis, 31, formerly of Knoxville.

An autopsy by Carter, supplemented by a skeletal examination by University of Tennessee forensic anthropologist (and "Body Farm" founder) Bill Brockton, indicated that Willis was killed by massive and repeated blunt-force trauma to the head. Willis's identity eluded investigators initially because no form of identification was found on his body, and the skin of his hands—including the fingerprints—had peeled off by the time the corpse was found. One piece of the missing skin was recently discovered by Brockton during a second search of the crime scene, said Carter, allowing the victim's prints to be matched to prints on file from an employment background check Willis underwent three years ago.

One source close to the investigation, speaking on condition of anonymity, said the slaying appears to be a hate crime, motivated by the victim's apparent sexual orientation. "He was wearing a sort of female dominatrix-looking outfit," said the source, "consisting of a long blond wig and a black leather corset, which most people would consider to indicate an S&M fetish or a quote-unquote kinky lifestyle. To some guys around here, a man in that kind of getup is like a red flag to a bull."

East Tennessee gay rights activists

have decried the slow pace of the investigation. "If a straight, conventional man or woman were killed in such a horrific manner, the police would leave no stone unturned," said Steve Quinn, coordinator of the Chattanooga Gay and Lesbian Alliance. "In this case, they seem more interested in sweeping the murder under the rug. The authorities here seem to consider homosexuals, transvestites, and transsexuals to be expendable, and that's an outrage." Knoxville activist Skip Turner added, "Craig Willis is a martyr in the struggle for sexual freedom. His bones cry out for justice."

Willis had moved from Knoxville to Chattanooga approximately six months ago, said Carter. He taught at Bearden Middle School for three years before moving to Chattanooga, where he had recently opened a karate school called Kids Without Fear. No one answered repeated calls to either Willis's home phone or the number listed for Kids Without Fear.

I was surprised the reporter hadn't contacted me, since Jess had mentioned my involvement in the investigation. I was also surprised he hadn't gotten wind of Willis's arrest record or proclivities. A few hours after Art phoned her with Willis's ID, Jess called him back to say that a search of his apartment had yielded hundreds of images of child pornography—in print, on CDs, and on his computer's hard drive. Some of the photos showed only nude children; some showed other adults with children; and some showed Willis himself performing sex acts with boys. A more seasoned or better-connected journalist would have gotten wind of the search, I felt sure, or at least the arrest record.

The story left me with very mixed feelings. I knew it might help the detectives to have more information than the general public now possessed. But it turned my stomach to hear Craig Willis, molester of children, described as a martyr to anything other than depravity and predation.

I wondered, too, about whether Jess had some agenda in releasing the information the way she did. Was she the unnamed source who referred to Willis's "kinky lifestyle," too? That didn't sound like the open-minded Jess I knew, but she could have said it to be deliberately provocative. I'd suspected she was frustrated with the slow pace of the investigation in Chattanooga. By framing the news in a way that sparked the anger of gay rights activists, was she hoping to ratchet up the pressure on the police? Jess was a smart woman and a gifted medical examiner, so I was sure she had thought carefully about what to say. She was also fearless and a bit of a maverick, though, and I hoped that she hadn't crawled out onto some limb farther than she should have.

CHAPTER 21

THE HEAD HAD BEEN simmering for three days down in the Annex before I took it out of the kettle for good. The hot water, bleach, Biz, Downy, and Adolph's Meat Tenderizer had done their work well: the remaining bits of tissue scrubbed off easily with a toothbrush; the bone had lightened to a deep ivory; and the aroma steaming off of it was like fresh laundry. Well, fresh laundry that had been mighty rank, for quite some time, before it went into the wash. Fresh laundry that could use another cycle or two. Still, the improvement was dramatic, and the results quite tolerable. I could take this skull back to Stadium Hall without offending anyone's sense of propriety or smell.

I set the skull and the top of the cranial vault on some paper toweling to dry, opened the valve that drained the kettle, and fished a few small bone fragments from the mesh screen in the bottom. I placed the fragments in a small Ziploc bag, then packed everything in a cardboard box, cushioned with more paper toweling.

Jess had called to say she was headed for Knoxville; she had two autopsy cases waiting for her in the cooler at the hospital, but before she tackled those, she wanted to see what information about the murder weapon I could glean from the skull now that it was stripped of its soft tissue. "Flesh forgets; bone remembers," she had said just before hanging up. It was a mantra of mine that I'd uttered enough times for her to remember, apparently. Her voice had regained most of its usual energy; either she was trying hard to sound cheerful again, or she'd managed to get some rest since I saw her looking so haggard in the morgue at the ME's office. I phoned Peggy, my secretary, and asked her to steer Jess to my office, which was at the far end of the stadium from the administrative offices, when she showed up.

I walked up the one-lane ramp from the Annex, which was down near Neyland Drive, to the service road that ringed the base of the stadium, and threaded my way beneath massive girders, cradling the box as if it were some precious gift. In a way, it was: the key, perhaps, to what had killed Craig Willis, and perhaps even to who had killed him.

I unlocked my office door and set the box on my desk, then switched on the lamp. Removing the lid, I reached in with both hands and hoisted out the skull. I set it on a doughnut-shaped cushion, one of dozens we had scattered around the classrooms and labs in the Anthropology Department, and swiveled the light and magnifying glass around to give me a good look. I had a theory, based on a cursory look in the Annex, but sitting on the window ledge beside me was the object I hoped would confirm it.

Just as I reached into the box for the top of the cranial vault, Jess Carter knocked on the doorframe and strode in. "Perfect timing," I said. "I just now got him finished. You want to take a look?"

By way of answering, she stepped to the desk and leaned down. Picking up the skull, she turned it this way and that, playing the ring-shaped fluorescent light over the contours from every possible angle. I stood back in silence, letting her take her time, make her own observations, formulate her own ideas and questions. Her eyes swept rapidly across the skull, then zeroed in on every fracture and indentation I had spotted. I had seen her work before; every time I did, it reminded me why she was one of the best medical examiners I'd ever worked with. Jess set the skull back on its cushion and subjected the top of the cranium to the same scrutiny, turning it over and over beneath the light. Finally she laid it down, finished with her examination, and turned to me. "Amazing," she said. "With all that macerated, contused tissue in place, the bone just looked like a big, mushy mess. Now it's easy to see discrete, individual marks left by a series of blows." She reached back down and picked up the skull again. "It looks almost like the killer used three different weapons," she said. She pointed to an indentation on the left parietal, the side of the skull. "Here," she said, "this indentation was made by an implement about an inch and a half wide, maybe a little more, with a flat face and parallel edges." I simply nodded; she wasn't asking anything yet, so I let her think out loud. "Here, in the frontal bone, there's a deep triangular gouge right in the center of the forehead." Again I nodded. "And the eye orbit looks like it was smashed by something broad and flat, three or four inches wide." There were other indentations in the bone as well, but she had pointed out the three most distinctive ones, and none of the others deviated from the patterns she had noted. "That doesn't make sense, though," she said. "Why would somebody strike a blow with one weapon, put it down, then strike a blow with another, and then trade that one for a third?"

I smiled. "Those were my questions exactly," I said. "Then I realized that it didn't have to be three different weapons; it could be one weapon with three different impact surfaces." She looked puzzled, so I reached over to the windowsill and produced my visual aid with a flourish. It was a piece of lumber, an ordinary two-by-four. First I laid the two-inch edge in the narrower indentation she had noticed first. It nestled down in the groove perfectly, its edges conforming to the parallel lines of the wound exactly. Then I laid the broad four-inch side against the shatterered edge of the eye orbit. Although numerous small shards of bone had splintered off, the basic fit was correct there, too. That left only the deep triangular notch in the frontal bone. I saw Jess staring at it, thinking hard; when I angled one corner of the board's end into the notch, she laughed with delight. "I'll be damned," she said, taking the two-by-four in her right hand and lifting the skull with her left. "Way back when I took the SAT? Only thing standing between me and an 800 on the math portion was those dad-blasted spatial geometry figures. Some things never change."

Just then my phone rang. "Hello, this is Dr. Brockton," I said.

"Dr. B., it's Peggy, I just wanted to let you know that Dr. Carter just showed up. She should be there momentarily."

"Thanks," I said, "but she's too quick for you. She's been here for five minutes already."

There was a long pause on the other end of the line. "I don't understand," Peggy said. "She just left my office a couple of minutes ago."

I turned to Jess. "Did you just leave my secretary's office two minutes ago?"

Now Jess looked confused. "I didn't go to your secretary's office; I came straight here. I parked right beside your truck, down by the end-zone tunnel, and came up this staircase right beside your office."

"Peggy," I said, "what was Dr. Carter wearing when you saw her two and a half minutes ago?"

"I didn't pay much attention. Um, maybe a navy blue suit? A dark skirt and jacket, anyhow, I think." I glanced at Jess; she had on olive green suede pants and a short-sleeved beige sweater.

"And she introduced herself as Dr. Carter?"

"Yes. Wait—no! She just said, 'I'm looking for Dr. Brockton,' and so naturally . . .'" She trailed off in confusion or embarrassment. "If that wasn't Dr. Carter, then who was it?"

"I don't know," I said as a red-faced, dark-suited woman burst through the door, "but I think I'm about to find out."

The woman stared at me with wild eyes, then she stared at Jess, and at the skull, and at the two-by-four Jess still held in her hand. She opened her mouth but no sound came out, so she closed it and tried again. On the third attempt, she managed to say, "Is that him?"

I exchanged an uneasy glance with Jess, then said, "Excuse me?"

"Is that *him*?" She pointed a shaking finger at the skull.

"Is that who?"

"Is that my *son*?" she shouted.

Jess spoke in a soothing, neutral voice. "Ma'am, who is your son?"

"My son is Craig Willis. Is. That. My. *Son*, damn you?"

"Yes, ma'am," said Jess, still in the same soothing tone. "We're pretty sure it is. I'm very sorry."

The woman looked at Jess as if truly seeing her for the first time. Her face radiated confusion, pain, and rage. "Who the hell are you," she spat at Jess, "and what have you done to him?"

"Ma'am, I'm Dr. Carter. I'm the medical examiner in Chattanooga," said Jess. "I performed the autopsy on the . . . on your son's body. Dr. Brockton helped us identify him, and is helping us determine how he was killed."

"You're Dr. Carter? The Dr. Carter who was quoted in the newspaper article that informed me my son was dead?"

Jess nodded but looked startled. "Yes, ma'am, that was me."

"You told the newspapers my son was found in women's clothing? You told the newspapers my son was a homosexual?"

"I said his body was found in women's clothing," said Jess. "That information had already been reported, back when the body was first discovered. I didn't actually say that he was a homosexual. I said one theory we were considering was that his murder might have been a homophobic hate crime."

"It amounts to the same goddamn thing as saying he was a queer," said the woman. "What gives you the *right*? Who do you think you are, to say things that destroy a young man's reputation? It's not enough that he's been murdered? You have to go and smear his name, too?"

I cleared my throat. "Ma'am—Mrs. Willis?— why don't you sit down in my chair here? I know this must be very upsetting to you." I took her arm gently; she shook me off furiously.

"Don't you dare patronize me," she said. "You don't know a damn thing about me."

"You're right," I said. "I don't. If I sounded patronizing, I apologize. I'm a little confused here," I added. "Normally the police notify the next of kin privately before a murder victim's identity is released. Did I understand you to say that you learned of his death from the newspaper?"

"Yes," she said. "I read it in the *newspaper*. And while I sat there reading it, a *television* crew came and knocked on my door, asking how it *felt*, knowing my son had been brutally murdered."

Jess's face was crimson. "Mrs. Willis, I am terribly sorry you were not notified personally. Our investigator did try to locate relatives, but on several leases and medical forms your son signed recently, he wrote 'None' in the blank where it asked the name of his closest living relative."

"That is a lie," the woman snapped.

"It may be," said Jess in an even, icy tone that set off warning bells in my head, "but if it is, it's his lie, not ours."

With startling quickness the woman darted forward. She slapped Jess across the face with such force that Jess fell across the desk. The two-by-four dropped from her right hand and clattered to the floor; the skull shot free of her left hand, arcing toward the filing cabinet beside the door. I made a lunge and managed to snag it just before it hit. The woman continued to rain blows on Jess, who seemed too stunned to even shield herself. I hastily set the skull down on the filing cabinet and took hold of the flailing arms, pulling the woman backward. She had begun to sob, great, heaving sobs that made her whole body shudder in my grasp.

"You will be sorry," she said to Jess. "You ruined my son's reputation. You will pay dearly for that." Jess just stared, dumbfounded, her face a mottled mass of splotches and scratches. The woman twisted in my grip to face me; her own face was contorted and quivering and frightening. "Did you do that to him? Did you turn him into one of your skeletons?"

"Mrs. Willis, we needed to know what sort of murder weapon to look for," I said.

"Damn you to hell," she said. "Give him to me."

"I'm sorry, but we can't," I said. "This is evidence in a murder investigation. We want to catch whoever killed him."

"Give him to me!" she shouted, and sprang toward the filing cabinet. I managed to wedge myself between her and the cabinet, blocking her path. Behind us, I saw Jess pick up the telephone and punch 911. "I'm calling from Dr. Brockton's office under the football stadium," Jess said. "We have a disturbed and violent woman here. Could you send an officer right away, please? . . . Yes, I'll stay on the line until help arrives."

Mrs. Willis backed away from me, her venomous eyes darting from Jess to me and back again to Jess. She pointed at Jess again. "You will be sorry," she said. And then she spun and hurried out the door.

Jess and I stared at the empty doorway in amazement, then at one another. "That . . . went . . . rather well, I think," said Jess. A moment later she began to shake. Another few moments, and she began to cry. She was still crying when the four UT police officers arrived.

CHAPTER 22

JESS STILL SEEMED SKITTISH hours after being attacked by Craig Willis's mother. If anything could soothe her, I figured, it would be a quiet dinner at By the Tracks Bistro.

By the Tracks was named for the railroad tracks that passed dish-rattlingly close to its original location. The restaurant had started small, but quickly won a devoted customer base through a combination of great food, attentive service, quiet ambience, stylish décor, and only slightly painful prices. It had long since outgrown its small beginnings and trackside location, but the name had stuck. Year in, year out, By the Tracks remained arguably Knoxville's best restaurant. Not its most expensive—that superlative belonged to the Orangery, a classic, chichi French restaurant a few blocks away. But I'd never found the Orangery particularly relaxing: every time I ate there, gussied up in my Sunday best, I half expected to be judged, found wanting, and tossed out as riffraff halfway through my meal. At By the Tracks, on the other hand, I could wander in without a reservation, wearing faded jeans and a polo shirt, and be certain of a warm welcome and a delicious meal. Their entrées ranged from basil-stuffed trout over Israeli couscous, at the fancy end of the spectrum, to the biggest and best sirloin burger in town, maybe in all of Tennessee.

Within five minutes after we settled into a booth, Jess was sipping a Cosmopolitan and visibly relaxing. Another drink, a half hour, and half a bacon cheeseburger later, she was smiling and laughing. My hope was that by the end of the meal I might be able to persuade her to stay at my house, but I didn't want to pressure her—that might undo all the good the meal had done—so I kept the conversation light. I couldn't resist telling her how beautiful and thrilling she had been the other night; she blushed and looked shy at the compliments. But she did not look displeased.

We had just gotten a crème brûlée for dessert, plus a coffee for Jess, when I saw her eyes lock onto something in the direction of the bar. Her expression froze; it seemed to contain equal measures of pain, fear, and fury. "Jess," I said, "what's wrong?" I turned and scanned the bar but saw nothing amiss.

"It's Preston," she said. "My ex. He's sitting over there at the bar. He's been watching us. That son of a bitch is *stalking* me."

I turned again. This time, I vaguely recalled having met the man at the corner of the bar once, several years earlier, at a forensic conference. He was a lawyer—a prosecutor, if memory served, which is probably how he and Jess first connected. "Do you want me to go tell him to get lost?"

"No," she said. "I need to deal with this." She pushed away the crème brûlée, drew a deep breath, and set her jaw. Then she slid out of the booth and stormed over to the bar. *I would not want to be in his shoes right about now*, I thought. Jess's hands flashed angrily as she spoke; I couldn't hear any of her words, but her tone carried, and it was not happy. I saw him shake his head vigorously, as if denying something—that he had followed her?—and then *he* seemed to go on the offensive. He pointed at me, and for a while they both sounded mad. Then his tone turned pleading, and her tone softened. She sat down on a barstool beside him. By now I was staring openly at the two of them; for her part, Jess was looking intently at his face. He reached up and wiped his eyes. She wiped hers.

Jess stayed at the bar for ten minutes going on eternity. When she finally came back to the booth, she would not meet my eyes. She sat down gingerly, as if the seat were wired with explosives. She didn't speak. "Talk to me, Jess," I said.

"He's in town for a DA's conference," she said. "Bob Roper, the Knox County DA, recommended this place. He swears he would never have come here if he'd had any inkling I'd be here with a date." She glanced up at me briefly, then dropped her eyes again. "I believe what he said."

Every alarm I had was ringing like crazy. "What else did he say, Jess? You seem more upset, in a pulled-in sort of way, than you did when you thought he was following you." I realized what my intuition was telling me. "You've just left me, haven't you? We barely got started, and it's already over. Is that it?"

This time she faced me squarely. She was crying a little, but she either didn't notice or didn't care. "Dammit, Bill, you're the last person I would ever want to hurt. You are the kindest, sweetest, smartest, most loving man I know. What you gave me the other night made me feel alive, and loved, and desired again for the first time in a long, long while. It was so lovely, and so healing. And maybe this is just a bump in the road." She drew a deep breath and shook her head. "I thought I was done with him, but now I'm not so sure. Shit, the guy still *gets* to me. Look what this one chance encounter has done to me." She gave me a small, sad smile. "The irony is, I could probably be happier with you. Preston doesn't actually *like* me all that much. And when I'm with him, *I* don't like me all that much." She gave me the half smile again, and I thought it might tear my heart out. "You, on the other hand, like me a lot. These past few days, I've liked myself, too. More than I have in . . . maybe *ever.* You see me through eyes of kindness, and when I see myself reflected in your eyes, I see myself a little more kindly, too." She slid a hand across the table, laid it tentatively on mine. Part of me wanted to clasp it and never let go; part of me wanted to fling it away from me. "I know I don't have the right to ask this, but could you just give me some space for a while, let me try sorting through what I feel and what I want?" I couldn't speak. I swallowed hard and looked down at the table, at our two hands. Neither of them seemed like mine anymore. "I worked with a therapist for a while when the breakup was at its worst," Jess was saying. "Maybe she can help me untangle the stuff that's underneath this. The deeper stuff—the stuff that seems to make it hard for me to choose things that would be good for me."

I considered trying to argue or reason with her, but I quickly concluded that any attempt to plead or pressure would only drive her farther away. I could behave stupidly, I could act pitiful, or I could strive for grace and dignity. When I opened my mouth, I landed somewhere in the murky middle of all three. "Are you leaving with him?"

"No," she said, nodding toward the bar. "He just left." I looked, and it was true; his stool was empty, and the restaurant's glass door was swinging shut. "I told him if he wants to talk, I'm willing to see a counselor with him. That's it—there, or not at all."

"But you're not leaving with me," I said.

"No," she said. "I'm leaving alone, and I'll drive back to an empty house in Chattanooga and cry all night, I expect."

"I guess I'm better off than I thought," I said. "I only have to drive about five minutes before I can curl up with the Kleenex box." I smiled, or tried to, to let her know that was meant as a joke. Amazingly, she laughed, though I wasn't sure if the laugh was at the joke or at my facial contortions.

"You dear, sweet man," she said. "I will call you when I figure out what the hell I'm doing, I promise. Even if I'm calling to tell you something that I think will be hard for you to hear."

"Swell," I said. "With promises like that, who

needs curses?" Again I approximated a smile. "Meantime, what about the casework?"

"Garland's back tomorrow," she said, then laughed briefly and added, "May God help you. And we've both done all we can do with the Willis case unless they make an arrest and it goes to trial." She was right; it was just that I would miss her terribly, even simply as a colleague.

Almost before I knew it, she had slipped out of the booth and stood up. She walked to my side of the table, gave me a quick kiss on the cheek, and said, "Thank you, Bill. You might not understand this or believe it, but I do love you."

And then she was gone.

CHAPTER 23

THREE DAYS HAD PASSED since Jess and I had parted. Three days with no call, no e-mail, no note in my in-box.

The gates to the Body Farm were slightly ajar, which probably meant that one of the graduate students was inside checking on a research subject. I parked in the slot closest to the gate—the Body Farm being the only place I could think of where the closest parking space was actually the least desirable, at least in terms of ambience—and swung the chain-link gate outward. As I stepped toward the inner wooden gate, something suddenly registered as odd, and I stepped back into the parking lot and did a quick scan. Mine was the only vehicle, I saw, anywhere near the gate, and that puzzled me. It was unlikely that a student would have arrived on foot: the research facility was three miles from the Anthropology Department by road, and road was the only way to get from one to the other unless you wanted to swim the Tennessee River, thereby shortening the distance to a mile. Someone could have walked over from the morgue or forensic center, but a half mile of access roads and parking lots separated the facility from the hospital. It wasn't inconceivable that someone had walked over from the morgue, but I had never known a student to do it.

As I reached the gate, I noticed a note wedged between two of the wooden planks. "Bill—I'm inside. Come find me. Jess." I scanned the parking lot again, more widely this time, but there was no sign of a fire-engine red Porsche.

I walked into the main clearing, half expecting to see Jess chatting with some graduate student she'd roped into letting her in. It was empty. "Hello?" I called. "Jess?" No answer. I took a short stroll downhill, along what remained of an old gravel roadbed where we generally set bodies that were brought here simply to skeletonize. Jess had sent a dozen or more up from Chattanooga over the past two years. She was building a skeletal collection for the ME's office down there, not to compete with ours, but simply for reference purposes and teaching material. I seemed to recall that we had two or three Chattanooga bodies skeletonizing at the moment, so it was possible she was checking on their progress.

The Chattanooga bodies were there, two of them, but Jess wasn't. One was down to bare bone, except for a few patches of mummified skin over the rib cage; the other had passed through the bloat and active decay stages and on to the dry stage, so it would soon be ready to process and send back as well. The cleaner one had been autopsied, I noticed; the top of his cranium, which had been neatly sliced off—by Jess, no doubt—sat on the ground to one side of the rest of his skull, looking a bit like an unusually smooth turtle shell. Judging from the prominence of the brow ridge and the smoothness of the cranial sutures, whose meandering joints had almost entirely filled in and disappeared, he was an older man. The robust bones of the rib cage and arms, and the large muscle-attachment points on the arms, spoke of great upper-body strength. But the leg bones didn't fit with this picture: they were delicate and spindly, like those of a thin, frail old woman, and one leg looked shorter and distorted. *Paralysis*, I thought at first. Then: *No. Polio.* Polio had cut a huge and tragic swath through an entire generation of American children in the 1930s and '40s and early '50s, attacking the myelin sheaths of muscles and nerves, warping young bones ruinously in a matter of days or weeks. I had considered polio virtually eradicated from the planet, much as smallpox had been vanquished, but lately I'd read a disturbing story in the *New York Times* about the disease's resurgence in India and Africa. Villagers there had grown suspicious and fearful about government vaccination programs. One rumor running rampant in Nigeria claimed that the vaccine contained a sinister American drug designed to sterilize unsuspecting African children. As fear and anger spread from village to village, causing public health workers to flee for their lives, the vaccination program was halted. Polio cases soon began spiking and spreading, setting back the global eradication effort by months or even years. *What fools these mortals be*, I thought. *And how mortal we fools be.*

I trudged back up the hill, through the clearing, and along the trail that led to Jess's experiment near the upper fence. Through the unfurling spring foliage, I began to catch glimpses of our research subject, still tied to the tree, the blond wig practically glowing against the gray-black bark of the oak. But where was Jess?

"Jess? Are you here? Jess, you're not hiding from me somewhere, are you?"

There was no answer. And as I got clear of the last thicket of underbrush between me and the big pine tree, I saw that Jess was indeed here, but I understood why she had not answered me.

Jess was against the tree, her naked body tied to the donated cadaver in an obscene parody of sexual intercourse. A blond wig and smears of blood partly obscured the face, but there was no doubt that it was Jess's face, no doubt that it was Jess's body. And no doubt that Jess was dead.

I had worked hundreds of death scenes, but never one where I had a personal stake, an intimate connection to the victim. That wasn't who I was or what I did: I was the forensic scientist, the dispassionate observer, the eagle-eyed Ph.D. summoned to solve the puzzle. I was not, never had been, and still—even as I stared at Jess's mutilated body—could not conceive of myself being the person who stumbles upon a scene that could tear out his heart, buckle his knees, burst a vessel in his brain.

My feet were locked in place, my brain scrambling wildly. My first impulse was to rush to Jess, feel for a pulse, pray that I'd misjudged the vacancy in her eyes and the stillness in her limp form. *No*, another impulse said, *don't touch anything, don't take so much as one step closer. It's a crime scene, and you shouldn't contaminate it.* Those, at least, must be something like the words that impulse would have used if my mind had been capable of wielding words, because I fought back the impulse to go to her.

So there I stood, rooted to the spot, for an instant that was also an eternity. Finally I felt one hand close around something hard in my hip pocket, and I pulled it out to see what it was. It was small and oblong and silver; I stared at it as if it were a mysterious artifact from some ancient or interplanetary civilization; finally I recognized it as my cellphone. Clumsily I pawed it open, struggling to remember and press the numbers 9 and 1 and 1 again. Nothing happened. I fought to recall how I had once used this device, in a former life; gradually I became dimly aware of the SEND button, and willed myself to press it. When I heard a female voice say "911," I nearly dropped the phone.

I stared at it dumbly. "This is 911, do you have an emergency?" What was I supposed to say—how and where could I begin to describe what I had, what I beheld? "Hello, can you hear me? Do you have an emergency?"

"Yes," I finally managed to say. "I do. Help. Oh God, please help."

The phone fell to the ground, and I sank to my knees, and I heard and saw nothing more, or at least noticed nothing more, until a strong pair of hands raised me to my feet. A police officer maneuvered his face directly in front of mine and said, "Dr. Brockton? Dr. Brockton? Tell us what happened here."

PART 2
AFTER

CHAPTER 24

THE UNIFORMED POLICE OFFICER led me down the path to the main clearing, just inside the gate of the Body Farm. A warped, weathered picnic table sat askew under a tree at one edge of the clearing; the patrolman took me there and set me on one of its benches. "Do you mind waiting here while we secure the scene and get some more people here?" I shook my head. "Are you all right?"

"Not really. But I'll manage. You do whatever you need to do."

I heard a series of sirens approaching, at least half a dozen in all. Someone had already stretched crime scene tape across the open gate; through the opening, I saw a fast-growing throng of officers— city police, UT campus police, and Medical Center security guards—as well as EMS personnel and firefighters. Heads leaned in through the gate, over the tape, peering at the facility. Peering at me.

After a while, a stylishly dressed man in a lavender dress shirt and yellow tie ducked under the tape and walked toward me. "Dr. Brockton?" I nodded. "I'm Sergeant John Evers," he said. "I'm an investigator in Major Crimes. Including homicides." He held out a suntanned hand and shook mine firmly, then handed me a business card. I pulled out my wallet and tucked it inside. "Can I get a brief statement from you here while things are fresh?"

"Of course."

"We'll want to talk to you in more detail downtown, since you're the one who found the body. But for now, just some basic information." He pulled out a pen and a small notepad, which he centered on one of the cupped boards of the tabletop. He took down my name, address, phone number, where I worked, and other data, then got to the particulars of where we were, and why. "What time did you arrive here this morning?"

"I think about eight," I said. "I was listening to the news on the radio, so it couldn't have been more than a few minutes after that."

He nodded. "And what were you doing here?"

"I work here," I said. "This is my research facility. The Anthropology Department's research facility, I should say."

"Yes, sir, of course. I meant, specifically, why had you come out this morning?"

"I came out to check on some research. To see what condition the body—the male body up there tied to the tree—was in by now." I explained how we had staged the research subject, and why. "I was doing the research for the Chattanooga medical examiner," I said. "Jess—Dr. Jessamine—Carter. I found her body when I went up there to check on my research subject."

"So you recognized the victim?" I nodded. "You knew Dr. Carter personally?"

"Yes. We had worked together on several cases over the past few years. And we were collaborating on a current case, involving a murder victim whose body was found tied to a tree down near Chattanooga. That's the death scene we were replicating here, so we could pinpoint the time since death more accurately for Dr. Carter."

"Did you see anybody else out here this morning when you arrived, either inside the fence or out in the parking lot?" I shook my head. "Driving away from the parking lot?" Again I shook my head.

"Was the gate open or closed when you got here?"

I had to think for a moment; my arrival seemed a lifetime ago. "It was open," I said. "That was the first thing out of the ordinary."

"It's normally locked?"

"Yes, with two locks—one on the chain-link gate, one on the wooden gate."

"What else was unusual?"

"There was a note for me on the inner gate." I suddenly remembered it was in my pocket. I reached for it, then caught myself before I touched it. "I'll let one of your evidence technicians get it out of my pocket and bag it. It's a note from Dr. Carter. Or at least, supposedly from Dr. Carter. Saying, 'I'm inside. Come find me.' It'll have my fingerprints on it, from when I pulled it off the gate and read it. But maybe it'll have the prints of whoever put it there, too."

He nodded, and drew a box around the word NOTE, with arrows pointing at each corner of the box, for extra emphasis.

"So when you found the note, what did you do?"

"I came inside and looked around, called Dr. Carter's name. I went down that way first"—I pointed to the lower area, where Jess sometimes put bodies to skeletonize—"and then I walked up that path leading to the research project. And that's when I found her. Her corpse. Tied to the other one."

"What did you do when you saw her?"

"Nothing, at first. I just stared. I couldn't process it; I couldn't think. Finally—I mean, it was probably only a minute or two, but it felt like forever—I called 911."

"And after you made the call, what did you do? Did you approach the body? Did you ever touch the body?"

I shook my head. "No. I know better than to disturb a death scene."

"How close were you?"

"Six feet. Maybe eight or ten."

"So how did you know she was dead?"

I looked up at him; met his gaze for the first time, really. "Detective, I've spent the past twenty-five years studying the dead. I've seen corpses by the hundreds. I recognize the vacant, clouded eyes. I know the difference between shallow breath and no breath; between an unconscious person and a lifeless body." I could feel my voice starting to rise, but it seemed to be someone else's voice, not my own; a voice that was beyond my control. "I know that when blowflies are swarming around a woman's bloody corpse, crawling in and out of her open mouth, I don't need to feel for a *pulse* to tell me that woman is dead."

Evers's eyes were locked on mine in horror and fascination. In my peripheral vision, I became aware of other eyes staring at me as well. I glanced toward the gate and saw a dozen people looking in my direction, their expressions all registering various degrees of shock. I took a deep breath and rubbed my eyes and forehead. "I'm sorry," I said. "This is very upsetting."

"I'm sure it is," said Evers. "No need to apologize. Listen, I need to go up the hill to the scene. And we'll probably be tied up here most of the day. But I'd like to talk to you in more detail tomorrow, if you wouldn't mind. Get more background on Dr. Carter, her colleagues, her activities. Okay?"

"Of course," I said. "Anything I can do to help. What time do you want me there?"

"Ten o'clock?" I nodded. "All right. Thank you, Dr. Brockton. Take it easy today. You've had quite a shock."

"Yes, I have. Thank you. Do your best on this one."

He smiled broadly, flashing me a band of teeth so white they'd have made a great ad for Crest. "I always do, Doc. I always do. Oh, one last thing. Sit tight for just another minute and let me find a forensic tech to get that note out of your pocket."

I stayed put, and he returned in a few minutes, accompanied by a forensic technician clad in a white Tyvek biohazard suit from head to toe. The technician used tweezers to pluck the note from my shirt pocket, then sealed it in a Ziploc evidence bag and labeled it. "You know where to go tomorrow, right?" asked Evers. I nodded. "Meantime, we'll try to keep a pretty tight lid on this. We'd appreciate it if you'd help us with that. If you get media calls, which you probably will, just refer them to us."

"I will."

Evers stood up, which I took to be my cue to do likewise. He walked me to the gate and raised the yellow and black tape for me so I didn't have to duck so far. He turned to a uniformed officer who was posted just outside the gate, holding a clipboard. "I'm not leaving," he said, "but he is. This is Dr. Bill Brockton of UT. Dr. Brockton was already inside when the scene was secured, so he's not on your log yet. You need to add his name; put 'N/A' as his sign-in time; and sign him out at"—he checked his watch—"nine thirty-eight." The officer nodded and obliged.

Twenty or more emergency vehicles, many with lights still strobing, jammed the northeast corner of the parking lot. Some were tucked into parking spaces amid the cars of hospital employees; others jammed the aisles between rows and filled the strip of grass along the east edge of the lot. A hundred yards away, in a taped-off area at the southeast corner, I noticed a gaggle of media vehicles—news crew SUVs, mostly, but also a couple of broadcast trucks, their antenna masts aloft. Crowding the yellow tape were half a dozen tripods topped by half a dozen cameras, their lenses all trained on me. I turned and walked around the back of my truck, opened the driver's door, and backed out of my parking space.

As I eased down the hill toward the exit of the parking lot, a black Chevy Tahoe emerged from the direction of the morgue and sped toward the Body Farm. As it passed, I caught a glimpse of the driver. It was Garland Hamilton: one medical examiner racing to a death scene where the body of another medical examiner awaited him.

CHAPTER 25

LIKE A SLEEPWALKER, I shuffled through my forensic anthropology class, which met less than an hour after I left the scene of Jess's murder. I considered canceling class, but if I canceled class, what was I to do for that hour instead? So I taught. Or went through the motions of teaching. At the end of class, I couldn't have said what topic I'd just spent an hour lecturing on. The only thing I noticed was that Jason Lane, my creationist student, was conspicuously absent.

After class, my autopilot carried me back to my office; luckily, the sidewalks and ramps from McClung Museum to the base of the stadium all ran downhill; otherwise, I might not have had the energy or will to make it. The two flights of stairs up to my sanctuary nearly overwhelmed me. Once inside, I closed the door—a rare gesture for me, and a sign of serious trouble. Slumping in my chair, I stared out the grimy windows, through the crisscrossed girders, at—what? Not at the river, although it continued to flow through downtown and alongside the campus. Not at the hills above the far shore, though they remained green and solid. Not at the sky or the sun, though they remained inexplicably, unfeelingly bright.

I could not recall ever before sitting in my office idly, doing nothing. It wasn't that I had nothing to do—I had a stack of tests to grade, I had at least a dozen articles to review for the three anthropology and forensic journals on whose editorial boards I served. Then there was the textbook revision I'd agreed to do nearly a year ago, a chore that always seemed to take a backseat to forensic cases. Cases like my forensic examination of Craig Willis's battered skull. Trouble was, I couldn't get past the fact that I'd been asked to conduct that exam and write that report by Jess Carter. And now Jess was dead.

Craig Willis's murder still needed to be solved; Jess's death might slow the investigation down, but it wouldn't stop it. In fact, my e-mail in-box already contained a memo indicating that Garland Hamilton would step in temporarily to fill Jess's shoes in Chattanooga, just as Jess had filled in for Hamilton here in Knoxville while his medical license was under review. But knowing that the wheels of justice would keep turning, however slowly, did not give me the strength to put my own shoulder to the wheel right now.

I opened the cardboard box that contained Willis's skull and lifted it out, along with the top of the cranial vault. Setting the skull on a doughnut-shaped cushion, I stared at its shattered visage as if some clue to Jess's murder might be encoded in the fracture lines etched in Willis's bones. A connection of some sort existed, I felt sure, but what, precisely, was the link? Or who?

Jess's body had been bound to the research corpse we'd used as a stand-in for Willis at the Body Farm. The research was meant to narrow down Willis's time since death. Did that mean that whoever had killed Willis also killed Jess? If so, why? Because he considered Jess a threat; because she was getting too close to the truth? But what *was* that truth? I had no idea who had killed Willis, and as far as I knew, neither Jess nor the Chattanooga police had any better insight into his murder than I did.

But if Willis's killer hadn't murdered Jess, then who had? Who else might have wanted her dead? As a medical examiner, of course, Jess had worked scores of homicides; in theory, any one of those cases might have prompted someone to seek vengeance—a relative of someone whom Jess's autopsy and testimony had helped send to prison, for instance. But the timing mattered, surely: Why *now*? Who *lately*?

My mind flashed back to Willis's mother, and the irrational fury with which she had attacked Jess. She had accused Jess of destroying her son's reputation by releasing the information about his being dressed in drag, and—if indeed Jess had been the unnamed source—by speculating that the murder might have been a homophobic hate crime. Could the rage she displayed in my office have intensified after she fled, escalating to the point of murder? She had parted with a vague threat directed at Jess, but in the heat of the moment, people often made threats they never carried out. Besides, if she were the one who killed Jess, why would she have posed Jess's body in that obscene position, bound to the corpse that was serving as a stand-in for her own son's body? That didn't seem to fit. Unless, I thought, by staging Jess's body that way, she meant to repudiate the theory Jess had mentioned—unless by killing Jess and tying her to the research corpse, she was saying, "Fuck you and fuck your demeaning theory about my son's death."

But what if there were no connection? What if whoever had left the threatening messages on Jess's voicemail had acted on them? In the dim, shifting light that had engulfed me in the hours since I found Jess's body, I could see things equally well— or equally poorly—from either angle.

Gradually I became aware of my telephone ringing. It had not even occurred to me that, rather than sitting and brooding alone, I could have been talking through what had happened with Jeff or Miranda or somebody else who cared about me. Fortunately, one of those people was now calling me. "It's Art," he said. "I just heard about Jess Carter. I am so sorry, Bill. I know you liked her and respected her."

"I did. More than that, too. We had—hell, I don't know what to call it, Art—we had started to get involved, I guess you could say."

"Romantically involved?"

"Yeah."

"Wow," he said. "Well, damn. I bet that would've been a good thing for both of you."

"I think so. Started off mighty nice, though I'm

not sure she was completely over her divorce yet. Might've gotten bumpy. But might've smoothed out again pretty quick. Guess we'll never know."

"Man," he said, "I thought I was sorry to hear the news before. Now I'm a lot more sorry. Is there anything I can do for you?"

"Nothing I can think of. I've got to go into KPD tomorrow morning for an interview."

"Why are they having you come in, instead of talking to you at your office?"

"I guess because I found her body."

"*You?*"

"Yeah. Lucky me. It was bad, Art. She was nude, and she was tied to that research corpse we had lashed to a tree. Like she was having sex with the corpse."

"Son of a bitch."

"Son of a bitch. Listen, Art, I'm gonna go now. Thanks for calling."

"You need anything, you page me. Even if it's the middle of the night. Especially if it's the middle of the night. It's liable to hit you hardest long about then."

A powerful sense of foreboding told me he was probably right.

CHAPTER 26

I WOULD NOT HAVE believed a single day could creep by so slowly. But then again, I would not have believed the nightmarish turn events had taken ten hours before at the Body Farm, either. What I found believable clearly had no relation to reality any longer.

Miranda was scrubbing the femur as if her life—or even her Ph.D.—depended on removing every molecule of soft tissue before putting it in the steam kettle to simmer. We had been working in the morgue's decomp room for an hour now, cleaning the bulk of the tissue off the bones of the research body that had been tied to the pine tree. The research body that Jess's body had been obscenely embracing.

Garland Hamilton had brought Jess's body over around noon, and KPD had released the scene at four-thirty. By five, all the cops and emergency vehicles were gone, and so, therefore, were the camera crews. As soon as the parking lot had cleared out,

Miranda and I drove up to the gate in the department's truck, collected the remains of the research body, and brought it into the decomp room to process. I blamed this research project, in some vague way, for Jess's death, and I wanted to rid myself and the facility of all traces of it. Besides, Jess was gone, and we had already pinned down Craig Willis's time since death to roughly one week before the hiker found the battered body on the bluff outside Chattanooga.

Neither Miranda nor I had spoken a word as we worked. For me, the shock and grief I felt over Jess's murder were overwhelming. I felt myself immersed, close to going under; the simplest acts—opening a door, flipping a light switch, speaking a sentence—seemed foreign, baffling, exhausting. Miranda had not known Jess nearly as well as I had; she might have been keeping silent out of deference to the pain radiating off me, although she, too, might have been too upset herself to feel like talking. A close brush with death seems to turn people into exaggerated versions of themselves, the same way a few drinks do: the mean get meaner, the sad get weepy, the talkative just will not shut up. So it wasn't surprising that two introverted scientists would fall silent when a colleague of both, and a love of one, had been murdered.

But there was another explanation for the tense silence that occupied the room, almost as palpably as if it were a third person: Jess Carter's body was being autopsied across the hall, in the main autopsy suite, by Garland Hamilton. He'd started two hours before, according to a morgue technician who greeted me with a stricken face upon my arrival. My guess was that unless Garland found something unusual, he would be finishing soon.

It added insult to injury to know that Jess's maimed body was being examined by a medical examiner I knew to be sloppy and incompetent. He might overlook or misread evidence, which could compromise the police department's effort to understand the crime and pinpoint the killer; conversely, he might imagine evidence where none actually existed, as he had in Billy Ray Ledbetter's autopsy, when he saw an accidental cut in the flesh of the back and interpreted it—or, rather, misinterpreted it—as a deep, lethal stab wound that zigzagged across the spine and threaded the rib cage before burrowing into a lung.

As I scraped a bit of tissue from the foramen magnum—the large opening at the base of the skull through which the spinal cord emerged—the scalpel slipped from my right hand; I made a fruitless grab for it, and the skull rolled from my left hand and thudded into the stainless steel sink, upside down. I stared down at it—the top of the cranium had nested into the drain, and the water pouring from the faucet was beginning to back up in the sink—and I could not think what to do. I stood transfixed by the rising water: Now it was filling the eye orbits; now the nasal cavity; now lapping at the teeth of the upper jaw. Miranda came and stood beside me; she laid one hand gently on my back; with the other, she leaned across the sink and shut off the water. "It's okay," she said gently. "You don't have to do this. Why don't you go home?"

"I don't want to go home," I said. "I know I won't like it there."

"Do you like it here?"

"Not really. But I don't hate it as much as I'll hate being home."

"Then stay," she said. "Just try not to break anything. How about you clean the rest of the long bones and let me do the skull?" Without waiting for an answer, she lifted the skull from the sink and took it to the other sink, where she had been working.

"I slept with her," I said, still staring into the now-empty sink. "With Jess. Last week, when I went down to Chattanooga to look at Craig Willis's body and go out to the crime scene. She invited me to her house that night, and we went to bed." I turned to look at Miranda and saw that she had reddened slightly. She bent over the skull and began scrubbing bits of tissue from its recesses with a toothbrush.

"Why are you telling me this?"

"I don't know. Because it was important to me. It was the best thing that had happened to me in a long time. It felt like the beginning of something. And now it's gone. She's gone."

She looked at me now, and her embarrassment had given way to compassion. "It's not your fault, you know."

"No I don't," I said, "and neither do you. You're trying to make me feel better, and I appreciate that, but I can't shake the thought that there might be some connection with me."

"Like what?"

"Like . . . I don't know. Maybe if she hadn't gotten involved with me, her ex-husband might not have flown into a murderous rage. Maybe if she hadn't been in my office that day when Craig Willis's mother showed up, that crazy woman would never have seen her and decided Jess was evil."

"Maybe if she hadn't gotten involved with you, Jess would have gone off her rocker and shot up a kindergarten. Maybe if she'd driven away from your office five minutes sooner that day, she'd have triggered a five-car pileup on I-75 that would have killed the medical researcher who's on the verge of curing cancer."

"What medical researcher? What are you talking about?"

"What I'm talking about is this," she said. "If you're going to play what-if—which, by the way, is a *huge* waste of time and energy, not to mention an act of supreme, center-of-the-universe narcissism—you have to play it both ways. If you're going to imagine yourself as an accidental villain, you have to give yourself equal time as an unwitting hero. As somebody who prevented God-knows-what dire disaster simply by doing exactly the things you did. And who knows," she added, "maybe the physicists are right; maybe there really *are* zillions of parallel universes. And maybe in those parallel universes, all the improbable scenarios we imagine really do happen, and all the wild conspiracy theories we imagine really are true."

She'd lost me by now, but at least she'd taken my mind off my misery for a minute. It was time enough to allow me a gulp of emotional oxygen, like a swimmer turning his head between strokes to bite a mouthful of air.

There was a rap at the door of the decomp and Garland Hamilton walked in, looking tense. He glanced at me, then eyed Miranda steadily. "Oh," she said. "I need to go . . . do . . . *something*." She laid the skull down on a tray lined with paper towels and hurried out.

"Tell me about it," I said. "Tell me about Jess."

"Are you sure?" I nodded. "She was killed by a gunshot to the head," he said. "Small caliber, probably a .22, maybe a .25. The ballistics guys will be able to tell. No exit wound—the bullet ricocheted around inside the cranium, so it chewed the brain up pretty bad. The good news, I guess, is that she died almost instantly once she was shot."

"Why do you say, 'once she was shot,' Garland? Is there some bad news besides the fact that somebody killed her?"

"It's possible she was raped," he said. "There were traces of semen in the vagina."

His comment hit me like a UT linebacker. Perhaps she had indeed been raped, but perhaps Hamilton had merely found residual traces of my own lovemaking with Jess from several nights earlier. I considered mentioning that possibility, but it seemed too personal—a violation not only of my privacy, but of Jess's, too.

"Anything else that might help? Fingernail scrapings? Hair or fibers?"

"Her nails looked clean, but I did collect a few hairs and fibers. Bill . . ." He hesitated. "I know you don't hold my work in the highest regard, but I gave this everything I had. I don't think any pathologist anywhere could have been more thorough than I was. The police have a bullet, a DNA sample, and hair and fibers to work with. I have a feeling they're going to find this guy pretty quick. As an ME, Jess was a friend and ally to cops. Jess was like family. They're going to work this hard."

"I hope you're right," I said.

"Count on it," he said.

It was 9 P.M. by the time I turned onto my street in Sequoyah Hills. It felt like 3 A.M. My heart and lungs felt filled with cement; my head hurt so badly I thought I might throw up; and every blink felt like burlap scraping across my eyes.

As I rounded the curve of the circle and my house came into view, I hit the brakes, hard, and my truck screeched to a halt on the asphalt. Four SUVs—one from each of the Knoxville television stations—were parked in front of the house. Several cameramen and reporters stood chatting in my yard. As I sat and pondered what to do, one of the cameramen swiveled his lens in my direction and everyone's head followed its lead. Soon all four video cameras were aimed at my truck, and I felt like an animal that knows it is being hunted.

Finally I forced down my fear and took my foot off the brake, idling toward my driveway. As I turned in, the cameramen took their cameras off the tripod and converged on my truck. The reporters followed a few feet behind, so as not to block the shot. I drew a deep breath, opened the door, and stepped out.

Even before I had both feet on the asphalt, one of

the reporters said, "Dr. Brockton, what can you tell us about the murder out at the Body Farm?"

"I'm afraid I can't talk about it," I said. "The police have asked me not to."

"Can you tell us who the victim was?"

"I'm sorry, I can't," I said. "They need to notify the next of kin before they release the identity."

"Did you know the victim?"

"I . . . I'm sorry, I can't say."

"Was it a man or a woman? Surely you can tell us that much?"

"No."

"How was he killed? How was she killed?" This time I just shook my head and headed along the curving brick walk toward my front door as cameramen scrambled to get ahead of me so they could capture my face.

As I put my key in the lock and opened the front door, the same reporter who'd asked the first question fired off a final one. "Do the police consider you a suspect, Dr. Brockton?"

That one stopped me in my tracks. Standing in my open doorway, I turned and faced the eight people and four lenses. "Good God," I said, "of course not." And with that, I stepped inside and closed the door.

CHAPTER 27

THE JUMBLE OF DRAB boxes that constituted KPD headquarters possessed just enough windows to highlight how blank and unbroken most of the walls were. The biggest expanse of glass was the entryway, which doubled as a corridor connecting the police department with the municipal traffic court. Outside, a mix of cops and traffic scofflaws smoked as equals.

I took a right inside the lobby and presented myself to the desk sergeant under glass. He nodded in recognition at my name, then buzzed someone to escort me upstairs. My escort proved to be a short detective with the build and the personality of a fireplug. Though I'd never seen a fireplug with a half-chewed toothpick dangling from what would be its face. If fireplugs had faces. Fireplug's name was Horace Bingham, a name I thought particularly unfortunate—particularly since he pronounced it "horse"—though I had the good manners not to call Horace's attention to the gracelessness of either his name or his enunciation.

Horace showed me into a cinder-block room outfitted with a table, three metal folding chairs, and a video camera high in one corner, then closed the door. Twenty minutes crept past.

The beep of my cellphone made me jump. It was Art.

"How are you? *Where* are you?"

"Funny you should ask. I'm in an interview room on the fourth floor of KPD, waiting for Detective Sergeant John Evers."

"Evers is working this?"

"Yeah. Maybe with the help of this fireplug-looking little guy."

"Oh, you mean Horse?"

"Yeah. Horse."

"Well, Evers is good. Best thing I can say about Horse is that he hangs back and lets Evers do most of the work. They got any leads that you know of?"

"They haven't said. I'm gonna suggest a couple." Just then the door opened and Evers walked in, accompanied by Horace. "Listen, they're here to talk to me. I gotta go."

"Hang in there. Call me later."

"Thanks, Art." As I folded the phone shut, I said, "Art Bohanan. He had good things to say about both of you."

Evers nodded and smiled briefly. "Sorry to keep you waiting, Dr. Brockton. We've been fielding a lot of media calls, as you might expect. Not much to say at this point; we try to limit what goes out, especially in the early stages of an investigation, but you still gotta give 'em a couple sound bites, or they get snippy."

"I hope you didn't release Dr. Carter's name? She's got an ex-husband that I know of; she might have other family, too, that ought to be notified first."

"We notified the ex-husband yesterday. He said he'd deliver the news personally to her mother. We had to release her name—we can't keep that under wraps once the next of kin have been notified. Beyond that, though, I just told them her death appeared to be a homicide, and that she was found at the Body Farm."

"Did you tell them I was the one who found her?"

"No. I just said one of the research staff had called 911 to report finding the body. They saw you walk out the gate, though; they all knew it was you. I told them half a dozen times, in half a dozen ways, that I couldn't comment on who made the report, or who the victim was, or how they'd been killed, or who might have committed the crime."

"Speaking of who might have committed it," I said, "can I mention a couple of names that have occurred to me?"

"Sure," he said. "But first, I need to start things off officially. We record every interview, both on that video camera up there"—he pointed behind him at the camera near the ceiling—"and on an audiocassette recorder." He pulled a small silver recorder out of his shirt pocket, pressed the RECORD button, and laid it on the table between us. "I'm also going to advise you of your rights."

"You're reading me my rights? Do you suspect me?"

"No, sir. And yes, sir. We do this with every single person we interview. I mean, at this stage, everybody's a suspect to some degree; our minds are completely open, and we're going to consider every possibility. And we'll read everybody their rights, just in case somebody unexpectedly blurts out a confession. If we haven't already advised them of their rights, we might not be able to use that confession in court. Does that make sense?"

"I suppose so. Still feels strange, though."

First he leaned down toward the tape recorder and said, "This is an interview with Dr. Bill Brockton regarding the death of Dr. Jessamine Carter." He added the date and the time the interview began, and then he read my rights off a laminated card he pulled from his wallet.

Evers asked me to recount yesterday morning's events again, in more detail, so I did. After he seemed satisfied with the amount of detail he had, he let me tell him about the threats Jess had received on her voice mail. "And when was this?"

I had to think about that. "Last Thursday," I said. "No, Wednesday. Same day as that protest at UT. She was on the news that night, and she called me Thursday morning to tell me she'd gotten the calls the night before."

"Did you actually hear these messages? Or did she just tell you about them?"

"She just told me about them. She called me from Chattanooga that night."

"How specifically did she describe them?"

"Not very. She said some were graphic sexual threats, and some were pretty sick death threats.

But she didn't give the particulars, and I didn't want to ask her to repeat them. Would you all still be able to get hold of those messages?"

"Maybe. If she didn't erase them. We can certainly check with the phone company to see if her voice mail was part of her telephone service. If not, we'll look for an answering machine at her house. Do you know whether she reported these threats to the phone company or the police?"

"I don't think so. I encouraged her to, but she didn't seem as worried by them as I was. She said she got crank calls and threats all the time." He nodded and made a note.

Next I related how Mrs. Willis had assaulted Jess in my office on Friday, after Jess had released her son's identity to the news media and had described his murder in a way that angered Mrs. Willis. "How brutal was this attack?" asked Evers.

"Not violent enough to cause any injuries," I said. "A few slaps is all, really, I guess. I pulled her off Jess pretty quickly. But if I hadn't, and if Jess hadn't called the campus police, I'm not sure what would have happened."

"And Mrs. Willis left voluntarily? Before or after the campus police arrived?"

"Before."

"So the campus police had no contact with this woman?"

"No," I said. "But they should have a recording of the phone call. Oh, and Peggy, my secretary, would probably remember her, because she gave her directions to my office. But Peggy didn't see the assault."

"In your opinion, did Mrs. Willis appear capable of murder?"

"That thought didn't occur to me at the time," I said. "But in hindsight, now that Jess has been murdered, I can't help thinking she did."

"Did she make specific threats?"

I replayed the woman's furious parting words. "I wouldn't call them specific, but I would call them threats. She said 'You'll be sorry' a couple of times, and 'I'm going to make you pay,' I think. Something like that."

"Did you think she was referring to violence, or to financial damages?"

"I didn't think about it at the time; I just wrote it off as angry words. Now, of course, I wonder if she meant physical violence."

Finally I told Evers about a third person who concerned me: Jess's ex-husband. I described the encounter at the restaurant, and how he seemed to be pleading with Jess; I told him how agitated she seemed afterward, and how she left moments later.

As he took notes about the restaurant encounter, Evers held up his left hand, a gesture he often used to signal me to slow down or stop. It seemed unnecessary, since two recording devices were capturing the interview verbatim, but perhaps he found it easier to refer to notes. He wrote a few more words, then he looked up at me. "This dinner you and Dr. Carter were having," he asked, "was that a business dinner?"

I felt myself flush. "Part business," I said, "part friendship. She was pretty shaken up when Mrs. Willis assaulted her in my office. I thought a good dinner at a quiet restaurant might help settle her down. Jess was a colleague, but she was also a friend."

"I notice you've referred to her several times as 'Jess' rather than as 'Dr. Carter.' How close a friend was she, Dr. Brockton?"

"Pretty close," I said. I hesitated, but decided he needed the whole picture. "And getting closer. At least, that's what I hoped. We had just started what I guess I'd call a romantic relationship."

"And how do you define a romantic relationship?" he asked. "Cards? Flowers? Daily phone calls?"

"We worked together," I said. "We liked each other. Lately, we'd gotten . . . much closer."

He kept his eyes on his notebook. "By 'closer,' do you mean sexually intimate?"

The question angered me. "What does that have to do with Jess's murder?"

Now he looked at me. "I don't know," he answered calmly. "What do you think it has to do with it? I'm just trying to piece together what was going on in her life just before she was killed. Sounds like you were one of the people closest to her. Sounds like you were a big part of what was going on in her life. Just before her death."

"Maybe; I don't know," I said. "She was a big part of what was going on in mine. I'm not sure I occupied as prominent a place in hers yet."

"Why do you say that?"

I told him what she'd said after she came back from talking to her ex; how maybe she wasn't finished with it—with him—after all.

"And did that bother you?"

"No. Yes. Some. She hadn't been divorced all that long—eight months, I think she said—so I guess it's not surprising that she might not've been completely over it. But until her ex-husband showed up at the restaurant that last night, she had seemed to be really opening up to me."

"That last night? Is that what you said—that last night?" I stared at him, confused that he was latching on to that. "Her body wasn't found—or wasn't reported—for three more days, Dr. Brockton," he said. "What made you refer to that as her last night?"

"I just mean it was the last night I saw her. Not the last night she was alive."

"Oh, I see," Evers said.

The interview ended shortly after that exchange, with a few questions about how soon I left the restaurant after Jess (about ten minutes, because the waitress was slow to bring the check); where I went afterward (straight home); and whether I tried to contact Jess that night or over the weekend (no, because she'd asked for some breathing room).

Evers thanked me for my cooperation and escorted me down to the lobby. We parted with mutual assurances to keep in touch and share any information that seemed meaningful. But as I crossed the asphalt to my truck, I felt shaken to my core, and not just because Jess had been murdered. I had spent a quarter of a century dealing with homicide detectives, and my experiences had been unequivocally positive: I liked giving them help; they liked getting it. Suddenly, for the first time, I had a glimmer of insight into what it might be like to be the subject of a detective's investigation, rather than a helpful advisor. I was relieved when I checked my rearview mirror and could no longer see the brick and concrete fortress that was KPD.

I took the long ramp that swooped downhill and fed me onto Neyland Drive. To my left, the river sparkled in the midday sun. That sparkle looked all wrong; the water should have been roiling, churning blackly, not rippling along as placidly as ever; as placidly as if Jess Carter's body were not, at this moment, on a gurney in the cooler at the Regional Forensic Center, the top of her skull sliced off, her chest slashed open, her heart and other organs bagged like offal at a butcher's shop. "Dammit," I said out loud. "Goddamnit to hell."

As I passed Thompson-Boling Arena and turned right onto Lake Loudoun Drive, I noticed blue lights behind me. I pulled to the curb to let the police car pass. Instead, it jerked to a stop behind me, and John Evers got out and approached my door. I rolled down my window. "What's the matter?" I said. "Has something else happened?"

"I need you to get out of the vehicle now," he said. "We're impounding this truck as evidence in a murder investigation, and I need you to come back to the station with me. I have more questions for you, Dr. Brockton. A whole lot more questions. And I need a whole lot better answers from you this time around."

CHAPTER 28

EVERS PUT ME IN the back of his car for the ride back to KPD. I didn't like how it felt back there. He waved off my efforts to find out why he had chased me down. "We'll talk once we're in the interrogation room with the tape rolling," was all he would say. I took it as a bad sign that he used the word "interrogation."

The interrogation room turned out to be the same room as the "interview room"; the only thing different was the atmosphere, which had turned distinctly hostile. Horace Bingham was already sitting in the same chair he'd occupied half an hour before; actually, for all I knew, he'd been sitting in it ever since I'd driven away. He was studying a yellow legal pad, and he did not look up as we entered.

Evers pointed wordlessly to the chair that faced the video camera, then laid the microcassette recorder on the table again. "Just as before, Dr. Brockton, we're going to record this," he said. He pressed the RECORD button and announced, "This is an interrogation of Dr. William Brockton, regarding the murder of Dr. Jessamine Carter." There was that word again, "interrogation." Evers gave the date and the time, then set the recorder down on the table in front of me.

"Dr. Brockton, let's go back to last Friday night at the restaurant," Evers said.

"Okay," I said. "I don't know what else I can tell you about it, but I'll try."

"Who was it who first saw her ex-husband sitting at a nearby table, Dr. Carter or you?"

"He was at the bar," I said, "not a table. She saw him. I had met him once, a few years ago, but I would never have recognized him."

"And she left you and went and sat with him."

"For a few minutes."

"Earlier you said it was at least ten minutes." He turned to Horace. "What were his exact words?"

Horace flipped through his legal pad, then read in a halting monotone, "Ten minutes. Maybe fifteen. Seemed like an eternity." Had I really said that? And had Horace written down every word I'd said?

Evers swiveled back to me. When he did, one of his knees grazed mine. He shifted slightly so our knees alternated, rather than bumping together. But in shifting, he also scooted closer to me. Uncomfortably close. "An eternity," he repeated. "That's a pretty long time, isn't it, Dr. Brockton? What did you think about during that eternity?"

"I don't know. I don't remember. I guess I wondered what he was doing there, and I wished he hadn't been. I worried about what this might do to

Jess, and to things between us. I worried about our food getting cold, too, I remember that." I tried to smile to break the tension between us, but he wasn't buying it, and that made the smile feel doubly false.

"Were there other people in the restaurant?"

"Sure. It was a Friday night. It was pretty full."

"Some of those people notice that your date had ditched you for a guy at the bar?"

"She didn't ditch me, and she wasn't my date, exactly."

"She wasn't? You were in a sexual relationship with this woman, and you took her out to dinner in a fancy restaurant. I'd call that a date. What do you Ph.D. types call that?"

"I wasn't thinking about it as a romantic evening. I was trying to cheer her up, make her feel better, after she got assaulted in my office."

Evers turned to the fireplug again. "You hear that? He wasn't thinking about it as a romantic evening. You just talked to that waitress, didn't you?" Horace nodded. "What was it she said about how he was acting? She said it looked kinda lovey-dovey, didn't she?"

Horace flipped back a ways in the legal pad. "She said, 'He kept touching her hand. He kissed her hand. I thought maybe it was an anniversary or something.' That's what she said." His stenographic skills were remarkable. Art had clearly underestimated Horace's contribution to the investigative duo's work.

Evers turned back to me again, scooting a little closer still. His knee was now nearly to my crotch, and he was leaning across the corner of the table toward me, looking me square in the eye. Without taking his eyes off mine, he swiveled his head slightly in the direction of his partner. "And did she say how the good doctor acted while his lady love was having the tête-à-tête with her ex-hubby, and how he acted after she came back?"

"She said, 'He seemed nervous at first, and then he looked more and more upset,'" Horace read. "'I asked if I could get him anything—a cup of coffee or a drink—and he almost bit my head off. When she finally came back to the table, it looked like maybe they were having a fight. Not a shouting fight—people don't do that in restaurants like the Bistro. One of those quiet fights where the couple just whispers but the woman still ends up crying. Except he was the one who looked like he was crying.' That's how she said he acted."

I felt myself getting angry. I tried to rein it in— Evers was clearly pushing me on purpose, trying to throw me off-balance, get me to say something he could use against me—and I wanted to be careful not to do that. "And what did she say about the ex-husband," I asked, "and how he acted when he saw her having dinner with another man?"

Evers smacked his palm down on the table, hard. It sounded almost like a gunshot, and it made me jump. It made the tape recorder jump, too. "I'm asking the questions here, Dr. Brockton, not you. But since you asked about him, I'll tell you something. We've already looked at Preston Carter. We always look first at the husband or the ex. And he's got something you don't have, Doc. You care to guess what that might be?" I shrugged and shook my head. I had an uneasy feeling what it might be, but I didn't want to say the word. "He's got an alibi," said Evers. "He is a deputy district attorney, and he has a damn good alibi."

He picked up the recorder and read the time off his watch, saying there would be a short break in the interview. Then he looked at Horace and cocked his head toward the door of the room. They walked out without a word. The door closed behind them gently, but even so, the sound of it clicking shut seemed almost deafening in the hard, empty room.

I pulled out my cellphone and hit SEND. My last call had been the one from Art, so the phone automatically dialed him. *Please answer*, I prayed, and he did. "Art, I'm scared," I said.

"What's wrong?"

"I'm not sure, but I've got a bad feeling." I told him how Evers chased me down and referred to my truck as evidence, and hauled me back in, and all but accused me of Jess's murder.

"You're right," he said. "Not good. I hate to say it, Bill, but I think maybe you better get a lawyer."

"Why? I didn't *do* anything. You think they think *I* killed Jess? You think they might be about to arrest *me*?"

"Probably not. Not yet, at least. But meanwhile, it looks like Evers has decided to put the screws to you."

"But dammit, Art, if I hire a lawyer, doesn't that just make me look guilty?"

"You already look guilty to him. And to a homicide cop, looking guilty and being guilty are virtually synonymous. Evers is looking for the best-fit explanation. And if he's decided you're it, he'll search like hell for other evidence that supports your guilt. He'll ignore things that suggest you're innocent, or he'll twist them around in ways that make even the innocent things look bad. Not because he's trying to shaft you personally. But because he's trying to piece together who committed a murder. And for whatever reason, you're starting to look like the key to the puzzle."

I knew Art was right. I'd spent years at crime scenes talking to cops like Evers, listening as they tried and discarded various theories. That experience enabled me to step back and look at this from his perspective, at least for one brief moment of clarity. "So I really do need to lawyer up?"

"You need to lawyer up."

"Who should I call?"

"David Eldredge is good," he said. "Smart. Respected. So is Herb Greene. Herb has cross-examined me three or four times in murder trials. Thorough. Kinda dull, though. A plodder. He's no Clarence Darrow. He ain't gonna win the hearts and minds of the jurors for you."

There was an uncomfortable thought buzzing around my mind. I tried swatting it away but it kept coming back. "There's another name occurs to me," I said, "though I shudder to think about it."

"Me too," he said, "but he's the first one I thought of. I just couldn't bring myself to say it."

We spat it out in unison: "Grease."

"Art, I swear, I would never have imagined I might stoop to hiring that guy. But then again, I never dreamed I might need to."

"I would never have imagined stooping to recommend him," he said. "Bottom line, though, is he's got the best win record, despite the worst clients."

"Yeah, but hiring Grease is like taking out a billboard ad along I-40," I said, "with my face and the words YES, I DID IT in ten-foot letters over Jess's corpse."

"Doesn't matter," he said. "If things get bad and you've hired a lawyer you respect, you might find yourself sleeping soundly in prison. If you've hired Grease, you've got a pretty good shot at tossing and turning in your own bed for the rest of your nights. Sure, everybody will assume you're guilty. Doesn't make it so, though. Suck it up and call the bastard."

"I'll think about it. Let me see how it goes once Evers comes back and starts asking questions again."

"Okay. Call me later. I don't know what I can do to help, but I'll try."

"You already have," I said. "Thanks."

"That's what friends are for. You want me to sing it?"

"I'd rather you didn't. Talk to you soon." I hated to hang up. Art's voice felt like a lifeline, and it was tough to let go. But I heard the doorknob rattling, and I knew I had no choice.

Evers and Bingham filed in and sat down, and Evers cranked up the recorder again. I felt his knee wedging itself between both of mine.

"Dr. Brockton, in your initial statement out at the scene, you told us you arrived at the Body Farm at approximately eight A.M. yesterday morning."

"Yes, that's right," I said.

"And you told us that again in our interview in this room about an hour ago, did you not?"

"I think so. I'm pretty confident it was around eight. Give or take a few minutes. Doesn't 911 automatically record the date and time of emergency calls?"

He ignored my question. "And before that, when were you last out there?"

"When was I last out at the Body Farm?"

"Yes, when? Think carefully."

I did. "Last Thursday afternoon. End of the day. A little after five. I was there to check on the condition of that research body. The one tied to the tree."

"You're saying you were last there one day before your dinner with Dr. Carter?"

"Yes, why?"

"And you're saying you were not out there at any time between Thursday night and Monday morning—yesterday morning—at approximately eight A.M."

"That's correct."

Evers smacked the table again. "You are *lying* to me, Dr. Brockton. And there is *nothing* I hate worse than being lied to."

"The hell I am!" I shot back in frustration. "What makes you think I'm lying?"

He swiveled and looked at Horace as if it were the most insulting thing anyone had ever said to him. "You hear that?" Horace nodded grimly. "You think I should tell him what makes me think he's lying?" Horace shrugged, then—as Evers continued to stare at him—nodded again. Evers turned back to me, his face so close to mine I could count the pores on his nose. "What makes me think you're lying, Doctor, is that I just watched a surveillance video that shows your truck—*your truck*, Doctor— driving through the gate of the Body Farm at five A.M. yesterday morning. Three hours before you called 911 to say you'd found her body."

"That's not possible," I said.

"Don't you *dare* fuck with me!" he shouted. Specks of spittle flew from his mouth onto my face. "It is on the goddamn tape! *Your truck*, Doctor."

I wiped my face. Evers's spit was mixed with a layer of sweat that had suddenly coated my fore-head.

"I was *not there*," I said. "I was at home, in my bed asleep, at five A.M."

"Can you prove that in a court of law?"

"Do I need to? Are you saying I'm a suspect?"

"Not *a* suspect, Doctor. *The* suspect."

"Should I get a lawyer?"

"Do you *need* a lawyer?"

"If you think I'm a killer, then I think I need a lawyer."

He suddenly leaned back, out of my face, and scooted his chair back, withdrawing his knee from between my legs. He drew a deep breath and blew it out between pursed lips. "Here's the thing, Doc," he said in a weary, regretful voice. "If you want to stop talking to me until you've got an attorney present, you have that right. Absolutely. No ques-tion about it. But if I shut off this tape recorder and stop this interrogation now, then from here on, I'm gonna come after you with both guns blazing.

Balls to the wall. If you'll tell me everything right now—tell me what went wrong, tell me how it escalated, tell me what made you do it—I might be able to help you. Might even be able to get you a deal for second-degree or manslaughter. Can't promise that, but I can recommend it. That's a onetime offer, though, and it ends the instant we stop talking."

I stared at him, and then at the impassive face of Horace, and then at Evers again. "You're asking me to confess to a murder I didn't commit?"

"I'm asking you to explain a murder you *did* commit."

"And this isn't what you'd call coming at me with guns blazing? Accusing me, spitting in my face, slamming things around, jamming your knee up my crotch?"

He smiled, in a sinister sort of way, and shook his head slowly. "Heavens no, Dr. Brockton. Not by a long shot. I have not yet begun to bear down on you. You think I've invaded your personal space? That was minimally invasive. I am fixin' to get maximally invasive. Wouldn't you agree, Horace?"

Horace considered it, then grinned nastily. "Y'all could share the same pair of grippers. If I was you, Doc, I'd try to clear things up right now. Tell us the truth. Don't make it harder on yourself."

I looked from one to the other and saw focused hostility and determination in both faces. I took a deep breath, then another. "Okay," I said, "I do want to clear things up. But this isn't an easy thing for me to say." Evers and Horace leaned forward; both detectives were practically in my lap now. "The truth is, I thought the world of Dr. Jess Carter. The truth is, I did not kill her. And the truth is—and this is the thing I have the hardest time saying to two police officers—I will not answer any more questions without an attorney present."

Evers slammed his hand on the table for the third time, but this time I did not flinch. Then he snatched up the recorder and said, "This interrogation was terminated when suspect exercised his right to counsel." He spat out the time and snapped off the machine with an angry click.

Evers stood up so abruptly his chair toppled backward, then spun and walked out of the room. Horace got to his feet more slowly.

"Are you finished with me?" I asked.

Horace snorted. "We have not even started with you," he said. "But you can go, for now. Have your attorney contact us at his earliest convenience." He said the last two words in a sarcastic sneer. He led me out of the room and to the elevator, and used his key to authorize the car to descend from the fourth floor down to the lobby. He pointed me to the front door. "We'll be seeing you, Doc," he said. "Real soon."

As I walked out the door into the parking lot, I realized I had no vehicle. It had been seized as evidence, and it would be combed for anything they could use against me.

CHAPTER 29

I COULD SEE BURT DeVriess's office gleaming on the far side of the valley from the hilltop where KPD hunkered. Lacking another way to get there, I set out on foot. DeVriess's office was near the top of Riverview Tower, a twenty-four-story ellipse sheathed in bands of green glass and silvery steel. Bands that were the colors of money.

The building soared above the river bluff at the south end of Gay Street, Knoxville's main drag. I crossed the valley to Gay Street on the Hill Avenue bridge, whose parabolic concrete arches spanned a messy knot of lanes and ramps where the Hill Avenue interchange tangled with James White Parkway and Neyland Drive.

Riverview Tower was one of a pair of side-by-side office towers built by the Butcher brothers, bankers Jake and C. H. Butcher, in the early 1980s, just before their financial empires collapsed in a rubble heap of criminal fraud. Longtime Knoxvillians still referred to the angular black-glass tower as "Jake's bank" and to the curving green and silver one as "C.H.'s place," but the buildings retained no connection to the disgraced bankers except as a fading stain on their architectural pedigrees.

I entered the lobby by way of the revolving door off Gay Street and rode the elevator up in the company of people in power suits and spring dresses. I was pretty sure I was the only one aboard who was about to be charged with murder, but then again, perhaps none of my fellow passengers imagined me as a fledgling felon, either.

The entrance to DeVriess's suite of offices spoke of money and sophistication befitting Knoxville's most successful defense attorney. Most high-end law offices were lined in an excess of walnut or mahogany veneer, but Burt's inclined more to chrome, frosted glass, and other touches of Art Deco. His receptionist, a correspondingly stylish woman somewhere in her thirties, looked up and greeted me with a smile. "Hello, may I help you?"

"Is . . . Mr. DeVriess in?"

"Do you have an appointment?" She took a quick glance at her computer screen.

"No, I'm afraid not."

"I'm sorry, we don't really take walk-ins," she said, looking genuinely regretful. "Would you like to make an appointment for a consultation, Mr. . . . ?"

"Brockton," I said. "Bill Brockton."

Her face brightened. "Oh, Dr. Brockton, of course," she said. "I knew your face looked familiar. I'm Chloe Matthews." She held out her hand and gave mine a firm shake. "Mr. DeVriess has a meeting with a client in just a few minutes, but I'm sure he'll want to say hello to you." She disappeared around a corner, and a moment later she reappeared with Burt DeVriess—my nemesis, on whose mercy I had come to throw myself.

"Hello, Doc," he said, giving me the simultaneous hearty-handshake-and-shoulder-pat combination that was supposed to underscore how very glad he was to see me. "What brings you clear up here?"

"Could I speak with you about . . . something?" I began awkwardly.

His eyes took on a startled expression, which he quickly masked. "Come with me," he said, turning and heading back down the hallway. As I followed, I made one final survey of my options, considering whether there might be some other way to protect myself. I came up dry again, and again I cursed the circumstances that had brought me to this.

Asking Burt DeVriess to represent me in a murder investigation might just be the hardest request of my life. Although I had testified for him on one occasion—when Garland Hamilton's botched autopsy had caused DeVriess's client to be wrongly accused of murder—my feelings for Grease could best be described as variations on a theme of loathing. DeVriess tended to defend the lowest of the low: child molesters like Craig Willis; notorious drug dealers; even one admitted serial killer. Cops and judges unanimously despised Grease. Yet his powers of pretrial maneuvering, courtroom confrontation, and media manipulation were so prodigious he nearly always succeeded in getting his clients off scot-free, or with remarkably lenient sentences. The serial killer's trial had ended in a hung jury, thanks largely to DeVriess's success in having the man's confession suppressed. As a result, the only thing keeping an admitted monster behind bars was a series of rape convictions.

It had run counter to every instinct I possessed to stop answering John Evers's questions—I'd spent years talking with homicide detectives, answering every question they asked as completely and candidly as possible. I told them everything I knew about crime scenes, bodies, bones, time since death, and manner of death. *Tell the truth, and let the chips fall where they may:* as a forensic scientist, I had always lived by that creed. It had served me well, and it had served the criminal justice system well. Now, I had forced myself to say to a homicide detective, "I refuse to answer any more questions without an attorney present." And now I had come to ask DeVriess to be that attorney.

Grease led me to an office walled in the same gleaming metal and frosted glass as the entryway and opened the door for me. Inside was a huge desk sculpted of similar materials. On its spotless glass top rested a sleek black phone, a sleek black laptop, a sleek black notebook, and a sleek black fountain pen. He ushered me in and closed the door, then motioned me toward a sleek chair of chrome and black leather.

We eyed each other warily, each knowing perhaps a bit too much about the other's business and sentiments. DeVriess spoke first. "What's on your mind?"

"I need an attorney," I said. "A criminal defense attorney." He waited. I thought I saw his eyes glitter. "The medical examiner from Chattanooga was killed sometime over the weekend. Her body was put at the Body Farm. The police seem to think I killed her." Still he waited. He wasn't making this easy for me. "I'd like to hire you to represent me."

He smiled at that. "Bill Brockton, you are the last person on earth I would have expected to find myself representing in a murder case."

"Well, I'm as surprised as you are," I said. "Astonished to be suspected of murder; amazed to be hiring you. But you have a remarkable track record. Good as you are at getting guilty clients off, you should have a pretty easy time representing an innocent man." As soon as the words were out of my mouth, I regretted them.

DeVriess looked away, then back at me. "Why, you smug, self-righteous son of a bitch," he said. "You have the nerve to look down on me, to *judge* me, while you come to me for help in a murder case? I ought to throw you out right now."

I felt a rush of shame, mixed with fear. "You're right," I said. "I apologize. That was rude."

"You're damn right it was rude," he said. "I do my best for every client I have. When I was admitted to the Tennessee bar, I promised to represent my clients to the best of my skill and abilities. Whether they're pure as virgins or guilty as sin, it's my job, my *duty*, within the American legal system, to fight like hell for my clients. You know why? Because the prosecution will fight like hell to convict them, whether they're guilty or not. You've seen that yourself—your DA friend Bob Roper tried to send Eddie Meacham to the chair for killing Billy Ray Ledbetter, even though that was an accidental death. If they decide they can convict you of this woman's murder, he'll try to do the same to you. After that Meacham case, you, of all people, ought to know better. Unless you're one of the twelve people in the jury box, or unless you're God the Father Almighty, you have no right to judge me or my clients."

Now it was my turn to be mad. I had apologized, and sincerely, but instead of accepting it, he had rubbed my nose in it and gotten up on his lawyerly high horse. "You know, that all sounds really noble, Grease. But I sat across from Susan Scott a few days ago as she howled like some dying animal. You remember Susan Scott, don't you? Mother of Joey Scott, little kid who was raped by your client Craig Willis? Joey Scott, who will spend years in therapy and still never completely recover? You're telling me I have no right to judge Craig Willis, a child molester caught in the act? You're saying I should feel a warm glow of civic pride that you cut him loose to prey on other kids? And you've got the nerve to call *me* smug and self-righteous?"

DeVriess's eyes flashed and his jaw muscles clenched and unclenched as if he were attacking a piece of gristle. For a moment I thought he might actually come across the desk at me. Finally he said, "Shit, Doc. Goddamnit." He looked away, and when he looked back at me, I could see pain in his eyes. "There's half a dozen cases keep me awake at night. That's number two on the list."

"Let me take a guess at number one," I said. "The case where the little girl was abducted, and then killed, while you delayed the search of the suspect's car?"

"Yes, damn you, that's number one. Are you satisfied?" He sighed wearily. "I like to believe that the good cases make up for the bad ones. Like clearing Meacham of a murder he didn't commit."

"Can't hurt," I said. "You just need some more like that."

"And is this a case like that?"

"Yes. I didn't kill Jess Carter."

"You know I'd defend you just as vigorously if you did."

"I know. I want to hire you in spite of that, not because of it."

"Defense lawyers have a saying, Doc: 'There is no client so dangerous as an innocent man.' Know why?"

"No; why?"

He thought a moment, then shrugged. "You know, it beats the hell out of me." He smiled ruefully. So did I. He picked up the phone and hit a button on the console. "Chloe, cancel the rest of my appointments for the afternoon," he said. "Yes, even him. And draw me up a letter of engagement with Dr. Brockton. Yes, the standard retainer, twenty thousand." I felt my sphincter muscles clench at the mention of the sum. "Thank you, Chloe." He set the handset back in its cradle. "Okay, tell me about it," he said, opening the leather notebook and uncapping the fountain pen. "Start at the beginning."

"Which beginning?"

"The beginning of the end. When things began to go wrong."

So I did. I started with the body Miranda and I had tied to a tree at the Body Farm for Jess, and I went on to tell about the creationist brouhaha, and Miss Georgia, and Craig Willis's raging mother, and Susan Scott's raging grief, and Jess's sweetness when she finally invited me all the way in, and her suspicious ex-husband, and her obscenely posed corpse. By the time I reached the end of the end—or at least the present moment—two hours had passed, the sky was dark, and I felt exhaustion and grief seeping into my bones.

CHAPTER 30

I TOOK A CAB from DeVriess's office to McGhee Tyson Airport and had the driver drop me at the doors to the baggage claim area. The Hertz counter was near, and there was no line, so I opted for that one. "I need to rent a car," I told the young woman behind the counter.

"Do you have a reservation?"

"No. Is that a problem?"

I thought I saw the corners of her mouth twitch. "Do we look swamped with business?"

I smiled. "This could be the first piece of good luck I've had all day," I said.

She entered my driver's license number and credit card into her computer, and five minutes later I was headed north on Alcoa Highway in a white Ford Taurus, which struck me as surely the most boring car to emerge from Detroit in decades. But my feet were still sore from my trek to DeVriess's office, so, boring or not, I appreciated the vehicle.

I passed the turnoff to UT Medical Center and

the Body Farm—a place that would forever be haunted by Jess's ghost for me now—and crossed the river, then took the Kingston Pike exit. The winding roads of Sequoyah Hills felt unfamiliar, probably because the Taurus handled differently from my truck. But maybe they felt unfamiliar also because the world had changed so completely in the past two days.

When the police impounded my truck, they impounded my garage door opener along with it, I realized, so I would have to leave the rental car in the driveway overnight unless I wanted to park, go inside, open the garage door, then drive it. The sequence of actions, which would have taken sixty seconds or less, loomed as overwhelming. The Taurus didn't strike me as a particularly tempting vehicle for car thieves, who could take their pick of Audis, Mercedes, Jaguars, and other high-end vehicles in other driveways in this part of town. As a security compromise, though, I paused on the front porch and clicked the keyless remote, and the vehicle locked with a diminutive beep.

As I stepped inside my front door, I heard and felt the distinctive crunch of broken glass underfoot. Switching on the light in the entryway, I saw glass littering the slate floor—dozens of shards and chips of it—and a rock sitting atop some of the pieces, a note attached to it with duct tape. I removed the note and unfolded it. "Now it's your turn to burn," it read. Below the words was a crayon drawing of a monkey engulfed in red and orange flames. I ripped the note in half, and was about to tear it into shreds when I realized that might be a terrible mistake.

I remembered the newscast the night of the creationist protest, and my surprise at seeing Jess interviewed at the scene. I also remembered the look of rage on the face of Jennings Bryan as he listened to Jess's sarcastic comments about his movement, his philosophy. And I recalled what she had said about the obscene and threatening phone calls she had gotten that evening. Had whoever made those threats actually followed through on them? And was I the next target?

I pulled out my wallet and fished out the card John Evers had given me, and dialed his number. He answered on the second ring. "Detective Evers? This is Dr. Brockton. Listen, I just got home, and I found something I thought you might ought to know about." I described the note, and how it had been delivered, and reminded him about the threats Jess had gotten.

"Okay," he said, "if you've got a ziplock bag, seal the rock and the note in the bag. Try not to handle them any more. Bring it in when you and your attorney come see us tomorrow."

I took a long, hot shower in hopes of unwinding. I leaned against the front wall of the bathtub enclosure, my head hung forward so the water beat down on my scalp and neck and shoulders. Fiber by fiber, the muscles let go, and I found myself slumping rather than leaning, then sliding down the tiles rather than slumping against them. The air had turned almost opaque with steam, almost solid, despite the exhaust fan I had switched on. When the effort to stand became too much, I switched off the water, wrapped my bright pink self in an oversize towel, and staggered into the bedroom. I fished a fresh pair of boxers from the top drawer of my dresser, sat heavily onto the bed, and laboriously threaded my feet through the waistband and leg openings. It took everything I had to stand back up and pull the shorts to my waist. As I bent to fold back the bedspread and top sheet, I could feel my eyelids drooping lower and lower.

And then I came wide awake, as heart-poundingly awake as I had ever been in my life. My white pillowcase was covered with blood. I stared at it, then yanked back the covers all the way to the foot of the bed. Both sheets were drenched in blood as well—mostly dried, but not entirely. And in the center of the bed was a pair of women's panties.

Even before the thought coalesced into words, I knew they were Jess Carter's panties. I also knew that I was about to be arrested for her murder.

I stumbled out to my living room and hit the REDIAL button on the phone there, which I had used to call Evers before my shower. "Evers," he answered.

"This is Dr. Brockton again," I said. My voice sounded distant and thready to me. "I think you need to send a forensic team out here to my house right now."

"I hate to burst your bubble, Doc, but I'm not sure there's any point," he said. "If we're really lucky, we might be able to lift a latent print from that rock or the note. But that's a long shot. Beyond that, I doubt there's anything for us to find."

"This isn't about the rock," I said. "Or the note. There's blood in my bed. A lot of blood. And a pair of women's panties."

There was a long silence on the other end. Then Evers said, "Where are you now? Are you still in the bedroom?" I told him I had come into the living room to call him. "You stay right where you are," he said. "Sit down and don't move."

"Okay, I won't," I said, and he hung up.

I needed to think, but I didn't feel capable of it on my own. *Call Art,* was all I could come up with. When he answered, I told him about the bloody sheets and the panties, and about the homicide detective and forensic team racing toward my house right now. He was silent.

Finally he said, "Somebody is setting you up big-time." He paused again. "Did you talk to DeVriess?"

"Yes. I just left his office an hour or two ago."

"Did he give you his cell number?"

"I think it's on the card he gave me."

"Call him. You should've called him first."

"My instincts just took over. The police were my first instinct. You were my second. Art, will they arrest me tonight?"

"Doubt it. Not tonight. You're going to be kinda hot for them to handle, being a forensic legend and all. They'll take this to the DA, and the DA will take it to the grand jury. But the Knox County grand jury meets three times a week, so they could take it to the grand jury tomorrow, and there could be a warrant for your arrest within a couple days. You were in a relationship with her; you were the one who found her body—at your locked research facility, no less; and now, there's blood and clothing at your house that suggest she was killed there."

"That's not all," I said miserably. "Evers claims to have a surveillance videotape that shows my truck entering the facility three hours before I found the body and called the police."

He was silent for an agonizingly long time. "This looks bad, Bill. The dumbest cop on the force could persuade a grand jury there's probable cause at this point. And Evers ain't the dumbest cop on the force. Hang up and call Grease right now."

I did. He cursed when I told him the police were on their way. "Dammit, Doc, I wish you'd called me first. We could have figured out a better way to handle this. Okay, they're going to ask for your consent to search your house. Do not consent. You probably need to allow them to enter and retrieve the sheets from your bedroom, but tell them that's all they're allowed to do without a warrant. They won't have any trouble getting a warrant, but at least it holds them off for a few hours. They're also gonna want to question you pretty hard. Tell them I'll meet you downtown at KPD. Do not—do not, not, *not*—answer any questions without me by your side. Promise me you will not."

"Okay. I promise."

"See you there." And then he hung up.

Moments later I heard the siren. It gave voice to something inside me—a rising wail of grief and rage and fear. The siren crescendoed as beacons of blue light began strobing through my windows, and then it died away. But the wail inside me did not.

CHAPTER 31

IT WAS 4 A.M., and I was so exhausted my entire body seemed to be humming like a high-voltage power line. DeVriess and I had been cooling our heels for two hours in the same KPD interview room where I'd already spent several hours earlier today. Only "today" had blurred into "yesterday." Or "tomorrow" had smeared into "today." It was as if I were trapped in a nightmare from which there was no waking. I imagined Rod Serling's metallic voice narrating how even the most respectable life could unravel in a heartbeat . . . *here* . . . in the Twilight Zone.

Finally the door banged open and Evers walked in carrying a file folder. He was still wearing the same outfit he'd worn eighteen hours ago—so was I, for that matter—but the starch had gone out of his shirt, and the man himself looked as rumpled and tired as his clothes did.

He went through the usual routine with the tape recorder, then said, "Tell me about the sheets.

Whose blood is that on the sheets? Whose panties are those?"

"I don't know," I said, "but my guess is, Jess Carter's."

"The blood, or the panties?"

"Both, I suspect. Again, I'm just guessing, but I'd say they're probably from the same person. And my guess is they're from Jess."

"You say you *guess* they're hers. Do you *know* they're hers?"

"No, I don't. But I do know that somebody killed Jess and put her body at my research facility, and I know that somebody put bloody sheets on my bed. Adding those two things together, I figure somebody's trying mighty hard to make me look guilty."

"Any idea why somebody might want to do that?"

"I've helped put a lot of people behind bars," I said. "Could be somebody just got out of prison and wants to get even with me. Jess has helped—Jess *had* helped—put a lot of people behind bars, too. Could be somebody wanted to kill Jess, and I just happen to be a convenient scapegoat. Maybe Mrs. Willis, who attacked Jess in my office. Maybe Jess's ex-husband. Maybe somebody from that creationist group—whoever threatened Jess last week and threw a rock through my window today."

"So what you're saying is, people are lining up to frame you for murder, is that right, Dr. Brockton? The whole world's out to get you?"

DeVriess spoke up. "Detective, you asked my client why somebody might want to make him look guilty. He has given you a reasonable answer to that question. If you're going to start browbeating him, we're out of here."

Evers sighed like a long-suffering saint. "All right, tell me the exact sequence of events when you arrived home this evening. Last night, rather." I did. "Where did you sleep the night before—the night after Dr. Carter's body was discovered?"

"At home. In my bed."

"On those sheets?"

"I don't know. The sheets I slept on two nights ago weren't bloody. I don't know if somebody replaced those with a bloody set sometime after that, or if somebody smeared blood on those same sheets after I slept on them." I thought of something. "That blood didn't look completely dry to me, Detective. Some of it was still bright red. If Dr. Carter was killed in my bed sometime Saturday or Sunday, the blood would have been dry and brown by Monday night."

"That's a good point, Detective," DeVriess chimed in.

"Not necessarily," said Evers. "That's a heavy bedspread. Thick enough to keep in the moisture for days. I've seen that happen before." Evers opened the file folder and pulled out a form I recognized as an autopsy report. I also recognized Garland Hamilton's handwriting on it. "Dr. Brockton, do you own a handgun?"

"No. I've never felt the need to have one. The director of the TBI tried to issue me one once, but I turned it down. When I'm working at a crime scene, I'm usually down on my hands and knees, my butt in the air and my nose to the ground. I wouldn't see somebody sneaking up on me in time to shoot them. Besides, I'm usually surrounded by armed police officers."

"What about for protection at home?"

"A lot of people end up getting shot with their own guns. Don't have one, never have, don't expect I ever will."

"So when we search your house—and we'll have that search warrant within the hour—you're saying there's no chance we'll find the gun that killed Dr. Carter."

A horrible thought occurred to me, and it must have occurred to DeVriess at the same moment. "Don't answer that," he said. "You don't know what else might have been planted in your home besides that blood."

"Are you saying we might find other incriminating evidence in your home?"

"Detective, my client can't speculate about what may or may not have been planted in the house in his absence. If we're down to hypothetical and rhetorical questions, I think maybe it's time for us all to go home and get some sleep."

"Fine, counselor," he said, "you can go on home. But Dr. Brockton? You can't. Your house is still secured as a probable crime scene. And we now have a signature on a search warrant."

"So where am I supposed to go?"

"Not my problem, Doc," he said. "Just don't go far."

I didn't. As DeVriess and I walked out the front door of KPD for the third time in less than twenty-four hours, I realized that not only did

I have no place to go, I had no way to get there. "Damn," I said. "They've stranded me again."

DeVriess shook his head. "Those bastards. You know they realize they're doing that. Just one more way to wear you down. You want me to take you to a hotel?" He pointed toward the bluff above the river, where the stepped-pyramid wedge of the Marriott reared against the skyline like some TVA hydro-electric dam that had missed its mark by a quarter mile. "Hell, let's get you a room there."

I shook my head. "I'm tired of being in other people's space," I said. "You're going to think I'm nuts, but would you be willing to drop me at my office over at the stadium? I've got an old sofa in there that I've spent the last twenty years breaking in. I can't think of anyplace I'd rather try to sleep right now than on that sofa, surrounded by my skel-etal collection."

He laughed. "You're right, Doc," he said. "I do think you're nuts. But come on, I'll drop you off."

There was no mistaking which of the handful of cars in the KPD parking lot was Burt's. Parked be-neath one of the sodium vapor lights was a gleaming black Bentley. It looked like what you'd get if you mated a Jaguar with a Rolls-Royce, and I suspected it was worth nearly as much as my house. The seats were upholstered in a butter-soft leather of silvery gray, and the dash was covered in what looked like burl oak, which I could tell, even in the dimness of the night, was not plastic. The door swung shut on what felt like jeweled bearings, and when the engine started, I could barely hear it, but what I heard sounded big and softly powerful. Burt pulled out of the lot and turned onto Hill Avenue, taking the same arched bridge I had crossed on foot a few hours before, on my way to hire him. Crossing the bridge in the Bentley, though, was like cruising in a luxury yacht.

I guided DeVriess through the labyrinthine route along the base of the stadium to the end-zone gate where a stairwell led to my office. Besides my pickup and UT maintenance trucks, few vehicles ever threaded this single lane of asphalt snaking among the girders and pilings; I was quite sure this was the first Bentley to do so, and probably the last. By the time the car stopped, I was half asleep in the leather.

"You want me to make sure you get in all right?" DeVriess asked.

I thanked him but refused. "I'll be fine," I said. It wasn't true—I was far from fine—but getting safely inside wasn't going to be the problem. It was being inside, and alone, that had me worried, and there wasn't a damn thing he could do to fix that.

As I unlocked my office and walked inside, I caught a fleeting glimpse out the window of expensive taillights disappearing into the labyrinth. And then it was dark, and I was alone. Pausing only long enough to step into my small bathroom and pee, then take off my shoes, I crawled onto the battered sofa beneath the bank of dirty windows. Even as I laid my head on the soiled armrest, I felt myself spiraling down into blackness.

CHAPTER 32

JESS WAS STRETCHED OUT *in my bed, lying on her back as we made love, her hands gripping the spindles of the cherry headboard. And then I looked in her eyes and saw that she was dead, and I got up and began refashioning the bed into a coffin for her. I fitted the wooden lid in place and began hammering the nails home. Tap, tap, tap. Tap, tap, tap.*

"Dr. Brockton? Are you in there?" *Tap, tap, tap.* "Dr. Brockton? Bill?"

I shook my head and rubbed the sleep from my eyes and the numbness from my face. Sunlight was casting short shadows from the girders of the stadium, which meant I must have slept until midday. Not surprising, maybe, considering the day and the night I'd just had, and the fact that I hadn't curled up on the sofa until nearly daybreak.

"Dr. Brockton?" As I hauled myself awake, I realized that I was hearing two different voices outside my door. One belonged to Peggy, my secretary; the other was less familiar, but finally I recognized it, and I knew this wasn't going to be good news.

"Yes, I'm here. Just a minute, please," I called out. I hurried into the small bathroom and rinsed my face with cold water, then straightened my mangled hair as best I could. Then I went and unlocked the door. "I'm sorry," I said. "I must have dozed off for a minute there."

"I tried your phone," said Peggy, "but I think you have it set on DO NOT DISTURB." She was right.

"Bill, we need to talk," said the woman with Peggy. It was Amanda Whiting, UT's general counsel.

"Come in, Amanda," I said, "have a seat. Thank you, Peggy." Peggy backed out, looking at me with concern and at Amanda with suspicion. "What's on your mind?"

"I know you've had a rough couple of days," she said, "and I hate to add to your troubles, but we have two major problems. As I feared, this creationist attorney, Jennings Bryan, has filed a civil suit seeking damages on behalf of his client. Your student Jason Lane."

"I am sorry," I said. "I wish I could hit REWIND and do that day's class over again. I hate it that I upset him so badly, and I hate it that UT is now bearing the burden and the expense of defending against a suit like that."

"That's . . . one of the issues we need to discuss," she said. "As you know, our policy is to defend academic freedom vigorously—when a professor is making a point relevant to the course material. In this case, it's been called to my attention that a tirade against creationism is not, in fact, pertinent to a class in forensic anthropology."

"Wait, wait," I said. "Are you telling me the university might not stand behind me in this?"

"I'm afraid I am," she said. "The trustees met in special session yesterday. They spoke with Mr. Bryan, and with the president of the faculty senate—who agrees, by the way, that you overstepped the bounds of academic freedom in this instance. In exchange for a letter from the board of trustees expressing a similar position, Mr. Bryan has agreed to drop the university from his suit."

"But he's not dropping the lawsuit altogether?"

"No. He now plans to sue you for actual and punitive damages."

"How much?"

"One million in actual damages. Three million in punitive."

"Four million dollars for embarrassing a kid in class?" She nodded grimly. "And the university's basically cutting me loose to fight this on my own?"

"I'm afraid so, Bill. I'm sorry to have to tell you this."

"Well. When it rains, it pours. Which reminds me, you said there were two big problems. What's the other big problem?"

"I can't imagine you'll be surprised to hear that it's the murder of Dr. Carter. I've been informed that you are considered a suspect in that murder. Bill, we're a school. Parents entrust their kids to our safekeeping. We have no choice but to suspend you until this is cleared up."

"Jesus, Amanda, whatever happened to the notion that a man is innocent until proven guilty?"

"Legally, that's the presumption," she said, "but we're a publicly funded educational institution, Bill, and the public holds us accountable to other, stricter standards." She glanced down at my desk, where I had photos of Jeff's boys. "Are those your grandkids?"

"Yes."

"If one of their teachers were a suspect in a child abuse case, wouldn't you want that teacher out of the classroom until the matter was resolved?"

If she had picked any other example, I could have argued with her. "Dammit, Amanda, you are taking away one of the last things I am clinging to for sanity right now." She looked regretful, but not regretful enough to change anything. "If you'll excuse me, I need to pack up some things," I said stiffly. "I'll be off campus within an hour. Thanks a lot, Amanda. It's been a swell twenty-five years." I turned my back on her and began to gather papers.

For months I'd been putting off a project whose deadline had come and gone: I'd promised a textbook publisher to revise and update my osteology handbook, which I'd written right after I began teaching, to help students identify bones in the field. But the combined demands of teaching, research, administrative duties, and forensic cases had made it impossible to set aside enough time to burrow into the revisions. Maybe now—barred from teaching, but not yet behind bars—I could finally get it done. I stuffed all the journal articles and research reports I'd accumulated as reference material into my briefcase, along with a triple-spaced version of the existing edition's text, then turned out the light in my office and closed the door. As I locked it behind me and headed down the stairs and out the east end of Stadium Hall to my parking space, I wondered if I would ever return.

My parking space was empty. Of course: my truck had been seized, and the Taurus I'd rented remained parked in my driveway, five miles away, thanks to my one-way trip downtown in a police car last night. "Dammit!" I shouted. "Is it too much to ask?"

A horn tooted behind me for a fraction of a second. I turned and saw Miranda leaning out the window of her Jetta. "Is *what* too much to ask?"

Relief swept over me. I nearly cried at the sight of her face, looking at me in the same open and friendly way it had for years. "Is it too much to ask for a ride home," I said, "and maybe a few kind words along the way?"

"Get in," she said, "you brilliant, handsome, kindhearted man."

Now I did cry.

CHAPTER 33

I PULLED THE RENTAL car into the driveway at Jeff's house, after checking my rearview mirror to make sure no one had followed me here. The double-width garage door was open, and inside, I saw both Jeff's Camry and Jenny's Honda minivan.

The front door was open, and through the glass storm door I saw Tyler and Walker in front of the television. I rapped on the door, then opened it and stuck my head inside. "Hey there," I called to the boys, "look who's here!"

Both boys turned in my direction. Walker was the first to scream, but a split second later Tyler joined him. Jenny came rushing out of the kitchen, an onion in one hand, a big knife in the other. When she took in the scene, the knife and the onion fell to the carpet. Jenny hurried over to the boys and knelt down, wrapping an arm around each. "It's okay, it's okay," she soothed. "Come in the kitchen with Mommy. Come on. Everything's okay. Nobody's going to hurt you."

A moment later Jeff emerged from the kitchen, looking embarrassed but angry. "God, Dad, I'm sorry," he said. "I wish you had called before you came."

Now it was my turn to be embarrassed. "I'm sorry," I said. "I didn't know that . . . that I needed to."

Jeff made a face. "Some of the kids at school . . . You know how mean kids can be. I guess some of the parents let their kids watch the news. We don't, but not everybody is as picky as we are about what their kids see. Anyhow. Obviously. They're . . . confused about you right now."

"Terrified of me, I'd say." He winced, but nodded in acknowledgment. "I guess this is not such a great place for me to take refuge from the media, then, is it?" He blanched, and looked nearly as terrified as the boys had. "I should be going, then." I turned and went out the front door.

He followed me out. "Dad, wait. Come on, don't just run away. What do you need? What can I do to help?"

I shook my head. "I don't know, Jeff. I don't know a whole hell of a lot right now. Everything I thought I knew—everything that seemed stable and reliable about my life—has imploded in the past few days. A woman I was starting to fall in love with has been killed, I'm on the verge of being charged with her murder, the university is suddenly treating me like a pariah, and my grandsons think I'm a villain out of some horror movie. I don't know what I need, or what anybody can do to help. It's like I've stumbled into the Twilight Zone, or some negative-polarity universe where every good thing I had and stood for has gotten twisted into its polar opposite."

"Tyler and Walker are little kids," he said. "They don't understand; they *can't* understand. But I can. And I'd like to help. Let's think about this for a minute. Do you need a lawyer?"

I shook my head. "I've already hired one."

"Who is it? Somebody good?"

I shrugged. "Yes and no. Burt DeVriess." He groaned. "I know, I know—he's the best of lawyers and the worst of lawyers. Believe me, I'm painfully aware what a Faustian bargain I'm making. But somebody has done a damn good job of making me look guilty. Now's not the time to be squeamish about Grease."

"Okay, I understand. You need a place to stay?"

"Yeah. I imagine KPD's forensics unit has moved into my house. And a small fleet of TV trucks has taken up residence in the street."

"Damn," he said, "I'm sorry. I know how painful this must be."

"Oh, I doubt it," I said. "Even I can't quite comprehend how awful this is."

He looked frustrated, and I saw him biting back something, and I felt bad for snapping at him in self-pity. "You're right, I don't," he said, "but I'd like to help. Let's figure out someplace quiet you could go, someplace off the grid." He thought for a moment. "You don't really need computer access or television, do you?"

"No," I said. "In fact, I'd prefer to be as far from TVs as possible."

"Here's an idea," he said. "What about a cabin up

at Norris Dam State Park? Remember that week you and Mom and I spent up there, back when I was about ten? Paddling a canoe around the lake, hiking the trails in the woods? That was great."

"It was," I agreed. "Cheapest vacation we ever took. Maybe the best, too."

"Jenny and I took the boys up there one weekend last fall. I don't think they've done a thing to those cabins since I was ten."

"Still lit by kerosene lanterns? Nothing but grills to cook on?" He smiled and nodded. "Sounds nice," I said. "But I probably need to be someplace with a phone. And I can't use my cellphone—I switched it off after the hundredth media call."

"That's easy," he said. "I've got an extra cell at the office; the seasonal tax accountants use it when they're working off-site at clients' locations. We can run by and get it, make sure there's a car charger for it. I'll go to the grocery store with you, if you want, help you load up a cooler with milk and cereal and sandwich fixings and stuff you can grill." He seemed to be building genuine enthusiasm for the idea, and I felt at least a bit of that energy flowing into me.

"I like it," I said. "Do me some good to get out of Knoxville and walk in the woods. Let's go."

He went inside to confer with Jenny. Five minutes later Jeff and I pulled our cars into the parking lot of his office, and in another ten we were cruising the aisles of Kroger, arguing the relative merits of hot dogs versus hamburgers, mesquite chicken versus honey ham, whole wheat bread versus seven-grain, and Honey Nut Cheerios versus plain.

A hundred fifty bucks after that, we loaded the trunk of the Taurus with a cooler laden with sandwich meat, milk, mayo, mustard, and pickles; bread and cereal; fruits and berries; and various members of the crunchy, salty food group. I thanked Jeff for the idea and the cellphone, and left the suburban McMansions of Farragut for the rustic cabins of Norris.

Jeff had called Norris Dam State Park on the way to the grocery store, and by great good fortune had snagged the only cabin available, which had just come open because of a last-minute cancellation. As I left Knoxville behind, I felt a bit of the weight drop from my heart. I found myself looking forward to a quiet week in a cabin where I could divide my time between revising my book and wandering trails beneath towering oaks.

Between Chattanooga and Knoxville, I-75 angled northeast; beyond Knoxville, though, it veered northwest, forsaking the Tennessee Valley for the Cumberland Plateau. And just at the edge of the plateau where the green waters of the Clinch River threaded deep wooded valleys, TVA had built the first of its network of hydroelectric dams in the 1930s, bringing electricity and industrial jobs to a region of rural subsistence farmers. Norris Dam State Park straddled the slopes on either side of the dam; the south side boasted modern chalets and a swimming pool; the north side, which I greatly preferred, had a rustic tearoom and primitive cabins. Mine, it turned out, was at the back of the loop road, right at the base of a trail leading up the hill into a huge, pristine watershed. I unloaded my groceries, brought in my bulging briefcase, and set off up the hill. By the time I returned two hours later, darkness was falling, my legs were spent, and I crawled into bed without eating a bite.

Next morning at six, I awakened to birdsong, and by seven I was immersed in my revisions. Papers sprawled across the entire top of a picnic table, anchored against the breeze by rocks that sparkled with quartz and glossy black streaks of coal.

DeVriess called at ten; I'd phoned him on the drive up the evening before and left the cellphone number on his voice mail. "I'm heading into court on a bank fraud case," he said, "so I only have a minute. But I wanted to pass along what I just heard by way of the grapevine. I was wrong about your friend Bob Roper, the DA."

"You mean when you said he'd prosecute me even if I were innocent, long as he thought he could win."

"Something like that. I underestimated Roper. He's recusing himself and his staff from your case—says it represents an irreconcilable conflict of interests and loyalties for the entire office."

"That's good news," I said. "Mighty decent of Bob."

"Maybe," said Grease. "Or maybe, next time he's up for reelection, he just doesn't want the voters of Knox County to remember him as the guy who nailed Dr. Brockton to the cross."

"Burt, you're too cynical."

"I defend the scum of the earth. Present company excepted, of course. Not a job for an optimist."

"Point taken. Practically speaking, what does this mean?"

"For starters," he said, "it means the Tennessee Conference of District Attorneys General has got to scout around and find some other DA to handle the case. Preferably somebody who hasn't worked with you."

"They might have to go to Middle Tennessee or even West Tennessee for that," I said. "I think I've testified for all the DAs here in East Tennessee."

"So depending on how long it takes to find somebody, we could be in limbo for a while. Weeks, maybe months."

"Ah. Then that's not such good news after all," I said. "I hate limbo. I'm suspended from my teaching job, I'm holed up in a state park, my grandkids think I'm a monster, and I keep waiting for the other shoe to drop."

"I'll press the court for a speedy trial, Bill, but I don't know that I have any influence."

"Well, do your best."

"Okay. I'll call you whenever there's news."

I forced myself to refocus on my revisions, and soon I was immersed again. I spent the rest of the morning combing through five years' worth of research papers on the pubic symphysis—the joint at the midline of the pelvis, where the left and right pubic bones meet—and updating my textbook's discussion of how features and changes in the bone at that junction could be used to estimate the age of a female skeleton with remarkable accuracy. After lunch, I switched to cranial fractures; one of the department's graduate students had just completed a fascinating thesis describing a series of experiments with skulls and a "drop tower" in the Engineering

Department: a platform attached to a vertical slide which allowed her to subject the skulls to measurable, precisely controlled impacts and compare the results. It was doubtful that a living person would ever be strapped to the drop tower and smashed to death—unless intradepartmental rivalries were far worse in engineering than in anthropology—but the data from the thesis could prove extremely useful in helping determine whether the force inflicted by, say, a baseball bat or a fall down a staircase was sufficient to cause a fatal fracture.

Absorbed in the science, I was blessedly oblivious for hours. Just as the light was fading and I was gathering up my papers for the night, the phone rang again. It was DeVriess once more. "There's good news and bad news," he said.

"What's the good news?"

"The good news is, you're out of limbo. They found a DA who can take the case. New guy down in Polk County. Doesn't know you from Adam. The Tennessee Highway Patrol actually picked him up in a chopper and set him down on the roof of the City County Building at noon today."

"I'm afraid to ask, but what's the bad news?"

"The bad news is, the other shoe has already dropped. The DA pro tem and Evers went to the grand jury this afternoon. I just got a courtesy call from Evers. Bill, the grand jury has issued a warrant for your arrest."

CHAPTER 34

IT WAS STILL EARLY April, but the midday sun hit me like a slap in the face from a mean streak of late August as I locked the front door of my house and pushed through the driveway's shimmer to the Taurus. Thirty-six hours after settling into a shady cabin at Norris Dam State Park, I'd been summoned back to Knoxville, back to the world of suits and ties and surveillance cameras and arrest warrants.

In the sweltering heat that engulfed me, the rental car's vanilla paint looked brilliant rather than boring. The American president might remain unconvinced about global warming, but I was a devout believer. Spring came earlier and earlier to East Tennessee, and fall hung on longer and longer before anything remotely approaching winter weather set in—for what seemed like only a few weeks—and then things began heating up again. By the time I got the car started and the air conditioner blasting, my T-shirt was glued to my skin, my dress shirt was beginning to stick to my T-shirt, and my suit coat was bunched and wrinkled.

Of course, global warming might not have been entirely to blame for the sweat. I was headed to Burt DeVriess's office, and from there, Burt was driving me to the Knox County Detention Center. I was turning myself in: surrendering voluntarily on charges of first-degree murder and—a charge I hadn't even thought to worry about—desecrating a corpse. Of course, if I got the death penalty for first-degree murder, there wasn't much way for the state to up the penalty for the second charge, so maybe it was just as well I hadn't sweated that one.

Burt had had to explain the proceedings to me three times before I retained all the details. Detective Evers and Michael Donner, the Polk County DA who'd agreed to fill in for Bob Roper, had spent a brisk twenty minutes summarizing the evidence against me for the grand jury. On the basis of the surveillance video, the bloody sheets, and hair and fibers linking me to Jess Carter's body, the grand jury had signed a "presentment," which prompted the Knox County Criminal Court clerk to issue a *capias* for me. "What's a *capias*?" I asked.

"Legalese for arrest warrant," he said. "You've heard the Latin phrase *carpe diem*, 'seize the day'? *Capias* is a noun form, but it means 'grab that sumbitch,' bottom line."

"But they're not coming after me with blue lights and handcuffs?"

"They will," he said, "if you make them. But I negotiated to drive you out to the booking facility

in my car so you can turn yourself in with some
semblance of dignity."

He had negotiated for more than that, as it turned
out. DeVriess didn't want me to have to walk in the
front door of the detention center, as he figured
there was a fair chance someone might leak the
news to the media. Instead, he worked out a deal
that would allow him to drive me into the booking
facility's "sally port," a lower-level entrance with a
big garage door, used by police cruisers and paddy
wagons transporting prisoners to court and back.
Normally only official vehicles were allowed in the
sally port, but Grease persuaded Evers to let him
drive me inside in his own car. Evers would meet
us there and accompany us into the sally port in his
unmarked Crown Vic, where I would be frisked,
then taken inside and fingerprinted and booked.
"Jesus," I said, "fingerprinted like a common criminal."

"Trust me, Doc," DeVriess had responded,
"you're being treated like a very uncommon criminal. This is what they call a high-profile booking,
which means you're getting the kid-glove treatment normally reserved for elected officials and
old-money millionaires." He'd paused. "Speaking
of money, Doc, we need to arrange for your bond."
My bail had been set at $500,000, a sum that had
made me gasp.

"Hell, I don't have that kind of money," I'd said.
"If I sold my house and my truck and what little
stock I own, I'm not sure I'd have it."

"It's okay. That's why God created bail bonds-
men." For the low, low price of $50,000—a sum

that would drain all my reserves and still tap my credit to its limits—a bail bondsman would post the required 10 percent of the bail. "The bondsman will need to put a lien on your property," DeVriess had added, "just in case you skip town and leave him on the hook for the other $450,000."

"I had no idea being a criminal was so damn expensive," I said. "You need to be rich to be a murderer."

"Not to be a murderer," he corrected. "Just to beat the rap."

When I reached DeVriess's office, his receptionist, Chloe, greeted me with a sunny smile, as if I were here to set up educational trust funds for my grandsons. "Hello, Dr. Brockton. Nice to see you again," she said. "I'll tell Mr. DeVriess you're here. Can I get you some coffee or tea, or a soft drink?"

"No, thank you," I said. "I have to sign some ruinous paperwork, but then I think we're gonna saddle up and move out."

Chloe smiled. "One for the road?" I shook my head, and she pressed an intercom button on her phone. "Mr. DeVriess? Dr. Brockton is here . . . I did, but he turned me down." She looked up at me and winked. "He seems itchy to saddle up and move out . . . All right, I'll bring him."

Chloe led me back to DeVriess's office. "Thanks, Chloe," he said, coming around the glass desk to shake my hand. Twenty grand bought a lot of courtesy, it seemed. "Bill, have a seat." I sat. "Let me go over the bonding agreement, and tell you what to expect out at the detention facility," he said. I found it hard to focus on the details of my financial destruction and impending arrest, but when he slid papers across the desk at me, I signed on the lines indicated by the cheerily colored tabs labeled SIGN HERE. After I had signed over all my assets, and perhaps my immortal soul, DeVriess said, "Okay, unless there's something I haven't covered, we should probably saddle up now." He smiled to make sure I noticed the echo of my words. I tried to smile back, to show him I appreciated the effort, but a grimace was as close as I could get. He dialed a number on his phone and said, "Detective? Burt DeVriess. We're heading out now. We'll see you out at the detention center."

We descended in silence to his car, which was parked directly beside the elevator. "I'll bet I'm the first Knox County prisoner ever delivered in a Bentley," I said as I opened the door. We left downtown on the James White Parkway, then bore east on I-40 to the 640 bypass, where we backtracked north and west a couple of miles. We got off 640 onto Washington Pike and angled northeast for maybe five miles. This corner of Knox County had been farm country for most of my twenty-five years in Knoxville, but I noticed that even here, condos and subdivisions were sprouting like fungus amid the weathered farmhouses.

DeVriess slowed and signaled a left, and we turned onto Maloneyville Road and threaded a small pocket of ranch houses. Then we came to an S-curve, and the road wound down into a wide valley. On the right, behind a fence of chain link and barbed wire, stood the old Knox County Penal Farm, a barracks of ancient concrete with a rusting tin roof and a square brick smokestack. Ahead—below and to our left—sprawled a new golf course and, just beyond it, a huge, multiwing complex. There were no guard towers, and there wasn't a perimeter of high razor wire, yet it was unmistakably a correctional facility. Confronted with the grim, tangible reality of it, I felt my stomach clench. "Jesus, I had no idea it was so big," I said. "How many prisoners are in there?"

"Right now? No idea," said DeVriess. "The capacity is 667. Any more than that, they're violating a federal cap. See that new cell block they're building right beside the golf course? That'll bring the maximum to nearly a thousand." He sounded sad as he said it. I glanced at him and he looked thoughtful, a word I had never associated with Burt DeVriess. "Did you know, Doc, that two million Americans are behind bars right now? Biggest prison population on earth." I did not know that. "We also have the highest incarceration rate of any nation. Six times higher than China, a place we like to believe is far more oppressive than we are."

"You sure about that statistic, Burt?"

"I study this stuff the way you study teeth and bones, Doc. The US of A is home to only five percent of the world's population, but one-quarter of the world's prisoners. Something's wrong with that."

He was right, though I didn't know precisely how. "Well, let's hope you can keep me from becoming prisoner number two million and one."

The main entrance was a large driveway to our left, marked by a seven-pointed star on a grassy embankment. The star was eight or ten feet across, labeled KNOX COUNTY SHERIFF. DeVriess continued past the driveway, past the main building, and turned behind a smaller building, a two-story barracks set inside a high fence. A basketball court was tucked into the angle formed by the L-shaped building. Just beyond this building, we bore left onto a one-lane driveway which circled back toward the central complex. The building's main entrance was actually at the front of the second floor; we were heading for a large garage door notched into the ground floor, almost like a basement garage. An unmarked Crown Victoria sat idling to one side. When DeVriess approached in the Bentley, the Crown Vic pulled up to a speaker and John Evers leaned out and spoke as if he were ordering fast food in a drive-through lane. With a thunk and a whir, the big garage door began rolling upward. Evers edged forward, into the dark opening, and DeVriess followed, practically on his bumper. When both cars were inside, the door whirred and clunked down again.

Three uniformed officers stepped from a curb to our right. One walked around to meet Detective Evers as he emerged from his car; the other two positioned themselves beside my door. Evers handed over a form—the *capias*, I guessed—to the officer I assumed was in charge, and then motioned to me to get out. As DeVriess and I opened our doors and got out of the Bentley, the two deputies stepped to either side of me, each grasping an arm. DeVriess started around the front of the car, saying, "Hey, *hey*, that is *not* called for. You take your hands off of my client." The two officers responded by tightening their grips.

Their supervisor hustled around and laid his palm on Burt's chest none too gently. "*You* listen up," he barked, "this is *our* facility. *Our* rules. We are extending every possible courtesy to Dr. Brockton, but he has been charged with murder, and we will not risk the safety of our officers. If he does not cooperate fully—if *you* do not cooperate fully—all deals are off, we put him in restraints and stripes, and we treat him exactly like every other prisoner. Is that clear?"

"Burt, it's okay," I said. "They're doing their job, and they're doing it right. This isn't a battle we need to fight." DeVriess looked unhappy, but he nodded and kept quiet, and the officers relaxed their grips a bit.

"Thank you, Dr. Brockton," said the officer in charge. "I'm Sergeant Andrews, by the way, the shift supervisor. We need you to step over here to this wall, please, so we can pat you down." The deputies steered me toward the spot he had indicated. "Please place your hands against this blue safety pad, shoulder height, far apart." I assumed the position I'd seen on television many times, and the deputies' four hands gave me a thorough going-over. One of them removed the small leather case clipped to my belt; he looked surprised and a little sad when he saw what was inside. It was my consultant's badge from the Tennessee Bureau of Investigation. I'd worn it partly as a gesture of vain pride, partly as a not-so-subtle message to the people booking me, and partly as a desperate effort to hang on to my sense of who I was and what I stood for in this world.

Once they were sure I wasn't carrying any concealed weapons, Andrews told me to empty my pockets, remove my watch and belt, and take off my dress shirt, leaving me in my T-shirt. On a clear plastic bag labeled INMATE PROPERTY BAG, he wrote my name, date of birth, Social Security number, and the date and time. Then he listed every item, including my TBI badge, and sealed them in the bag with a self-adhesive strip along the bag's top flap. Then he had me sign the bag to indicate that the inventory was right. Down below, I noticed another line where I would sign—presumably within an hour—when they gave me back my property and released me. In this part of the machine, at least, the wheels of justice appeared to be well-oiled cogs.

I heard Andrews telling Evers and DeVriess to pull forward when the garage door ahead of Evers's car was raised. But before that happened, I was escorted from the sally port and into the building's interior through a glass door labeled INTAKE.

The room was large, clean, and brightly lit by fluorescents. It was also equipped with at least three video cameras that I could see. I'd already noticed several on the roof of the facility as we approached— they swiveled, tracking our trajectory—another camera outside the sally port, and a couple inside the port. "Y'all sure have a lot of cameras," I said to my escorts. "Must be quite a command post if you've got a monitor for every camera."

The deputies glanced at each other in surprise. Most prisoners didn't engage in such conversation, I gathered. "Yes, sir," said one, "it's a pretty advanced system. Made by a company called Black Creek. We've got over two hundred cameras, so there's no way to have separate monitors." He pointed at the three cameras suspended from the ceiling of the main intake room. "Central Command has a touch-screen computer system that shows the position of every camera on every floor. All you do is touch the icon for the camera you want, and the video feed from that camera pops up on the screen."

I nodded. "Sounds smart. You archive the images on videotape, or on a big hard drive?"

"A monster hard drive," he said. "We brought this system online a month ago. We've saved every image from every camera since, and we've only used a fraction of the storage capacity so far."

"Well," I said, "if I'd known I would be on so many cameras and archived for posterity, I'd have gotten a haircut this morning."

He laughed, but suddenly he seemed embarrassed, as if by joking about my arrest, I had reminded him why I had been arrested. "We need to go in here and take your picture and get your fingerprints," he said, pointing to a small room off one corner of the intake area.

Two technicians occupied the room. One instructed me to stand with my back to one wall—"Put your back against the X," he said, "and look at that X on the opposite wall." That X was fastened to the top of a camera which snapped a photo that soon appeared on a computer screen.

"I don't have to hold a sign with an inmate number on it?"

"No, sir," he said in a tone that implied I'd asked the dumbest question he'd heard in a long while. "Computer puts that in automatically now. Okay, now turn and face the X on that wall," he said, pointing to my right. "And now turn and face the X on this wall." And so, in a matter of seconds, I had mug shots on file.

The other technician belonged to the guild of fingerprinters. It was a guild that had gone high-tech. The sheriff's intake facility had two comput-erized fingerprint scanners, labeled CROSS MATCH. The fingerprint technician had me lay the four fin-gers of my left hand on the scanner's glass—a print he called a "four-finger slap," then the four fingers of my right hand, then each thumb. Then he rolled each of my ten digits across the glass, some more than once, when the Cross Match computer in-formed him the print was unacceptable because of a "vertical gap." After he'd printed all my fingers, he removed a black cover from a clear plastic cone lo-cated to the left of the flat glass plate. Through the plastic, under the wide base of the cone, I saw wires leading to a small black rectangle that was emitting green light. "What's that?" I asked.

"Palm scanner." He had me wrap my palms around the cone, one hand at a time, the tip of the cone rising up between my thumb and forefinger. Beneath the cone, the scanning head—the rec-tangular box—rotated around a central axis as the green light brightened, illuminating the ridges of my palms. I thought I was finished then, but next he had me lay the edge of each hand on the cone—my "writer blades," he called them.

"That's very thorough," I said. "Now you send these off to the TBI and the FBI to see if I'm already in their criminal database?" He nodded. "My friend Art Bohanan says he can get an answer in an hour or less. Is that right?"

"Oh, often in ten minutes or less," he said, "at least from the TBI."

"The wonders of modern technology," I said. "We done now?"

He looked a little sheepish. "No, sir, not quite. We also have to do what's called a 'major crimes package' on you, Doc."

"What does that mean?"

"That means we have to break out Old Betsy here," he said, pointing at a large and dusty wooden box that was shoved underneath the counter where the mug-shot computer sat.

"What's Old Betsy? You fixing to shoot me?"

"Naw. Old Betsy is an old-fashioned ink-on-deck fingerprint kit. Besides the scans, we have to take ink impressions—slaps, rolls, tips, palms, writer blades, and wrists."

"How come? You've already scanned most of those. Anyhow, I thought the fingerprints were what really mattered."

"Funny thing," he said. "A lot of criminals are really careful about not leaving prints from their fingertips. But they don't think anything about the edge of their hand, or their wrist. These ink impressions will be sealed in an envelope and hand-delivered to the lead investigator. They'll give the investigators and forensic techs more to look for at a major crime scene."

"Good thinking," I said. "I just wish they knew where the crime scene was. Where Dr. Carter was murdered." Suddenly he, too, looked uncomfortable. I seemed to be having that effect on people a lot these days. He didn't say much as he took the prints in ink, and when he'd finished and handed me some moistened towelettes to clean my hands and wrists, he seemed relieved to turn me over to my next handler, a pleasant female clerk who asked a series of routine questions—my name, address, age, date of birth, Social Security number, some basic medical information, and the like—and typed in my answers in a clatter of keystrokes. She also transferred some information from the arrest warrant Detective Evers had handed over upon our arrival.

As she typed, I noticed a fairly steady stream of uniformed personnel passing through the intake area, in ones and twos, with no apparent purpose. Finally it dawned on me that they were sightseeing, and that I was the sight they had come to see. The thought made me flush with a mix of humiliation and anger, but I did my best to act nonchalant. Eventually I started nodding and saying hello, and that seemed to even the scales: the sightseers, caught gawking, now looked as ashamed as I felt.

After the intake clerk had finished her flurry of typing—producing more keystrokes, in less time, with fewer visible results, than anyone except maybe an airline ticketing agent—she looked up and smiled at me. "Okay, I think we've got it. I believe Sergeant Anderson will be here for you shortly. Would you mind having a seat in this room over here?" She indicated a small side room separate from the larger intake room. I pointed at the main room, where three prisoners in stripes lay sprawled on stainless steel benches.

"You don't want me where those other guys are?"

"No, sir," she said. "They told us you're a 'high-profile.' That means you're segregated from the other prisoners." She gave me another smile, and it seemed genuine. Even here, in the seamy underbelly of society, there was a class system, and DeVriess had negotiated me into the upper crust.

"Well, thank you for your kindness," I said. "It's good to know I'm a VIP among murder suspects. Just so you know, I really didn't kill Dr. Carter."

Now she, too, turned crimson and ducked her head. *Damn*, I thought, *me and my big mouth again*.

I slunk to the bench and sat down. Within five minutes Sergeant Anderson appeared. "Dr. Brockton, your bond has been posted and we're going to be releasing you from custody now. If you'll follow me, we'll step across the hall and get you going."

An automated glass door at one side of the intake area slid open, leading to an elevator and a staircase. Beyond those, another door slid open before us, admitting us into an area labeled RELEASE. Release was virtually a mirror image of Intake except for the lack of the mug-shot and fingerprint stations. Another clerk at a computer desk—also a pleasant blond woman—handed over my possessions, along with a Sharpie marker. I used the Sharpie to sign the line at the bottom of the bag, indicating that all my property had been returned to me. It took some strength to pull open the top of the bag, and when I did, I noticed that a series of thin red stripes along the top got ripped to hell. Even our jails had adopted tamper-evident packaging. That was a good thing, I supposed; it could be the reason my TBI badge wasn't going to show up on eBay during my murder trial.

I put on my shirt, watch, and badge, and Andrews led me out a glass door and into the sally port. The door, likewise labeled RELEASE, mirrored the Intake door some fifteen feet away. Anderson raised his radio to his mouth. "We need one-sixty-two," he said, and I heard an electronic lock click open in a steel door set into the wall beside the garage door. He ushered me out, blinking, into the brilliant Tennessee sunshine, where DeVriess sat idling in his car. On the embankment above, at the edge of the facility's parking lot, I saw a thicket of television cameras, and I guessed that one of the sightseeing deputies inside had tipped off a cousin or girlfriend who worked at one of the stations. I got in with as much speed and dignity as I could combine, and Burt backed down to a spot where he could turn around. Then we retraced our route along Maloneyville Road, Washington Pike, and the expressways until we pulled into the garage beneath Riverview Tower once more. Burt dropped me at my rental car. As I opened the door of the Bentley, he reached over and took my arm to keep me there a moment longer. "Those reporters will probably show up at your house in a few minutes," he said. "You might want to go back to the cabin for another night or two."

"Damn. You're probably right."

On the drive back to Norris, I mentally replayed

the experience of being booked for murder. Aside from the extra set of prints for the "major crimes package," nothing about the process seemed to have any relation to the terrible outrage inflicted on Jess. I might just as well have been getting booked for shoplifting. For that matter, it wasn't that different from the paperwork for a minor surgical procedure at an outpatient clinic; a proctoscopy sprang immediately to mind. The criminal justice system—like my own forensic work—contained relatively few moments of high drama, I realized, widely spaced by long intervals of boredom and drudgery.

During my hour and ten minutes as an inmate—I had been promised I'd be out in an hour, but I figured I'd asked at least fifteen minutes of questions along the way—I had moved along a carefully orchestrated assembly line, like a car chassis moving through the factory. I had traced a big U, with one side of the U corresponding to Intake and the other side to Release, with a short hallway connecting the two at the base. Some of the procedures seemed silly, such as surrendering and inventorying my personal effects only to reclaim them a mere seventy minutes later. But there was an elegant symmetry to the process, too, a satisfying sense of ceremony or ritual.

I'd gone in one side, stripped of almost everything I had, and had come out the other, where everything was restored to me. I wondered if there was any hope of that same symmetry holding true in the rest of my life. I couldn't see it yet. I hoped that was merely because I was still locked on the "Intake" side of the nightmare.

CHAPTER 35

TWENTY-FOUR HOURS AFTER I'D gotten dressed up for my arrest, I put on the same outfit once more and climbed into the Taurus. I felt odd and conspicuous—ashamed, almost—to drive through the rustic cabins and campground wearing a coat and tie, especially two days in a row. The fancy getup seemed as inappropriate here in the woods as shorts and a T-shirt would have seemed at a symphony concert. But once I got to the funeral, I would blend right in.

I had not known Jess was religious; for that matter, I still didn't, but the location of her memorial service—St. Paul's Episcopal Church—suggested that either Jess or whoever arranged her funeral was. How strange, I reflected as I approached the outskirts of Chattanooga yet again, to know someone's flesh as intimately as I had recently come to know Jess's, yet to know nearly nothing about their spirit, or at least their beliefs. *So many things I'll never get the chance to learn about her*, I thought, and the realization sent me spinning down another dark spiral of grief.

St. Paul's was located in downtown Chattanooga, three blocks from the convention center and practically alongside U.S. 27, the elevated expressway that skirted the western edge of the business district before crossing the Tennessee River and angling northeast up the valley of the Tennessee River. I took the second downtown exit, which fed me north onto Pine Street; I was early, so I was able to park at a meter directly across the street from the church's main entrance.

St. Paul's was set above street level, and the entrance was beside a tall bell tower of red brick, rising from a gray limestone base. Episcopalians, I'd observed, tended to have a flair for architecture, along with the money to indulge it. As I crossed the street to the front steps, I noticed several police cars at the curb. Technically, Jess wasn't part of the police department, but she was part of the extended family of law enforcement, and the code of honor extended to her: You turn out to honor your fallen comrades. The unwritten, darker corollary, I'd noticed over the years, was that the more shocking the death, the bigger the turnout, as if a show of posthumous solidarity might somehow make up for the tragedy that had struck down one of their own—or prevent the next one.

As I topped two flights of steps and reached a brick plaza just below the double wooden doors into the nave, I noticed two uniformed officers flanking the entrance. I thought perhaps they were giving out programs, but their hands were empty, so I decided they were simply some sort of honor guard. One of the officers looked my way; I made eye contact with him and nodded somberly. He stepped forward to meet me. "Dr. Brockton?"

"Yes, hello there," I said, holding out my hand and reading the name MICHAEL QUARLES on a brass bar on his chest. "Have we worked together before, Officer Quarles?"

"No, sir," he said, "we haven't met. Dr. Brockton, I'm sorry, but you're not allowed here."

"Excuse me?"

"You're not allowed to be here."

"What do you mean?"

"Just what I said, sir. You're not allowed to enter the church; in fact, you're not allowed anywhere on the church property, so I'll have to ask you to go back down these steps."

"This is Dr. Carter's memorial service, isn't it?" He nodded once. "She was a colleague and a friend of mine," I said.

"Maybe so," he said, "but there's a restraining order, signed by Judge Avery, that bars you from entering this church or setting foot on this property today. So I'm asking you—no, sir, I'm telling you—to leave the property now."

I stared at him, dumbfounded. "Who requested this restraining order?"

"Assistant District Attorney Preston Carter." Jess's ex-husband.

"This is not right," I protested. "He has no grounds for this."

"Way I hear it, you've been charged with her murder," he said. "I'd call that pretty solid ground.

In any case, we're here to enforce a restraining order that bars you from this property. I'll give you to the count of three to comply; if you do not, I will take you into custody, sir."

"Who can I talk to about this?"

"One."

"I need to be in there."

"Two."

"*Please*. I am begging you."

"Three." He stepped forward and took my arm. I shook off his grip; without taking his eyes from mine, he reached to the back of his belt, where I knew police carried their handcuffs. Holding up both hands, I began backing down the stairs. He allowed me to retreat. A small group of onlookers who had gathered at the foot of the steps parted to let me pass. Some of them glanced at me furtively; others stared openly.

I noticed Jess's receptionist at the edge of the group, her eyes rimmed in red. "Amy," I said, "*please* see if you can get me in there." She ducked her head and hurried up the stairs, and the rest of the small crowd followed suit.

The two policemen were still watching me. I looked from one unyielding face to the other, then finally shook my head and walked across the street to the Taurus. As I pulled away from the curb onto Pine Street, I rolled down my window and stopped to give the officers a long last look, which they returned without expression. Then I took my foot off the brake and eased north on Pine, toward the STOP sign at Sixth Street. As I turned right onto Sixth, I took a final look back at the church and I thought

I saw Officer Quarles speaking into the radio mike that was clipped to his shoulder.

Two blocks east, Sixth intersected Broad Street, the main boulevard through the heart of downtown. A right on Broad, followed by another right onto Martin Luther King Boulevard, would take me back to highway 27, and from there to I-75 North, and to Knoxville. But I did not turn right; instead I turned left onto Broad Street, away from my route home. I parked at the first meter I came to, fed in five quarters I fished from the change tray, and started walking toward St. Paul's. Then I turned back to the car; I took off my suit coat and my tie and put a UT cap on my head. My clothes—black pants, a blue shirt and tie, and black wingtips— looked too dressy for the cap, but I hoped I could pass for a tourist or casual passerby if a policeman didn't look too closely.

Where Sixth met Pine, I looked left toward the front of the church. I didn't see any police on the sidewalk, but just to be on the safe side, I continued down Sixth, past a high-rise nursing home named St. Barnabas, then doubled back through an alley that ran between the nursing home and the back of the church. An iron gate behind the church opened onto a small playground; to one side of the playground, a door led into what looked like a wing of classrooms. I tried the gate and found it locked. Looking around, I saw no one, and I gripped the uprights and prepared to scale it. Then I thought of all those windows in St. Barnabas, and all those rooms filled with elderly people whose chief entertainment might consist of staring outside in search of something interesting. I hurried up the alley to Pine, and turned onto the sidewalk bordering the church.

Ten yards down, I came to a side entrance to the classroom wing. A pair of wooden doors, up half a dozen stairs, was set into a deep archway sheltered from the view of anyone near the main entrance. I trotted up the stairs and studied the doors. They were an old-fashioned kind that met in the middle, with no pillar between them. The lock was in the right-hand door; my hope was that the church custodian had forgotten to engage the vertical bolt that anchored the left-hand door to the floor. If that was the case, a good tug might be enough to swing both doors outward and apart, even if the crash bar was locked. As it turned out, I got even luckier than that. I smelled the aroma of fresh varnish on the wood, and I noticed that a small wedge had been placed between the doors to keep one slightly ajar so the wet varnish wouldn't glue them together. I opened the wedged door just enough to slip between the varnished edges, then pulled it quickly shut behind me.

My educated guess, my educator's guess, had been right—I was in a wing of classrooms which I hoped would connect with the nave. I set off down the hallway to find that connection. The hall smelled of musty wax and dirty paper wrappers, the unmistakable scent of crayons that had been gripped by countless little hands. A large puppet theater was tucked into an alcove in the hall, beside a poster of Noah's ark, jammed with animals. The door of the first classroom featured a poster of Jesus, with the caption "Let the little children come unto me." Inside the room were miniature wooden chairs and tables, as well as something that resembled a wooden rowboat on rockers. With a jolt, I suddenly remembered one exactly like it from my own childhood, and the tune "Row, Row, Row Your Boat" popped into my head from fifty years before, sung in the voice of Miss Eloise, my sweet-tempered kindergarten teacher.

After three children's rooms, the last equipped with playpens, cribs, and several cushioned rocking chairs, the hallway intersected with another hall and a stairway. Even before I could hear it, I felt the deep thrumming of a pipe organ down the passage to the left, its bass notes resonating in my core. I passed through a thick doorway arch, which led into an older part of the building; there, a curving passage hugged what I guessed must be the apse of the nave, the semicircular area behind the altar. I turned left into the curve, and within twenty feet I found an arched wooden door helpfully labeled NAVE. It was slightly ajar, and I put an eyeball up to the crack and eased it open another few inches. What I saw made me jump back from the doorway, as if a snake were coiled inside at eye level. Not ten feet away stood the high altar, and to one side, facing me, was the organist. Another ten feet beyond him, farther to my left, was the first row of people, their pew marked with a white bow. I recognized the face of Jess's ex-husband; on the same pew with him, but several feet away, sat a woman who looked like a seventy-year-old version of Jess. It was her mother, I realized, and it saddened me to think of a mother burying her child. Behind them, blue-suited police officers sat shoulder to shoulder, three pews deep. Behind them, I noticed with a start, was an elegant black woman; her face was half hidden by the broad brim of a hat, but I suspected the face belonged to Miss Georgia Youngblood. Her choice of seat—immediately behind dozens of muscled policemen—virtually confirmed my hunch. I eased the door shut. This vantage point would give me an unmatched view of the service, but it would also leave me dangerously exposed.

As my mind and my pulse raced to the accompaniment of the pipe organ, the music gave me an idea. I'd toured a number of Gothic cathedrals in England and France, and most of them had a balcony or mezzanine ringing the entire nave. I wondered if there might be one in this church, since it was neo-Gothic, and I decided to risk another look. I eased open the door again, less than an inch this time, and was rewarded with a glimpse of dark archways twenty feet up. A set of silvery gray organ pipes filled some of the arches, but most of them looked empty, and they appeared to ring the entire apse. I hurried back to the hallway crossing and staircase, and climbed four flights to the upper level. Again turning left, I found another old-fashioned wooden door. This one wasn't labeled, but it was directly above the other one, and when I laid my hand on it, I felt the wood quivering in time to the organ's bass notes. At the top of the door—out of the reach of the Sunday school students—was a small latch, the kind found on screen doors throughout Tennessee.

Unhooking the latch, I pushed open the door

and found a dark, narrow passage, eight or ten feet long, leading to the arches I'd seen from below. To my left, as I felt my way toward the nearest arch, I could hear one set of pipes; looking across the apse through the narrow arch ahead of me, I saw the other set. In addition to the rumbling bass notes and high trills and all the intervening octaves, I could hear the rush of air through pipes, and the clicking of valves deep within the organ's mechanism. The arch gave me a bird's-eye view of the altar and the soaring marble structure that topped it, like a twenty-foot-high dollhouse.

A white-robed priest stepped slowly into view, carrying a brass urn about a foot high. He set the urn on a wooden stand in front of the altar, and I realized with a shock that the urn must contain Jess's "cremains," the hokey contraction funeral directors had coined for "cremated remains." From my research, I knew that her cremains—ground-up bits of crumbly bone, whose minerals were the only things to survive the heat of the furnace—would probably weigh somewhere in the neighborhood of five pounds. I knew the chemical composition was mainly calcium, seasoned with a host of trace elements. And I knew that Jess, her essence, was not among the trace elements inside that urn.

As the priest ascended the stairs to the altar itself, the music reached a crescendo that set my very teeth buzzing. Then the music fell away, and the priest began to speak.

"In the midst of life we are in death," he began. "From whom can we seek help? From you alone, O Lord, who by our sins are justly angered."

A chorus of voices rang from the nave beyond. "Holy God, holy and mighty, holy and merciful Savior," the congregation recited, "deliver us not into the bitterness of eternal death." *Ah*, my heart answered, *but what about the bitterness of empty life?* I would have traded places with Jess if I could.

The priest began to chant, a high incantation that had no discernible melody, and I lost the thread of its meaning, circling back instead to the opening words of the service. "In the midst of life we are in death." *No, that's backward*, I thought. *In the midst of death, Jess and I were most alive. It was our daily bread.* We were oddities, she and I: a doctor who never had a live patient, and an ivory-tower professor immersed to his elbows in death and dismemberment. Could we have made an odd life together, I wondered, sharing space and hearts and bodies in Knoxville or Chattanooga or somewhere in between? *The power couple of the dead set*, I thought, and smiled at the grim humor even as tears sprang to my eyes for the loss of what might have been. I knew I was grieving for something that never really existed except in my imagination, but the loss cut deeply all the same.

As the congregation read a response to some prompting I hadn't heard, I shifted my stance, and when I did, I kicked a chair hidden in the dark catwalk. It grated on the stone floor, and the priest looked up in my direction. As he registered my presence, his eyes widened with surprise, then narrowed sharply. I realized that the police had probably briefed him about me, the forbidden intruder, and I suddenly pictured him interrupting the service—Jess's service—to have me hauled away. I clasped my hands in front of my chest in a gesture of prayer, a gesture whose sincerity I hoped he could see. Maybe he did; maybe he saw sorrow etched in my face, or tears streaking my cheeks; maybe he simply didn't want to interrupt the service. At any rate, his expression softened, and he turned back to his text. "O God of grace and glory," he read, "we remember before you this day our sister Jessamine. We thank you for giving her to us, her family and friends, to know and to love as a companion on our earthly pilgrimage. In your boundless compassion, console us who mourn." He never looked at me again, but at that moment he seemed to be speaking to me, speaking *for* me, alone among the crowd.

At the end of the main service, the priest invited the mourners to join him for a brief burial service in the courtyard beside the nave. Then he lifted the brass urn from the altar and processed out the nave.

Retreating into the maze of hallways and stairwells, I made my way by blind reckoning in the direction the priest had indicated. I soon found myself in an elegant lobby just outside the parish offices; then, down a long, sunny hallway, I glimpsed windows looking out onto an enclosed garden. At the garden's center was a sunken circular courtyard inlaid with black and white tiles that formed the pattern of a labyrinth, a symbol of spiritual pilgrimage. To one side, in a raised bed of flowers and hostas, stood a statue of an angel, and in one edge of this plot was a freshly dug hole, perhaps a foot square. The priest stood there with the urn, and the tightly bunched crowd faced him. I recognized

Preston Carter in the group; I also saw the woman I'd known at a glance to be Jess's mother. She held her head high, almost defiantly—another recognizable echo of Jess—but her face told how much the show of strength was costing her. She kept her distance from Carter, which I took as a sign that she had not forgiven him for whatever had caused the rift between him and Jess.

The priest began to speak, and I crept to a window to catch his words. I got there just in time to see him pour the urn's contents into the ground. He straightened and then raised both hands in a gesture of blessing. "In sure and certain hope of the resurrection to eternal life through our Lord Jesus Christ," he said, "we commend to Almighty God our sister Jessamine, and we commit her body to the ground. Earth to earth, ashes to ashes, dust to dust. The Lord bless her and keep her, the Lord make his face to shine upon her and be gracious to her, the Lord lift up his countenance upon her and give her peace. Amen."

"Amen," I whispered. "Sleep well, Jess."

CHAPTER 36

I SLIPPED OUT THE church's side door and made it back to Broad Street undetected—more to the point, unarrested—and had just climbed into the Taurus for the sad drive back to Knoxville when I heard a soft, familiar voice. "You not speaking to me?" Miss Georgia was decked out in a sleeveless calf-length black dress that simultaneously covered and stunningly packaged her willowy body. A hint of cleavage showed at the neckline; the naughtiness was somehow both undercut and underscored by a panel of sheer black mesh stretching from the neckline up to her throat. The outfit was topped off by a pair of black gloves and the broad-brimmed black hat I'd seen in the church, trimmed with a spray of black feathers. Miss Georgia raised a stiletto-clad foot to the running board; the movement caused a long slit in the dress to open, revealing a stocking top, a garter, and several inches of bare thigh above the stocking. It was an elegant, womanly thigh, and it startled me all over again to recall that Miss

Georgia was not actually a woman. "Dr. Bill, I'm sorry about your friend," said Miss Georgia. "I saw it on the TV, and I cried and cried. She a classy lady."

"Yes, she was," I said.

"How come the po-lice not let you in the church, Dr. Bill? Everybody talkin' 'bout that after the fun'ral. You loved her, didn't you?"

I nodded. "I think maybe I did, or I could have. I was just beginning to find out."

"You did; it was all over your face that night at the club. She crazy 'bout you, too—I axed her, and she told me so. Anybody deserve to be in there at that woman's fun'ral, it was you. You and her mama. Who tell the po-lice to keep you out?"

"Her ex-husband," I said. "I think he thinks I killed her. So does Detective Sergeant John Evers. So does the district attorney."

"You?" Miss Georgia threw back her head and cut loose with her high, cascading laugh, whose femininity was undercut slightly by the prominence with which her Adam's apple bobbed into view. "Dr. Bill, you as meek as a baby lamb," she said. "No way you do something bad to a woman, 'specially a woman you in love with. I got me a mind to go find that ex-husband and bitch-slap some sense into him. Bitch-slap me some po-lices, too." She grinned lasciviously. "Some of them white-boy po-lices? They just *dyin'* to be bitch-slapped by a long-legged Nubian goddess."

I smiled in spite of myself. "I appreciate your willingness to take up for me, Miss Georgia, but I don't want to drag you into my troubles."

"Sweet Jesus, did somebody say *drag*? Tha's one of my most favorite words. I am all about drag, and draggin', and bein' dragged. Next time somebody start messin' wif you, they gonna find theyself messin' wif me. Then *they* be the one in a mess."

"Okay," I said. "Next time the police—the *po-lice*—mess with me, I'll holler for help." She gave me an exaggerated wink of approval.

"Dr. Bill, I done found out somethin' 'bout that case you and Miss Jess was workin' on."

There was a deli near the corner—Ankar's Downtown—so I suggested we get a bite to eat while we talked. "You *know* I gots to watch my girlish figure, but I would just love some sweet tea," she said. I held the door for her, then ordered two teas and a bag of chips, and we headed for a booth that looked out of earshot of the handful of other customers. Heads turned as we walked through the deli; Miss Georgia beamed at all who stared, as if accepting tribute. And in a way, maybe she was.

Once seated, she took off her gloves, laid them on the table, and drew a sip of tea through a straw so as not to smudge her coral lipstick. "Oh my," she sighed, "that is refreshing." I took a swig of mine and popped a potato chip in my mouth. It was a thick, kettle-cooked chip, so it crunched loudly. Miss Georgia crinkled her nose in disapproval.

"You said you found out something," I said. "Tell me."

She reached down under the table and produced a folded piece of paper which I guessed had been tucked into the top of her stocking. When she unfolded it, I saw the forensic sketch artist's two renderings of Craig Willis, in drag and in men's clothing. "I axed some of my friends—girlfriends and boyfriends—about this *person* you and Miss Jess was wondering about," she said.

"Oh," I said, "we identified him by his fingerprints after I talked to you." I described finding the skin from the hand, and how Art had donned the skin like a glove in order to take prints.

"Dr. Bill, that is just *fascinating*," she said. She sounded like she meant it, and I was grateful for the compliment. "One of my boyfriends, he recognize the picture—the regular picture, not the one in that tatty Dolly Parton outfit—and he say, 'That guy is not a drag queen; that asshole motherfucker is a chicken hawk.' 'Scuse my French, Dr. Bill."

"Chicken hawk? What's a chicken hawk?"

"Iss a bird. And iss a pedophile. Chicken hawk swoop down and grab li'l baby chickens. They's even a damn chicken-hawk support group, calls isself 'Nambla.' Stand for 'North American Man-Boy Love Association.' Nambla say men should be able to have sex with boys of any age, long as the boys consent." She paused, then added, "Whatever 'consent' mean to a six-year-old chile."

"You seem to know a lot about this," I said.

Miss Georgia looked away. When she looked back, I saw deep-seated hurt in her eyes. "You know that tree it talk about in the Bible—the tree of good and evil?" I nodded, startled—Art and I had discussed it, in the same context, a few weeks ago, or a lifetime ago. "Somebody make me eat some fruits off that tree a long time ago," she said. "You choke down something like that, it stick with you for life, Dr. Bill."

I felt a wave of compassion for Miss Georgia, but I didn't want to pry and I didn't know a graceful way to express it. Instead, I simply told Miss Georgia about Craig Willis's arrest for child molestation in Knoxville, shortly before he moved to Chattanooga; she nodded. "See, thass what I'm talkin' about. I tole you that night at Alan Gold's I'd remember if I seen anybody in that sorry-ass drag-queen getup."

"So a chicken hawk couldn't also be a drag queen?"

For the second time in as many minutes, Miss Georgia looked uncomfortable. "Don't never say never, Dr. Bill. They's some mighty twisted people in this world. And queers be some of the twistedest." I studied Miss Georgia for any hint of irony in her expression, and detected none. "But my friend, he say he cannot imagine this guy in drag."

"But that's how he was dressed when he died," I said.

"When he die? Or when y'all *find* him?"

"But what's the—" Suddenly I saw what she was getting at. "You think maybe whoever killed him dressed his body in drag for some reason?"

"Mm-hmm."

"How come?"

"You the forensic genius, Dr. Bill. Why you think?"

"To make it *look* like a hate crime?"

"See, baby, you know it. It just takes you a while

to *know* you know it. Sort of like the way you was slow to know you love Miss Jess."

"But surely whoever killed this guy knew he was a pedophile," I said. "So wouldn't it still be a hate crime?"

"Yes and no," she said. "Different kind of hate. So different kind of crime."

Something was crystallizing in my mind. Slowly, to be sure, but definitely. "So if it's a different kind of hate," I said, "and a different kind of killing, that means . . ." Miss Georgia nodded encouragingly. "That means a different kind of killer, someone killing for a different reason."

"Dr. Bill, you so brilliant," she said.

"Oh, stop," I said. "Now you're patronizing me." Miss Georgia's laugh pealed throughout the deli, causing another round of head-turning. "So instead of just some redneck yahoo who's enraged by a man in drag, we're looking for someone who hates pedophiles. Maybe somebody he molested who wanted revenge?"

Miss Georgia looked doubtful. "You think some li'l boy done turned killer?" She shook her head. "That fella not old enough to have victims what be growed up. Besides, a boy been molested might turn molester his own self. Shit flow downstream, we say here in Chattanooga. Y'all might not say that in Knoxville, being upriver and all."

"Well, Craig Willis sure flowed downstream," I said. "But if it wasn't someone he molested, then who?" Miss Georgia rolled her eyes and drummed her fingers on the table. Finally I got it. "A parent." Then I thought of my grandsons, and how enraged

I would be if someone molested them. "Or a grand-parent." And then I thought of Art, and his quiet fury at the predators he was stalking day in, day out, and of what he'd told me about the officer who caught Craig Willis in the act of molesting Joey Scott; I wondered how it might have affected that officer to see Willis set free without so much as a trial. "Or a frustrated cop."

Miss Georgia beamed at me. "Now you usin' that big ol' brain of yours, Dr. Bill." She took another sip through her straw, then frowned at the thin plastic tube. "I can't get no satisfaction through this straw. I guess I just be out of practice suckin' on things." She winked at me, then put her lips into a pout and wrapped them around the straw again. "Oh, the hell with it," she finally said in a huskier voice. She extracted the straw and dropped it on the table, then hoisted the glass and drained it in three larynx-pumping gulps. Then she set down the glass and looked at me with an expression I hadn't seen on her face before. She looked shy, and scared, and utterly free of the dramatics and affectations she hid behind so much of the time. "Dr. Bill, could I ax you something? Iss a highly personal matter."

It was hard for me to imagine what could be more personal than some of the conversational ground Miss Georgia had already trampled with abandon. I nodded nervously. "Go ahead."

"I've had some surgery. I got these boobs; maybe you noticed?" I nodded again. "As a first step, you know, toward seeing how I might like being a real woman."

"And?"

"I think I want to go the rest of the way."

"Does 'the rest of the way' mean what I think it means?"

"If you thinking Lorena Bobbitt, it do," she said. Then she shook her head. "Actually, iss a lot more complicated than that. Iss called 'sex reassignment surgery,' and they don't just whack everything off. They kinda split everything open, and turn it inside out, and do some serious tuckin'-in. They do empty the marble bag, and take out most of the hydraulic tubing, if you know what I mean. But they make you a vagina and even a little clitoris, with nerve endings and everything." She got a wistful look on her face. "I've seen pictures; I could look like a real woman. Make love like a real woman, too. Do everything but have periods and have babies, and who wants to mess with all that?"

"The surgery sounds pretty drastic," I said. "Are you sure that's what you want?"

"Pretty sure, Dr. Bill. I been trying to get out of this male body ever since I hit puberty. The fit just don't seem right, you know?"

"Well, I don't know, but I reckon you do," I said. "But you wanted to ask me something?"

"They's a plastic surgeon up in Knoxville at the UT hospital, supposed to be pretty good," she said. "He trained over in France with the doctor pioneered this fancy operation." She hesitated. "I got me an appointment a while back. If I come up there and have this done . . ." She trailed off.

"Yes?"

"Would you come visit me in the hospital, Dr. Bill?"

I laughed. "That's it? That's what you were worried about asking me? Good Lord, Miss Georgia. Wild horses couldn't keep me away."

As we left the deli and headed back to my boring white car, Miss Georgia took my arm. And when I got in, she leaned in and kissed me on the cheek. I kissed hers, too. It felt smooth and soft—like a real woman's—and it was the most human, compassionate, comforting moment I'd experienced in the five days since I'd found Jess's desecrated corpse at the Body Farm.

I decided not to take the interstate back to Knoxville; instead, in hopes a different route might distract me from thoughts of Jess, I took U.S. 27, which crossed the river a half mile downstream from the glass-peaked aquarium. It had been years since I'd taken 27; the highway had been mostly four-laned since then, but the surrounding countryside remained virtually unchanged. The road roughly paralleled I-75—both of them angling northeast from Chattanooga—but while 75 ran through the broadest, flattest part of the Tennessee Valley, 27 lay about twenty miles to the west, skirting the base of Walden Ridge, the mouth of the rugged Chickamauga Gulch, and the eastern escarpment of the Cumberland Plateau.

Forty minutes north of Chattanooga, highway 27 bypassed Dayton, and on a whim, I angled left into the business district. On the north edge of the four-block downtown, I saw an elegant old courthouse on my left, three stories of brick with a bell tower rising another two stories above the main structure. It hit me with almost physical force:

this was the courthouse where Williams Jennings Bryan and Clarence Darrow had tried the case of John Scopes, the high school science teacher arrested for teaching evolution in 1925. Had I subconsciously chosen this route so that I would pass this historic spot, site of a debate that remained as unresolved today as it was eight decades ago? Probably, I decided.

There were plenty of parking spaces along Main Street, and—irrefutable proof that Dayton was a small town—no meters to feed. I pulled into a spot directly across from the courthouse and strolled across the shady lawn toward the front doors. To the left of the entrance stood a life-size bronze statue on a pedestal; the inscription identified it as William Jennings Bryan, U.S. senator and three-time presidential candidate, nicknamed "the Great Commoner" for his affinity with ordinary folk of the time. Already famous for his dire pronouncements about the nihilistic implications of evolution, Bryan was recruited as the celebrity spokesman for the prosecution. I looked around for another statue; surely there was one of the lead attorney defending Scopes, Clarence Darrow. Darrow, like Bryan, was considered a titan. To his admirers, he was "the Great Defender"; to his detractors, "Attorney for the Damned." If there was a statue of Darrow, it was well hidden.

As I puzzled over the sculptural imbalance, an older gentleman emerged from the courthouse, approached me, and said hello. "Where's Darrow?" I asked. "Seems like they ought to have both lawyers out here."

"Anybody wants to put up the money, we'd be glad to have him," the man said. It turned out that he was the volunteer curator of the Scopes Trial Museum, housed in the basement of the courthouse. The courthouse had just closed, but when he found out I was passing through from out of town and hoped to see the courtroom, he graciously offered to let me look around not just the courtroom but the museum as well.

Stepping into the courtroom was like stepping back in time. The room occupied the entire second floor of the building; high windows lined every wall; the stamped-tin ceiling was the perfect counterpoint to the scuffed wood floor. Even the seats— old auditorium-style wooden seats bolted to the floor—were original. I sat in one of the front-row seats, imagining Darrow and Jennings hammering away at one another, and at one another's philosophies: Darrow's fierce belief in human free will and self-determination, Bryan's dogged belief in the necessity of divine salvation. They staked out their positions in their opening arguments. "Scopes isn't on trial," Darrow proclaimed; "civilization is on trial." Bryan set the stakes even higher, claiming, "If evolution wins, Christianity goes."

I had long known that the trial was a media boondoggle; what I hadn't fully realized, until I explored the exhibits in the basement, was how thoroughly orchestrated a publicity stunt it had been, from start to finish. Tennessee's 1925 antievolution law was real enough, and so was the ACLU's interest in challenging it. What was nearly pure hokum was the trial itself. It was the brainchild of local businessmen, Chamber of Commerce types who dreamed of putting Dayton on the map in a big way. When similar challenges to the new law began gathering momentum in other, larger Tennessee cities, the Dayton boosters maneuvered to get the date of the Scopes trial moved up, so Knoxville and Chattanooga wouldn't steal Dayton's thunder. Even the defendant, earnest young John Scopes, was a ringer: Scopes taught chemistry, not biology; he was persuaded to play the part of educational martyr as his contribution to the town's economic salvation. Several students were carefully coached to confirm that, yes indeed, Mr. Scopes taught that man was descended from apelike ancestors. At one point, when a technicality came to light that threatened to nullify the charge against Scopes, Darrow—the Great Defender!—hastened to assure the court that the defense did not *want* the charge dismissed. Darrow hoped for a guilty verdict, one he could appeal all the way to the U.S. Supreme Court. In short, the noble script of *Inherit the Wind* notwithstanding, this landmark case in American jurisprudence was as carefully choreographed as any professional wrestling exhibition.

As planned, evolution lost in the local court, so presumably Christianity won. But the victory, even at the time, rang hollow. Bryan—who'd taken the witness stand to defend the truth of the Bible—was portrayed in the press as a "pitiable, punch-drunk warrior." Six days after the trial, the Great Commoner died in a house on a side street in Dayton.

Finding out how thoroughly the "landmark" trial was a sham and a gimmick was a bit demoralizing; I hated to learn that our court system was as susceptible to self-serving manipulation and grandstanding as, say, political campaigns. On the other hand, the debunking did put my banana cream pie in a broader historical perspective. If Bryan was the Great Commoner and Darrow the Great Defender, maybe—just maybe—history would remember Brockton as the Great Meringuer. At the very least, I might be able to land a celebrity endorsement deal with Sara Lee pies.

CHAPTER 37

THE DAYLIGHT FILTERING THROUGH the dusty screens of the cabin was even dimmer than usual when I awoke the morning after Jess's funeral. I rolled across the lumpy mattress and pressed my face to the window. Through the grime on the glass and the dust and cobwebs on the screen, I thought—though it was hard to be sure—that I saw dark clouds scudding above the treetops. That meant I would have to work on my textbook revisions indoors, by kerosene lamp. Although the image seemed romantic, in an Abe Lincoln sort of way, I knew that a day of hunching over to read fine print by flickering lamplight would leave me with knotted shoulders and a screaming headache. As I wrestled with my choices—the case of cabin fever I'd get if I didn't work, versus the aching head and neck I'd get if I did—the cellphone Jeff had loaned me began to ring. The display read PRIVATE NUMBER, so I considered not answering—what if a reporter had somehow gotten hold of the number? By the third ring, though, I decided I was being excessively paranoid. Somebody *was* out to get me, and I did want to be cautious, but I didn't want paranoia to run away with me.

"Hello?"

"Bill? It's Art."

I felt my shoulders relax, not simply because it wasn't a reporter, but because it was someone who actually still had faith in me. I'd called and left my number on Art's voice mail and Miranda's voice mail; I'd also given it to Peggy, my secretary, and Burt DeVriess and his assistant Chloe. That small circle of people, plus Jeff, seemed to represent the sum total of human beings whose loyalty and faith I retained. It wasn't many, but they were all good people to have in my corner. Well, Burt DeVriess was an unsavory person to have in my corner, but nonetheless a crucial one.

"Hi, Art. How goes the pursuit of the pedophiles?"

"I set up a date yesterday with one of my boy-friends. We were supposed to meet at the food court at the mall. He stood me up. I'm feeling rejected."

"You think he got suspicious? Figured out that Tiffany was really a cop?"

"Maybe. But I think he's just skittish in general. I sent him a hurt-feelings e-mail last night, and he wrote back to apologize. Made some lame excuse about work. Sometimes it takes two or three times before these guys follow through—I'm not sure if they're just chickens, or if they have some tiny shreds of conscience. But I've told him we need to take a break from each other for a week or so."

"You playing hard to get?"

"No. I've taken some time off, actually. I thought maybe there might be a higher and better use of my investigative talents."

"Higher and better than catching child molesters? What would be better than that?"

"Figuring out who killed Jess. Figuring out who's setting you up. I'm off all week. How about we rough out some sort of plan?" Art's generosity astonished me and moved me. "Bill? You still there?"

I had to clear my throat before I could speak. "Yeah. Yeah, I'm here. Thank you, Art. Thanks."

"You'd do the same for me, wouldn't you?"

"Yes," I said, "I would."

"Okay, then, we're even. You got any bright ideas for how we track down this diabolical killer?"

"Not so far."

"That's okay," he said. "I didn't figure you would. Lucky for us, I do."

"That is lucky. Whatcha got?"

"I keep thinking the Willis murder must be tied to Jess's," he said. "No pun intended. Jess had just released Willis's name to the media, and it's the one case you and Jess were working on together. Right?"

"Right. I keep thinking about Willis's mother. The way she acted was really strange. It's like she was less upset over the fact that he was dead than over the way Jess described him to the media. Almost as if his reputation were more important than his life."

"Grief's a funny thing, though," he said. "People express it in wildly different ways. That could've been some weird version of denial."

"Maybe," I said, "but if so, then killing Jess might have been an extension of it—taking that assault on Jess to the extreme. That would fit with the threatening note that got thrown through my window, too."

"But didn't you say that came from one of those creationist protesters?"

"Looked that way," I said, "but maybe she was trying to throw me off the scent. Then again, there's another possibility."

"Namely?"

"The cop that caught Craig Willis in the act. Given that he rushed in, didn't follow procedures, and even roughed the guy up a bit, he sounds like a bit of a cowboy. Might he be capable of killing Willis, once the case got thrown out?"

"Maybe," said Art. "The line between good cop and bad cop can be mighty easy to cross. You bend a rule here and there, pretty soon you're breaking 'em right and left. Be a mighty big leap, though, to go from exterminating a pedophile to murdering a medical examiner—and then framing a forensic scientist for it."

"Hmm. That does seem like a stretch."

"Tell you what," he said. "Let me try to track him down and have a talk with him. If nothing else, he might have some ideas about other folks who may have wanted Willis dead, and whether any of them were capable of the rest of this stuff."

"You want me to go with you?"

"Naw," he said. "Let me talk to him, cop-to-cop. You think you'd be taking a chance if you went and talked to Mrs. Willis?"

I felt more nervous than I cared to admit. "I'll be okay," I said, hoping Art would think better of it, try talking me out of it. He didn't.

"Let's touch base after lunch," he said. "I'll give you a call around one unless I hear something from you before then. By the way, do you know where Mrs. Willis lives?"

"Um, no."

"That's okay. I just happen to have her address handy." He read it off—she lived on a street of small bungalows near West High School, and I knew the neighborhood well.

Relieved not to be facing a day of flickering eye-strain, I downed a bowl of Cheerios (Honey Nut, which I'd chosen over Jeff's objections), took a quick shower in the bathhouse, and donned a pair of khakis and a polo shirt for the trip to Knoxville. I was still the best-dressed person in the park—a truly startling distinction for me—but at least I'd scaled back from church clothes (and arrest clothes) to business casual.

One lane of I-75 South was closed for repaving, so traffic was crawling today. The drive back to Knox-ville, which normally took thirty minutes, required nearly an hour this time. I got off at the Papermill Drive exit—also a bottleneck, as it had been for a couple of years now, during a massive interchange reworking—and wound through small residential streets to Sutherland Avenue, the main artery that led to West High and Mrs. Willis's neighborhood. I had just parked across the street from her house when she emerged from the front door. She was wearing work clothes—blue jeans and a dingy T-shirt and boots—and carrying pruning shears. She headed for a hedge of boxwoods lining the front of the yard and began hacking at the new growth with a vengeance.

My camera was in a bin in the passenger-side floorboard; on impulse, I fished it out and zoomed in on her face. She looked nearly as angry as the day she had stormed into my office, and the look brought the altercation back vividly into my memory. *You know,* I thought, *I bet there's a lot of rage inside that woman. Any mother whose son turns out to be a child molester, and then gets murdered—be enough to turn anybody pretty hateful.* I snapped a few photos, then stowed my camera and got out of the car.

"Mrs. Willis," I called as I crossed the street, "could I talk to you for a minute?"

She turned slowly, and when she recognized me, her eyes flashed. "What do you want?"

"I'd like to talk to you about Dr. Carter," I said.

"Dr. Carter's dead," she snapped, "and I'm glad. And you're going to jail for killing her, and I'm glad of that, too."

"I didn't kill Dr. Carter," I said. "I had no reason to."

"I don't give a damn," she said. "I'm glad she's dead, and I hope they give you the death penalty. The paper said they might try."

The conversation was not going quite the way I had hoped it would. I tried to imagine what Detective John Evers would do if he were interrogating Mrs. Willis, but the only thing that came to mind was the feeling of his knee crowding the space between my legs, edging up toward my crotch and making me extremely uncomfortable. It was not a tactic I could use with a woman—especially a woman holding a pair of pruning shears.

"I think there might be a connection between your son's death and Dr. Carter's," I said, hoping to appeal to her more maternal instincts. "Dr. Carter and the Chattanooga police were working to solve his murder when she was killed." She didn't say anything, but she lowered the shears to her side. I took that as an encouraging sign. "You got any idea who might have killed him?"

"I already talked to them detectives from Chattanooga," she said. "Like I told them, I can't imagine why anybody would have wanted to kill Craig." I could think of some reasons, but it didn't seem wise to mention them at this particular moment.

Something Miss Georgia Youngblood had said to me about pedophiles occurred to me—the phrase "Shit flow downstream," which had gotten linked in my mind somehow with the phrase "Each one teach one"—and I wondered if Mrs. Willis could shed any light on her son's pathology. "Mrs. Willis, can you think back to when Craig was about ten years old? Do you remember him at that age?"

"Of course I do," she said. "I remember him at every age. Why?"

"I'm wondering if maybe something happened around that time. Something that might have been very frightening or upsetting to him." Her eyes darted back and forth as she thought, and it seemed to me that she fixed on something, because they stopped darting and she looked away, her jaw clenched. "An incident, maybe, that might explain things that have happened more recently."

She looked at me now. "What kind of incident? What are you talking about?"

I didn't see any alternative but to put it out there. "Maybe an incident in which . . . in which an older male might have . . . done something to Craig. Something sexual." She stared at me. "The reason I ask," I floundered, "is that sometimes, when that happens to a boy, after he grows up, he . . . might be inclined . . ."

Even if I could have put the rest of the sentence into words, I didn't get the chance. With a low snarl, she flung herself at me, pruning shears and all. Luckily, she didn't wield them point-first; instead, she swung them like a club or a baseball bat, and I was able to put up a hand in time to block the blow and grab the shears. We wrestled over them for a moment, but I was considerably stronger than she was, and it wasn't hard to take them from her. When I did, she came at me with her fists, as she had done to Jess. I dropped the shears and grabbed her, spinning her around so her back was to me, and wrapped her in a bear hug, pinning her arms to her sides.

"Let me *go*!" she cried. "Let me go or I'll scream. I'll scream bloody murder, and they will haul you away in *handcuffs*."

She had a point there. I could imagine the lead-in to the nightly newscast: "He's already on trial for *one* murder. Did Dr. Bill Brockton try to commit *another* today?" I let her go, but as I did, I placed a foot on the pruning shears lest she grab them and use them more effectively this time. "Don't you care who killed your son, Mrs. Willis?"

She glowered at me, her chest heaving, tears beginning to run down her face. "Of course I care," she said, "but nobody else gives a good goddamn. You think I don't know how the police feel about . . . people like Craig?"

It was an admission of sorts. "No matter what they think," I said, "they'll still try to solve his murder."

"Bullshit," she said. "I wouldn't be surprised if the cop that arrested him was the one that killed him."

I was startled that she'd thought that through, although I suppose I shouldn't have been. She'd undoubtedly spent far more time turning over the possibilities in her mind than Art and I had. "Who else could have?"

She gave me a look of undisguised contempt. "Gee, Mr. Fancy Ph.D., let's think about that." She shook her head. "It's done. Nobody will ever be caught. Get the hell out of here and don't come back. If I see you again, I'm calling 911. In fact, if you're not gone in thirty seconds, I'm calling 911. Maybe even if you are."

I bent down and picked up the pruning shears. Suddenly she looked frightened. With an underhanded toss, I lobbed them over the hedge and up near her front porch, just in case she was still inclined to take another run at me. Then I held up one hand and backed away, across the street, and got into the Taurus. I locked the doors first, then started the engine. As I eased away from the curb, I glanced back just in time to see Mrs. Willis hurling the pruning shears in my direction. They hit the trunk lid with a scraping clatter that I knew had left a nasty gouge. *At least it's a rental*, I thought. Then I remembered that I had declined the supplemental insurance.

Once I was safely out of the neighborhood, I paged Art. He rang me right back. "Hey, how'd it go with Mrs. Willis?"

"Not so good," I said.

"You mean she didn't confess?"

"That's one way of putting it."

"What's another way?"

"Let's just say that if all you've got is a pair of pruning shears, everything looks like a hedge."

"Oh, *that* good?"

"That good."

"You lose any body parts?"

"No. Only the last of my dignity. You get a chance to talk to the guy that caught Craig Willis in the act?"

"Not yet. He's kinda hard to reach."

"Because?"

"Because he's been in Iraq for the past four months. He's in the Guard, and his unit got called up right after the Willis thing."

"Damn. So I guess that clears him, huh?"

"See, I *knew* you had a knack for detective work," Art said. "You got a Plan C?"

"Maybe," I said, "but I don't much like it. Tell me what you think." I laid it out for him.

Art didn't much like it either, but he agreed we needed to grit our teeth and give it a try at the end of the day.

CHAPTER 38

I WAS LUNCHING ALFRESCO—WOLFING down a drive-through deli sandwich at a picnic table in Tyson Park, a long strip of grass and trees near the UT campus—when the cellphone rang. The display read BURTON DeVRIESS, LLC. When I answered, I was pleasantly surprised to hear Chloe instead of Burt on the other end. "Dr. Brockton?" My bubble was swiftly burst. "Mr. DeVriess would like to speak with you. Can you hold while I put him on the line?"

"Sure, Chloe," I sighed, "though I'd rather talk to you."

"But you need to talk to him. I hope you're doing well."

"I'm still a free man, so things could be worse."

"That's the spirit. Hold on for Mr. DeVriess."

I held on. I'd been holding on a lot lately. Mostly by my fingernails. "Bill? It's Burt. How are you?"

"Ask me at the end of the phone call. What's up?"

"Can you come in this afternoon? I'd like to go over two pieces of evidence we've obtained in the course of discovery."

"What kind of evidence?"

"It's good-news and bad-news evidence. Which one you want first?"

"Hell. Give me the bad news first."

"It's an exhibit the prosecution will try to make hay with at trial. It's the video from the surveillance camera on the roof of UT hospital."

"The one that's zoomed in on at the gate of the Body Farm."

"Exactly. About three hours before you called 911, that camera shows what sure looks like your pickup truck driving through the gate and into the facility."

"I'll tell you what I told Evers. That's impossible. I wasn't there. I swear to you, I was not there."

"Nevertheless. I've looked at a copy, and I have to say, if it's not your truck, it's a dead ringer for it. Any chance somebody could have borrowed it that night without you knowing?"

"I don't think so," I said. "During the daytime I usually leave it in the driveway, but at night I lock it in the garage. And the garage door opener clatters pretty loud—I'm almost certain that would wake me up."

"Hmm," he said. "I'm not sure you need to volunteer that part on the witness stand. Anyhow, I've got a video and audio expert coming in to examine the original tape, see if he can find any basis for challenging it. Might be good if you were here, too."

"I'd like to see it," I said. "I can't believe how thoroughly this deck is getting stacked against me. So what's the good news? Instead of the death penalty, they're only seeking life without parole?"

"Ha," he said, followed by an actual laugh. "Glad you haven't lost your sense of humor. No, it's a little better than that. Something we can use to create reasonable doubt in the minds of the jurors."

"What? Tell me."

"It's the voice mails Jess got after she was on the TV news sticking up for you and evolution."

"The ones where some guy threatened to do nasty things to her? I'm surprised she didn't erase those right away."

"Maybe she figured she should hang on to them in case he kept harassing her," he said. "So she could prove to the phone company that these weren't just typical prank calls."

"Whatever the reason, I'm glad she saved them," I said.

"Me too. This expert I'm bringing in should be able to compare your voice to the voice mails and establish that it's not your voice making those threats." He paused. "Bill, there's no reason we shouldn't get him to do that comparison, is there?"

It took a moment for me to grasp what he was implying. "Jesus, Burt, of course not. I did not make those phone calls to Jess."

"Just making sure," he said. "I've listened to the messages. The voice doesn't sound like yours, and it's not your style. They're pretty strong stuff—sadistic sexual threats, and some pretty sick death threats. If I were a juror and I heard some creep threatening her like this, I'd wonder whether the killer might be this guy instead of the mild-mannered Dr. Brockton."

"You think jurors think like you?"

"Hell no. Nobody thinks like me. But I'm able to think like jurors when I need to."

"I hope your crystal ball is right about this."

"Self-fulfilling prophecy," he said. "I'll plant those seeds of doubt and then fertilize like hell."

I'd seen Grease in action enough times to know what he meant—and know he'd be good at it. "Fertilize how—with a couple truckloads of bullshit?"

"Doc, you cut me to the quick," he said. "My bullshit's so incredibly rich it won't take but a shovelful."

Now it was my turn to laugh. "What time is your expert coming in?"

"Two o'clock. Can you make it?"

"What else have I got to do? I've been suspended from teaching, and the police haven't exactly deluged me with forensic cases since they arrested me for murder."

"Damned shortsighted of them," he said. "I'll see you at two."

The next two hours passed with excruciating slowness. Finally, at one-fifteen, unable to wait any longer, I headed for DeVriess's office. Even taking the long way around the UT campus, I pulled into the parking garage beneath Riverview Tower a good twenty minutes early. *Too bad*, I thought. *Worst case, I'll have to sit in the waiting room for a while. No worse than sitting anywhere else. Maybe better—Chloe's always nice to me.*

As I stepped into the elevator and punched the button for DeVriess's floor, I noticed a slight man pushing a large, wheeled case in my direction. It didn't take a rocket scientist to realize he wouldn't be using the stairs, so I held the elevator for him. The case—actually two cases, one atop the other—bumped over the sill and into the car. "Thanks," said the man. He was breathing hard and had broken a sweat. He didn't look muscular enough to be a deliveryman, and his shirt and tie suggested that he was a professional of some sort. The fact that the tie was a clip-on suggested that the sturdy black cases contained computer gear of some sort.

"That's quite a load you've got there," I said.

"Yeah," he said. "Weighs more than I do. Plane fare for it costs more than mine, too, time I pay all the excess baggage charges."

"Computer hardware?"

"Sort of," he said. "Video and audio equipment. Plus a computer."

That would explain why he'd glanced at the elevator console and not pushed a button: he was bound for the same floor I was, and the same lawyer's office. I was on the verge of introducing myself when it occurred to me that I didn't know a graceful way to do it. "Hi, I'm Bill Brockton, accused murderer?" Or maybe, "God, I hope you're good enough to save me from the electric chair?" So instead I decided to focus on him. "What do you use it for?"

"I do forensic video and audio analysis."

"You mean like enhancing recordings?"

"I'm careful not to call it 'enhancing' in court,"

he said. "The word 'enhancing' makes it sound like I'm adding something to it. What I'm really doing is subtracting—filtering out noise, static, and other interference—to extract the best possible images and sounds from what's already recorded."

"How much difference does that make?"

"You'd be surprised," he said. "Or maybe disappointed, if you watch *CSI*. On shows like that, video analysis is like magic—they take these really crappy, blurry images and zoom in by about a factor of ten, and hit a button and suddenly the image is razor-sharp. Doesn't work that way in real life—if you start out with a crappy camera and a worn-out tape, you can't end up with a great image. But TV makes people think you can."

"I've heard that called 'the *CSI* effect,' I think," I said.

"Exactly," he said. "The public—and jurors—now expect miracles from people in law enforcement. They think all this razzle-dazzle, instant-answer technology that some scriptwriter has made up must really exist. And if a prosecutor can't produce that sort of thing in court, they tend to discount the evidence."

"What about the defense?"

"Funny thing," he said. "On TV, it's nearly always the cops and prosecutors pulling the rabbits out of the high-tech hats. So the jurors expect more bells and whistles from them than they do from the defense."

This gave me some comfort.

The elevator stopped on Burt's floor, and I held the door button again while the man levered and bumped his gear over the threshold. Then I squeezed past him so I could open the door to Burt's suite of offices. "Thank you," he said. "That's very nice of you."

"Maybe you can do me a favor sometime," I said with a smile.

Chloe looked startled to see me coming in with the video consultant. "Well, hello, Dr. Brockton," she said. "You're here early."

"I am," I said, "and look who I found wandering around on Gay Street." She looked confused. "I'm kidding, Chloe," I said. "We just happened to ride up on the elevator together."

Her relief was almost palpable. "Hi, you must be Mr. Thomas," she said. "Welcome to Knoxville. I'm Chloe Matthews, Mr. DeVriess's assistant. I hope your flight was good?"

"It was fine," he said. "We circled Atlanta quite a while—a thunderstorm had blown through, and the planes were stacked up—so it was nice to be up in first class." I raised my eyebrows at Chloe but she ignored me. "I had just enough time to make my connection to Knoxville," Thomas was saying. "Fortunately, my gear made it, too. I wouldn't be much good here without it."

"And you've already met Dr. Brockton," she said.

"Not exactly," I said. "On the ride up, we just talked about TV and reality, and the difference between the two."

"Oh, then let me introduce you," she said. "Dr. Brockton, this is Owen Thomas, our forensic audio and video expert. Mr. Thomas, this is Dr. Bill Brockton. He's . . ." She floundered here.

". . . the reason you're here," I said.

"He's a *famous forensic scientist*," she said. "That's how I was going to describe you."

I smiled. "Chloe, you're not a very good liar. Mr. Thomas, I've been charged with a crime. A murder, in fact. The prosecution says a surveillance video shows me and my pickup truck delivering the body to the place where it was found. I'm hoping you can prove them wrong."

Thomas looked uncomfortable, and I couldn't say as I blamed him. "I'll do my best to clarify the tape," he said. "Whatever it shows, it shows. Like I told Mr. DeVriess, I don't really think of myself as working for the defense, or for the prosecution; I think of my role as clarifying the truth."

"Good for you," I said. "That's my philosophy, too. You know, when I'm not on trial for murder. As a forensic anthropologist, I usually get called by the prosecution, but not long ago I testified for Gre—for Mr. DeVriess—and helped him clear an innocent man of murder charges. I'm hoping he can do that again this time."

Burt DeVriess turned a corner of the hallway and strode into his reception area. "You guys having this meeting without me?" He shook my hand and then introduced himself to Thomas.

"Let's go back to the conference room," Burt said. "That'll be better than my office. My office is too bright for looking at video."

The conference room was on the opposite side of the hallway from Burt's office; it was an interior room, with no windows except for a wall of Burt's trademark frosted glass along the hallway. A fair amount of daylight bled through from Burt's window and frosted-glass wall, but he lowered a set of blinds in the conference room, and the daylight vanished. "That dark enough?"

"Oh, plenty," said Thomas. Burt flipped on a set of Art Deco wall sconces, and the room took on a high-design feel, with the light itself looking like something sculpted. Between the Bentley, the first-class airfare, and the décor, I began to suspect that my $20,000 retainer was likely to be merely the first of several installments.

"How long do you need to set up?" Burt asked.

"Seven minutes," Thomas said. The clip-on tie was not just for effect.

"Okay, we'll be right back. Bill, come across the hall with me and let's talk trial strategy." I followed him into his office, where the bank of windows revealed a rain squall moving up the river channel in a wall of solid gray. As it advanced, it enveloped the railroad bridge, the graceful arches of the Henley Street bridge, and the bright green trusswork of the Gay Street bridge, Knoxville's favorite venue for suicidal jumpers.

I watched, mesmerized, as the storm seemed to obliterate the river itself, the banks, and Knoxville's very downtown. It was as if the storm marked the edge of the earth—an edge that was drawing closer with every passing second. Suddenly sheets of rain began to lash the office tower; the force of the water and the gusts driving it made the plate glass tremble. I stepped back, close to the door. "You ever get nervous up here during a big storm?"

Burt looked out at the window just as a streak of lightning arced across the hills lining the river's far bank. A smile creased his face, and I could hear him counting the seconds—"one Mississippi, two Mississippi, three Mississippi, four Mississippi"—until the thunder rattled the windows. "Naw," he said, "I love the storms. Wish I could bottle some of that energy and carry it into court with me."

"I think maybe you do," I said. "You've pretty nearly fried my hair during a cross-examination or two."

"Come on, Doc," he said. "I have always handled you with kid gloves on the witness stand."

"Then you're the iron fist in the kid glove."

He smiled and shook his head. "Just wait and see what I do to some of the witnesses in this case. Then you'll appreciate how gentle I've been with you."

"So who do you plan to tear into? Do you know who the prosecution will be calling yet?"

"Some; not all. They'll use Evers pretty hard. He usually does a good job on the stand. He's thorough, he looks good—that matters, believe it or not—and it's hard to get him rattled. They'll call a couple of hair and fiber people to talk about finding your hair in Dr. Carter's house, in her bed. Finding her blood and hair on the sheets from your house." The sheets still seemed like a nightmare I couldn't wake up from. "Probably the thing that will do the most damage, though, is Dr. Garland's testimony about the autopsy. She suffered a lot before she died, and the jury will want to make somebody pay for that."

"And I'm the only option they've got."

"Unfortunately," he said, "for this particular office, you're running unopposed. Unless that wasn't your semen."

"So how do we counter all that? Hell, at this point, if I were on the jury, *I'd* probably vote to convict me."

"We stipulate to the things we can't fight, and we whittle away at everything else. We stipulate to your hair and fibers in her bed. We stipulate to your semen in her vagina."

"But that wasn't related to her death," I protested. "That was a night of pure . . ." I stopped; the words would have made it sound cheesy or corny, like the mass-produced sentiment on a Valentine's card.

"All they need to do is make it *look* related," he said. "Their theory of the crime is a three-act play: Act one, you have a fling with her. Act two, she dumps you for her ex. Act three, you kill her in a jealous rage. It's very simple, and it plays well with juries. The DA will drive home any evidence that appears to support that version of events. By not contesting some of that evidence during the prosecution's case, we give it less airtime in the courtroom, so it carries less weight with the jurors."

"And what about when it's our turn?"

"When it's our turn," he said, "we'll offer up a multitude of other explanations, other people who could have wanted to kill Dr. Carter. Her ex. Relatives of people she helped send up for murder. Whoever was leaving her nasty voice mails. Hell, by the time it's over, I'll have the jurors wondering if the DA or the judge might have done her in. Remember, we don't have to prove who actually did it; all we've got to do is create reasonable doubt that *you* did." He checked his watch—a European-looking thing that probably cost half my retainer—and said, "Let's go see if this video guy is worth his three thousand a day."

"Three thousand a day? That's a lot," I squawked. "Hell, that's twice what I charged you to clear Eddie Meacham."

He smiled. "And half what I'm charging you. You're right—it *is* pretty high." DeVriess's phone intercom beeped. "Yes, Chloe?"

"There's a police officer here." I must have looked panicky, because I noticed Grease making soothing motions at me with one hand.

"Ask him to have a seat; tell him we'll be with him as soon as we finish double-checking the video equipment." After Chloe clicked off, he answered my unspoken question. "He brought over the tape from the surveillance camera. Can you believe it? KPD wouldn't trust me with the tape."

I laughed. "That elevates my opinion of KPD's judgment quite a bit."

He stuck out his tongue at me—not the sort of gesture one expects from a high-priced attorney in pinstripes—and led me across the hall to the conference room.

Half the tabletop was now covered with equipment. I recognized a Panasonic VCR and a computer keyboard, but the keyboard appeared connected to a clunky television set. Also connected to that was a slim vertical gizmo, about the size of a hardback book, whose brushed-silver housing sprouted a thicket of cables from the back. It was labeled AVID MOJO. There was also a microphone on a stand.

"Before we look at the video," said DeVriess, "let's get the doctor's voiceprint." Thomas nodded.

"What voiceprint?" I asked.

"We've obtained the threatening messages that were left on Dr. Carter's voice mail," said Grease. "We'll want to suggest that whoever left those messages could be the one who killed her. We need a sample of your voice, saying the same things, in the same way, so we can rule you out. This should carry a fair amount of weight with the jury."

Burt nodded at Thomas, and Thomas played the first message, one sickening phrase at a time. Jess had said they were graphic, but she had spared me the details. "I can't say that," I said.

"You have to," said Burt. "We need an apples-to-apples comparison—your voice saying the exact same words, same inflections, same pacing. Don't worry, we won't play this in court."

"Is there any chance the prosecution could play it?"

"I'd object strenuously to that," said DeVriess. "I think I could block that. It would be irrelevant and prejudicial."

"I'm really not comfortable doing this," I said.

"You'll be a hell of a lot less comfortable if the jury votes to convict you, Doc," he said. "Besides, these messages could point to whoever really killed Dr. Carter. By proving you didn't leave the messages, maybe we encourage the police to investigate other possibilities."

I still didn't like it, but I cooperated. Each of the messages took me several tries—I stumbled over some of the words and phrases, they were so repugnant—but I got through it. The messages began as litanies of sexual perversions; by the last couple, they were vicious, misogynistic death threats. "Yuck," I said when it was over. "I feel like I need to bathe in Lysol now. I hate to think how Jess must have felt when she heard these."

Owen had watched his computer screen impassively as I read the threats, but he, too, looked relieved to have put the distasteful task behind us. He closed the computer program he'd used to record my voice, unplugged the microphone, and coiled the cable neatly. "Okay, that's out of the way," he said. "Now let's see what we can see on the video."

DeVriess punched the intercom button on a phone that had been shoved precariously close to one edge of the table. "Chloe, would you mind showing the officer back to the conference room? Thank you." He turned to Thomas. "Tell us a little about the system," he said. He eyed Thomas's clip-on tie. "But only a little."

If he felt insulted, Thomas didn't show it. "This is a turnkey system called dTective," he said, "from a company called Ocean Systems. They start with an Avid video editing system—the thing most TV shows are cut together on—and they develop hardware and software tools to customize it for forensic work. They've sold well over a thousand of these to police departments all over North America, including KPD, here in Knoxville. Most of those are desktop or rack-mounted systems. They call this version the 'Luggable'; I call it the 'Hernia-Maker.'" So he had a sense of humor. I liked that.

Chloe appeared in the doorway and ushered in a uniformed officer who was carrying a videotape case in one hand. Thomas reached out a hand for the tape case; the officer frowned, then handed it over grudgingly.

Thomas opened the case and studied it. "And this is the original tape, right?"

"Right," said Burt, as if the police officer weren't even there. "You wouldn't believe how hard I had to fight to get this. The DA's office and KDP insisted you could work with a copy. I told them the original was the best evidence, and reminded them we're legally entitled to the best evidence."

He nodded. "Absolutely," he said. "I'll show you why in a minute." He clicked the computer's mouse, and the screen lit up. I had expected it to show a TV-like image from the UT surveillance camera, but instead it was a normal Windows screen, just like on my computer, except that it had a lot more program icons on it than my machine's handful, and most of these looked unfamiliar. He clicked on one of the icons, and the screen filled with several horizontal bands, and a pair of dark circles that looked a bit like maps of the night sky, and a rectangle several inches square. He reached out a hand and Burt gave him the tape case, which he flipped open. He looked at one edge of the tape and frowned, then used a thumbnail to pry out a small tab of black plastic.

"Hey," barked the officer, "what the fuck are you doing?"

"That's the RECORD tab," Thomas said. "If you want to make sure the tape doesn't accidentally get erased or recorded over, you have to remove that tab. Your video guy should have done that the moment he got the tape." He popped the tape into the machine, then hit PLAY. The small rectangle on his screen turned blue, with numerals, just like my television at home did when I put a tape into the VCR. Then the images began, a series of seemingly unrelated images, each on-screen for a fraction of a second, like a visual burst of machine-gun fire. After a few seconds, though, I detected a pattern. The images cycled past in a regular sequence, which I gradually recognized as hospital entrances, parking garages, and—the one that most caught my eye—the Body Farm's gate. It was as if the pages of a dozen different books had been shuffled together at the book bindery, and to follow one story, you'd have to read one page, then flip forward ten or twelve pages to pick up the thread again. Suddenly my truck flashed past a couple of times, and I lunged toward the VCR's controls to hit PAUSE. Thomas reached over and batted away my hand.

"Don't touch that," he snapped. "Do not touch that." The officer grabbed my arm and pulled me back several feet.

"I just wanted to pause it on the truck," I said.

"Do *not* touch the controls," Thomas said. "Every time you start or stop or pause a tape, you damage it. Do it enough times, all you're left with is snow." He glanced in Burt's direction. "This is one reason I hate having clients in the room," he said. "It always complicates things."

"I'm sorry," I said. "It won't happen again. Promise. I just didn't know."

"Okay," he said grudgingly, then—less grudgingly—"Okay, but you're on probation." It sounded like maybe I wouldn't get kicked out after all.

"Well," I said, "that sure beats death row."

He snorted, and Burt laughed; the cop frowned. "We'll look at everything a frame at a time in a minute," Thomas said. "This pass, I'm just reviewing the tape, and optimizing the levels. Then we'll digitize it—load it into the computer's hard drive—and once we've done that, we can pause, or stop and start, as many times as we want without hurting anything. Okay?"

"Okay," I said. "I am sorry."

"If it makes you feel any better, cops make that mistake all the time," he said with an apologetic glance at the officer. "They get to the spot on a tape where an incident occurs—a convenience store shooting or a bank robbery—and they stop and start and rewind and slo-mo, and by the time the case comes to trial, the tape's useless. I make two passes, three at the most, without ever stopping the tape anywhere in the event sequence."

As he talked and the images strobed by, he slid and clicked the mouse rapidly, and the computer's cursor flitted from one pull-down menu to another. As it did, I noticed slight changes in some of the images flickering past—dark images got brighter, washed-out images got toned down, and some colors seemed to fade while details got crisper in shades of gray. After a few minutes, the dark, nighttime shots gave way to sunlit images, and I noticed police vehicles and uniformed cops at the Body Farm. Thomas looked at Burt and asked, "We're past the event sequence now?" Burt nodded. Thomas hit STOP and rewound the tape to the beginning, then hit PLAY again.

"How are we going to tell anything meaningful from that jumble of images?" I asked as they flashed past again. "It looks like they wired a whole bunch of cameras to one VCR."

"That's exactly what they did," he said. "It's called multiplexing. Saves a lot of money on recording decks and tape. In an ideal world, you'd have a separate tape for each camera, recording in real time, and you'd archive all the tapes. But if you did, you'd end up with seventy thousand tapes a year."

"That's a lot of tapes," I conceded.

"A video camera records at thirty frames a second, and it looks like they have sixteen cameras, so in this setup, each camera grabs one frame of video about every half second. Not a bad compromise."

"But everything's all jumbled up," I said.

"Patience, my friend," he said. "There's a tool in dTective called 'Deplex' that demultiplexes the feeds—separates them, like unraveling a rope into individual strands—so we can play the video from one camera at a time."

After he'd recorded the entire nighttime sequence, he stopped and rewound the tape once more, then ejected it, tucked it back into its case, and handed it to the police officer. "Okay, we're done," he said. "Thanks very much." The officer nodded; he hesitated, almost as if hoping to be asked to stay, then turned and left.

"You're done?" I asked. "But we haven't looked at anything yet."

"I just meant I'm through digitizing the original," Thomas said. "Now we'll work with this digital copy. And if something terrible happens as we're working with it, all we lose is a copy, not the original."

"How come UT's still recording on videotape," I asked, "given that even home video cameras are starting to record on memory cards and hard drives?"

"Storage space and data quality," he said. "One hour of images from these cameras would require seventy-two gigabytes of storage. Multiply that times twenty-four hours in a day, times thirty days in a month, and pretty soon you'd need a supercomputer to store it all. You can save space by compressing the images, but when you compress, you lose a lot of the details. To use a nontechnical analogy, the image quality goes from being more like a glossy photographic print to being more like a newspaper photo, which turns into a grainy collection of dots if you look at it closely. More and more surveillance systems are going to digital," he acknowledged, "but nearly all the big Las Vegas casinos—which spend millions on security—still think tape is better." He did more clicking, and sixteen postage-stamp-sized images came up on the monitor. "Okay, there are the sixteen camera angles, separated by the deplexer. Looks like it's camera nine that we're interested in." He clicked on the thumbnail showing the Body Farm's gate, illuminated by the streetlights in the parking lot, and that image enlarged until it filled about half the screen.

He scrolled forward, and as a few cars flitted past the edge of the picture, I saw that the deplexer had indeed plucked this one strand of footage from the multitude of others. "That's amazing," I said. "How does it do that?"

Owen looked over his shoulder at me. "There's a nerdy technical term for it," he said with a twitchy smile. "We call it 'magic.'"

Suddenly a pickup entered the frame and nosed toward the Body Farm gate. He paused, and as I took in the truck's profile—a bronze General Motors pickup with a matching camper shell—I felt the floor drop from beneath me. "Oh Jesus," I breathed. "How in bloody hell . . ." Evers had told me the tape showed my truck, but until this moment, I had dared to hope he was wrong.

The driver's door opened, and all three of us leaned toward the screen. The atmosphere in the room was as charged as the storm crackling outside the office tower, and my heart had crawled so far up my throat I could almost feel it on the back of my tongue. Was I about to see my own face on the camera? By this point, I halfway expected that.

Instead, I saw no one's face. The man—at least, it appeared to be a man—was wearing a cap, pulled low over his eyes. Dark pants, a light-colored shirt. His head was bent down and turned at an odd angle. "Pause it," I said, and I devoured the image. "He *knows*," I said. "He knows there's a camera. He even knows where it is. Look how he's careful to keep from turning his face toward us."

This realization thrilled me. For the first time since Jess's death, I felt something shift subtly; I felt I had something to work with; a tiny piece of the puzzle. I wasn't completely powerless any longer. "You son of a bitch," I said to this man who had killed Jess Carter and set me up. "You sorry son of a bitch. I am coming after you."

I spun my index finger at Thomas and he started the footage again. The man walked up to the chain-link gate and fumbled with the lock. Then he swung the gate open a foot or two and stepped toward the inner, wooden gate. "He's got keys," I said. "That bastard has a set of keys. Who the hell is that?" In my mind, I began reviewing every male who had been issued keys to the facility over the past few years, since the last lock change. There were only a handful—a couple of faculty members and four or five grad students—and it seemed inconceivable that any of them could have killed Jess and laid the blame at my feet.

Suddenly an idea hit me with the force of an electric shock. "Go back, go back," I said. "Let me see that again." This time, I wasn't looking for the face; this time, I was looking for breasts, for female hips, a female gait. Could we be seeing Miranda? She had keys to the facility and even to my truck, and she had once, on a case several months ago, seemed jealous of Jess. Had that jealousy festered into something more sinister? I couldn't believe it, but neither could I ignore the possibility. As I studied the figure's silhouette and gait, I was relieved and deeply ashamed to see that both were unambiguously male.

"What is it?" Burt asked. "Did you see something?"

"No," I said. "I was afraid I might. I was wrong."

The man climbed back into the truck and backed out of the frame. "Where's he going?" Burt asked.

"He parked too close to the gate," I said. "He had to back up so he could open it. I would never make that mistake." Neither would Miranda, who drove into the gate more often than I did these days.

"Good," said Burt. "I'll be sure to ask you about that on the witness stand."

"But won't the DA say that I was just trying to look like I wasn't me?"

"Maybe," Burt said, "but if you were smart enough to act dumb about this, wouldn't you be smart enough not to drive your own damn vehicle?"

"Wait a minute," I laughed, "you've already got me confused."

He smiled and took a bow. "Confusion, my friend, is only a hop, skip, and a vote away from reasonable doubt."

The man walked back into the frame, again keeping his head down and turned slightly to the right, away from the camera. He swung the chain-link gate outward and the wooden gate inward, then walked back to the truck and idled through the gate. Then the wooden gate closed behind him. Burt pointed to the time code in the upper right corner of the screen; it read 5:03 A.M. "Pretty shrewd," he said. "Early enough that nobody else is out and about yet."

"The hospital shift change isn't till seven," I agreed.

"But it's close enough to daybreak so the guy watching the camera feeds will figure that crazy Dr. Brockton is up really early today. Those guys all know what your truck looks like, right?"

"Sure," I said. "They've seen me drive in there hundreds of times. Hell, I've given every campus cop and hospital security guard a tour of the place."

"And this guy knows that somehow," Burt said. "Knows they know your truck."

Owen scrolled forward in the clip until the man opened the wooden gate and pulled out. This time, he pulled far enough forward to clear the chain-link gate. As he closed both gates behind him, I studied the truck more closely. This time it was angled slightly down the parking lot, slightly downhill, so more of its roof was exposed. "I'll be damned," I said. "Stop."

"What?" Burt asked.

"Look at the roof of the cab."

"What about it?"

"What's that dark patch?"

Owen worked his mouse, cranking up the brightness and doubling the size of the image. "It's a moonroof," he said.

I laughed. Wildly. Hysterically.

"What's so funny?" asked Burt.

"My truck . . . doesn't *have* . . . a roonmoof," I gasped. "A moonroof."

"You're sure?" said Burt.

"Sure I'm sure. It was an option, but it cost an

extra five hundred bucks, and I was too damn cheap."

Burt, Thomas, and I exchanged high fives.

"Oh *God*, I feel better," I said.

"Me too," said Burt. "I actually *believe* you now."

"You didn't before? You acted like you did."

"It's a courtesy thing," he said. "My clients always claim they're innocent. I aways pretend to believe them. It's more convenient all the way around. Not many of them are telling the truth." He looked me in the eye. "Doc, I'm really glad you're one of the exceptions."

Owen cleared his throat. "Are we through bonding? Shall we look at the rest of this?"

"Sure," I said. "Let's see what else we can see." I could feel excitement stirring, the same excitement I often felt at death scenes whenever I began finding clues in decaying flesh and damaged bones.

What we saw was another handful of details that would clearly refute the prosecution's claim that this was my truck. The wheels had five spokes; mine, I knew—I had recently had to replace one— had six spokes. One headlight angled crazily down and toward the right. "That's good," said Thomas. "Headlight spray patterns are as distinctive as fingerprints. Unless yours are misaligned in that same way, that's very persuasive. And if we can find a truck like this, with a headlight spray like this, we've nailed it."

"Even if we can't," said Burt, "we can get footage of the Doc's truck in that same spot at night and show how his headlights differ, right? And show he's got no moonroof?"

"Right," said Thomas. "This will blow the jurors away. Jurors *love* this shit. This is nearly as good as *CSI.*"

I no longer begrudged Thomas his $3,000 a day. He had earned it just now, I figured, and then some. In fact, he'd earned every damn cent I had forked over to Burt DeVriess so far. "Will you tell all this to Evers and the DA, or wait and spring it at the trial?" I asked Burt.

"Actually, I'll file a motion to dismiss as soon as I get Owen's report," he said. "We'll get some good press. But the judge won't dismiss the case. Too much other evidence. No judge in his right mind would dismiss a case against a guy whose bed is drenched in his dead lover's blood." He shook his head. "A shame those sheets didn't just disappear."

"I play by the rules," I said. And then I thought of something else. "This guy knows that, too. He was counting on that. Counting on the fact that I'd call the cops when I found the sheets. Giving me the rope he knew I'd use to hang myself."

"Then that tells us even more about him," Burt said. "Maybe a name will pop into your head in the wee small hours. Maybe Evers will have another, friendlier chat with us. Maybe he'll start asking and thinking about who else might have done this. Start casting his net a little wider."

Burt clapped Thomas on the shoulder; Thomas flinched, either from the force of it or from the violation of his boundaries. "Okay, I think we're done for now," Burt said. "How soon can you send me that report?"

"I'll write it on the plane and e-mail it to you tonight. That soon enough?"

"Yeah, that'll do; thanks. Chloe will be in touch once we have a trial date. I'm gonna go start drafting that motion." As he left the conference room, Burt yanked up the blinds, flooding the room with light. It was that scrubbed version of sunlight that follows a hard spring storm. I took it as a good omen.

CHAPTER 39

AFTER I LEFT DEVRIESS'S office, I sat for several minutes in the cool darkness of the building's parking garage, considering where to go next. I still had several hours to kill before my rendezvous with Art and our evening's errand. Normally I would simply go to my office on campus, which was only a couple of miles away, or home, which was no more than five or six. But I'd been asked to stay away from the one, and I was anxious to avoid the reporters that I feared were at the other.

I'd brought my briefcase, stuffed with the journal articles that would help me update my textbook's discussion of long bones. But where to work? The downtown library felt too public, too exposed; so did the restaurant across the valley from Burt's office, Riverside Tavern. The last thing I wanted was to be gawked at, pointed at, intruded on, even in the unlikely event someone simply wanted to wish me well. In the end, I drove back to Tyson Park, where I spread my papers on a slightly sticky picnic table under a shelter, in case another storm blew through.

Not long after I settled in, a car drove through the park and stopped when it drew alongside the shelter. I glanced up just long enough to recognize the markings and light bar of a police car, then redoubled my focus on my papers. After idling beside the Taurus for an interminable ten minutes, the cruiser left. But it circled back at regular intervals over the next three hours. The vigil made me feel both vaguely guilty and unfairly persecuted. I wondered if this was what homeless people felt like—people whose days stretched out before them, with no comfortable, welcoming place to spend them. I had money in my pocket and a roof over my head, of course—two roofs, if I counted my house and the rented cabin at Norris—yet neither place felt like home.

I willed myself to concentrate on the bones of the human arm and leg. In the two decades since I had written the first edition of my textbook, Americans' average stature had increased by a fraction of an inch. Consequently, the femur and other long bones had also grown ever so slightly; as a result, a femur whose dimensions would have identified it as unequivocally male twenty or thirty years ago might now be that of a tall woman instead. The changes were slight, but not insignificant. I thought of the creationists, and what they might make of the trend. If we were created in God's image, would Jennings Bryan and his followers take this to mean God was growing, too?

The reading and revisions took me until dark.

When I could no longer see to read or write, I gathered up my papers and drove out of the park and along the Strip, the stretch of Cumberland Avenue whose restaurants and bars bordered one edge of the UT campus. I went back to the same deli I had visited at lunchtime; the turkey sandwich had been good, and the drive-through window afforded me some privacy. This time, feeling daring and in need of variety, I ordered a corned beef. Then—undercutting the boldness of the impetuous sandwich choice—I pulled into the farthest, darkest corner of the lot to eat. The sandwich was fine, but I was preoccupied. I wasn't looking forward to what I was about to do. My only consolation was that Art was doing it with me. Halfway through the sandwich, I lost interest and put it back in the bag. Then, with more than a little trepidation, I drove to KPD headquarters, where Art stood waiting for me under the floodlit flagpole. He got in without speaking—clearly he wasn't looking forward to this any more than I was—and I headed toward Broadway and Old North Knoxville.

I'd called Susan Scott earlier in the day to find out what time her son went to bed. "Joey's bedtime is nine-thirty," she had said. "We usually watch *America's Funniest Home Videos* at eight-thirty, and I read a chapter out of *Harry Potter* to him. He's nearly always asleep by nine forty-five."

"I know it would be late," I'd responded, "but could my friend Art and I come by at ten? I'm sorry to ask, but I think it's important. And I'd like to come when you and your husband can both be home."

She had hesitated, and I could almost hear her trying to decide whether to ask why. She didn't ask, and I was grateful, as I hadn't been able to come up with an explanation that sounded anything short of crazy or terrifying. "All right," she had said. "Bobby's working a lot of overtime, like I told you, but he's usually home by eight or nine. I'll turn on the porch light for you when Joey's asleep."

It was nine-thirty when Art and I pulled up to the curb across the street from the Scotts' house. The honey-colored lamplight shone from every window on the front of the house. It made the old Victorian look like something out of a Currier & Ives print—*Home Sweet Home* or *Cozy Sanctuary* or something equally sentimental; not the sort of place you'd ever imagine hearts had been shattered and young psyches scarred. We sat in silence. I was grappling with myself, wondering whether this was really necessary; I was pretty sure Art was, too. After a few minutes, the light in one of the second-floor windows winked out, and soon after, the front-porch bulb snapped on. Just enough of its light carried into the dimness of the car to illuminate Art's face a bit. It looked sad and drawn. "We could just drive away," I said. "Leave it alone."

He was silent for a long time. "We could," he said. "Don't think I wouldn't love to. But if we look the other way this time, what happens next time? And the next? Once you cross a line, it gets easier the next time, and the next and the next. And pretty soon you don't even remember where the line was. You and I have spent a lot of years playing by the rules. We believe in 'em, even though they don't always seem fair. You know that. That's why you called Evers instead of burning those sheets, or tying them around a cinder block and chucking 'em in the river."

"I know," I said. "And isn't that working out swell for me?"

"It ain't over yet," he said. "Too soon to give up on the system. You've got a shrewd lawyer, and if anybody in this city can get a jury that's inclined to give the benefit of the doubt, it's you."

"Yeah," I said with more than a trace of irony in my voice. "The greatest legal system in the world. And at its pinnacle there's my lawyer, Grease DeVriess."

"Hey, I didn't say it was perfect," he said. "But in this case, maybe Grease can actually do a good deed. Bootstrap himself up from the lowest circle of hell to one of those mid-level circles."

"If clearing my name means making the afterlife easier for Grease, I'm not so sure I want to be acquitted," I said, and Art laughed quietly. "You're a good man, Bill," he said. "You ready?"

"No. But I guess we'd best go do this anyhow."

We got out of the truck, easing the doors shut quietly. Down the street, a dog barked once, then fell silent. We eased wordlessly up the walk and up the stairs, and I knocked softly on the front door. It opened in seconds, and Susan Scott faced us nervously. Behind her stood her husband Bobby. She had said he was a contractor, and judging by his build, he wasn't just a foreman, he still did a lot of labor himself. He stood about six-three, with broad shoulders and bulging arms. He had a hint of a beer gut, but underneath it, he still had the body of an athlete. When he shook Art's hand, I saw Art wince, and when he shook mine, I understood why.

They led us to the sofa, where Art and I had sat when we delivered the news of Craig Willis's death to Susan Scott the week before. They sat in closely spaced armchairs, holding hands between the chairs.

"I'm not sure where to start," I said. "You might have seen me in the news lately." They both nodded, looking embarrassed. "Somebody's working hard to make it look like I killed Dr. Carter, and they're doing a pretty good job of it. We're trying to figure out who, and why."

Susan looked confused, and I could hardly blame her. "When you called, you said you had some new information about Craig Willis."

"We do," said Art. "And we're thinking there might be some connection between that case and Dr. Carter's murder."

"How on earth would those be related?" asked Bobby.

"Not sure," Art replied. "But Dr. Carter was murdered right after we identified Craig Willis's body. Willis's mother was very upset at the news stories about her son's death. She felt like Dr. Carter had ruined his reputation."

"Christ, give me a break," said Bobby Scott. "That guy was a piece of shit."

"Bobby!" his wife exclaimed.

"I can't help it, Sue. You know it's true, and you feel the same way. I'm glad he's dead, and I wish the papers had printed the rest of his story."

"A day before she was killed," I said, "Dr. Carter was in my office at UT. Craig Willis's mother came in and physically attacked Dr. Carter. We had to call the campus police."

Susan put a hand to her mouth. "You think maybe she killed Dr. Carter?"

"Don't know," Art said, "but we're concerned that Mrs. Willis might be unstable, and might pose a risk to anyone who's connected to her son's case." He reached into his shirt pocket and took out a photograph. It was a print of one of the photos I'd shot earlier in the day, at Mrs. Willis's house. "You haven't seen her in the neighborhood, have you? Or anywhere near Joey's school?" He handed the photo to Mr. Scott. He took it in his free hand, studied it a moment, and shook his head. Then he handed it to his wife. She looked at it much longer, then shook her head as well, and handed the photo back to Art. Art, too, looked at the photo. He held it under the floor lamp that was at his end of the sofa, and angled the picture back and forth to catch the light. His face took on a look of infinite sorrow, and when he looked up at Bobby Scott, I could see tears gathering in the corner of Art's eyes. I could feel them welling up in mine, too. "Mr. Scott," Art said, "how did you cut your thumb? And when?"

Bobby Scott looked startled, and then nervous. "With a utility knife on a job," he said. "Stripping electrical wire. About a week ago, I'd say."

"I'd say more like three or four weeks ago," Art said. "Just before that night you spent away from home? It's healed up pretty well—just a faint scar by now, I'd say, judging by this thumbprint." Bobby

Scott flushed. "Mind showing me your thumb?" said Art. Scott extricated his hand from his wife's, but he did not show his thumb to Art; instead, he put both hands on the arms of his chair, leaning forward and looking ready to jump up. The fight-or-flight reflex had clearly kicked in like a turbocharger.

His wife was looking from Art to her husband to me. "What's going on?" I could see confusion and panic rising in her. "Somebody please tell me what this is about," she said. Her voice was taut as a guitar string on the verge of snapping.

"When Craig Willis was killed," I said, "his penis was cut off and shoved in his mouth. There was a bloody thumbprint on the penis. The thumb had a pretty big cut down the center."

She turned and stared at her husband. The looks that passed between them—her unspoken and frightened questions, his angry and apologetic answers—nearly broke my heart. She began to shake, and to weep. "Oh God, Bobby," she said, "what have you done? How could you do this to us? Oh God. Every time I think it can't possibly get any worse . . ." She clenched a fist and bit into the side of her index finger with enough force that I expected to see the skin tear open. "I can't take it," she sobbed. "I can't. I can't. I have tried so hard. So fucking hard. But I can't take any more."

Bobby Scott dropped to his knees in front of her. Now he was crying, too. "Baby, I'm so sorry," he said. "I did it for Joey. And I did it for all the other kids I knew would suffer the same thing he did. And I thought I was doing it for you and me, too. I thought it was the only way to get some justice, so I could quit being so furious all the time. I never thought . . . I never dreamed . . . Oh, baby, I'm sorry. So sorry." And he buried his head in her lap and sobbed. She sat there, stunned and unmoving, and I thought, *This is when this marriage lives or dies.* And finally she laid her hands on his head, and stroked his hair, and leaned forward to cradle him in her arms and her bosom, and they grieved together.

After they were cried out—and it took some time—Bobby raised his head and turned to Art. "So what happens now? Are you here to arrest me?"

"No," said Art. "I think it's best if you turn yourself in and confess." He grimaced, but then slowly nodded. "Things might not be as bad as they seem," Art said to Susan. "With a good lawyer and a reasonably understanding DA, there's a shot at a pretty decent plea bargain. Could be out in a year or two. Other possibility, if it goes to trial, is an acquittal. Sometimes juries ignore the letter of the law in favor of a higher form of justice. Even cops and prosecutors sometimes hope for that. No guarantees, but speaking as a cop, that's what I'd hope for in this case. And speaking as a parent, I know how I'd vote if I were in the jury box."

"Me too," I said. "I need to ask you something, Bobby. I'm pretty sure I know the answer, but I have to ask anyhow. Did you kill Dr. Carter? To cover your tracks?"

He shook his head. His face looked ravaged, but it looked open and honest. "No, of course not," he said. "I could never kill an innocent person.

I'm sorry she's been murdered." He pointed at the photo Art still held, as if from a lifetime ago. The photo we'd used to trick him into giving us a fingerprint. "What about her?"

"She's maybe mad enough," I said, "and maybe crazy enough. But the reality is, she's not strong enough. I found that out today, when she came at me with a pair of pruning shears. Whoever killed Dr. Carter carried her body fifty yards up a hillside. No drag marks. A sixty-year-old woman couldn't have done that. Hell, I'm not sure I could've done that. Gotta be a pretty strong man. Besides, there's a surveillance video showing a man."

He shook his head again. "I swear to you, on my son's life, I didn't kill Dr. Carter."

"I believe you," I said. "I think you're an honest man. A decent man who got pushed past his breaking point. Can I ask you something else?" He nodded mutely. "Why that out-of-the-way trail in Prentice Cooper State Forest? That took some doing, and it must have been risky, too."

An odd, sad smile flitted over his features for a moment. "Joey and I went camping down there. It was right before he . . . We hiked that trail, and saw that TVA place across the river gorge, and the next day, before we drove home to Knoxville, we went over there and toured the place. It was the last time and the last place I saw Joey really happy. Purely happy."

"It won't be easy," I said, "but I think maybe you all can still be okay. I hope you'll try." I looked at Susan, who still seemed shell-shocked. "You two must love each other very much," I added. "And you still need each other. And Joey still needs you both."

We talked a few more minutes—lawyers and court proceedings; the nuts and bolts and cogs of the Rube Goldberg machine that was the legal system—and then Art and I left. As we reached the end of their sidewalk, I looked back. They were standing on the front porch, dark forms silhouetted in golden light, each with an arm around the other's waist. Despite the hard row ahead of them, I envied them in that moment. They had one another.

Art and I did not speak on the drive back to KPD. He got out wordlessly and trudged to his car, looking ten years older and tireder than I'd ever seen him look. He might have thought the same about me if I'd been the one crossing the pavement beneath unforgiving sodium lights.

I grieved the whole way back to the cabin at Norris. For the first time since Jess's death, I wasn't grieving for her, or feeling sorry for myself. The horizon of my grief had broadened enough to take in others, and to allow me to recognize that my pain was far from unique, and far from the heaviest burden to be borne.

CHAPTER 40

MY CELLPHONE RANG AT seven the next morning; it took some groping to find it in the early morning darkness of the cabin. "Bill, it's Burt. Listen, I got Owen Thomas's report last night, and it's great. Besides writing up the video analysis and e-mailing a movie highlighting the differences between your truck and the mystery truck—that's what we're calling it from now on—he also did some additional voice analysis that's very interesting."

"Interesting how?"

"Well, after he confirmed that it was not your voice on Jess's voice mail, he downloaded a couple of TV news stories covering the creationist protest. One of the creationists—the lawyer who's really pulling the strings—used a few of the same words in his interview as the guy on Jess's voice mail. So Thomas was able to do some comparisons."

"Jennings Bryan used profanity and death threats in his TV interview?"

"No, no; words like 'the' and 'we.' A few paired

words—'will wish' and 'had never,' I think. Anyhow, it's not enough to be conclusive, but based on the waveforms and the spacing between words and so on, he says there's a strong possibility that it was Bryan who left those messages for Jess. So we'll turn that over to the DA and Detective Evers, and push them to interrogate that guy. See if they'll haul him in and make him repeat the messages verbatim, just like Thomas made you do. If he doesn't, I'll beat him over the head with that omission at trial—make the jury think the cops ignored other suspects in order to railroad you. Meantime, I might just go have a chat with Mr. Bryan, friendly-like, and see if I can persuade him to drop that lawsuit against you."

"You mean blackmail him?"

"Heaven forbid!" he said. "We attorneys call such negotiations 'alternative dispute resolution.' Sounds far more ethical."

"Can you also build the voice analysis into your motion to dismiss?"

"No, because it's not the same as the video evidence. The prosecution isn't claiming that it's your voice in those messages, but they *are* claiming it's your truck on the video. Don't worry, the motion is plenty strong. As I said, I don't expect it to be granted, but we can get a lot of mileage out of it. If you're willing to help."

"Help, how?" I could hear alarm bells ringing in the back of my mind.

"I'd like to take this evidence to the court of public opinion. Start rehabilitating your image before the trial starts; start planting those seeds of doubt right away. I'd like to hold a news conference and share the motion and the surveillance video and Thomas's findings with the media."

I'd witnessed Burt's press conferences in numerous other trials, and always before, his flamboyant theatrics had struck me as unseemly. They still did. "Is that really necessary?"

"Is it necessary? No," he said. "Is it helpful? Absolutely. So far, everything that has come out in the media has been released by the prosecution or the police. And so far, everything makes you look guilty as sin." He had a point there, I had to admit. "This surveillance video—together with Thomas's written report and his DVD highlighting key differences between your truck and this mystery truck in the video—will make everyone realize that you're the victim of an elaborate setup."

It sounded good, but I knew not everyone would react as Burt was predicting; some would react as I invariably did, dismissing the entire performance as grandstanding. "I don't know, Burt."

"Bill, you're paying me—and paying me a lot—for the benefit of my experience and legal skill, right?"

"Right . . ."

"Every bit of experience and skill I have tells me this is a crucial step toward building a strong defense for you. A courtroom trial doesn't occur in a vacuum. The judge, the prosecution, and I will all bend over backward to pretend that it does; to pretend we've got a jury completely untainted by news coverage. Truth is, that's bullshit, and we all know it. Our side is way behind so far, Bill. We have to start getting some good licks in."

I still didn't like it, but it made sense. Just as Burt's other ploys had made sense, I supposed, to his other clients. I recalled the old saying about not judging another man until you'd walked a mile in his moccasins; at the moment, it felt like I was running a marathon in some mighty stinky footwear, with something unpleasant squishing up between my toes. "Damn," I said. "Okay, go ahead."

"I think we need to take a couple more quick steps in your rehabilitation, too," he said.

"What steps?" The word underscored that squishy feeling between my toes.

"You need to be with me at the press conference. Then you need to move back home. Come out of seclusion."

"Come on, Burt," I said. "There were cameras all over the death scene, and my house, and the booking facility, and my house again. How can you ask me to live in that kind of fishbowl?"

"There'll be a big flurry of interest when we file this motion and release the video analysis," he said, "but it'll die down in twenty-four hours and things will stay quiet until the trial. You need to start acting like an innocent man again. Take a cue from Bill Clinton, Ronald Reagan, Dick Cheney, and all those other Washington bigwigs. Even when they're being accused of all manner of evil, they smile and wave for the cameras. And people think, 'That nice man—he couldn't have done those dreadful things!'"

"Would I have to answer questions at the press conference?"

"No, I'll head that off at the start. Just hold up a

hand, and look regretful that I'm not allowing you to comment. It's all part of the game, Bill. If you can think of it as a game, maybe it won't be so intolerable. And if you'll play by the media's rules even a little bit—give them some footage to help fill that gaping hole they have to fill every night—they'll stop painting you as a villain. You'll be surprised how the tone of the coverage will shift. I've seen it a hundred times."

"Okay, counselor," I said. "You win."

"That's good," he said, "because Chloe's already called all the news outlets to tell them the plan."

I just shook my head. "Incredible. Where should I meet you, Machiavelli, and when?"

"My office. One forty-five. We'll walk to the City County Building to deliver the motion at two, and hold the press conference outside right afterward. That gives the TV stations plenty of time to get the story on both newscasts tonight."

"And you really think this will help?"

"It has to," he said. "This could be our one shot before the trial. Once the DA sees we're fighting back, he might ask for a gag order. Or maybe the judge will decide to impose one on his own. In any case, we have to swing for the fence."

At one-thirty, I pulled into the garage at Riverview Tower. Upstairs, Chloe greeted me warmly. "You ready for your close-up?" she said.

"Don't rub it in," I said. "I really hate doing this."

"I know," she said. "Not everybody basks in the limelight like Mr. DeVriess does. But this will help things, it really will. I have a friend who works at the *News Sentinel*, and she says this is the talk of the newsroom. They're assigning three investigative reporters just to look for that truck and dig up other story angles they might have missed. Oh, and *Larry King* and *20/20* have already called."

"*Larry King? 20/20?!* How the hell did they get wind of this already?"

"We've had high-profile cases a time or two before," she said. "We don't call people at the national level very often, but when we do, they know it's a good story."

"Lord, what have I done? I should never have let him talk me into this."

"Yes you should. Can I tell you something, just between us?" I nodded warily. "If you tell Mr. DeVriess I said it, I'll get fired."

"My lips are sealed," I said, holding up three fingers in the Boy Scout sign.

"I don't always respect our clients, and I don't always like what Mr. DeVriess does for them. But you're different. And he knows it. What he's doing might help save you." She looked suddenly shy. "It might help save him, too. Does that make any sense?"

"You mean make up for some of his other cases? Redemption?" She nodded. "Stranger things have happened," I said. "Especially lately." I heard DeVriess's office door open and his Italian shoes clicking down the hall. I held a finger to my lips and gave Chloe a conspiratorial wink. She winked back. I hoped the image of her wink, and the generous impulse behind it, could carry me through the surreal gamesmanship of the next hour.

"Keep up," Burt said as the elevator reached the

lobby. "Walk briskly, with purpose. Smile, but not too big, and nod occasionally to acknowledge the cameras. Hold up a deferential, apologetic hand every third or fourth question." With those instructions, we pushed out the lobby door onto the sidewalk of Gay Street, into a waiting mob of reporters. I saw cameras from all the local TV stations, as well as CNN and Fox News. I counted a dozen or more still photographers, too, as well as what I estimated at close to a hundred spectators. Where had they all come from? And why?

I followed Burt's instructions to the letter, partly in hopes of creating the desired effect, and partly to have something to do besides flee or hide my face like a minister arrested in a prostitution sting. Burt brushed off all questions on our way into the City County Building, pausing only to say, "As soon as we file this motion to dismiss, we'll have a statement, and we'll distribute copies of the exculpatory evidence we're basing the motion on."

It took a grand total of sixty seconds to file the motion in the court clerk's office. The staff there gave Burt a look of weary forbearance—they had been through this routine with him countless times before—but I noticed several of them eyeing me closely. As we left the building, Burt led the media horde to a set of steps at one side of the plaza, where he—and I—could ascend and display ourselves to better advantage. The clamor of questions was almost incomprehensible. Burt held up both hands, signaling for silence, and as if on cue, a thicket of microphone booms swung into position above his head. "We have just filed a motion to dismiss all charges against Dr. Bill Brockton," he said. "We have dramatic new evidence that proves conclusively— contrary to what the prosecution claims—that it was *not* Dr. Brockton's truck that entered the Body Farm in the hours shortly before Dr. Carter's body was found." Another round of questions roared, but Burt ignored them and continued with his script. "That truck—the mystery truck—was driven by someone intent not only on killing Dr. Carter but also on destroying Dr. Brockton. When we solve the mystery of that truck, we'll solve the mystery of Dr. Carter's murder." DeVriess glanced to one side, and Chloe emerged from the crowd. "We have some additional information in these briefing packets, including technical details of the video analysis and a broadcast-quality DVD that shows the surveillance footage and then highlights irrefutable differences between Dr. Brockton's truck and the mystery truck." He nodded at Chloe, and she began handing out glossy black folders which I noticed were imprinted with the name of Burt's firm in raised gold lettering. They were the Bentley version of folders, I thought with a wry smile.

Burt wasn't quite finished. "We call on the court to dismiss all charges," he said in a voice worthy of the pulpit. "We call on the district attorney to stop using Dr. Brockton as a scapegoat. And we call on the Knoxville Police Department to find this mystery truck, and the real killer, and bring him to justice for this terrible crime." With that ringing pronouncement, he grabbed my elbow and practically dragged me back to his office.

The event was simplistically scripted, it was cynically staged, and it was brilliantly effective. During the five-thirty newscast, which I watched in the living room of my own house, I flipped back and forth among all the Knoxville stations, and caught the phrases "mystery truck," "mystery man," and "mystery killer" more times than I could count.

We hadn't won yet—not by a long shot—but DeVriess was right: it was time to start acting like an innocent man, and he had just made that possible for me.

CHAPTER 41

IT WAS TEN O'CLOCK when my cellphone rang. I checked to see who was calling, and was puzzled to see a 423 area code. Chattanooga. "Hello," I said warily.

"Dr. Bill? Hey, I see you on TV this evening."

"Well, hello, Miss Georgia. I didn't know I made the Chattanooga news, too."

"Naw, baby, I see you on the Knoxville news. I be right here in the same town as you. My cellphone just think it's still in Chattanooga. How you doin', Dr. Bill?"

"How am I? Well, let's see," I said. "The woman I was falling in love with has been killed, I've been charged with murder, I've been barred from the university, and my grandkids scream when they see me now. On the bright side, my sleazy defense lawyer is the lead story on all the local TV stations tonight, and a video expert can prove it wasn't my truck that drove into the Body Farm the night Jess's body was put there. So I suppose things could be worse."

"We can't bring Miss Jessamine back, Dr. Bill, but we gon' clear up all this other mess. You wait and see."

I wasn't sure what part Miss Georgia saw herself playing in setting the record straight, but I appreciated her faith. "I hope you're right, Georgia," I said. "How about you?"

"Well, less see," she mimicked. "My weenie and my 'nads done been chopped off, I got a hundred stitches in my bottom, and I done traded in my little silk thong for a big ol' Depends. But I be a real woman now, Dr. Bill, so I be just fine. My ass hurt like a motherfucker, but iss a good hurt. I be going home in a couple days, doctor say."

"Congratulations," I said. "I'm glad you've finally got what you've been wanting for so long."

Just then my landline rang. "You need to answer that, honey-lamb?"

"I'll let the machine get it," I said. "Probably a reporter, or somebody phoning to call me a murderer or an infidel." When my greeting finished playing, though, I was startled to hear Garland Hamilton's voice. "Bill? Are you there? It's Garland. If you're there, Bill, please pick up."

"Georgia? Sorry, I need to take this." I laid down the cell and grabbed for the receiver.

"Guess you're not there. Listen, I've got something that sheds some new light on Jess Carter's murder," Garland was saying, "and I thought—"

I snatched up the receiver. "Garland? I'm here. What have you got? Tell me."

"Oh, Bill, I'm so glad you're there. Hey, congratulations, by the way—I saw the news about the surveillance video," he said. "That will help your case enormously."

"Thanks," I said, "I hope you're right. Now tell me what you've found out."

"I don't think I should over the phone," he said. "Is it too late to come see you? Are you already in bed?"

"No," I said. "I'm not sleeping much these days. Too many ghosts under the bed."

"I understand," he said. "Strictly speaking, I shouldn't be talking to you at all, but I have a bombshell that could clear your name overnight."

"Jesus, Garland, what is it?"

"I need to show it to you. You want me to come over now? Or would you rather wait till morning?"

"God, no. If you've got something new on Jess's murder, please come now."

"Okay. I'm calling from the car—I just left the morgue. I know you live somewhere in Sequoyah Hills, but that neighborhood is like a maze to me, especially at night. Can you stay on the line with me and talk me in?"

"Sure. Where are you now?"

"I've just gotten off Alcoa Highway, and I'm heading west on Kingston Pike. I'm almost to the light at Cherokee Boulevard."

"Okay, turn left on Cherokee." From there, I guided him through a series of turns past ivy-wrapped stone mansions and glassy contemporary boxes. I had to close my eyes to visualize the route; I'd driven it so many thousand times over the years, I'd long since ceased to pay attention to the street names or the landmarks. Finally I steered him onto my street. I looked out the front window and said, "Okay, I see your headlights. I'm hanging up now; I'll flash the porch light for you." I did, and a moment later I heard the thunk of his Tahoe's door closing.

I met him at the door and pumped his hand. "Thank you for coming," I said. "I can't tell you how much I appreciate it. Come in, sit down, and for God's sake tell me what you've got."

"Hang on a second," he said. "You know it would get me in a lot of trouble with the district attorney if he knew I was here?" I nodded. "You didn't tell anybody I was coming, did you?"

"No, how could I? I was on the phone with you until thirty seconds ago."

"What about that telephone message? You better erase that, just to be on the safe side. The police could come back with another search warrant."

"Really? I would never have thought of that." I walked to the answering machine and deleted the last message. "I'd make a lousy criminal."

He laughed at that. "Yes, you would, Bill. Indeed you would."

"So tell me. What is it? What have you got?"

"I think you'd better sit down," he said. "This is going to blow you away." I sat. "What would you say if I told you I had the gun that killed Jess?"

I was sitting perfectly still, but my mind was racing. "I would say . . . that's amazing," I said. "Where was it? Who found it? Have the police already done the ballistic tests? Were there fingerprints on it?"

"There are fingerprints," he said.

"Have the police run them yet? Is there a match?"

"They haven't had a chance. But I can promise you they'll find a match in the system."

"How can you be so sure?"

"Because the prints will be yours."

I stared at him, trying to follow, but failing. "I don't understand."

"No. But you will." He reached behind his back and produced a small handgun, which he pointed at my chest. "This is the murder weapon," he said. "I shot Jess with it. Now I'm going to shoot you with it. Not quite the end I had in mind for you—I was so enjoying the thought of you spending time in prison with killers and rapists you helped send there. But your lawyer and his video expert have seriously lowered the odds of getting you convicted. So I think it's safer to go with Plan B."

Suddenly the puzzle pieces fell into place, and I felt stupid for not having suspected Garland Hamilton—tall, strong Garland Hamilton. The one person whose work and whose woes involved both Jess and me. He knew where the hospital surveillance cameras were placed, knew how to plant evidence on a corpse, knew my truck, knew my habits, knew my strengths well enough to turn them against me. Hell, he even knew where a spare key to the Body Farm was stashed at the Forensic Center. "You killed Jess and framed me for her murder? Why? Out of spite?"

"Oh, 'spite' doesn't begin to do it justice," he said. "Something like 'implacable hatred' or 'black-hearted vengeance' would be much closer to the mark. Was it Hamlet who said, 'Revenge is a dish best served cold'? I've been letting this chill for months. You have no idea how humiliating I found it to be made a fool by you over the Ledbetter autopsy. Not once, but twice: first in court, and then before a board of medical examiners—my professional peers."

"But they didn't take your license," I said. "What harm did that do you? You got your job back."

"Only temporarily," he said. "The board made that clear when they called to impose my punishment. The governor himself told the commissioner of health to ease me out. And I'll never get my reputation back. It's ruined. You ruined it."

"I can see why you might hold a grudge against me," I said slowly, "but why Jess?"

When he smiled, I felt icy fingers clutching my soul. "Why Jess? So many reasons why Jess." He cocked his head. "Did you know she was about to be made state medical examiner?" I shook my head. "All the MEs in Tennessee are about to be rolled into a statewide organization, and the beautiful, brainy Dr. Carter had been tapped to head that organization. So six months from now, I would have been out, and Jess would be in. Farther in than I had ever been. I'm surprised you didn't know."

"It wasn't my business," I said. "She'd have had no reason to tell me."

"Then she probably also didn't tell you that she and I had a fleeting romance once."

"You? When?" The thought of it turned my stomach.

"A year or so ago. Right after she and her husband separated. She made it clear afterward that I was just a revenge fuck. I never forgave her for that. But she did have a gorgeous body, didn't she, our Jess?"

I made a lunge at him; he struck me with the pistol, then kneed me in the groin. I sank back into the chair.

"But you want to know the third reason, the main reason, why I killed Jess?"

"Yes. Why?"

"You."

"Me?"

"You. You were falling in love with Jess; she was falling in love with you. That made her your Achilles' heel, your most vulnerable spot. I followed you to her house that night in Chattanooga. Being out of a job at the moment, I had plenty of time to keep tabs on you. I saw you spring up the stairs to her house like a teenager going on a date; I saw her come to the door and welcome you in; Christ, I even heard the two of you moaning up there in her bedroom. It took every ounce of willpower I had not to walk in and shoot you both in her bed. But I kept my eyes on the prize."

"And what prize was that, Garland?"

"Making you suffer."

"Well, you've certainly done that," I said. "But if you kill me, too, the police will match the bullet to the one that killed Jess. They'll know that whoever murdered me also murdered Jess."

He laughed and shook his head. "As you said, you'd make a lousy criminal, Bill. You're not going to be murdered; you're going to die by your own hand. Tragic, really: Bill Brockton, driven to suicide by his guilt over murdering Dr. Carter, his despair over losing his reputation, his fear of going to prison and getting manhandled by some of his old friends."

"Go to hell," I said. "I will never commit suicide."

"Call it assisted suicide, then," he said. "The criminalists will find your prints, and only your prints, on the gun. The autopsy—*my* autopsy—will find powder burns and even a nice, round contact impression from the muzzle, which you held tight against your skull as you pulled the trigger." As he said it, he jammed the gun into my temple. "It's a terrible thing, losing one's hard-earned reputation, isn't it, Bill? We have that experience in common now." He smiled and added, "Just like we have Jess in common now."

The sight of him disgusted me, and I looked away. And when I did, I saw a glimmer of hope. It was the tiny green diode on my cellphone, the one that blinked every few seconds during a call. *Georgia*, I realized. I had been talking to her on the cell when Hamilton called, and I never hung up. Was there a chance she was still on the line? *Please, God, let her be listening; please let someone hear me die; please let someone know the truth.*

It was a long shot, but it was the only shot I had. "So tell me more about how you killed Jess," I said.

"With pleasure," he said. "Pun intended. Where shall I begin?"

It was the same question I'd put to Burt DeVriess the night I'd hired him. "At the beginning of the end," I said. "When you abducted her, or broke into her house, or whatever you did when you made your move."

"Hmmmm," he said, as if savoring a fond memory. "It was that night the two of you had dinner at By the Tracks. That row of shops facing the restaurant? I was on the sidewalk, behind one of the columns, right in front of her car. Jess came out of the restaurant alone. She hit the remote to unlock her car and got in. I stepped out from behind the column and got in with her. It was so easy."

"Then what? Where did you take her? Your house?"

"I have a large wine cellar in my basement—a concrete room within a concrete basement. Very secure, and very quiet. No sound gets in; no sound gets out."

I thought I should ask for more details about Jess's death, but my courage failed me; I couldn't bear to hear the details of her suffering. "The hair and fibers—my hair, my carpet, my bedspread—how did you get those onto her body before the autopsy?"

"I didn't," he said. "I wrote them into the autopsy report, but I didn't collect them until the next day. That rock through the window of your front door?" I nodded; the note had an antievolution message on it, so I'd assumed it was thrown by one of the creationist protesters. "My little Trojan horse. The broken window let me reach in and unlock the door, put blood and some of Jess's hair on your sheets, then collect some of your hair and tell the police I found it on Jess's body. The police had no reason to doubt me."

I was just about to ask where he'd found a truck so nearly like mine for transporting Jess to the Body

Farm when a series of low beeps sounded from the bookshelf beside him. It was the low-battery warning on my cellphone, and I kicked myself for not having charged it in the car earlier in the day. Hamilton whirled in the direction of the sound, and his eyes spotted the blinking light on the cell. Keeping the gun pointed at me, he sidled over, picked up the phone, and held it to his ear. Then he flipped it closed. "You son of a bitch," he said. "Time's up." He stepped toward me and raised the gun to my right temple.

Just then the front doorbell rang. Hamilton and I both jumped, and I was surprised his trigger finger had not reflexively tightened enough to fire the gun. "Now what?" I asked.

"Now nothing," he said. "Stand still and don't make a sound or I'll shoot you."

"You're going to shoot me anyway," I said. "Why shouldn't I make you do it when there's a witness within earshot?"

"You stupid son of a bitch," he said. "No matter what, I walk away clean. You called me on the phone, distraught and suicidal. I raced over and tried to talk sense into you. Just as I was about to persuade you to hand over the gun, someone rang the doorbell, and you panicked and pulled the trigger. There is no scenario I cannot explain."

There was a loud knock on the door. "Bill? You awake?" The voice was familiar, but I couldn't quite place it. "Bill?" The volume was getting louder. "Hey, Bill—come on, let's go!"

At the word "go," the living room window closest to us shattered, and then the world seemed to explode. I seemed to be falling, but curiously—even as I felt myself hit the floor—the image that remained frozen in my gaze was of my front door, and of Garland Hamilton standing beside me, his hand and the stock of a pistol just visible in my peripheral vision. *So this is what it's like to die of a gunshot to the head*, I thought.

And suddenly my vision unfroze, just in time for me to see a squad of police officers, wearing body armor and carrying automatic weapons, pouring through my front door. One of them flung himself over my body, and two of them grabbed Garland Hamilton, who appeared as dazed as I felt. Two more pointed weapons at Hamilton's chest.

One of the policemen spoke into a shoulder-mounted radio mic. "All clear in the house," he said. "Suspect is restrained. No casualties."

A moment later, Detective John Evers—whose voice it was I'd heard at the door—strode in. He surveyed the bizarre scene, studying Hamilton for a long moment, then reached down to help me up. "You okay?" he said.

"I guess maybe I am," I said. "I thought I'd been shot in the head. Evidently not."

He laughed. "Stun grenade. It's nice when they work like they're supposed to."

"Where the hell did all you guys come from?"

"You have some character calls herself 'Miss Georgia Youngblood' to thank for the cavalry," he said. "She heard you and Hamilton on her cellphone, called 911 on a landline from somewhere at UT Medical Center. Gave the dispatcher your name and my name, then held the cellphone up to the mouthpiece. The dispatcher patched me in, and I pulled the SWAT guys in pretty quick."

"Amazing," I said. "You got here just in the nick."

"Looks like I owe you an apology, Doc," he said.

I smiled. "Nice to hear you say that," I said, "but actually, you don't. Any good homicide detective would've come to the same conclusions you did. Hell, even I was beginning to suspect myself. And you just saved my neck. I just hope you can build as strong a case against this piece of shit as you were building against me."

"I think we can manage that," said Evers. "All 911 calls are recorded. So we've got Hamilton's confession on tape."

"Does this mean the murder trial is off?"

"Yours is off," he said. "His is on." Evers grinned, and for the third time in a week, I heard him reciting the Miranda rights. Only this time, he was reciting them to Hamilton, not to me.

EPILOGUE

MY ARMS AND LEGS ached from wrestling the wheelbarrow up the trail that led from the Body Farm's main clearing to the spot where I'd found Jess's body that unforgettable morning. This was my third load of topsoil, and I'd lugged up a load apiece of sand, lime, and peat moss. The ground at the base of the pine tree had been stained nearly black by the volatile fatty acids leaching from the research body; that meant the soil was so acidic no vegetation would grow there for at least a year, maybe two, without some help. And I wanted vegetation to grow there.

I'd come close to cutting down the tree, knowing I would never be able to look at it without remembering the sight of Jess's body, without feeling the loss of her. "You *should* remember her," Miranda had said when I told her of my plan to fell the tree and chainsaw the memory into two-foot lengths. "I know it hurts right now, and maybe it always will. But she deserves to be remembered, and not just the easy parts. Her life intersected with the Body Farm. So did her death. Don't try to erase that. Find a way to honor it."

It had taken me a while to process that. Eventually, though, I realized that what Miranda said was right, and important. Surprisingly wise, too: How could someone half my age possess twice my wisdom? She had shrugged off that complimentary question when I put it to her. "I wasn't as close to her as you were," she said. "That makes it easier for me to see this clearly—to see her, and see you, and see you in relation to her. That's all. You know this stuff, too; you just don't realize you know it yet, because there's still too much pain heaped on top of it." Again I'd marveled at her insight.

"Woof," I groaned as I staggered the last few steps toward the base of the pine tree. I let the wheelbarrow topple sideways, and half the dirt spilled out into a small pile, alongside the other piles of soil, sand, and peat moss. A pair of shovels reached into the barrow to scrape out the rest.

"I offered," said Art, who was wielding one of the shovels, "but would you let me? Oh no. You had to do it all yourself."

"He needs the exercise," said Miranda, wielding the other shovel. "And his demons need exorcising."

Art looked me up and down. "I can see how you might benefit from the workout. You got demons need exorcising, too?"

"That might be a bit dramatic," I said. "It does help to do something physical. Maybe to overdo it, too—maybe sore muscles will take the place of the ache inside. Distract me from it, anyhow."

Art and Miranda began turning the dirt, mixing the piles of topsoil with the other ingredients. Then they began raking it around the bases of the creeping juniper and mountain laurel we'd positioned around the pine tree. "You're gonna have to water this every day, you know," Art said. "Be a lot safer to transplant this stuff in the winter, when it's dormant."

"I know," I said, "but it seemed important to do it now. You wait too long to create a memorial, the memory starts to slip away. Be easy to get sidetracked, forget the point, maybe never get around to it." I looked at Miranda. She was studying me as I said it, and she smiled. I smiled back and gave her a small nod of gratitude.

Art paused and leaned on his shovel, then reached into his back pocket and took out a handkerchief, which he used to mop his face and neck. "What do you think's taking them so long? You think they got lost?"

"Naw," I said. "She's probably flirting with the stone carver." Just then I heard the solid thunk of expensive car doors closing down in the parking lot. "Speak of the devil," I said. "I do believe they're here."

My belief was confirmed moments later by a voice wafting up the hill from the gate. "Dr. Bill? Yoo-hoo! Where y'all at, Dr. Bill?"

"We're up here, Miss Georgia," I called. "Follow the path through the woods. And watch your step!"

A minute later Miss Georgia wobbled into view, her stiletto heels sinking slightly into the ground at each step. "Dr. Bill, you need you some sidewalks out here, baby," she said. She fanned herself with an embroidered hanky. "Not to mention a crop-dustin' with some air freshener. Land *sakes*, this place got a powerful aroma."

"Sorry," I said. "We don't get many ladies of your caliber out here. Where your men friends?"

"They be along directly. They restin' halfway up. That thing they carrying be heavy. Least, they *say* it be heavy."

I introduced Miss Georgia to Art and Miranda.

Miranda shook Miss Georgia's hand. "Thanks for coming to Dr. B.'s rescue," she said.

Miss Georgia smiled, but I saw her sizing up Miranda at the same time. "You in love with Dr. Bill, too, girlfriend?"

Miranda smiled back. "I just pretend to be, so I'll get good grades. Truth is, I'd hate to lose my dissertation advisor this late in the game."

Miss Georgia laughed. "We gon' get along *fine*," she said.

I heard a snapping of twigs and a chuffing of breath, and Burt DeVriess and Detective John Evers staggered off the trail in our direction, a large square of black granite swaying between them. "Damn, Doc, I hope you know CPR. This sucker's heavy."

"I told 'em to make it extra thick, once you said you'd pick it up for me," I joked. "You can set it down right there. Bend your knees, not your back." He and Evers set the slab down, and as they straightened up, DeVriess groaned and puffed out several breaths in a row.

"Babycakes, you be needin' some mouth-to-mouth

resussification?" Miss Georgia took a hopeful step in his direction, but Burt waved her off with a laugh.

"Thanks, Miss Georgia, but I think I'll pull through on my own."

Evers swapped handshakes with Art, then introduced himself to Miranda, who said, "I might still be mad at you for arresting Dr. B."

Evers shrugged. "Hey, I'm just a dumb cop," he said. "You have to admit, though, he looked like a killer and quacked like a killer." Miranda nodded grudgingly. "Would it help any if I told you I testified to the grand jury yesterday, and single-handedly persuaded them to indict Dr. Hamilton for first-degree murder and attempted murder?"

Miranda beamed. "That helps. Be sure to tell me when the trial is so I can come throw rotten vegetables at him."

DeVriess cleared his throat in my direction. "Just so you know, Hamilton asked me to represent him," he said. I looked away. The news itself didn't particularly surprise me; after all, Grease was the most aggressive defense attorney in Knoxville, and he was my choice when *I* was the one charged with Jess's murder. What shook me was how betrayed I felt. "Doc," he said quietly, "I turned him down."

"*What?*"

"I said no." This, *this* was surprising. He grinned as a smile dawned across my entire face. I felt it wrap all the way around to the back of my head, and from there down my neck, into my shoulders.

"Why, Grease," I said, "you've restored my faith in humanity. If I didn't know better, I'd say you had rejoined the human race."

He held up a hand in protest. "Now, don't go thinking I've turned soft," he said. "It's an unwinnable case. For starters, there's your testimony about what he told you the night he tried to kill you. And you, by the way, are a wet dream of a witness for the prosecution. Not just a forensic legend, but a wrongly martyred and freshly redeemed one, too. There's the blood they found on the floor of his wine cellar. There's even a receipt for the gun, which he bought at a pawnshop on Broadway."

"On Broadway?" asked Art. "That wouldn't be Broadway Jewelry & Loan, by any chance?"

"I think so; why?"

"Because," I laughed, "if he bought it there, he bought it from Tiny, who's an undercover cop. So there's another good witness against him."

"He's getting some karmic payback, that's for sure," said DeVriess. "But what really nails him to the cross is the confession Miss Georgia here captured on, um, her cellphone."

I noticed Art studying DeVriess with a glint in his eyes. Clearly he was not feeling as forgiving as Miranda. "Well, here's a case I'm sure you'll want," he said. "I just arrested a forty-year-old Scout leader. Online solicitation of a minor for sexual purposes. He promised to teach little Tiffany all the joys of love. When we searched the car he drove to the rendezvous, we found handcuffs, a gag, a digital Nikon, and a broadcast-quality video camera." Art shook his head in disgust. "His name's Vanderlin," he said to DeVriess. "We just booked him an hour ago, so I'm sure you could still nab him as a client."

DeVriess shook his head. "Thanks, but no thanks," he said. Art stared at DeVriess, then at me.

"What's the matter, Burt," I teased, "is this case unwinnable, too?"

"Oh, I'm sure I could win it," he said, "but I've got my hands full right now. I've agreed to represent Bobby Scott in the murder of Craig Willis."

This was news, too. A year earlier, DeVriess had gotten Willis off the hook for molesting Scott's own son. "None of my business," I said, "but can they afford you? I had the impression they were pretty tapped out from all the therapy bills."

"We . . . worked something out," he said sheepishly.

"You're taking the case pro bono," I marveled, "aren't you? Tell me again how you're not going soft."

"I'm not. Really," he said. "Just think how much publicity I'll get for winning this case. 'Vengeful Dad Goes Free,' the headlines will say. 'Homicide Was Justifiable.' Hell, I'll probably be able to double my hourly rate once I get him acquitted."

"Burt, don't ever take the witness stand yourself," I said. "You're a shitty liar."

He looked slightly embarrassed. And immensely gratified.

I took Art's shovel from him and began scooping out a flat, shallow depression in the freshly spread earth, in a space we'd left amid the creeping juniper and laurel bushes. When I had the spot to my liking, I tore open a bag of pea gravel I'd brought. I poured a thin layer of gravel across the bottom of the circular hole, then a thicker layer around the rim. Then I bent down and lifted one edge of the granite plaque DeVriess and Evers had lugged up the hill, so it was standing vertical. Art and Evers stepped forward to help me, but I shook my head. "Thanks," I said, "but I'd like to do this myself."

Rocking the stone slab up onto first one corner, then another, I walked it over to the bed of gravel I'd laid. I fussed with the stone's placement, lining up the bottom edge so that the corners would be equidistant from the rim of the circle, then eased it down to horizontal. I rotated it a fraction of an inch clockwise, then a smaller fraction back the other way, squaring it up with the pine tree and the plantings. Then I knelt down and spread more of the pebbles around it so the rough-hewn edges jutted up by about an inch all the way around.

I stood up and stepped back for a better look. As I did, Miranda came and stood close beside me on my right. I felt her take my right hand in her left, and then felt Art put an arm around me from the other direction. Evers and DeVriess and Miss Georgia Youngblood stepped forward, forming a circle around the marker, and I noticed hands clasping all around, heads bowing toward the inscription chiseled into the granite.

IN MEMORY OF DR. JESS CARTER
WHO WORKED FOR JUSTICE

WORK IS LOVE MADE VISIBLE

"Sleep well, Jess," I whispered for the third time in as many weeks.

We stood in silence. Somewhere overhead I heard the high, sweet song of a mockingbird.

The spell was broken by the beep of a pager. Hands came unclasped and reached into pockets, fumbled at belts. "I'm sorry; it's mine," said John Evers. He stepped away, and a moment later I heard him talking quietly on his cellphone. When he returned, he caught my eye. "That was Dispatch," he said. "Fisherman just found a floater under the Henley Street bridge. Pretty ripe, apparently."

"Suicide?"

"Not unless the guy shot himself in the back of the head on the way down. Could you come take a look?"

My adrenaline spiked even before he finished asking. "Let's go," I said, starting down the path toward the gate. After a few steps, I stopped and looked back. Evers drew alongside me and turned, too. Miranda, Art, Burt DeVriess, and Miss Georgia Youngblood remained circled around Jess's marker—around Jess herself, it somehow seemed. At the same time, I felt their presence—friendship, maybe even love—encircling me as well. And not theirs alone: I felt Jess, too, around me and deep within me. The force of it—the gift of it—made my breath catch.

"You okay, Doc?"

"Yeah," I said. "I'm fine. Just fine."

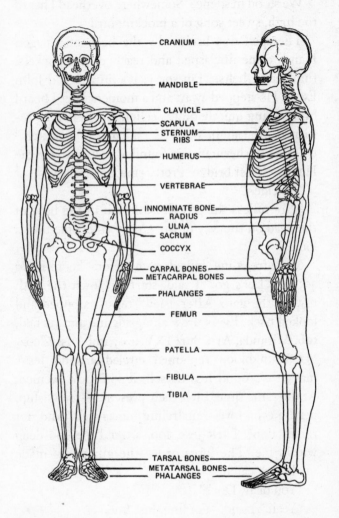

CRANIUM

MANDIBLE

CLAVICLE
SCAPULA
STERNUM
RIBS

HUMERUS

VERTEBRAE

INNOMINATE BONE
RADIUS
ULNA
SACRUM
COCCYX

CARPAL BONES
METACARPAL BONES

PHALANGES

FEMUR

PATELLA

FIBULA

TIBIA

TARSAL BONES
METATARSAL BONES
PHALANGES

Reprinted from *Human Osteology: A Laboratory and Field Manual* (fourth edition), by William M. Bass. © Missouri Archaeological Society, Inc., 1995.

THE SKULL

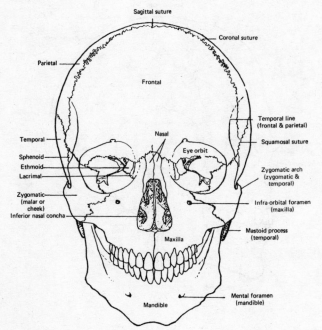

Sagittal suture

Coronal suture

Parietal

Frontal

Temporal line
(frontal & parietal)

Nasal

Squamosal suture

Eye orbit

Temporal

Sphenoid

Ethmoid

Zygomatic arch
(zygomatic &
temporal)

Lacrimal

Zygomatic
(malar or
cheek)

Infra-orbital foramen
(maxilla)

Inferior nasal concha

Mastoid process
(temporal)

Maxilla

Mandible

Mental foramen
(mandible)

THE SKULL

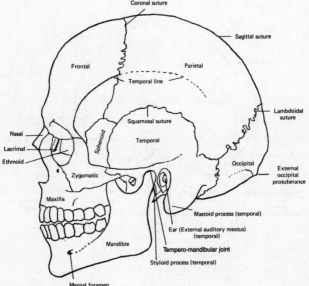

Coronal suture

Sagittal suture

Frontal

Parietal

Temporal line

Lambdoidal suture

Nasal

Squamosal suture

Sphenoid

Lacrimal

Temporal

Ethmoid

Occipital

Zygomatic

External occipital protuberance

Maxilla

Mastoid process (temporal)

Ear (External auditory meatus) (temporal)

Tempero-mandibular joint

Mandible

Styloid process (temporal)

Mental foramen

ACKNOWLEDGMENTS

Advances in the science of forensic anthropology, which plays a crucial role in the cases in this series, would not have been possible without the research and experimentation by my many graduate students. To them, I offer my greatest respect.

After the publication of *Carved in Bone*, I was surprised at the number of people who bonded with the characters in that first novel. Now, though, as we've worked on this second one, I've become much more attached to our characters, too—so much so that I miss those who are not around. As I shed tears for one of them, I reflected that I could not have found a better writer to collaborate with than Jon Jefferson.

To my wife, Carol, who has difficulty separating the fiction from the facts in the Body Farm novels, I offer my sincere thanks for her support. Carol claims she knows who the student is that Dr. Bill Brockton kissed in *Carved in Bone*. I say, "Carol, this is all fiction." She says, "Art Bohanan is not fiction."

—*Dr. Bill Bass*

My forensic discussions with Bill Bass, and my lunches with Bill and Carol, rank high on my list of life's delights. It's always fun when the discussion in our restaurant booth makes nearby heads turn . . . or makes Carol's cheeks go crimson. Art Bohanan—real-life fingerprint expert and children's advocate—has been remarkably gracious about letting us borrow from his cases and his causes, and we're proud to dedicate this book to the memory of his son.

Knoxville Police Department investigators Tom Evans and Tim Snoderly shared their time and insights generously, as did the staff at the booking and detention facility of the Knox County Sheriff's Office, especially Sgt. Robert Anderson.

From one side of the courtroom, criminal defense attorney David Eldridge—as smart as Burt DeVriess, but far less slippery—coached me on defense strategy; from the opposite side, Assistant District Attorney Jennifer Welch helped me untangle the Gordian knot of criminal-court procedures.

Forensic technology is getting more sophisticated all the time; for sharing their time and technical expertise, I thank forensic audio and video consultant Tom Owen as well as Doug Perkins and John Laycock of Ocean Systems.

Elaine Giardino, parish administrator of St. Paul's Episcopal Church in Chattanooga, kindly escorted me through the nooks, crannies, and staircases of her lovely church. I explored the nooks and crannies of the Hamilton County medical examiner's facility thanks to Tom Bodkin, the staff forensic anthropologist there (another of Dr. Bass's bright and successful protégés), and his boss, Medical Examiner Frank King, M.D. In Knoxville, at the Regional Forensic Center, I also owe a debt of gratitude to Knox County Medical Examiner Sandra Elkins, M.D., who drives a sports car but does not, as far as I know, resemble Jess Carter in any other personal respects.

For insights into the Scopes trial, I extend my gratitude both to University of Missouri law professor Douglas Linder (who has a fascinating series of websites about great trials) and to Richard Cornelius, a Scopes historian and the curator of the Scopes Evolution Trial Museum in Dayton, Tennessee.

I'm grateful to JJ Rochelle, John Craig, David Brill, and Sybil Wyatt, dear friends and true; to my sister Sara, for seeing me through a move to Baltimore; and to sweet, smart, sassy, and ever-capable Cindy.

Our agent, Giles Anderson, continues to do a spectacular job of keeping us off the streets and happily writing. We have a wonderfully supportive team at William Morrow: Sarah Durand, editor extraordinaire; crack publicists Seale Ballenger, Eryn Wade, and Buzzy Porter; marketing geniuses Rachel Bressler and Kevin Callahan; and sales wizards Brian McSharry, Michael Morris, Mike Spradlin, and Carla Parker. We're also grateful to everyone who succeeded in getting us *off* those shelves, including booksellers who have recommended us and—especially—readers who have responded so warmly to Dr. Bill Brockton, Art, and their sundry partners in crime.

Finally, profound gratitude to Seabiscuit, who galloped through these pages with me and helped make them smarter and better. What a beautiful, brilliant ride.

—*Jon Jefferson*

Turn the page for a sneak peek into the next thrilling case from the Body Farm . . .

CUT TO THE BONE

Coming soon in hardcover from William Morrow

Murder is as old as the human species, but the forensic work of the Body Farm is a modern weapon in the war on crime. Back in 1992, Dr. Bill Brockton—the promising young chairman of the Anthropology Department at the University of Tennessee—wages a baffling, deadly battle of wits with a sadistic serial killer, one who seems to be circling ever closer to Brockton himself. In CUT TO THE BONE, Brockton finds his lifelong research mission . . . but risks losing everything he holds dear.

"DAMN THAT ALBERT GORE," I said, slamming the kitchen door and tossing the newspaper onto the table.

"What on earth has Albert Gore done to you?" Kathleen didn't look up; her gaze remained intent on the steaming coffee she was pouring into her mug.

"He's gone and made me waste a perfectly good haircut." Kathleen turned and raised her eyebrows—her way of asking me to elaborate. I picked up the *News-Sentinel*, fresh from the driveway, and read her the story.

VP Possibility Gore Skips Knox Trip

Sen. Albert Gore Jr., asked everywhere he goes about speculation he may be asked to be presidential candidate Bill Clinton's running mate, abruptly canceled a speaking engagement in Knoxville for today and went to his rural home in Carthage.

The Tennessee Democrat, who ran unsuccessfully for president in 1988, is one of several candidates reportedly being considered as Democrat Clinton's vice presidential candidate.

My wife's spoon clinked against the side of the porcelain cup as she stirred in a dollop of half and half. "And the connection between the presidential election and your haircut is what, exactly?"

"I told you," I grumbled. "I'd wrangled five minutes with Gore during his visit to UT this afternoon. Now I've gotten all fancied up for nothing."

She turned and surveyed my hairline with amusement. "You're calling that buzz-cut *fancy*?" She laughed. "Besides, you get your hair cut at 6:30 a.m. every Wednesday, come hell or high water. An eighth of an inch a week. Albert Gore had nothing to do with that . . . *coiffure*." I grunted. She was right—my standing appointment fell on the day of Gore's abortive visit purely by coincidence—but I wasn't ready to quit sulking, as Kathleen could tell, judging by her next question. "What's the real reason you're so crabby?"

I sighed. "I was hoping to put a bug in Gore's ear about some research funding," I admitted. "Begging for a little scrap from the pork barrel. The University of Tennessee hired me to build the Anthropology Department, but they don't give me enough money to buy books, let alone bricks and mortar."

"We're not exactly living high on the hog over in Nutrition Science, either," she pointed out, reasonably enough; Kathleen's research on dietary deficiencies in low-income children was chronically underfunded, and after three years of scraping by, she'd begun to wonder if she was wasting her Ph.D. in Knoxville. "Look on the bright side," she said. "If Clinton *does* pick Gore, and if they win in November, we'll have a vice-president from Tennessee. He'll be in a better position to help."

"Bullshit," I grumbled. "Being vice-president is not worth a bucket of warm piss."

"Bill Brockton! Don't be such a potty mouth." I noticed a slight smile tugging at her mouth as she caught the inadvertent pun.

"Hey, those aren't *my* words. That's a famous quote. From an American vice-president, no less."

She eyed me dubiously. "*Which* American vice-president?"

"I can't remember," I said. A serendipitous afterthought made me grin. "Which just goes to prove the point."

THE DEADBOLT OF my office door *thunked* into place just as the phone began to ring. I pulled the key and turned toward the stairwell, but the phone nagged at me, shrilling and scolding, as if it sensed my presence and even my indecision. I wavered, the key still in midair. A new secretary was scheduled to report for duty at the beginning of the fall semester, but until then, I wasn't just the Anthropology Department's chairman, I was also its receptionist, mailsorter, and message-taker, and I was a sorry excuse for a temp. "All right, all *right*," I muttered, unlocking the bolt and flinging open the door. "Hold your horses." Leaning across the midden of mail, memos, and other bureaucratic detritus, I snatched up the receiver. "Anthropology Department," I snapped.

"This is Sheriff Jim Cotterell, up in Morgan County," drawled a voice that I recalled from a case two years before. "I'm trying to reach Dr. Brockton."

"This is Bill Brockton," I said, my annoyance dissipating. "Good morning, Sheriff. How are you?"

"Oh, hey there, Doc. I'm hangin' in; hangin' in. Didn't know this was your direct line."

"We've got the phone system programmed to put VIP callers straight through to the boss," I joked. "What can I do for you, Sheriff?"

"We got another live one for you, Doc. Another dead one, that is." He chuckled at the joke, one I'd heard a hundred times in a decade of forensic fieldwork. "Some fella from Oak Ridge was up on Frozen Head Mountain yesterday, fossil-hunting— that's what he says, leastwise—and he found some bones up at an old strip mine."

I felt a familiar surge of adrenaline—it happened every time a new forensic case came in—and I was glad I'd turned back to answer the phone. "Are the bones still where he found them?"

"Still there. I reckon he knew better'n to mess with 'em—that, or he didn't want to stink up his jeep—and you've got me trained to leave things alone till you show up and do your thing."

"Glad to hear it, Sheriff. Have you seen the bones? You sure they're human?"

"I ain't seen 'em myself—they're kinda hard to get to—but my chief deputy seen 'em yesterday evening. He took Meffert from the TBI up there with him. Him and Meffert both say it's a human skeleton. Small—maybe a woman or a kid—but human for sure."

"Meffert? Bubba Hardknot?" Just saying the words made me smile. The Tennessee Bureau of Investigation agent who was assigned to Morgan and Campbell counties had a name befitting a character in a British costume drama: Wellington Meffert IV. Meffert's nickname, on the other hand—"Bubba Hardknot"—sounded like something from a hillbilly comic strip. Average the two names together and you might get something that sounded fairly normal, which I supposed was the point. "Bubba's a good man. If he says it's human, I expect it is."

"Me and Bubba figured there weren't no point calling you out last night," Cotterell went on. "Tough to find your way up that mountain in the damn daylight, let alone pitch dark. Besides, whoever it is, they ain't any deader today'n they was last night."

I smiled, tucking away the line for possible future use. "Couldn't've said it better myself, Sheriff." I checked my watch. "It's 8:15 now. How's about we meet you at the courthouse around 9:30?"

"Me and Bubba'll be right here waitin'. 'Preciate you, Doc."

TYLER WAINWRIGHT DIDN'T even glance up when I burst into the bone lab. The Anthropology Department resided in the bowels of Neyland Stadium, a long, curving hallway of classrooms, faculty offices, and graduate-student cubbyholes. The osteology laboratory lay two flights below, notched into the structure's lowest level: in the descending colon, you might say, of the stadium's bowels. The left side of the cavernous room was filled with sturdy metal tables, shallow specimen trays, lamps with large magnifying lenses encircled by fluorescent lights. The right side was filled with dozens of shelving units—and thousands of cardboard boxes of bones. Each box measured one foot square by three feet long, and each one contained the skeleton of an Arikara Indian who'd lived and died in the Great Plains in the 1700s or early 1800s. I'd spent years' worth of summers in South Dakota excavating the Arikara skeletons, staying one step ahead of rising river reservoirs being filled by the Army Corps of Engineers. When I'd moved to Knoxville three years before, the thousands of bone boxes had occupied nearly as much space in the moving van as my household goods.

The bone lab had one exterior wall, which held a big bank of grimy windows; through the grit, the windows offered a scenic view of the steel girders and concrete footing of the stadium's grandstands. The lab's opposite wall, obscured by the shelves of bones, adjoined the football field itself, smack at the center of the south end zone. If *that* wall had been made of glass, the department would be awash in cash, because we could sell field-level, goal-line tickets to UT's home football games.

Tyler laid down the bone he'd been scrutinizing and picked up another. "Hey, Dr. B," he said, once the steel door had rebounded off the wall and slammed shut. "Let me guess. We've got a case."

"How'd you know?" I asked. "How'd you even know it was me?"

"Elementary, my dear Watson," he said, affecting an exaggerated British accent. "*A*, it's 8:15 on the Monday after a holiday, which means nobody's here but me and you and a bunch of dead Indians. *B*, any time the door bangs open hard enough to rattle the whole stadium, it's because you're really pumped. *C*, you only get really pumped when the Vols score a touchdown or somebody calls with a case. And *D*, football season doesn't start for two months. *Ergo*, you're about to haul me out to a death scene."

"Impressive powers of deduction," I said. "I *knew* there was a reason I made you my graduate assistant."

"You picked me for my powers of deduction?" He pushed back from the lab table, revealing a shallow tray containing dozens of pubic bones, each numbered in indelible black ink. "I thought you picked me was because I work like a dog for next to nothing."

"See?" I said. "You just hit the deductive nail on the noggin again."

THE BIG CLOCK read 9:05 when Tyler and I arrived at Wartburg's town square and pulled behind the courthouse to park. "Damn, we made good time," I marveled. "Forty minutes? Usually takes an hour to get here from Knoxville."

Tyler glanced at his watch. "Sorry to burst your bubble, but it's actually 9:27. I'm guessing that's one of those clocks that's right twice a day."

"Come to think of it," I recalled, "seems like it was 9:05 two years ago when I was here, too."

The stuck clock only added to the charm of the Morgan County courthouse. A square, two-story brick structure built in 1904—back when Wartburg still hoped to prosper as a community of industrious German immigrants—the courthouse started in simplicity but ended in elegance. Its boxy lines were broken, at the four corners, by square towers that projected slightly from the sides, each tower topped with a small pyramid of a roof. The finest architectural flourish, though, was a graceful white belfry rising from the building's center. The sides of the belfry consisted almost entirely of open arches, topped by a four-sided cupola. Each side of the cupola—north, south, east, and west—proudly displayed a six-foot dial where time stood still. I suspected that it wasn't just eternally 9:05 in Wartburg; I suspected that it was also, in many respects, still 1904.

THE ROAD INTO the abandoned strip mine consisted of a pair of rocky ruts angling up the northern flank of Frozen Head Mountain. It was obvious at a glance that my UT truck, with two-wheel drive and only eight inches of ground clearance, wouldn't be up to the challenge. I parked and locked it on the shoulder of the two-lane blacktop, hoping no local yahoos would steal or trash it, and Tyler and I shifted our gear—a body bag and a plastic bin containing the camera, evidence bags, trowels, gloves, tweezers, clipboards, and forms—into the back of the sheriff's four-wheel drive Bronco.

Sheriff Cotterell and Special Agent Hardknot rode up front; Tyler and I sat in the back like prisoners, behind a wire-mesh screen, as the Bronco began lurching and lunging up the track. "Last time I had a ride this rough," Tyler shouted over the whine of the transmission and the screech of clawing branches, "I was on the mechanical bull at Desperado's, three sheets to the wind. I hung on for thirty seconds, then went flying, ass over teakettle. Puked in midair—a comet with a tail of vomit."

"If you need to puke now," Cotterell hollered back, "give me a heads-up. You ain't got no winder cranks or door handles."

"I'm all right," Tyler assured him. "Only had two beers for breakfast today." He was probably joking, but I wouldn't have staked my life on it. Tyler loved beer the way I loved forensic cases: in frequent, copious quantities.

Eventually the Bronco bucked to a stop beside a high, ragged wall of stone, and the four of us staggered out of the vehicle onto what might have been the surface of the moon, if not for the kudzu vines and scrubby trees. "Watch your step there, Doc," Cotterell warned over his shoulder as he and Meffert led us toward the looming wall. The warning was absurdly unnecessary—not because the footing was good, but because it was so spectacularly bad. The jagged shale debris left behind by the strip-mining ranged from brick-sized chunks to sofa-sized slabs.

"I'm glad y'all are leading the way," I told the backs of the lumbering lawmen.

"Be hard to find on your own," said the sheriff.

"True, but not what I meant," I replied. "I figure if anybody's going to get snakebit, it'll be the guy walking in front. Or maybe the second guy, if the snake's slow on the draw."

"Maybe," conceded Meffert. "Or maybe the two crazy fools stickin' their hands down in the rocks rooting for bones."

"Dang, Bubba," I said, wincing at the image he'd conjured. "*That'll* teach me to be a smart-ass."

"Man," muttered Tyler after a hundred slow yards. "Every step here is a broken ankle waiting to happen." The bin of gear he was lugging didn't make it easier to see his footing or keep his balance. The trees were too sparse and scrubby to serve as props or handholds; all they were good for was to obscure the footing and impede progress.

"Bubba," I huffed, "you came out with the guy that found the bones?"

"Yup," Meffert puffed. The TBI agent appeared to be carrying an extra twenty pounds or so around his middle.

"He said he was hunting fossils," I went on. "You believe him?"

"Seemed believable. Name's Ro-*chelle*. Some kind of engineer at the bomb factory in Oak Ridge. Environmental engineer. Maybe that's how he come to be interested in poking around old strip mines. Fossils plus acid runoff—a two-fer for a guy like that, I reckon. There's damn good fossils right around the bones. I'll show you directly." He paused to take a deeper breath and reach into a hip pocket. "Yeah, I believe him," he repeated, mopping his head and neck with a bandana. "He come into the sheriff's office and then brung us all the way back up here. No reason to do that except to help, far as I can see. Hell, that shot his Sunday right there."

"You never know," I said. "Sometimes a killer will actually initiate contact with the police, insert himself in the investigation."

Meffert shrugged.

"More than that, sometimes," I pointed out. "An FBI profiler told me about a California serial killer back in the seventies, Ed Kemper—'Big Ed'—who hung out in a cop bar. When he finally confessed to this string of murders and dismemberments, his cop-buddies thought he was joking."

Meffert shrugged. "This Rochelle guy seemed okay," he said. "He's got a federal security clearance, for whatever that's worth. But like you say, you never know."

Fifty yards ahead, I saw yellow-and-black crime-scene tape draped around an oval of scrubby foliage and rugged shale. "Did somebody actually stay out here overnight to secure the scene?" I asked.

Cotterell made a guttural, grunting sound, which I gradually realized was a laugh. "*Secure* the *scene*? Secure it from *who*, Doc?"

MEFFERT WAS RIGHT about the fossils. Just outside the uneven perimeter of crime-scene tape lay a flagstone-sized slab of black shale, imprinted with a lacelike tracery of ancient leaves. Beside it, angling through the rubble, was a stone rod the length of a baseball bat. Its shape and symmetry made it stand out against the random raggedness of the other rocks, and I stooped for a closer look. Thousands of diamond-shaped dimples dotted the entire surface of the shaft.

"I'll be damned," I said to Tyler. "Look at that. A lepidodendron."

"A what?" Tyler set down the bin and squatted beside me. "Butterfly fossil?"

I nudged it with my toe, and it shifted slightly. "Close, but no cigars. Your Latin's rusty."

He laughed. "My Latin's nonexistent."

"Butterflies are Lepidoptera—'scaly wings.' This is a lepidodendron—'scaly tree'—a stalk from a giant tree fern. Ferns a hundred feet tall. Carboniferous Period. That plant is 300 million years old if it's a day."

Tyler grasped the exposed end of the fossil and gently tugged and twisted, extricating it in a succession of rasping clinks. He sighted along its length, studying the intricate geometry of the diamond-shaped pattern. "You sure this is a scaly stem? Not a scaly snake?"

"Those scales are leaf scars," I said. "Also called leaf cushions. But they do look like reptile scales, for sure. Actually, circus sideshows used to exhibit these as fossilized snakes. You're a born huckster, Tyler." I stood up, scanning the ground ahead and catching a telltale flash of grayish-white, weathered bone. "But enough with the paleo lesson. We've got work to do. Let's start with pictures." Tyler laid the fossil aside carefully and opened the equipment bin.

Early in my career, a detective at the Kansas Bureau of Investigation had taught me a crucial forensic lesson: You can never have too many crime-scene photos, because working a crime scene requires *destroying* it. The KBI agent's approach to crime-scene photography sounded like something straight from Bonnie and Clyde's bank-robbery playbook: "Shoot your way in, and shoot your way out"—start with wide shots, then get closer and closer, before eventually reversing the process as you're finishing up and leaving the scene. Tyler had been quick to master the technique, and even before we stepped across the tape at the strip mine, he had the camera up and the shutter clicking. It wasn't unusual for Tyler or me—sometimes both of us—to come home with a hundred 35-millimeter slides from a death scene, ranging from curbside shots of a house to frame-filling closeups of a .45-caliber exit wound.

As Tyler shot his way in, so did I, shooting with my eyes and my brain rather than a camera. As I zoomed in on the skull, I reached out to pluck a seedling that was growing beside it, obscuring my view. As I began to pull, the skull shifted—bone grating against the rock—and I froze. "I'll be damned," I said, for the second time in ten minutes. The seedling, I realized, wasn't growing *beside* the skull; the seedling was growing *from* the skull. Not only had I never seen such a thing before, I'd never even imagined it. Wriggling my fingers gently beneath the skull, I cradled it, then lifted and twisted, tugging tendrils of root from the rocky crevices below. The seedling was a foot tall, the fronds of black locust leaves reminding me of a fern; as I held it up, with Tyler snapping photographs and the sheriff and TBI agent looking on, I felt as if I were displaying a bizarrely potted houseplant. "Bubba," I said, nodding toward the bin, "would you mind unfolding and unzipping that body bag?" Meffert scrambled to comply, spreading and smoothing the rubberized fabric over the uneven rubble as best he could. The sheriff held the lower end of the bag tight as the deputy tugged the C-shaped zipper across the top, down one side, and then across the bottom.

They folded the flap open and I set the skull inside the bag. "You gonna just leave that tree in it?" asked Meffert.

"For now," I said, laying the skull on its side and tucking the seedling beneath the zipper. "When we get back to UT, I'll take it over to a botanist—a guy I know in the Forestry Department—get him to cut it open and count the growth rings. However many rings he finds, we'll know she's been here at least that many years."

"Huh," Meffert grunted, nodding. Suddenly he added, "*Watch* it!"

Just as he spoke, I felt a sharp pain on my wrist. I looked down in time to see a wasp pumping the last of its venom into the narrow band of skin between the top of my glove and the bottom of my sleeve. "Dam*na*tion," I muttered, flattening the wasp with a hard slap. "Where the hell did *that* come from?"

"He crawled out of that skull, Doc," Meffert said. "Looka there—yonder comes another'n." Sure enough, at that moment a second wasp emerged from the foramen magnum, the large opening at the base of the skull, and took flight. Meffert's hand darted downward, and by the time I realized what he was doing, he had caught and crushed the second wasp in midair, barehanded. "Sumbitches must have 'em a nest in there." He swiftly dispatched two more in similar fashion. We watched and waited, but no more emerged.

"You're quick, Bubba," I said, rubbing my wrist. "You that fast on the draw with a gun?"

He smiled. "Ain't nobody ever give me a reason to find out."

"Well, watch my back, if you don't mind."

I turned back to the postcranial skeleton, scanning the bones from neck to feet. "Y'all were right about the size," I said. "Just guessing, I'd say right around five feet. And female," I added, bending low over the flare of the hip bones. "And young."

"How young?" asked Sheriff Cotterell.

I hedged. "Be easier to tell once we get the bones back to the lab and finish cleaning 'em up."

"Any chance this is an old Indian skeleton?" the sheriff asked hopefully. "Make our job a hell of a lot easier if she was prehistoric."

"Well, she's lying on top of this busted shale," I pointed out. "If she's prehistoric, this is the world's oldest strip mine."

WE RODE IN silence down the winding mountain blacktop road toward Wartburg. Tyler was absorbed in the fossil he'd brought back, his fingers tracing the intricate diamond patterning, as if he were blind, examining it by touch alone.

For my part, I was brooding about the TBI agent's parting shot—a good natured joke, no doubt, but it had stung. Just after my arrival in Tennessee, I'd been called to a rural county in Middle Tennessee, where a decomposing body had been found in a shallow grave behind a house. The remains were in fairly good shape, as rotting bodies go—pink tissue still clung to the bones—and I'd estimated that the man had died about a year before. The dead man turned out to be Colonel William Shy, a Civil War soldier killed in the Battle of Nashville. "Don't feel bad, Doc," Meffert had joked when he mentioned it. "You only missed it by a hunnerd-something years. Too bad that colonel didn't have a big ol' tree growing outta *his* head."

In hindsight, there were logical reasons I'd missed the time-since-death mark so badly. Col. Shy had been embalmed, and until modern-day graverobbers had looted the grave, the body had been sealed in an airtight cast-iron coffin, which kept bugs and bacteria at bay. But those explanations sounded more like excuses than I liked. They were also precious little comfort in court, I'd learned from humbling cross-examinations by hostile defense attorneys, delighted to rub my expert-witness nose in my whopper of a mistake.

Determined never to repeat the error, I'd searched the scientific literature thoroughly for more information about the processes and timing of human decomposition. But apart from a few musty articles about insect carcasses—dead bugs found in bodies exhumed from old cemeteries—I'd found virtually nothing. The good news was, I wasn't the only forensic anthropologist who was flying by the seat of his pants when estimating time since death. The bad news was, *every* forensic anthropologist was flying by the seat of his pants.

The interesting news, I realized as Tyler and I reached the base of the mountain and the road's hairpin curves gave way to a long, flat straightaway, was that the field of human decomposition was fertile ground for research, and I caught the first, faint glimmers of an idea dawning.

The sun was low in the sky, a quarter-moon high overhead, when Tyler and I passed through Wartburg's town square on our way back to Knoxville. We were surrounded by frozen moments in time: The clock; the town; the fossilized fern, its diamond-dimpled pattern captured 300 million years ago; the girl for whom time had ceased, sometime after wildcat miners had ravaged the mountainside, sometime before a germinating seed and a nesting wasp queen had staked their claims to her, thereby drawing her back into the circle of life.